I0641332

# AN ANGEL NEVER PRAYS

A Dak Donahue Novel

# Steve Dwight Nichols

An Angel Never Prays

This book is a work of fiction and the product of the author's imagination. Names, characters, places, events, incidents, business entities, religious entities, and organizations are used fictitiously. Any resemblance to actual places, organizations, business entities, religious entities, incidents or persons is entirely coincidental.

Books

1. Murder and the Preacher's Wife

2. The Sinner's Reckoning

3. The Good Samaritans

4. The Last Revelations: The Beginning of the End

5. The Inception War

6. Tanger Gold

7. To Kill a Blueblood

8. An Angel Never Prays

9. A Demon Never Prays

# Prologue

Dak stepped forward, "We need you to entice the army out of the fort. He will not expect us to scale down the cliff this time of year. I am counting on him not fearing us. He has us outnumbered four to one. The Dark Master is arrogant, he will want to kill us and that will be his undoing. We do not have time to wait them out. We must return to Cliff Tops."

Dak looked at Trey, "You Trey are in charge. You men will do as Trey commands. This is my order to you as the King of Cliff Tops and the commander of this mission."

# Chapter 1

Hulk and Trey were tired as they led the group north on the road into Zenith Point. The two men knew the horses were spent as the two warriors talked about how the new government in the area near Harpers Ferry Harbor needed law enforcement. Hulk looked at Trey as they dismounted, "Without a federal police force and with dishonest men acting as the sanctioned authority, Harpers Ferry Harbor will be nothing but a city full of organized crime. Someone with integrity needs to be placed in the position to be the Federal Marshall."

Trey looked at his friend, "Are you considering being part of the federal police force in the south?"

Hulk did not say anything for a few seconds. After they dismounted they walked their horses to the front of the large home in Zenith Point. "I am not certain what I will end up doing. I was considering planting my flag somewhere and leaving my mark on this earth. I am like Dak. I do not see my future living in Cliff Tops. I do not believe the Queen will gift the property in her realm to us. My parents and your parents received a small parcel in comparison. Dak has made us all part owners in his ranch, and I am already wealthier than my parents. I love the people of Cliff Tops, but I do not desire to live there."

Trey tied his horse to the rail, "Dak and Zenith are going to stay here at their home. They do not wish to raise the kids in Harpers Ferry Harbor. I believe Zenith likes the warmer climate compared to Cliff Tops."

Hulk smiled at his friend, "What about you? I noticed you settled in on the one whore name Jazmine."

Trey smiled, "I did like her company. I really liked her body. Other than me paying her for sex, we have nothing in common. I believe I will return to Cliff Tops to visit. I might visit Mrs. Daisy's house in Harpers Ferry Harbor in the future and check on Jazmine, but I might stay here in Zenith Point with Dak. What is your brother going to do?"

Hulk shook his head sideways, "I have no earthly idea what that boy is going to do. He does not seem to be motivated to do anything except what we are now doing. He is not interested in starting a ranch or working for a government. He will most likely return home. He might end up working with you and Dak here at Zenith Point. I believe Robin Hood and I will travel back to Harpers Ferry Harbor and work with Vulture in the New Republican Army."

Dak and Zenith started riding into the front compound. The group had spread out over four hundred yards and talked between themselves as they rode. The extra months they spent trying to assist with establishing a government in the south was exhausting. The trip took seventeen days, and the weather had turned cold. The conversations riding north were curt with everyone looking forward to being home. Zenith noticed the home had been well maintained, and the staff was happy to see them. Dak noticed the herds of cattle and goats had increased as they rode through the fields leading to the gate of their home. He could see through the open barn doors that the hay had been stacked in the dry for the winter. He knew his employees had been working hard. They each gave their horses to the stable boy and followed Zenith into the home.

Juan was excited to report the herds had multiplied, and they were able to sell cattle and sheep monthly to the two northern cities. He then hesitated and reported some of the cattle had been stolen.

Dak liked Juan's nature. He was a humble small-framed man, and he appeared to try to be appeasing when faced with bad news. Dak had always found Juan to be honest and a good-natured person. Juan rubbed his hands together which appeared to be a nervus gesture, "The cattle are missing from the southern herd. We have tracked the cattle to the Forge River. Sir, the men that took them appear to be bandits. We cannot fight them. I hope you understand. When we realized some of the cattle were stolen, we moved the rest of the herd north into the north pastures. We watch your herds and try to keep them safe, but we are not soldiers."

Zenith looked at Juan, "No one is blaming you, Juan. We will ride out in two days and check on the herd, but tonight we will eat and rest."

Dak noticed Zenith did not mention the bandits. Dak added, "I will stop the problem. This type of activity must be stopped. There is nothing worse than a thief."

"Thank you. Do I need to summon the sheriff from The Midnight Hole?"

Dak smiled, "So the Midnight Hole now has a sheriff?"

Juan tried to smile, "Yes Mr. Dak. The mayor hired Tom Brimmer to be the sheriff two months ago."

Dak thought for a second trying to remember if he knew Tom Brimmer, and he could not recall. "No Juan, we will handle this on our own. Did the people of the Midnight Hole vote on the sheriff or did the mayor hire someone of his liking?"

"No. There was no voting. The mayor started his own general store and opened up a corral and built a gambling house with a bar." Juan looked at Dak, bowed his head and walked out of the room.

Zenith looked at Dak, "He seems frightened of you. Why is that?"

Dak smiled, "I have no idea, but the cattle thieves need to be scared of me. I will tell Hulk to have the guys ready to ride in the morning two days from now. Then, I want to head north to see my kids." He looked at Zenith, "I do not trust the new mayor. By the description of the mayor, he sounds like he is greedy and is using his position as mayor to further his own agenda. Listening to my tribe's elders talk for years, that type of greed is what caused the demise of the old world."

Zenith looked at Dak, "As long as there are people, there will be greed."

***

Hulk looked up from the cattle tracks on the west side of the Forge River. "There appears to be four horses pushing the cattle west. One of the horses has a cracked horseshoe on the right front leg. The tracks are five to seven days old. There is no mistake. We are dealing with cattle thieves. Juan's men did not cross the river. I can clearly see the metal horseshoe tracks following the cattle."

Zenith looked apprehensive and frustrated, "They are headed toward Ryan O'Neil's Ranch."

Dak looked at his friends and then at Hulk, "Follow the trail and let us see where the trail leads. I do not wish to jump to conclusions, but I do not care for Ryan O'Neil."

Hulk mounted his horse and rode out in front of Dak and the others looking at the ground following the tracks. Dak looked over at Zenith as they rode, "O'Neil lost one son in the battle with the Normand army. He then fled west and hid and waited for the Normand Army to retreat. Once the Cliff Tops Army and the New York Army pushed the Normand Army south out of the region, he returned to his ranch. He claimed additional acres from his neighbors, and the rumor was he stole cattle. I believe he could be the cattle thief. I met him once on the Continental Trail as we were heading North. I decided I did not like the ill-mannered man. He suffers from little man syndrome and trying to impose his will on others."

Zenith looked forward as she rode, "I noticed when you decide you do not like someone, they end up dead or have a hand cut off." She remembered the bandit at the ALE House located north of Merlin.

Dak glanced at his wife and then focused on the path ahead. "My conscience is clear. There is no one innocent." Zenith knew he was repeating what she had mentioned to him after they had escaped Merlin, and Dak was forced to kill a teenager who was trying to kill him along the snow-covered trail in the northwest territory.

Zenith announced, "The cattle thieves must be stopped and brought to justice. If they are not stopped, the problem will grow."

10

Hulk led the group for four hours as they ascended the hill overlooking the green valley with the creek running from the north. He could see the ranch as he sat still on his horse from the apex of the ridge close to a quarter mile away. Hulk looked at Dak with a frown. "There is no mistake. The cattle were driven to that ranch. I have followed the one horse with the cracked horseshoe all the way from our field into the Forge River. You saw me locate the trail once we cross the river, and the trail leads directly to that ranch."

Trey was looking through his binoculars and announced, "I count fourteen cowboys."

Tommy Boy said, "There is a large herd west of their ranch house. There will be additional men we need to consider. The cowboys are breaking the wild horses. If they see us, what are you going to do?"

Robin Hood smiled, "What do you think he is going to do? He is going to do what he always does. He is going to take his cows back and maybe kill those cowboys."

The seven riders rode slowly toward the ranch. Dak saw Mr. O'Neil walk out on his front porch as he stood waiting for them to get closer. The cowboys picked up their bows and other weapons as they observe as Dak, Zenith, Trey, Tommy Boy, and Hulk ride in a line followed by Juan who rode behind Dak and next to Robin Hood. Dak pulled his horse to a stop and the others stopped their horses a few feet further back.

They placed their shields in front of them and had their arrows loaded on their bows. Mr. O'Neil yelled, "Who are you, and what do you want? This ranch is private property, and you are trespassing."

Dak rode closer, within fifty feet and looked at Mr. O'Neil. He hesitated to respond. "You do not remember me? We met once on the Continental Trail after the battle of New York. You were an obnoxious, ill mannered, unfriendly asshole then. I can see you have not developed better manners." Dak stared at the man.

O'Neil shifted his weight and tried to remember when he had met this man sitting on a horse with a shield protecting his left flank with high quality multiple swords and two knives, one in a boot on the left leg and one strapped around his chest with the knife position across his belly. O'Neil tried to make out the face shaded by the hood covering his head. He motioned with his hand for his men to stay in position. "I do not recall meeting you. Mister, you need to get off my land."

Dak glanced at the cowboys holding their swords. "I cannot do that. You see, me and my posse are tracking four cattle rustlers, and the tracks lead us here to your front porch."

Dak noticed a small female toddler with long dark hair, walking barefoot onto the porch. "Hi gran paw."

O'Neil turned to the child and tried to shield her from Dak. "Sady dear. You need to go back inside." The young man came out the front door and quickly picked her up and held her. A lady with long dark hair then rushed out on the front porch and took the child from the younger man and carried her back into the home.

"How dare you accuse me of being a cattle thief. You need to turn around and leave mister or my men will bury you and your posse in the graveyard."

Dak did not move. He stared at Mr. O'Neil. The man standing next to Mr. O'Neil looked to be younger. Dak thought he had the same body type as Mr. O'Neil. The son asked, "Who are you? Under whose authority are you making these false accusations? We will not tolerate being accused of thievery. We have a sheriff to investigate these matters. You are not the authority licensed to make an arrest. You need to get the hell out of here."

Dak looked at the son, "Who are you?"

He aggressively stepped forward and pulled his sword as his father reached and grabbed his right forearm to hold him in place. Mr. O'Neil was being cautious as he tried to figure out who this bold man was sitting in his front yard with his hood pulled over his head and several weapons attached to his body. He said, "I am Jessie O'Neil. You do not come on my property and accuse me and my family of wrongdoing. I will report you to my wife's father, Mr. Tom Brimmer, our sheriff. Now, I asked you a simple question. Who are you?"

"Well Jessie O'Neil, my name is General Dak Donahue."
Dak then adjusted his vision to the father, "So, Mr. O'Neil, it
appears you are calling my tracker a liar. He has reported to me
my stolen cattle led by four men from this ranch have taken my
cattle. One of the cattle thieves is riding a horse with a
fractured horseshoe on the front hoof. I believe we can inspect
your horses and locate the horse thieves. Then, we would have
the proof for your sheriff, Mr. Tom Brimmer. However, I do
not see the need for us to contact your brother-in-law." He
adjusted his vision to the son, "I am prepared to save your
sheriff the embarrassment of hanging his kinfolk."

Mr. O'Neil's son looked at Dak, "How dare you?"

Dak glanced at the cowboys and adjusted his shield to the
side between himself and the threat of their arrows. "Because I
know what cattle thieves look like when I see them, I am not
going to leave here without the problem being remedied. There
is a very good chance the undertaker is going to have to bury
you and your son. I do not need the assistance of the county
sheriff to hang cattle thieves. Those are my cattle, and I am
testifying before you and our Lord that you, your son, and your
men are all cattle thieves. The punishment for your crime is for
us to hang the guilty by their necks. After I have hung each of
you, I will contact Mr. Tom Brimmer, the sheriff, and tell him I
hung his scum son-in-law for stealing my cattle. If he is an

honest man at that point, he will thank me for saving him the time."

Mr. O'Neil seemed nervous as his demeanor changed. He glanced at the cowboys standing next to the corral. "Listen here Mr. Donahue, I know nothing of stealing any of your cattle. I have some new cowboys working for me, and there could have been an honest mistake. I thought you were down south fighting the Normand army."

Dak responded, "Yes, I was down south fighting while cowards like you, your son and your cowboys hid in the mountains. I understand how mistakes can be made. I am a reasonable man."

The son declared, "We are not cowards."

Mr. O'Neil held his son in place and then stepped forward with his palms upward to his side, "How many cows are you missing?"

Dak stared at Mr. O'Neil and spoke loudly, "Juan, how many cattle are we missing?"

Juan was sitting close to fifty feet behind Dak on his horse. "Sir, we know of fifty-two cattle taken from the southern field."

Dak said, "That would be fifty-two cattle."

Mr. O'Neil looked at Dak. "Yes. I am certain there was an honest mistake. Your southern field joins my property. My newly hired cowboys would not have known that the property line stops at the Forge River. I can assure you; this will not happen in the future. You can wait here, and I will have my men bring up fifty-two cattle from our southern field."

"No sir." Dak hesitated, "We will not wait here. You will drive the herd of fifty-two cattle back to my field no later than five tomorrow, or I will return and burn this place to the ground and leave your worthless ass and any men who oppose me on the ground for the wolves to eat. This is the only warning you will ever receive from me, and you and your men in the future better not ever step one foot on my property." Dak turned and rode past his posse and headed home.

Mr. O'Neil stood and watched Dak ride toward the apex of the ridge. He then watched Zenith, and the others turn their horses and follow. The young man whispered, "I will have the boys from the lumber camp and cowboys from the north field attack them in the open prairie and then we will bury them. I will end this here and now."

Mr. O'Neil acted like he did not hear his son's comment. He yelled for his foreman to come at once. The man jogged to the front porch. "Manie. Take six men, round up sixty-two of our best cattle, and drive them to General Donahue's ranch. Take them to Zenith Point and have them there by two tomorrow."

"Yes Sir."

Mr. O'Neil turned and grabbed his son by his shirt collar and pushed him against the wall. His face was red with rage and wrinkles appeared in his forehead. "If you ever steal any more cattle, I will disown you. Those men are warriors. They would kill our cowboys with little effort. You do not cross General Dak Donohue and live to tell the story. Do you understand?"

"Hell. We had them out numbered three to one, and one of them is a female. We need to hit them now before they ride off our property and obtain more men."

Mr. O'Neil slapped his son as he held him pushed against the wall of the home. He clinched his jaws, "You fool. That smaller rider is a Merlin Blueblood. A veteran fighter with several hundred kills to her credit. All those soldiers are killers. The best you and these cowboys could do is make them sweat before they killed every damn one of us. Now, you do as I say."

# Chapter 2

The three riders were noticed as they fast approached from behind the hill in the far horizon. The young boy walking across the top of the stone wall yelled, "Three riders, three riders."

The two workers walked from the barn and viewed across the meadow and saw the three riders approaching on a fast gallop. The one worker repeated the alarm "Three riders." He turns to the main complex building to verify if the people in the compound reattacks to his warning as he and others watch the three riders' approach. The three rode the horses into the compound in front of Zenith point and met Juan at the front door of the main complex. Juan listens to the lieutenant and then turns and walks into the large main room and reports, "We have three riders from the New Republican Army. They have an urgent message for Mr. Dak."

Dak glance at Juan and then commands, "Send them in at once."

Dak walks to his window and appears at three men sitting on horses in the front courtyard. He observes the three men are not in uniforms and dressed like ranchers with each having a sword which is the brand standard issue in the New Republican

Army. He observes them as they stretch their backs and legs once they dismount and then as they take short steps; he concludes they are tired from a long ride. He notices the one in the front appears to be in charge and says to himself, "Professional soldiers." Two of the men stepped behind the front man as they approached Dak. Dak watches the three men as Juan holds the door for them. After Juan closes the door, "I am Lieutenant Washburn and my two sergeants, Jones and Hatfield. We are from the New Republican Army. General Vulture has sent us. Here is his confidential report from the asset inside Southern City."

Dak knew this was the information he had been waiting to receive. He also knew at great risk to his friend Veronica; she and her network of people had sent the information of the location of the Rogue Blueblood master.

Dak looked at the men, "Lieutenant Washburn, I will provide you and your men rooms to rest, food and resupply you for your journey back to Harpers Ferry Harbor." Dak reached for the cylinder with the map and description of the hidden information. "Lieutenant Washburn, how many spies died bringing us this information?"

The lieutenant looked at Zenith as she entered the large room. They then looked at Hulk, Trey, Robin Hood and Tommy Boy as they walked into the room. Dak announced, "This is Lieutenant Washburn and his two sergeants, Jones and

Hatfield. They have arrived from Harpers Ferry Harbor and are delivering us the intel on the Rogue Bluebloods." They all shook hands. "Juan, please show these men a room to rest and prepare food for them."

Lieutenant Washburn looked at Dak, "There was one messenger that slipped through the Normand lines. We did not ask about the risk, or how many people died to bring us the information. We will rest for two days and then we must report back to our command center in Harpers Ferry Harbor."

Trey looked at Lieutenant Washburn, "Is Jasmine still working at Mrs. Daisy's? Please give her a message. I will be coming back through Harpers Ferry Harbor in the summer and look forward to seeing her." The men all smiled knowing Jasmine was the pretty dark skin prostitute Trey had enjoyed many nights being entertained with her.

Zenith shook her head no with a smile, "Is that all you men think about? There has to be something more important than Tom Catting around. Why not ask about the training of the fighting men?"

Robin Hood smiled, "He is speaking of motivating the fighting men." Robin Hood smiled and looked at Zenith, "Speaking of Tom Catting around, I have a list of women in Mrs. Daisey's working establishment and the Catch One Home of the Night Cats I need you to provide them my condolences and apologies. I am sorry I had to leave, but I also will return in the summer."

Lieutenant Washburn smiled, "I will be happy to provide all your correspondence to the sad women of Harpers Ferry Harbor. I am certain your correspondence will cheer them up."

Zenith said, "For heaven sakes. What a waste of government resources. Those whores will be okay."

***

Dak looked at the fire as he stood with his right hand resting on the hearth while his friends were sitting in the great room and announced, "We will ride to Cliff Tops tomorrow. I want to see my kids. Juan said Mr. O'Neil and his son, and several cowboys pushed sixty-two cows in the field at two today. I gave the ten extra cattle to Juan and his men for their bonus. The New York tribe is still buying close to fifty cattle from us a month."

Trey said, "I doubt they will steal anymore cattle from us."

Hulk looked at Trey, "I believe Mr. O'Neil did not realize his son was a cattle thief."

Zenith smiled, "I did not bother unleashing my sword. As soon as that cute little girl walked onto the porch, I knew what Dak was not going to do."

Trey smiled, "I believe Dak has a soft spot for kids."

The group smiled with Hulk toasting the group and saying, "I will drink to the soft spot."

Dak looked at Trey, "I hope your parents understand why Veronica is not with us. The information she has provided us is a game changer. Not only has she confirmed the Rogue Bluebloods existence, but she has reported the approximate location. She however did not report the number of resistant fighters and is suggesting there is only a couple of Rogue Blueblood warriors protecting the Master Blueblood. We must attack now before he masses an army."

Trey looked up from his chair, "My parents will have to understand. The news could have been worse. I still worry about her and wonder if her sacrifice is worth her risk."

Robin Hood declared, "Hell yes. We all love Veronica. We could have all been killed along with the army we had assembled if not for her. Veronica saved a lot of lives. With King Solman signing the treaty and suspending the war, we can concentrate on taking out the evil empire at the top."

Dak looked at Robin Hood, "I hope you are not so gullible to believe that the treaty signed by King Solman will keep his armies from marching further north. All we can do is show others why you do not sign a treaty with the Normand empire. They will break that treaty when the time suits them. The news of the war has spread, and everyone will hope the treaty will provide peace. Without an established army to at least defend ourselves, the Normand empire will not honor the treaty. They have that army for one reason and that is to conquer what they desire. The only chance I see is to decapitate their leadership."

Tommy Boy looked at Dak, "What are you suggesting?"

"I am going to Cliff Tops and suggest we attack the Normand Empire. We must slow them down, and secondly, I agree with Veronica. The wars are not going to be halted until we destroy the hidden menace. We must find the head of the snake and cut the head off. We must locate the cult and annihilate them. You know the soldiers in Harpers Ferry Harbor are not going to be able to accomplish what we must do."

Hulk shook his head no. Dak noticed, and he looked at Hulk, "You do not agree?"

"I do not believe we will have any meaningful assistance coming from Cliff Tops. My mother does not agree with us. She will not endorse any mission going south with the standing treaty. She will advise the Queen of such. Besides, the only men they have that can fight, need to stay on guard to protect their city. If they had additional men, they would be riding with us now. Your request will be futile."

Dak adjusted his hand on the hearth, "We need a few good additional soldiers, but I only need one man from Cliff Tops to ride with us. I must let them know how dire our situation has become. My mother will not agree with me. Her advisors will also not agree with me. She and I do not agree on the new world. She will not announce my birth right position as being her heir to her throne. She believes in an isolated world position with Cliff Tops. If the people in the middle of the continent fall to the armies of the south, we will be next. We have no choice but to support the people of Harpers Ferry Harbor. We must locate the Rogue Blueblood Master and take him out. If he is allowed in time, he will grow in strength, and we must act now. I am going to suggest we attack King Solman but all I need is Samuel to ride with us."

Trey smiled, "You are cunning. You are counting on them denying your request to attack King Solman and in return you will settle for Samuel to ride with us. I like that strategy."

Hulk clinched his jaws, "So, for us to need Samuel, you expect the worst when confronting the Rogue Master."

Zenith announced, "We do not know what to expect. We do not know their numbers. We will need Samuel. He is the only one who has experience hunting a Rogue Blueblood."

# Chapter 3

As Dak approached the city of the Midnight Hole, he noticed the city was growing. He looked at Zenith and Hulk, "The town has built several new buildings. Notice the hospital, the sheriff's office, the courthouse, and the new church under construction. We are now looking at a two-church town."

As they rode, they noticed several groups of people in the city working with horses, building a home, and merchants on both sides of the street. There were kids playing baseball in the open area near the street. Zenith said, "I never noticed so many people living in this area. Wow. Two churches. Must be a disagreement over Christ."

Hulk saw three men riding toward them. "I believe we are going to meet the new sheriff, Mr. Brimmer. Maybe he is also a preacher."

Dak and his group approached the Continental Trail and the gate leading to the large tunnel. He slowed his horse as the sheriff and his two deputies pulled even. The sheriff smiled, "You must be Dak Donahue."

Dak did not smile and looked at the sheriff and sized him up to be a competent man. "You must be the newly appointed sheriff, Mr. Tom Brimmer."

He kept smiling as he looked at Zenith, Hulk, Robin Hood, Trey and Tommy Boy, "And these others must be your partners. I have heard a lot about you guys. You are famous."

Dak did not respond, and he and the others stared at the sheriff and his two deputies. Tom looked at each of them with a smile as the two deputies had neutral expressions. "Well, I was hoping to meet you, your wife, and your men."

Dak looked at the sheriff, "I met some of your family two days ago. You need to do a better job. I will not tolerate cattle thieves. We however were able to resolve our dispute without me hanging the thieves. I told your brother-in-law, Mr. O'Neil not to ever step a foot on my property, and the next time he and his men are caught stealing my cattle I would hang them."

The sheriff looked a little upset with the comment. "Speaking of property. I was asked to mention to you about your unpaid property tax which is past due. As you can see the town is growing and everyone must pay their fair share."

Dak clenched his jaws, "We were not provided an opportunity to vote on you as a sheriff or who would be the mayor of the Midnight Hole. I own my property with my partners. We live in our own country. The country is called Zenith Point. We do not owe any levied taxes to anyone. We are not part of the Midnight Hole community, and therefore your rules do not apply to us. Sheriff, you can report that mandate to your mayor. If the mayor or you declare any other mandate, then we will consider your actions an act of war against our country and my sovereign nation. I will send your mayor a letter explaining our relationship. Now Sheriff Brimmer, I would suggest you get the hell out of our way."

\*\*\*

Dak hardly talked with the captain of the New York Tribe as he met him at the gate entrance. The captain tried to be friendly and asked for updated news on the treaty. Dak changed the conversation and requested the captain to have Zorro report to Cliff Tops tomorrow at noon. The group rode slowly north toward Cliff Tops.

The group was happy to see their village where they had such fond memories growing up. They proceeded into the small city followed by the children and town folks watching them. The main road housed the fourplex, blacksmith shop, church, and several other cottages. They all dismounted, and several of the town's people were present to meet them. They greeted their family and friends with hugs and kisses. Queen Vicky ordered a banquet to celebrate the festive moment.

There was drinking and dancing in the cheerful celebration which took place in the late afternoon. Dak looked at his mother as they were sitting at the head of the table in the church which was turned into the banquet hall. The tables for eating were lined in the middle of the room full of the town people sitting and eating in the festive environment. "I will spend time with my kids tonight and then tomorrow at noon we will need to meet. It is good to be home. We can talk tomorrow." He glanced at his mother, "It does not look like anything has changed since I left. The cottages along the road coming into town have not changed."

Vicky smiled as she faced her son. "The Ryan family had twins. Our city is growing slowly which is a good thing. Most the people under my realm are happy. They work hard and are secure." She hesitated while looking at Dak, "You made it right before the winter storms hit. The last snow has about melted. The larger storms are coming. We are speculating another cold winter will come our way."

"We were in a hurry to reach you before the winter storms. We had to deal with some cattle thieves once we returned which took four additional days. The south and mid region are full of lawless cutthroats. The large cartels run the areas, and there are constant battles between the cartels. You live here in your fortress with no concern about the people of the south." He looked at his mother, "Certainly, you will have another cold winter. The weather has been bitterly cold every winter I have been alive."

Vicky smiled, "We are celebrating your return, and the success of the treaty. That was the best news I have heard. We vet the people coming across our borders. We cannot have a secure realm unless we have a secure border. If they do not offer us something, they are not allowed to stay." She looked at Dak, "We do have crime. Just last week two of Mr. Dotson's chickens were stolen."

"Two chickens being stolen. What a crime wave." He smiled, "Yes, the treaty. Mother, the treaty might not be worth the paper it is written on. I will meet with you and the council tomorrow. I requested the presence of Zorro. You will not like hearing my report. We must act. This is not like the old days in the old world. There is no one holding the strong in check. We will be attacked." Dak walked over to Zenith and his two sons. Vicky watched as the four placed on their heavy coats and Dak carried Drake and Zenith carried Denzel as they headed for their room in The Dive.

# Chapter 4

Dak enjoyed his family time. He relaxed and enjoyed the laughter as he wrestled with his boys and then he would tickle them. He and Zenith played with their two sons until late in the night, and the four slept in the same bed. They slept until late morning and were late eating breakfast. Dak tried not to think about the war, but after he and Zenith had enjoyed their time with their twin sons, both knew they had to protect them. He looked at Zenith, "Hulk was right, asking for military assistance from Cliff Tops is not going to be successful. They have only a few extra men. I am counting on The New York Tribe which can spare a few, but I need their best men for the mission."

Zenith kissed him as Drake and Denzel watch their parents, and she told Dak she would spend time with the boys. He thought of Zenith and his relationship with his wife, and how he enjoyed spending time with her and their two sons. "I am fortunate to have you as a wife." He kissed each son on the forehead and smiled at her, "Be careful while I am gone. Mom said they had a crime wave last week. Mr. Dotson had two chickens stolen." He smiled and walked out of The Dive toward the church as he dreaded every step. As he walked down the decline, he thought of his two sons, and how the Lord had blessed him. He also thought of the weight of the war that was on his shoulders and now a secret deadly mission where he would attack a Rogue Blueblood Master. He could not walk away from his commitment to his family, friends, and village. He knew he was the only one who could hunt and then exterminate the Blueblood Master. He reluctantly accepted what he and Zenith had planned to assassinate a Rogue Blueblood Master.

The meeting was scheduled to be a closed meeting with only the Board of Directors of Cliff Tops and a few guests. He noticed the four horses tied to the bar in front of the church and knew Zorro and his three men had already arrived. As he walked through the double doors, he knotted his head to Quincy, the long-term city guard posted at the door entrance. He also smiled at Quincy knowing Quincy had been the first guard to be hired by his mother to protect and serve his mother's realm over fifteen years ago. Little Jimmy had taken a liking to Quincy and his buddy and been a mentor to both men. Quincy was teenager when he survived the Transitional Period and settled to live in Cliff Tops. Dak then nodded to Zorro as he walked into the meeting. He then smiled to himself as he read out loud the wooden sign placed at the interior entryway to the sanctuary, "Board of Directors". Zorro was dressed in a leather uniform carrying a white ivory handle sword on his side. He was sitting next to his two commanders and advisor. Zorro sat in the front row of the bench seats and smiled at Dak. Dak walked over to him, "Nice to see an old friend. How is one kidney working out for you?" He shook hands with all four men.

Zorro stood and smiled, "If not for you, I would not be alive and here today. Please let me know what I can do for you." The two men smiled at one another.

Dak said, "I can only pray you do not lose the other one in another battle. Otherwise, I might have to give you one of mine." The two men hugged. Dak then said, "I do need maybe ten of your best men to accompany me and my men on a secret but dangerous mission to the west coast."

"Certainly, I can spare you ten men for your mission."

"I will talk with you after this meeting." Dak walked to his seat next to Hulk.

Wayne walked over to Dak and greeted both Hulk and Dak.

Dak mentioned, "I read the sign positioned at the sanctuary entrance. I find it humorist that Cliff Tops has formally named a Board of Directors to work with Queen Vicky."

Wayne smiled, "The name Board of Directors sounds more metropolitan and attractive to outsiders. We grew by two-hundred people over the past sixty days and a couple hundred over the past year. The board is the same people as before plus Barney Simpson, the man who was elected to represent the people of Meadow Bottoms." Dak stopped smiling. Hearing the name Meadow Bottoms brought back sorrowful memories of him decapitating the man name Sie. Wayne noticed the mood change with Dak and turned and walked to his seat as the Queen entered the room.

Dak noticed his mother dressed in an expensive looking attire which was form fitting to her beautiful body. Her appearance was noticeable as she came through the double doors. She seemed to be concentrating as she walked toward her chair. She said hello to Delores and Wayne as she took her spot at the end of the table. Most of the talking between the others stopped as she approached her chair. He noticed her confidence in herself and the respect from the other council persons as she was the Queen of Cliff Tops, and her realm included several surrounding villages and over forty-two-thousand square miles. Her realm reached a three-day horse ride west and north. The distance to the great gorge which separated Cliff Tops, and the New York tribe was south fifteen miles. Only the board members were seated around the large table with the invited guest sitting in the front rows of the church pews. Vicky started the meeting by sitting down in the end seat at the table. She pointed to Wayne.

Wayne stated, "Let the meeting begin. I would like to welcome our visitors along with our board members. We are thankful to have our glorified friends from the New York Tribe and our soldiers returning from the war."

Vicky wanted to show Zorro she did have a democracy, "I would like to mention our government bylaws have been written and reviewed by my Board of Directors. Since a large amount of our growth has occurred in the community of Meadow Bottoms, they will hold an election every year, and they will vote for their representative. Otherwise, I will appoint all other board members in my realm. According to our census, our community grew by six-hundred people over the past year, which is a good thing. One of the changes added to our bylaws is that each new citizen must pledge to follow the laws, pay taxes, and agree I am the Queen before they are granted citizenship. If they fail to pay taxes, follow the laws and accept me as the Queen, they will be subject to be punished and then escorted out of my realm." She glanced at the two men from Meadow Bottoms to make certain they agreed with the bylaws. "Now, I will get to the point of this meeting, Dak please update us on the war down south." She looked at her son.

Dak looked at his mother as he stood. "I will submit the copy of the treaty executed by King Solman and those representing the New Republic. The original is being housed in the city of Harpers Ferry Harbor with the newly formed government." He handed the papers to his mother. "I can assure you the Normand army will not honor the treaty. It is similar to what they have signed with other governments. They have broken all the prior treaties, and they will break this one. Their armies will come north."

Vicky looked at the treaty and scanned the document rather quickly as the contents of the treaty were short and to the point. The boundary lines were noted and located over one-thousand miles south of the Midnight Hole. She noticed King Solman's signature as being the king of the Normand Army and Dak signed his name as being the general of the north armies representing the New Republic. The treaty had several witnesses who had signed the document. She handed the treaty to Delores to review.

Delores was fast to ask, "Why agree to the terms?"

Dak looked at Little Jimmy and Mia and did not answer Delores's question. He felt saddened for their concern for their daughter, Veronica. He also knew Trey had updated his parents on their daughter, and her decision to stay in Southern City. The parents were excited about her being pregnant and devastated with the fact her marriage was forced, and her husband was the King of the Normand Empire. Dak then looked at Delores. "Veronica saved a large part of our army and maybe me by making the decision to leave with her husband, and her goal for each side to sign the treaty. This provided us enough time to withdraw our men to safety across the rivers and re-establish our front lines. She also negotiated to have one-hundred-twenty-seven POWs returned to us." He paused and made eye contact with both Mia and Little Jimmy. "For that, we will always be grateful to Veronica."

Dak then added, "I would suggest we attack King Solman and the Normand army before they attack us. We need to hit them with squads of attackers and then retreat. Ambush them and fight a guerilla war against them. We need to break their spirits and drive them back across the Plains of Jellico. Their army and their boundary lines keep being pushed north closer and closer to us. Every time the battles end with them signing a treaty and securing additional land. This is the third time they have signed a treaty and pledged not to attack the north. Two prior times they broke the treaties, and they will break this one. We can attack them and make the attack look like they started the battle, and they broke the treaty, not us. The New Republic has soldiers, but most have started returning home to their tribes but have sworn an allegiance to fight those bastards." Dak could tell almost everyone in the room was surprised with his recommendation. His mother and Samuel were among the few who did not show emotion with his recommendation. Dak noticed Barney Simpson, the representative from Meadow Bottoms grinned and stared at the table surface during his presentation.

Delores announced, "Based on what I know and the fact we are made to be part of this treaty, I cannot vote for an attack. I understand they have us out numbered ten to one. Why attack if we cannot win? We need to make certain they break the treaty, not us. We do not want to have a reputation of not being honest. We need to strive for peace not war." She then looked at Vicky with concern and then looked back at Dak. "Are you still the general of the Northern Armies?"

Dak ignored Doloris a second time, "I have tried to set up organized groups to run that part of the world. They need to be governed, and they need to be united. There are several warlords, cartels, bands of outlaws, and cut-throats in the region. There are even some Midlanders led by a man named Vulture that have fought alongside us. We have taught these men and women how to fight, and how to kill. Some are very good at both, and we need them fighting alongside us in the future battles. However, until the next battle, they have elected to be mercenaries or make a living being outlaws using their swords to advance themselves financially. They have no love for the Normand army, but there is a concern for the meek and righteous people in the south who choose to live in the middle of our continent. There is a need for a federal police agency and a federal court to be established. However, for the present, the strong survive and the weak are killed. The strong are called warlords, and they will also send their men north. Doing nothing is not going to work."

Hulk looked at his father, Billy Ray, and then at his mother, Delorse. "We have no choice. If we wait, the Normand army will destroy us and those armies south of us. They have broken every treaty they have signed, and you know this to be true. I have personally watched as those Normand bastards butchered innocent children, women, and men in their path. I am not certain you understand the threat they present to us." Delores was taken back by her son's description and the language he used to describe the war as the look on her face turned grim.

Delores looked at Dak, "Why did you sign the treaty? The purpose of the treaty is to promote peace. It does not sound like you have any intention to abide by the treaty."

Dak looked irritated, "The peace we have is temporary and is a delusional concept at best. Peace will not last. The Normand Army out flanked our army. In doing so, they secured over one-hundred prisoners. We lost over four-hundred men in less than one hour just in one battle. They have us outnumbered ten-to-one with a better equipped army and better trained soldiers. Some of our soldiers are young teenagers and others are old men. We fought with what we had. Our initial plan and the only hope as I saw the plan was for us to retreat over the next four months and fight them as we headed north to Beech Grove. Allow them to believe they are pushing us north. This would minimize our losses. At that point, I was counting on the New York Tribe and Cliff Top warriors to enter the war.

I intended to seek help from the New York army and the army from Cliff Tops to hold the line at Beech Grove." He turned and looked at Zorro.

Zorro answered, "We would have responded to your request, and we would have fought to hold the line."

Dak added, "Then, I planned to attack the Normand army from the south by traveling by sea and through the underground network south of Harpers Ferry Harbor and destroy their supply lines. Trap them in the winter weather. We cannot fight them and win in the open ground. They have too many well-trained soldiers. My men failed to burn the Waldo Bridge which crosses the Broad South River. At that point they moved over three-thousand troops across the bridge in one day, and we could not withdraw our other troops fast enough from the plains and mountain regions. They had an opportunity to march directly to Harpers Ferry Harbor and cut off several thousand of our troops." He paused. Dak did not want to talk about the failure of his army. He blamed himself for the defeat.

Mia looked at her husband, Little Jimmy, and then Dak. She knew she was not on the Board of Directors and was not allowed to speak, "What will happen to Veronica if we attack her husband's army?"

Dak took a deep breath, "Mia, I am afraid the same thing will happen to her if we do not attack. I do not believe she is safe, and no one was more aware of the risk than Veronica. I do not believe Board of Director and the Queen of Cliff Tops understand the threat we are under. I cannot convey the need for action by this realm any clearer."

The audience could tell Dak was frustrated with clinched jaws as he spoke, but he also was trying to be amiable as his hands were palms up to his side as he talked and made eye contact with the people in the room. His mother knew he did not like the debriefing and the meeting with the board members. She also observed he was avoiding eye contact with the two men from Meadow Bottoms as Barney Simpson was sitting at the last seat on the table furthermost from her but closest to Dak as he stood and spoke. The other man from Meadow Bottoms was sitting in the first row of the church pews observing the meeting. The Queen had not considered the city representative, Barney Simpson, and her son meeting in this room for the first time sense the capital punishment of Sie. She knew her son had decapitated Sie, a man from Meadow Bottoms, in front of that community. She also knew Dak despised being questioned by people who were not in the battles fighting to the death. Dak looked at Samuel standing in the back of the room, "May I talk to you in private?"

Samuel nodded his head yes. The people in the room saw Dak turn to Samuel and ask him to meet in private. Queen Vicky suspected there was more to Dak's plans as she ignored the request.

Dak turned back to the table with the board members, "I have nothing else to report. I assume there is nothing further you need from me." He looked at Wayne and his mother, the Queen, and walked briskly past Quincy out the rear pushing both double doors open with force. Samuel followed him along with Hulk.

The three men walked into the street and turned to face one another, "The Board of Directors is not going to vote to break the treaty," declared Samuel.

Samuel could tell Dak was frustrated as he observed Dak's reactions as Dak dropped his gaze to the mud-and snow-covered street, "That does not seem to surprise you."

Hulk smiled and answered, "Not one bit." He looked at Samuel. "We know our parents. They are not going to like what we suggest. Their minds are already established, and all have been persuaded by the old-world events. This is the new world here and now. They refuse the change needed."

Dak noticed the two hatchets in their sleeves on Samuel's back. He was also carrying a knife in his boot and a new looking sword which was made with a wide curve hanging in the sleeve strapped to his hip. The blade was not straight like other warriors in Cliff Tops and looked to be made with a heavier gauge of metal. The curved blade would make fighting more difficult with a Sai Sword, similar to his, to block a forceful swing and lock the blade during combat.

41

Dak refocused when Samuel added, "The request to attack the Normand Army and break the treaty was just a show?"

Dak smiled, "Yeah, it was a show. Meeting with you is what I need. We have a covert risky mission planned and with or without the board's blessing we are going to move forward. We are leaving in two days, and I need your assistance. The people in the south and mid regions have moved forward and elected a government and some are preparing to fight for their freedom. However, they cannot win against the army of the south. They will need our assistance. In the meeting, I tried to wake the Queen and her board members up to the reality of the world down south. They need to spend time preparing men for war."

"Your battle strategy was a sound plan. I like the strategy behind the plan. The Normand army would have been too poorly supplied the further north they traveled. Their supply lines coming from Southern City would have been a liability for them. You would have trapped them in the cold winter and destroyed their will to fight and destroyed their army."

Dak looked at Samuel, "The plan did not work. There were several moving parts to the plan, and all had to work with precision. The problem was control. I cannot order the farmers and ranchers to fight. The area will need to develop a government and pledge allegiance to their government. There were some unknowns dealing with the people down south.

Some appeared to be undermining the war effort and either not willing to fight or not willing to pay taxes to support the war. I was surprised some seemed to think everything would be okay once the Normand Army was in control. They would have been sympathizers and willing to supply the Normand Army food during the winter. In addition, my commanders will not follow my orders. Step one in my plan was to burn the damn Waldo Bridge, and we failed. We set our defense line on the south side of the bridge to transport needed animals and crops across from the south to feed our army but most importantly stop their push north at the river. We could have forced them to fight us as they crossed the river." Dak turned his head in frustration.

Wrinkles appeared on Samuel's forehead and his jaw clenched, "I would have beaten any commander who did not follow my order. They would understand what I command is a requirement and not open for negotiation. I would have stripped the landowners of their land and resources if they were unwilling to contribute to the war effort. You cannot partially enter a war and try not to hurt someone's feelings. You must persuade, with force, everyone to do what you demand to crush the enemy."

"Then, we would have treated them the same as the Normand Army would treat them. The people need to be willing to fight for their freedom. If they are not going to fight, then why should we go south and die for their families and their property?" declared Hulk.

Dak thought about Hulk and Robin Hood breaking from the squad and killing those Normand soldiers along the coastline after the treaty had been signed. Hulk's decision had worked, but he had specifically ordered Hulk to follow his commands. He then thought about Vulture not burning the Waldo Bridge which allowed the Normand Army to advance across the river. He did not answer Samuel. He pulled his coat tight to protect against the cold wind. He glanced at the ice-covered ground with the three-day snow which had turned brown from the mud in the street. He wanted to stay on point with Samuel.

Dak glanced at Samuel, "Samuel, we have located the Blueblood cult operating in the southern part of the continent. I believe the nest is located near the port city of Tanger. I now know this cult controls King Solman and maybe has links to Senator Dale in Merlin. How would you suggest we pinpoint the exact location of the cult?"

Samuel smiled, "Your mother told me last night she thought you had located the Blueblood cult, and you would go after them. We never could locate the cult leadership in our investigation from the city of Merlin. We were told of their existence prior to the bombs being dropped a year before the Transitional Period. After the Transitional Period and once we were able to leave our pods, we were told we would need to locate the cult and exterminate them. We, however, did not have information required to locate the cult, and we hoped they were killed along with the other non-survivors in the world. As you know the world immediately after the Transitional Period was in turmoil with everyone trying to survive."

"How did the Queen know I knew of the location of the hidden Blueblood cult?"

"The Queen is a smart lady. She also knows her son." Samuel smiled at Dak. "Wisdom comes with age. I have made mistakes on the battlefield which cost men their lives. I have also learned the importance of diplomacy, and how to be a politician. You, young Dak and Mr. Hulk, will need to learn from your mistakes and gain wisdom as you age."

Samuel glanced at both men. He then added, "Like I told you before, we in Merlin hunted the Rogue Bluebloods for the first five years after the Transition Period. Only a few first-generation Bluebloods knew I was ordered to hunt the rogue sect and exterminate them. At first, we tried to keep the information a secret because we did not know if they survived. Our people were afraid if the normal humans found out about the Rogue Bluebloods, they would not differentiate between us and them. We never were able to establish their origin. We suspected they originated in the old country of Germany. There was no record of them coming from our pods. One arrived in Merlin from the south, and then a second and then a third.

They were easy to spot. We could track them by following the dead bodies they left in their path. They were psychopathic, some deformed, most outcast, very violent, and very hard to kill. However, a few were not disfigured and were very charming in talking with the people, but then they were very impulsive and would kill an entire family for no apparent reason. The testimonies from witnesses we interviewed were graphic, even for an area that was in constant violent turmoil."

"The Blueblood leadership in Merlin at that time was all first-generation Bluebloods, and we knew the Rogue Bluebloods were pure evil and had to be destroyed. We petitioned the Merlin Senate to allow us to travel out of our realm to hunt the Rogue Bluebloods. The normal man could not kill them. They were too good with a sword. At great risk to ourselves, we hunted them trying to exterminate all we could locate. I knew we never located all the Rogue Bluebloods. We found a few loners, but we never located the master or maybe masters. There could be more than one pod, and we knew they were located outside our realm. The Rogue Bluebloods are difficult to predict and hard to locate. They quickly evolved and understood we were trying to exterminate them. The master can hide in plain sight, and I believe they are very good at blending into any environment. They all have pointed ears unless they have been altered by a surgeon. Most of the soldiers have tattoos with piercings, all have eyes of demons, and are truly monsters. To understand them you must first understand the maker because they were created with different traits. Although most are soldiers, some were meant to be leaders. The soldiers were engineered to be controlled by the masters. The Blueblood Senate was too fast to say we killed all of them. The Merlin Senate changed with the revolution and nine of the first-generation Bluebloods became the Merlin Senate. Now, the Blueblood Senators have changed with the election of the second-generation Bluebloods. The second-generation Bluebloods do not have the perfect DNA, and their DNA, I believe, is contaminated."

Dak looked concerned, "How would that be possible?"

"I do not know, but the second generation does not have the same characteristics. We had two Bluebloods who survived the Transitional Period. They were programmed by the maker to excel in genetics, and both were murdered. When they were killed, we lost our understanding of how we were made. The normal humans were blamed and executed before a trial. I never was convinced the two humans were capable of killing the two Bluebloods."

He looked at the ground and hesitated. "Senator Dale claimed he was from a pod similar to mine, but everyone died except him. We could not verify his statements. I never trusted that man." He looked at Dak with a serious expression, "The Rogue Bluebloods will not be easy to locate, but if they are hiding near the City of Tanger, the people in Tanger will know they are close. The citizens of Tanger will live in constant fear. That much evil is impossible to hide and exterminating them will be extremely risky. You will need my help."

Samuel looked down at the ground and then stared into Dak's eyes. The realization had occurred to him why Dak had asked to speak to him outside, "That is why you asked me out here. You need my help to track them and then kill them."

"We were successful in intercepting the gold shipment headed to Southern City which bought us needed time, but we must stop the cult. Yes, I need your help to hunt them and exterminate them with prejudice. As long as they are out there, there will be no peace. For our village to survive and the north to survive, we will have to eliminate the threat coming from the south. We know the cult is located on the west coast of our continent. The problem is twofold. First, we must locate them before the spring and the Normand army attacks the north. We cannot cross the mountain range located southwest of Harpers Ferry Harbor during the winter months. The elevation gain in the gap of the mountains is close to nine-thousand feet, the trail is steep, and now will be covered with ice and snow. It is difficult enough during the summer months, but I can assure you the mountains cannot be crossed in the winter. We have created a path called The No She Trail which crosses through a low gap in the mountain range and is surrounded by nuclear contaminated waste areas. The trail takes you around mountains and is rough, time consuming, and strenuous. Wagons cannot pass, and the horses must be walked around the cliff ledges with blinds over their eyes."

"The Normand Navy has control of the ocean and has total control in the south. The oceans north are frozen this time of year and not passable. So, our second alternative is to proceed west and cross the Midlander's territory before the winter storms and then proceed straight south and find a pass through the mountains and desert to the port city of Tanger. The message we received from a spy indicated the meeting with King Solman and his master was in a bay on a ship located approximately fifty-miles south of Tanger. I agree the locals must have a clue the neighbors are Bluebloods, and we will need to solicit their help. We will need to be back in Cliff Tops by early spring to defend against the possible armies coming from the south. I believe Cliff Tops must be guarded at all times. However, if we are successful in killing the Rogue Bluebloods, the Normand army may stand by the treaty."

Samuel looked confused, "The No She Trail? Is that a name from the old world from a country called China?"

Hulk smiled, "No. Robin Hood came up with that name because there are no females on the trail." Samuel smiled at Dak and then Hulk.

"You mentioned a spy. Who is your spy inside the Southern City feeding you this information?"

"Veronica is one source inside Southern City. The city is very large, and there are those who oppose the King's rule. At great risk the spies sent us communication outlining we must stop the cult."

"I will help. I know we need to kill the Rogue Bluebloods. Let me look at your map."

Dak unfolded the map and showed Samuel the territory. "I do not believe the area west is contaminated by nuclear waste as we have been told. When Zenith and I returned from Merlin, we went north into the frozen tundra. There were no nuclear waste pits in that area. As Hulk and our group crossed to Merlin, there were four nuclear pits as we crossed the plains and the mountain regions." He pointed to the area.

Samuel said, "You will need to update your mother on this mission. She is the Queen, and she needs to know. I will explain to her the importance of the mission. Dak, you will need my help. There are other details about the Rogue Bluebloods you need to be made aware. We did discover certain characteristics before the Transition Period about the Rogue Sect. Which we set in our pods waiting for the Transitional Period to pass, and we hoped they all died." He glanced at Hulk, "Killing one Rogue Blueblood is dangerous and trying to eliminate a nest of them will be costly. Let me warn you. Some of your hunting party might not return."

He hesitated with clenched jaws. "Let me be clear. I know Zenith is very good in battle, but she will be no match for a Master Rogue Blueblood. I know the two Blueblood trainers in Merlin. There was always talk with the Blueblood apprentices and other army personnel about how good they were in combat training. They never competed in the war game tournaments in Merlin, so the cadets and other soldiers speculated on who was the best. Especially the second and third generation Bluebloods would talk among themselves, and they were consumed with the speculation which of the two trainers were the best. The citizens, army personnel, guards, and even the Merlin Senators concluded the two trainers could beat me, all the citizens known to be good with a sword, guards, and the soldiers. However, in secrecy, I would meet the trainers in the arena just the three of us. We respected each other, and it was important for the cadets in training to believe those two were the best warriors. But we would compete." He stared at Dak. "I could beat both in a match individually or at the same time. I have killed five of the male Rogue Bluebloods and one female but never a Master Rogue Blueblood. The five soldiers were better than the two trainers. Dak, the Rogue Bluebloods can discern your weaknesses, and they were engineered to attack a weakness. They will be able to smell your fear, and your fear will make you hesitate and be indecisive which will be your downfall." He kept his jaws clenched and stared at Dak without blinking, "They will unhinge you, and they will show no mercy. They cut the ears and other appendages off their prey and hold them as trophies. The Rogue Master will do whatever he must to survive. He will sacrifice his own soldiers. He will kill whomever he must for his survival. There will be no limits for his means of survival. This was part of the DNA package when the masters were created. The soldiers were programmed to follow orders and be followers. The scientist that created them in the lab tried to find a balance between being a cold-blooded killer and a follower. The soldiers were created to kill but also to follow the command of the master. They have in their DNA package the physical abilities I have, but their advantage is they have no ability for empathy or mercy toward their enemy. We must do this together."

Hulk looked at both men with a questionable expression, "Damn." He then reflected on the Battle of Harpers Ferry Harbor when he ran up the stairs and saw the blood spread across the floor from the dead six guards and General Cuez lying on the floor.

Dak broke Hulk's reminiscing when he said, "I know all about the fear you speak. The fear turns to anger, and the anger leads to hatred. The hatred is the emotion one must fight to overcome our loving nature to brutally kill the opponent."

Dak's eyes narrowed and wrinkles appeared on his forehead as he then stared into Samuel's eyes. "I understand we will have casualties, but we must endure. Those born in harmony die in harmony."

Samuel's posture relaxed, and he glanced at Hulk and Dak, "The Rogue Bluebloods were not genetically programmed to love and that is their one huge advantage. They do not know fear, remorse, or live with regret. The soldiers were designed to follow orders, and a few were programmed to be masters. There is only one master the soldiers will obey. That will be our target. Once a master is killed, the soldiers will separate and then they can be tracked and killed, or they might kill one another fighting for control."

Samuel hesitated, "Did you know your mother has sent a spy to the Asian Continent?" Dak could not hide his surprise. Samuel then added, "She is planning to take out the man named Zanbar who she now is convinced sent the three assassins. She believes, as does Wayne and the rest of her team; Zanbar sent the three assassins to kill your mother. It has something to do with your mother's prior life working in the CIA. None of her group will openly talk about the past. If Wayne or Billy Ray mentioned anything about that time period, the subject is intentionally vague. I have been unable to pin any of them down on any facts."

Dak was in shock. He never thought his mother would try to kill someone. He looked at Samuel, "My mother and I do not agree on the politics of our new world. However, I must protect the Queen. Who is her spy?"

Samuel was not certain he should mention the spy's name. He hesitated, "Captain J.J."

Hulk blew out air, "He is not from that region. He will not have reliable information, and I do not trust him. He is the one who brought the three assassins to Cliff Tops, and he never told us until we confronted him. We have a man who is from Israel. He can get us into the country unseen. He has no love for the Persians. For a fee, he and his associates will be able to assist with killing this man named Zanbar, but first we need your help taking out this nest of Rogue Bluebloods. Time is running out."

The horn from the watchman located in the tower on the cliff sounded. The three men jerked and looked in the direction of the watchtower. The elderly guard was standing in the watchtower looking through his binoculars toward the sea. Walter yelled and held up one finger, "One unidentified small merchant ship northeast about two miles out."

Dak looked at Samuel, "Who would be crazy enough to sail this far north this time of year?"

Samuel announced, "Wayne confirmed last week all our boats are dry docked. We have no one out at sea. It must be a foreigner."

The three men walked to the cliff and at first did not see the tiny ship. Hulk watched the position of the watchman and the direction of his binoculars. He finally exclaimed, "There it is, about thirty degrees northeast." They observed the ship sailing close to a mile out in the rough waters. The small sailing vessel was bobbing up and down like a cork in a fast-running creek with the sail almost disappearing in the swell of the waves. Zenith and Billy Ray were the next two to arrive. Wayne and Vicky walked next to the group on the cliff along with Zorro and many others. Hulk pointed in the ship's direction. Wayne looked confused, "Who would be that crazy to sail from the north in thirty-foot-high swells in this ocean? They must be lost."

Vicky announced, "I do not believe they are lost. You better go meet them on the dock and see what they desire. You need to notify Doc Johnson. There could be a medical emergency. The arrival of a small sailing vessel this time of year is concerning. We need to follow our quarantine protocol."

Wayne looked at Vicky understanding the ship could be hauling people with a deadly virus. He walked toward the lift as he pulled his cloth face mask down around his mouth and nose.

Dak announced, "Zenith and I will go with you." Wayne motioned for the lift operator to lower the lift to the beach below. He motioned for four men to come with them.

The group stood on the dock and watched as the one-man crew on the boat worked the sails and was trying to keep the sailing vessel from ramming the ocean side of the jetty wall. The large waves and cold weather were brutal for the sailor. The sailor threw a rope to the men on the jetty to pull the sailing vessel further into the jetty and onto the stationary dock. They noticed the sailor bend over as he held the rail and seemed to be exhausted as the boat cleared the jetty rock wall and was guided past the underwater large metal barriers staged in the opening as the boat coasted into the jetty and the smoother waters. The sailor then lowered the two sails.

Vicky and the large gathering of folks stood on the cliff area and looked down as the one sailor on the boat threw a second rope to the men of Cliff Tops to secure the vessel to the inside of the jetty and the dock. The sailor then jumped over the rail and landed on the dock. Wayne and two other men pulled their swords and approached him. Dak and Zenith also approached with caution.

Vicky and the others observed from the cliff top as the sailor fell on the dock at Wayne's feet. Wayne turned and pointed to the cliff top people to prepare the medical team.

Dak and Zenith both knelt next to the sailor. Wayne turned to his four men, "Secure the vessel to the dock and search it." Two men boarded the vessel and two of them worked to better secure the boat with additional ropes to the cleats on the dock, and they also placed the soft buoys along the dock and the side of the vessel. As the other two men entered the cabin, Wayne ordered, "Burl let me know what is in the storage bins and see if you can discern the home port."

Dak asked, "Mister, who are you?"

The sailor at first did not respond and closed his eyes and then opened them. The sailor was exhausted. Zenith noticed the blue eyes and quickly reached for his hood and pulled the fur cap off his head revealing the two-pointed ears and blond hair. She excitedly announced, "This is not a he. She is a second-generation Merlin Blueblood. I recognize her. She is nineteen years old, and her name is Dominique Vandergriff. We need to get her inside." Zenith looked puzzled and then glanced at Dak and shook her head no with a puzzled expression.

Dak picked her up and carried her across the dock and the beach to the lift. Dak spoke loudly to the lift worker, "Hurry." Zenith tried to obtain her pulse by holding her wrist as they ascended the cliff. Once on the top of the cliff, Trey, and Tommy Boy carried her to the fourplex. Zenith noticed every few feet, Dominique would open her eyes and moan as she appeared to be in pain. Doc Johnson ran over to her side and looked at her and felt her head for a fever and held her wrist as the men were carrying her. "She might be going into shock. There is a faint pulse. She could be dehydrated. We need to get her warm and administer an IV with your blood, Zenith."

The sailing vessel was secured with ropes to the dock, and the two guards came out of the cabin to meet Wayne. Burl said, "Sir, there is one dead body in the cabin. The man is frozen and must have been dead for several days. There is very little food and water. The four heating oil cans are empty. There is no cargo. The map they were utilizing has their path marked with them going north around the pole from Merlin. She was on a one-way voyage to our city."

The other man then added, "They were traveling light with no weapons, very little food, and nothing of value. The storage containers are empty. There is only the one map of the northern oceans. They do have reinforce sails to assist with the increase wind velocity and to generate elevated speed."

Wayne ordered, "Secure the vessel on the beach. Dry dock it. The sailor will not be able to leave until spring. Bring the dead body to the top and secure the body in the jail." He then turned and walked quickly to the lift area waiting on the next trip.

The teenager was laid on the table in the fourplex. Mia held up her head and provided water. Dominique opened her eyes and drank the water. Her voice was raspy, "Where am I?"

Dolores leaned over her, "You are in the city of Cliff Tops."

She closed her eyes and appeared to be straining to speak, "I need to talk with Zenith and Queen Vicky."

Zenith came to her side and bent over her face, "Dominique, we will provide you with food and water. Doc Johnson will set up an IV for me to transfer you a half pint of my blood. Your blood pressure is low, and you are dehydrated. You need fluids. Why are you traveling this far by yourself? Why take the chance this far north in this weather?"

She whispered, "Your father sent me. The other crew member was an older man who volunteered for the mission and died a few days ago. We ran out of heating oil. I knew I could not turn back, and I kept going north around the continent. I need to talk to you and Queen Vicky in private." Zenith felt the ominous feeling about her father. The bad news was coming with regards to him being discovered by Senator Dale.

Zenith spoke to those in the room. "Tell the folks out front she sailed around the north pole. Clear the room." Dak walked next to Zenith as everyone left the room. Zenith looked closely at Dominique, "You can tell me with him present. Dak is the son of our Queen. Queen Vicky is here."

Vicky walked next to the bed on the opposite side of Zenith and Dak.

Dominique looked tired, hungry, and her face was red from being exposed to the ocean's cold winds. Her lips were covered in sores caused by the freezing weather. She whispered, "I have some very bad news. The army from Merlin has been ordered to cut through the waste land across the Midlander's territory on a direct path for Cliff Tops. They mean to conquer you. Your father told me to advise you to cut the patrols off between the large nuclear waste pits. The patrols will not be equipped to enter the nuclear waste areas. They know there is a trail, and they will send patrols of men to find the way followed by their army. If you can stop the patrols, the main army will not be able to advance. I knew I must reach you before the winter storms, so you could prepare."

Dak stepped forward and leaned in next to Zenith and stared down at the female, "When?"

Her voice was raspy. "They will leave Merlin in early spring."

Dak clenched his jaw, "How many Blueblood soldiers, and how many men in the army are headed this way?"

"Eight-hundred men with an additional one-hundred Blueblood soldiers, all third generation Bluebloods."

Dak felt a sudden feeling of despair. He looked at the female Blueblood. She could hardly hold her head up as she spoke. He could tell she was exhausted from the trip. "Let us get you warm with a hot meal and allow you to sleep. Our doctor will set up an IV for you. We have much to discuss when you wake."

# Chapter 5

"I asked you here to update me on your plans. I know you are planning another mission."

Dak looked out the window and thought about his mission. "Are you certain the invitation was a request? It felt more like an order, mother." The two stood still letting the air clear.

"I also would like to remind you; Delores is a board member. She is one of the chosen people in charge of my realm, and she is also one of my dearest friends. I have known her for a long time. I did not raise you to be disrespectful. You will show her respect and not ignore her when she asks you a question. She has photographic memory and is one of the most educated people in this part of the world. I trust her with my life."

Dak turned to his mother in a harsh tone, "I was the general of the northern army. I was appointed by my peers. Yet here in your city, I am treated like a child. I do not live under your realm, mother. Therefore, I am not beholden to take orders from you. You might want to consider that before you start ordering me to do something. I have provided you direction in dealing with the army of Merlin and yet you have time and time again chosen not to listen. I have suggested you make alliance with the tribes in the middle of the continent. You have time and time chosen not to listen to me." He turned and looked back out the window, "You will no longer hold the opportunity over my head for me to be the king of Cliff Tops when you step aside." She could see the clenched jaws and the directness of his eyes as he stared at her and then turned and peered out the window.

"Why come here and update me about this mission? Why not leave from Zenith Point?"

He turned back to the Queen. "Mother, we know who is behind the wars. There is a cult led by a team of Rogue Bluebloods. They control King Solman. We have now confirmed they are affiliated with Senator Dale in Merlin. We have their gold and at some point, they will come for their revenge and their gold. Your realm better be prepared. Before the Blueblood Master obtains so much power he cannot be challenged, I must leave on this mission to locate him and execute the beast. We will attack him and catch him unprepared before he surrounds himself with a large army."

Dak hesitated and faced his mother, "The cult's home base is on the west coast near the Port of Tanger. I must locate them and will exterminate them."

Vicky looked at her son, "So, Dak you are planning to leave on this mission? We need to prepare for the soldiers attacking across our west border. Did you not hear what the sailor reported? I cannot allow all these soldiers to leave. We need them here to fight with us. We need to be prepared for a siege."

She stared at her son, "And as far as holding the title of the King of Cliff Tops over your head, I will make the decision when I am ready who will be my successor. You are not ready to be a king."

His face turned red with the last remark. "Mother, if we cut the head off the snake, there might not be soldiers attacking you from the west. Me, my wife, my crew, a few men from both Cliff Tops, a few from New York Tribe, and Samuel will be leaving in two days. We will be home before the attack of the Blueblood army in the spring."

Vicky hesitated and realized now why Dak had returned to Cliff Tops. He needed Samuel. "Do you really believe if you kill the cult master, this action will stop the invasion from the west by the government of Merlin?"

"I do believe once we kill the cult leadership, there will be no war, but if we fail, you need to prepare to repel the best army on the planet. The soldiers and the army from Merlin will be nothing like the Normand army. They will roll across the Midlander territory and kill all that oppose them. I will need Samuel on this mission for us to be successful. He is the only one who has experience hunting and executing the Rogue Bluebloods." He watched his mother to verify her facial expression if she would allow Samuel to be part of his mission.

"Where did you obtain this information on the cult?"

Dak looked at his mother, "Veronica. She has sacrificed more than anyone for us. I do not believe you understand what we are facing. Veronica was adamant we must undertake this mission, and I believe her. We cannot sit here and wait. We must be on the offense, or I can assure you, we all will be killed. The Normand army, the large army in Merlin, and the Midlanders all have bigger and better armies than us. Our part time warriors are no match for these three large armies. I have tried to unite the north against the threats, and my efforts have been futile. The northern tribes do not trust one another and are led by warlords and people from the old world who are self-serving. They handle things like the old-world governments handled them. They wish for me to agree to their concessions before they commit their wealth and people to war. I was faced with trying to establish fighting men to confront the Normand army. I did not have time to meet with the different groups and discuss their concessions. I assumed the people in that area would fight for their freedom. I will not make that mistake in the future."

Vicky stared at Dak while she processed his answer. She also knew his comment about the old world was directed at her. "What about the Midlanders? You know they protect their territory. They do not allow outsiders crossing their designated land. Since the Transitional Period, they have elected to turn their backs on the old world and anyone that lives by the rules of the old world. They will enforce their creed and kill anyone who crosses into their territory."

"I know mom. I do not see another way. We will attempt stealth, but if we are confronted with an entanglement of Midlanders, we will then try diplomacy. Fighting the Midlanders will be the last choice." Dak walked to the map on the table. She could tell he was irritated. He then looked at his mother, "I have fought next to Midlanders. One of my captains, a man named Vulture, lived near the Midlander territory. Some of them agreed to fight with us. They are fierce warriors, and I need all the fierce fighters I can find. Captain Vulture has indicated the Midlanders blame the old-world abomination on the old industrialized system and the greed of the people of that era. The B12 Virus was made by Artificial Intelligence (AI) and released on the world to cleanse the human population. The bombs then were launched in retaliation to kill the masses of people in response to the release of the B12 virus. All the countries who owned bombs fired their bombs. There was no one innocent in the old world. The chaos in the world resulted in the death of the planet. You know the history of the world geographically re-shaping. The world has been cleansed. The Midlanders have pledged to never return to an industrial world. They choose to live a simpler life. If the Midlanders discover you are the only realm that has coal, and you start using the coal to modernize and start an industrialized country, I do believe they will attack you. They will never allow the world to go back to the old ways."

"You have changed."

Dak stared into his mother's eyes, "I have changed. This is the world we live where there is no mercy and the meek are killed or forced into slavery. You and your council need to adapt. The old world is a thing of the past, and it will never be reestablished. War is coming, and you better be ready for the harsh reality and stop living in the past. I do not agree with you and your board members. Therefore, I do not choose to discuss the future with them. I do not mean to be disrespectful to Delores, but I do not agree with her ideology. And given your weakness in the world, and the lack of a strong army, I would suggest you change your position. War is coming north."

He turned and looked out the window, "I did listen growing up to some of the stories of the old world. Wayne and Billy Ray would discuss a city in the north which they nicknamed Gotham. In the city of Gotham, a man was arrested fifty-five times and released back into society. He then stabbed two people on a subway once he was released the last time. He had a history of being a thief, a violent gangster, a drug user and yet in the city of Gotham the government released him back on the streets to harm others. I would hang the man and leave him hanging by his neck for a week for all to see after his first time being caught stealing, and then he would not be able to commit the other fifty-four crimes. In addition, he would serve as a deterrent for others who would be persuaded not to steal."

The Queen looked perplexed trying to figure out if her son was being honest or was he really that jaded. She knew the liberal cities in the old country of the United States had gone too far to the left and the nation had started to erode from the inside. The liberal party had controlled the mainstream news media, and the people were fed political propaganda which resulted in the decline of the morals of the nation and hindered the respectable judgement of the voting public.

He turned and hesitated. "One other thing. You have told me that my father was selected randomly as a doner, and you did not know him. You also told me that me and my friends were all enhanced by an old-world process to align and cleanse our chromosomes, so we would never contract over fifty childhood diseases. Evidently, our intelligence and athletic abilities were also enhanced."

She looked at her son with one eyebrow raised, "Yes. Delores, Mia, Casey and I all checked into the process to purify you and their kid's DNA. During that time period the world was just starting to understand Artificial Intelligence, and we utilized the technology in our pregnancies. We felt we needed to research the technology and then act accordingly. Our actions were the right thing to do."

"I understand by listening to Billy Ray and Wayne talk over the years that Artificial Intelligence was utilized to destroy the world?"

She explained, "The technology was used worldwide, and some very bad people misused the AI programs."

"We all are thankful, but I do not believe you randomly selected a donor for me. You never do anything randomly. Your prior husband who was shot and killed was a mild-mannered man. I have heard your friends, and you describe him. I do not have his traits. I am a warrior and have the heart of a warrior. This is where I excel. Who was my father?"

"I will tell you one thing. I loved my late husband, and he was gifted intelligently. I watched him die after being murdered," she expressed in an angered voice. Her jaws were clenched, "I do not know the identity of your father. I swear this to you. I do know you are my son, whom I love. I do not wish for you to have to make the type of decisions I made. Taking someone's life, even if the killing is justified, can wear on your psyche. You must learn compassion to be a leader. Greed is one of the worst sins, because greed leads to the seduction of the other sins."

"Mother, I am way past the psyche concerns. You have no way of knowing what it is like to butcher someone with a sword, knife, spear, or hatchet. That is normal for me. I am a berserker. I will champion this mission because the mission is the right thing to do. I do not consider myself to be greedy. I desire to live with my family a humble life of hunting, fishing, and ranching. We have no other choice." He turned and walked out.

# Chapter 6

Dominique opened her eyes and glanced around at the ceiling and walls of the room. As she looked, she observed the wood burning stove with the fire burning hot. She noticed several blankets on her and a large fur bedspread on top. She pulled her left hand from under the blankets and ran her hand over the top bedspread as she felt the softness of the fur. She thought back to her trip and how close she came to dying at sea. Three days prior to her making the trip to Cliff Tops, her sailing companion froze to death. She had tried to ration the heating oil, and she used the last of the oil the prior day. She felt grateful she was now in the warm bed. She quickly remembered sailing into the jetty and viewing the large cliff covered in ice, snow, and the men on the dock before passing out. She thought, "Did I talk briefly to a man on the dock?" She turned toward the door when she heard someone approaching from the hall.

"Well, good morning sleeping beauty. We wondered if you were ever going to wake up." Mia smiled and walked to the window. "Maybe you would like to see out the window? The sun is big and bright this cold morning." She opened the drapes and allowed the sunlight into the room.

Dominique felt relief with the happy spirit of the small lady who entered her room. She immediately reached out with her telepathic powers. Her telepathic powers provided her the ability to detail a person's aura. Her ability to sense the qualities in a human. The small lady was one of good will and her aura was a loving nature. She relaxed and asked, "Where am I? How long have I been here?"

Mia sat down on the side of the bed and smiled, "Honey, you sailed into the jetty two days ago. You are at Cliff Tops. The most northern city of our continent. You have slept for twenty-seven hours. We asked our doctor to look at you. He recommends we cover your exposed skin and lips with lotion. Your lips have started to heal. I am sorry your companion did not make it. On the Queen's orders, we buried him."

"He was a nice man who loved to sail. He volunteered to come on this mission with me, and without him I could not have made the journey through the northern passage." Delores walked into the room followed by Wayne both holding cups of coffee. Dominique looked at the two.

She again reached out with her psyche senses and felt the aura of the two, and both were loving. Wayne smiled, "My name is Wayne, and I am the City Manager. We are pleased to see you are now awake. Let me know if you need anything. We anticipate you to have a full recovery. I will go tell the cook to make you some eggs and such. You need to eat."

"I would like to see Zenith. I need to tell her about the war to come."

Delores smiled, "My name is Delores. I am one of the council members. You need to rest and recover. Your body needs time to heal. The war can wait. I will notify Zenith you are awake."

Dominique watched Delores and was confused by her lackadaisical attitude with regards to the Merlin army. She thought, "How can she not be concerned?"

\*\*\*

Zenith walked into the room and smiled as Dominique was eating the last of three eggs. She set her cup of goat milk down on the tray. "How are you feeling? That must have been one heck of a journey. You are the talk of Cliff Tops."

"Thank you for helping me. I am hot with all these blankets and the fire. This room is toasty." Zenith reached over and removed the large fur blanket and pulled down the other blanket. Dominique sat up in the bed and positioned a pillow behind her back pressed against the headboard and was impressed by Zenith's friendly actions to assist her pulling down her fur blanket. "A Blueblood warrior would never assist someone. In Merlin, the Blueblood warriors were taught actions of helping others were a sign of weakness. Yet you choose to assist me. Why is that?"

"I have learned it is better to give then receive. You are welcome. Normally people complain about being cold here in the north. It takes an extended period and a strong positive mental attitude for one to become acclimated to the cold weather. You really must embrace the bitter cold wind. The spring, early fall, and summer are something to cherish. The mountains, ocean view, rivers and vast open lands really are beautiful, but the winter is another story. I am still trying to acclimate." Zenith sat on the side of the bed and smiled. "I am anxious to know how my father is doing."

Dominique looked at Zenith, "Your dad is doing what he can. Your parents and my parents go way back. The four were in the same pod in the Arctic during the Transition Period. My parents aspire for me to be someone who makes a difference, and not a follower. I overheard the conversation with my parents and your father, and I volunteered to locate you here in Cliff Tops. None of the adults at first would agree, but they soon realized I had an opportunity to travel and not be noticed missing. I was scheduled to travel to Israel located in Asia for school. Instead, I came here."

"You sailed around the north of our continent. You are only the second sailor to ever accomplish that task. Why did you volunteer for such a hazardous trip?"

"They needed someone you would trust. The route is three months faster. I knew I needed to help, so I volunteered. There are those in the Blueblood community that do not agree with the rule of the Merlin Senate. They dislike what has happened in our city."

Dak, Tommy Boy, and Trey walked into the room. Zenith glanced at the three and then turned and smiled at Dominique. "These are the men who carried you to this warm room."

She smiled and tried to sense each of their aura which two of the men were normal for humans. "I remember being carried along the top of the cliff. Thank you."

Tommy Boy and Trey both said, "You are welcome."

Zenith turned to her husband and the two men, "Dominique is a student of science. She is one of the few who elected not to enter the training to become a Blueblood Warrior. Her father and mother are both educators and work in the medical industry. She was going to go to Israel and study but came here instead."

"My parents are both scientists. They try to manufacture better medicines and are classroom instructors."

Zenith noticed Dominique suddenly showed signs of fear and alarm as she stared at the door to the hall.

Samuel walked into the room. Tommy Boy and Trey stood to the side to allow Samuel an area to enter. Dominique looked at Samuel as Samuel asked how the sailor was getting along.

Dominique pulled the covers upward as she set straight in the bed as fear resonated in her eyes as she said, "No, not him. He will kill us."

Dominique looked alarmed at Zenith, "I thought I could trust you. Your father told me to seek you out. You would do the right thing."

Dak stepped forward and was alarmed as he observed her action, "No one is going to harm you. Samuel will protect you."

She noticed the two hatchets strapped to his back and the sword in the sleeve on his side, "He is one to fear."

Samuel noticed the unmistakable look of sudden panic on Dominique's face. "Come on guys, we have work to do. We will check on you later." Samuel smiled and walked out. Trey and Tommy Boy both smiled and followed Samuel.

Dak looked at Zenith with a questionable expression. Zenith motioned with her head for him to leave the room. He then turned to Dominique, "We have some books on science that survived from the old world. I will go retrieve a couple, and you can read them while you recover." He walked out of the room and could be heard walking up the stairs to his mother's chambers.

Mia walked over to the bed and picked up the tray of empty food. She smiled, "Queen Vicky will be in to see you soon. Girl, you do not have anything to worry about. Queen Vicky will not allow anyone to harm you. You are free to do what you desire."

Zenith added, "Samuel will be leaving with me on a mission tomorrow. We must hurry and beat the harsh winter. The people in this tribe will take good care of you. You are our guest."

"When will you return?"

"The spring of next year."

"No, you cannot leave me. Your father said you must protect your tribe and these people."

"You will learn to trust these people. You need to be taught how to fight, protect yourself, and your friends. You have the skill set to be a warrior. It would appear to me; you also have other skills very few other Bluebloods encompass."

She stared at Dominique waiting for her to respond. When Dominique did not answer, Zenith added, "I know you are very brave. You just sailed a small sailing vessel several thousand miles through some of the roughest ocean waters in the world." Dak walked back into the room and handed the book of science to Dominique. She laid the book on the bed next to her. She again extended her psyche ability directly at Dak to sense his aura. She knew she could not sense another Blueblood's aura, but his man was not a Blueblood. There was a small trace of the unknown she could detect but not solve.

Zenith watched Dominque closely as her facial expression changed as she stared at Dak concentrating.

Domingue turned to Zenith, "Zenith, you do not understand. You were a natural at fighting. You received those genetic traits from your parents. That is the way the maker designed the first-generation Bluebloods, so the offspring would be warriors. You were the highest-rated female to ever complete the trials to be a Blueblood Warrior. In addition, your skill ratings were higher than ninety-five percent of all the male students." She looked at Zenith and smiled, "Plus, you are so pretty. All the guys still talk of you, and how you are the prettiest female ever. I have been told Apollo still has your picture hanging in his locker. He still has not accepted a mate because of his feeling for you. My father was able to reattach his right hand for him in the surgery center after his mishap in the tournament. The rumor was that you two were to be paired after you were granted your warrior status. He still desires you."

Zenith smiled, "Some would question if I actually completed the trials, and the incident was no tournament he lost. It was a trail-by-comeback. A battle to the death. I am glad to hear Apollo recovered from the trial by combat." She glanced at her husband and then turned back to Dominique, "Apollo is a bully and self-absorbed man. His pride in himself is not appealing to me. I do not believe he has empathy for others. The Makers erred on certain aspects of genetic breeding." She stared at Dominique. "Some of the most important traits such as empathy, compassion, and love were ignored. A Blueblood has to be disciplined and be willing to learn how to have compassion and love for others. The characteristic has to be taught, and the Blueblood has to be willing to learn. It is easier to be psychotic. I love my husband, and I was so happy he won and spared Apollo's life. The Merlin Senate was going to have Dak murdered. Senator Dale is a Rogue Blueblood. He is not from one of the sanctioned pods that survived the Transition Period. He is no doubt psychotic."

Dominique looked surprised at Dak, "You are the man who beat Apollo in the senate ring? In a trial by combat. You spared his life?"

Dak smiled, "That would be me. I did not know he had desires for Zenith. If I knew, I would have killed him." He developed a large smile as Zenith quickly turned and looked at him with a frown and the wrinkles appeared on her forehead, "I am kidding. What? Can a guy not joke?"

"Your mannerisms do not depict that of a warrior. I mean you are not like Samuel. You seem so simple yet mysterious to me. Great warriors do not go out of their way to retrieve a book for someone. A great warrior orders someone else to retrieve the book." She then glanced at Zenith, "I mean he does not act like a great warrior."

Dak looked at Dominique, "Looks may be deceiving but that is the nicest compliment anyone has bestowed on me in a long time."

Zenith smiled, "Dominique, I can assure you Dak is not simple, and these people here at Cliff Tops are not simple-minded. You need to give them a chance, and Dak, I believe, is the best warrior on the planet. I believe he is better than the Blueblood training instructors in the academy. He is better than Samuel."

Dak smiled, "You ladies certainly know how to feed the male ego. My head just grew so large, I might not be able to fit it through the bedroom door."

Dak smiled and looked at Dominique, "Samuel has only killed one person since he started residing here in Cliff Tops. The man he killed was an Asian assassin sent to kill our Queen. Zenith is right. You need to learn how to defend yourself. A person in the new world is defined by how well he or she can utilize a weapon, and there is no better instructor than Samuel to teach you. But unfortunately, he is leaving with us on the mission. I will ask Billy Ray to teach you. He taught me and my friends."

"The book I provided you may help you learn how to combine certain elements to form other materials. We need someone to forge lightweight metals and develop better arrows for use in battle."

"I do not wish to spend my time trying to develop tools to kill. I do not believe in killing others," Domonique announced as she shifted positions in the large bed. Zenith noticed she then looked at Dak and seemed to be concentrating.

Zenith smiled, "The Blueblood empire is marching to destroy us. King Solman and the Normand army have tried to kill us. We killed the Persian assassins trying to kill our Queen. The Midlander tribes will kill us if the opportunity presents itself. The southern part of this continent is full of bandits and cut-throats. I can appreciate your position, but someone must fight and protect the meek. Once you have children, you will change. You will desire to have your children protected. Your gifts are to help others through research and medicine, but you need to branch out. You need to be proficient to defend yourself, and you have the skill set to learn how to see things before they happen. My gift was to be a warrior, and I kill those who need to be killed and protect the innocent. I believe in doing what is right, and these are my people."

"Samuel is known as the human slayer; a killer of many people. I do not trust him."

Dak looked at Dominique, "Samuel is direct in the way he approaches people or missions and has a code he follows. He believes in the chain of command. He is tough but fair to his soldiers. He will listen to his wife, the Queen of Cliff Tops."

Dominique shifted in her bed a second time and stared at Dak, "That is the problem. No one is innocent based on the laws in Merlin. The people who survived the civil war are guilty of being a rebel if nothing else and that alone places them in the crosshairs of the now established government. If any Blueblood speaks out against the senate, we will be arrested for insurrection. Samuel and his men were the enforcers of the Blueblood law. He was brutally efficient in carrying out the senate's warrants. I thought he was dead."

She then extended her stare at Dak, "What about you? What do you believe?"

Dak smiled, "I believe in doing what is right, what is morally correct, and protecting those who cannot protect themselves."

Mia stepped forward, "You need to rest. If you would like, I can assist you to the restroom."

Dominique was surprised to hear Mia's voice. She was small in stature and easy to go unnoticed. "Are you my handmaid?"

Mia laughed, "Of course not. I have volunteered to assist you and nourish you back to good health. You met my son, Trey. He carried you into your room from the top of the cliff. We all try to help one another."

"He is huge, and you are so tiny."

Mia smiled, "You have not met Trey's father. I also have a very beautiful daughter. Her name is Veronica, and she lives in Southern City."

"Southern City! What is she doing living in Southern City? Is that not the command center of the Normand Army? I thought they were attacking your city."

Mia smiled, "My daughter is the Queen of the Normand Army."

"What! I do not understand. She is the Queen of the Normand Army? I thought you were at war with the Normand army. I need a flow chart to keep track of all these people and their titles."

Zenith and Dak laughed along with Mia. Dominique looked at Zenith, "I wish you did not have to leave. Zenith, I trust your father. He and my parents work together trying to make Merlin a better place. The city is in turmoil, and we believe some very corrupt individuals are in control. Someone is killing the first-generation of Bluebloods. My parents live in constant fear."

Vicky walked into the room. She smiled at Dominique, "How is our world traveler doing today? We are so happy you are doing better."

She immediately felt the loving warmth of the Queen's aura. "I was always convinced that Zenith was the prettiest female. All the Blueblood men and men in Merlin would talk about her beauty. I am not so certain now after meeting you if she is the prettiest female."

Vicky smiled and stood beside of the bed, "I can assure you the men in Merlin are correct. Zenith is prettier than I."

"But you are married to Samuel?"

Vicky glanced at Dak and Zenith, "Yes. He is my husband and the father of our two daughters. He will be leaving tomorrow with my son and several of my son's friends along with Zenith on a very important mission. We will take care of you, and if you need anything, ask me or Mia. We thank you for risking your life to bring us the plans of the army in Merlin. We will start preparing. If the secret mission is successful our people are undertaking, it may prevent bloodshed and the loss of thousands of lives. If we are attacked, we will fight. In the spring if you would like to return to Merlin, we will have your vessel prepared for you. Is there anything you need?"

"Dak provided me with this book to read and suggested I train to be a warrior. I guess I am stuck here until spring."

# Chapter 7

Zenith walked over next to the Queen. They both watched as the four children were playing in the playroom. Zenith said, "I need you to understand, I will stand by Dak at all times. We are scheduled to go on this mission, and we are leaving tomorrow. You know I am a warrior like your husband. Dak is the leader of the group of friends. Dak's friends love him and look to him for leadership."

Vicky glanced at Zenith, "What is on your mind? Speak now and speak plainly."

"I have watched Dak become totally consumed as the general in the New Republican Army as he was named the general of the army by his peers. I can tell you he needs time to grow into that leadership role. I am a warrior, and I have been trained as a warrior since I was their age. Dak is a great warrior. He might be the best fighter I have ever seen, but he must learn how to be a leader of people. This mission is too important. We must win. I believe you need to order Billy Ray to go on this mission as the leader of this mission?"

Vicky watched as Drake tackled his cousin, Kindle. She stepped forward, "Drake you do not push other people down. Now go sit in the corner." She turned to Nancy, "You must make certain they learn to be thoughtful of others and respect others." Nancy assisted Kindle to her feet, "Yes, my Queen."

Vicky turned to face Zenith, "I will order Billy Ray to lead this mission, but at some point, you must stand up to Dak and have a conversation with him about how you feel. You are his wife and the mother of his two children. As a wife, you must talk to your husband and be honest; otherwise, your marriage is hollow. He must be made to understand your position."

Queen Vicky turned and watched the kids. She then turned back to Zenith, "One more thing. What do you know about Domingue and her abilities?"

Zenith was surprised with the nature of the question. "She is like her parents. She is a student of science. Her parents both worked in the medical ward, and both were outspoken about the violence committed by the Blueblood army against the people of Merlin. They view the conduct of the army and federal police in Merlin different from the military and the now established Senators in Merlin."

"Samuel reported to me her abilities are more of the psyche ability. Samuel indicated there were a few Bluebloods that were equipped in their DNA structure by the creator, the ability to read a human's aura. He felt her reach out to the others in the room with her sense driven ability when he first walked into her room. Samuel indicated he can feel others on a very small scale, but her ability to do this is off the chart."

Zenith was now cautious. She thought back to the encounters and Dominque's reaction when she met each person and how she became fearful of Samuel before he entered her room. She knew he was approaching. "I have only heard rumors of this ability. The Blueblood leadership kept certain things secret. The Blueblood leaders wanted to use their abilities to the fullest in dealing with the normal humans. I do not know of her abilities. She never was in any of my classes or social gatherings. She spent her time mostly growing up with her parents. I recall once my father mentioned she was not normal, but he did not elaborate. I just figured none of us Bluebloods are normal."

***

The riders all gathered and were hugging their spouses, children, and friends. Vicky noticed the temperature was rather warm for the season. She held her two daughters by the hands, Kindle and Kenzie, and their father kissed both on the heads. Samuel kissed Vicky and then mounted his horse and waited as Vicky allowed the two girls to walk into the fourplex for a snack with the help of the daycare provider.

Dominique walked onto the porch and stood next to Vicky as the two girls ran past her inside as the daycare worker hurriedly walked to catch the running kids. She watched the riders gather in the street to start the journey. Vicky glanced at Dominique from her peripheral vision, "Dominique, should you be out of bed? You need to rest."

"I am starting to regain my strength. I have been reading the book Dak provided. I have some ideas about forging metals. I also decided I would like to take fighting lessons. Can Billy Ray teach me?" Vicky turned enough to see Dominique more clearly, "I am guessing you met Ivan Chezon?"

"What makes you ask?"

Vicky smiled, "I have known Ivan for years. There are several females prettier than I, and you are one of them. I knew you had met him with that statement. It was a message to me; he is doing okay. We go back before the Transitional Period in the old world."

"Yes, we met right before my voyage. He said he knew you, and I should mention how pretty you are." Dominique hesitated and whispered, "He said the scene of you walking up the stairs in Von Salkowski's home will always be etched in his memory. Do tell, or is that another secret message?"

Vicky smiled and thought back to over twenty years ago to the job when she worked for the CIA. She killed Von and several of his guards with hidden pistols while in the nude. She recalled meeting Ivan that day standing with a pistol aimed at Ivan in the kitchen, and Ivan seemed to enjoy the view of her standing in the nude even with the gun aimed at his chest. She recruited him to work for her in the CIA that day. "I will ask Little Jimmy to teach you. He is very patient and a great warrior. He was my bodyguard during the old world. Besides, Billy Ray elected at the last minute to lead this mission and spend time with his two sons."

Dominique turned and glanced at Vicky, "I talked with Dak and Zenith in-depth about the mission. I wanted to go with them. Dak said he was leading the mission. He was nice but said I could not go. Does he know Billy Ray is going to be leading the mission?"

Queen Vicky turned to face Dominque, "I understand you have the ability to see inside someone. I understand you have the ability to see the true nature of a person. You are psychic."

Dominique turned and faced the group about to leave. She glanced at the riders and thought about being dishonest to the Queen. "Yes, I can interpret the aura of a normal human. I cannot however interpret the aura of a Blueblood. I can sense a Blueblood's present but not read their profile of their aura. It is not easy to be a psychic. I spent a great deal of time becoming disciplined to develop my ability."

"What have you learned since you have arrived here in Cliff Tops about my people?"

Dominique glanced at Dak. "Everyone is good natured and most people of age who lived through the demise of old earth live with regret which is normal. I can feel their pain of life.

However, there is one I could not read, and I believe you know which one I am referring."

They both watched as Dak hugged his sons, and his two boys were kissed by Zenith. Drake and Denzel ran to Queen Vicky as they were finished saying goodbye. Trey and Tommy Boy both mounted their horses, and each pulled the lead rope for a horse in tow carrying additional supplies. They rode their horses behind Samuel and waited. Hulk said goodbye to Delores, and Robin Hood said goodbye to his little sister and parents, Eric of Newport, and Casey. They mounted their horses and pulled behind them another horse with supplies and walked them in behind the others.

Dak walked over to his mother and smiled at Dominique. Dominique walked back inside with his two sons and their daycare worker. "Mother, I will see you before the next spring."

Vicky was stern as she peered at Dak, "You are a great warrior, and we are counting on your return. We will need you if we are attacked. I am very proud of you. You are my son."

Dak nodded, "We will return." He stared at is mother considering her last remark.

Vicky looked at the men waiting on horseback in the line ready to leave. "There are a couple of men from Meadow Bottoms who will accompany you. Barney Simpson wanted them to gain experience in war and contribute to our fight."

Dak looked at the two men and was frustrated, "Mother, neither man graded very high in the mandatory military training. They are not qualified. I am not going to babysit them. This is not a mission to send inexperienced warriors. We will be riding fast and hard for long stretches at a time. I need proven warriors, and they are nothing like the warriors from the New York Tribe and our men. I have hand-picked our men and the men from the New York Tribe for this mission. The men I have picked are good men and have fought bravely in battles. Those two men are going to be a liability."

"We have to make concessions."

"I do not make concessions. This mission is too important. I am responsible for their lives, and the lives of my other warriors. This is a clandestine mission, and I can only hope the mission is still a secret. They have no idea what they are going to be facing."

"I placed Billy Ray in charge of this mission."

Dak could not conceal his anger. "What! I am in charge. I will lead this mission."

The Queen turned to face Dak. "You do not have enough experience to lead such an important mission. You should have never been placed in charge of the Northern Army. You confessed your failure with the Broad South River and allowing the Normand Army to take the Waldo Bridge and cut off your fleeing soldiers. You also did not allow for the

Normand Army to attack you from the north by ship and cut off your retreat. I have discussed this with Billy Ray, and he will lead this mission."

Dak abruptly turned to the Queen. His face was red with anger and his jaws were clenched, "Billy Ray sat back hundreds of yards at the Battle of Harpers Ferry Harbor and only joined the fighting once we had won. He killed two Normand soldiers, and one of them was already injured. I on the other hand killed over sixty combatants plus one Blueblood General. You do not have the right to tell me he should lead this mission."

Vicky faced Dak and did not back down. "I have ruled. Being a leader is more than swinging a sword, and we won that battle."

Dak knew the mission was more important than winning this argument, and he needed Samuel. Dak walked to his horse and mounted the horse. He rode past the two men from Meadow Bottoms and became enraged as he passed them as he rode to the front of the line and waited.

Billy Ray rode his horse to the front of the line and looked at Dak. Zenith mounted her horse and waved goodbye to their kids as they peered through the kitchen window. Zenith rode to the front of the line with Dak looking over at Billy Ray, "Mom said you are in charge." Billy Ray studied Dak and could tell he was angered as he rode forward.

Dak then said very quietly so only Zenith could hear him, "I am to take orders from you at least until we clear her realm. You may think you will lead the way General Claiborne."

Zenith responded, "Dak, this will help you concentrate on the mission, and Billy Ray can concentrate on the men, the food supply, and the logistics on the mission. He can also provide a second opinion if one is needed. This is a good thing."

Dak shifted in his saddle and looked the other way thinking about what Zenith had just mentioned, and how she did not take up for him or seemed surprised. He bit his tongue as they proceeded south.

# Chapter 8

She felt the ship move in the waves as she shifted her position. She reminisced about her childhood thinking back to her home growing up with her four male friends and her younger brother, Trey. She and Dak were the oldest, born a few days apart. Then, Hulk and Robin Hood were months younger. Her younger brother, Trey was eleven months younger than her and Tommy Boy, Hulk's younger brother, was the youngest of the group. Her parents had always insisted she, being the only female, had to be included with the group of males, not only in school but in hunting, fishing, and training to be a soldier. She always gave her all in the activities competing with the males, and she never backed down. If one of her male counterparts beat her the prior day, she would show up the next morning waiting again to compete. She deliberates her pregnancy, and her actions being a mother of a daughter, "How will I act as a mother. Will I allow a daughter to hunt and fish? Will I allow my son to travel overnight on hunting trips at the age of nine without adult supervision?" Her thoughts drifted to the group traveling all over their realm hunting and camping in the wilderness. They would return the spoils of hunting and fishing to the tribe's hungry members.

Veronica heard someone approaching the cabin door and her thoughts fast forwarded to the present. Michael entered, "My Queen, the dock of Tanger is a half mile north of us. We should be docking in forty minutes. Are you certain my Queen we should be docking here in Tanger? The city has a recent trade agreement with the Normand Army with cattle and such." He held his palms up and looked concerned.

Veronica looked at her most trusted guard. She knew he was anxious about them entering the port in Tanger. "We have discussed our options. We must hide somewhere and then proceed across the mountains in the spring. There is a trail called The No She Trail." She smiled as she thought of her childhood friend, Robin Hood, naming the trail as they struggled to cut through the mountains the prior year. "I do not see another alternative. We know what we must do, and what we face. I will need to give birth in the next few weeks. You and the other guards must protect me and these children with your lives."

"Yes, my Queen." He hesitated, "Captain Whitehead has indicated, Tanger has a busy port. Sailors stop at the port to resupply on their journeys going north and south. Someone might talk." He turned his eyes and made eye contact with Veronica. "There are too many unknowns about the people of Tanger. They will not allow a person to visit their city longer than a couple of days while a ship is being repaired or cargo is being loaded or unloaded. According to captain Whitehead, the people of this city are not friendly. There sheriff and his deputies are firm with their quarantine laws. Some of our crew will be allowed to travel just to the diner for a meal but no further into their city."

"Merlin is the next major port north of Tanger, and I cannot go to Merlin. The Bluebloods in Merlin will kill these kids and my child. They have a sworn law to protect their genetic code. They will kill any half breeds. I do not dare go any further north of Tanger. We do not know how far south from Merlin the Blueblood government-controlled territory extends. The boundaries change weekly."

Veronica looked at Stone while he slept under his cover and only the top of his head appeared, and then noticed Vaughn and Mica were awake playing with wooden wagons and horses provided to them by the church. "Can you take Mica and Vaughn to the deck for ten minutes, and ask one of the other guards to watch them?" Veronica knew the boys loved to go on the deck of the ship and learn about the sailing vessel. Her guards would carry them to the deck on nights in the warm weather and show them the stars and allow them to man the wheel. However, as they sailed further north, the cold wind created less deck time for the children. Veronica was aware the captain classified her five guards, herself, and the four children as castaways. He had no manifest showing them as passengers. She knew his life and the life of his crew were on the line to smuggle them through the Normand army patrolled waters. Captain Whitehead took payment from the church of Southern City and agreed to transport the group north and away from the search parties of the Normand army stationed in Southern City. Captain Whitehead was able to avoid the Normand fleet as they sailed from the Southern City harbor north along the west coast by proceeding out to sea further out of the traditional shipping lanes. Veronica knew Michael and the four other guards were loyal to her. Michael announced, "The boys will be watched. They love being on the deck of the ship."

Veronica looked at Michael. "There is something I have not told you. We are sailing into hostile waters of an unknown enemy. We have no other choice. I have my concerns with regards to the captain of the ship and the crew members telling someone where I am hiding. There will be a generous bounty offered for my location. But I am also concerned with my prior visit near the city of Tanger and meeting the Rogue Blueblood, Damon about fifteen miles south of Tanger. A renegade Blueblood would not be in the area of Tanger by himself. There must be others."

Michael looked at the two sleeping kids and then back at Veronica. "We will protect you with our lives. We must blend into the town and go unnoticed." He looked into Veronica's eyes, "Is there something else bothering you?"

"Damon, I suspect might have lived in Tanger. He appeared too quickly to have come from the north. He was not on one of the three ships when the ships set sail from Merlin. We will need to be careful. There could be other Rogue Bluebloods in the area."

\*\*\*

Veronica emerged from the cabin with her cape pulled over her head and pulled tight around her body which concealed her identity. The weather was cold. Winter had arrived. Veronica looked at Michael, "This time of year, in this part of the continent, the nighttime temperatures will dip down in the upper thirties. In the newly formed high mountain ranges to the west of Tanger, the temperatures never get above twenty degrees with some of the mountain ranges being as high in elevation as fourteen-thousand feet. The newly formed mountains were developed by the earthquakes and the earth's crust shifting to form two continents on earth. Those who survived the Transitional Period are now faced with groups fighting for control over the shortages of raw materials. This occurred close to nineteen years prior after the deadly B12 virus had killed over five billion people worldwide, and the nuclear war which killed millions of others."

Michael looked at his Queen, "Yes, my Queen. I understand the history of our new world. The newly formed mountains are uncharted. I understand we cannot flee across them until summer."

"As you can see, I am very nervous about what I face, and what we must do to survive. I trust you, Michael and your men, but this is not going to be easy."

As the boat was docking, Veronica walked next to Captain Whitehead, "In addition to the amount of payment the church provided, here is your bonus of one Merlin gold coin. I will provide you one additional Merlin gold coin in the spring if you and your crew can keep this a secret."

The captain looked at the Merlin gold and recognized that the value of coin's worth was more than twenty times that of the small gold coins he normally traded. He looked at Veronica, "I can assure you my lady, I will collect that fee next spring. I wish you well with your pregnancy. I would not suggest you off board here in Tanger. This is not a good place. I have heard there are witches in those mountains. The tells us sailors hear are not good about this place."

She knew Captain Whitehead had to be suspicious about her, her five guards, and the four children. He had smuggled the group out of Southern City in the dead of night without asking any questions. "Why help me? Why help us?"

Captain Whitehead was a middle-aged man who spoke with an Asian accent. He never smiled but seemed nice. "I lost my family in the Transitional Period. I lost my friends in the wars after the Transitional Period. The church saved me. I owe a debt to the church in Southern City. I have no love for the Normand army. King Solman is a vicious king. I am trying to do what I can. This dock in Tanger is port of the West Coast Shipping Alliance. The city of Tanger has agreed to follow the rules set forth by the other ports along the west coast with the two major ports in Southern City and Merlin making most of the governing laws. I have signed to be part of the West Coast Shipping Alliance. We must follow the rules. You may leave my ship for a short period of time, but you will be forced to return. You are not listed on my manifest. Please understand, I have no paperwork for you, your men or the children." He held his hands out to his side. "I understood I was to take you to Merlin and there you, your men, and children would be processed as migrant workers."

She knew if the children were ever discovered to be half Blueblood, they would be hunted by countless groups. She knew she needed to protect them. She also knew her husband, King Solman, would not rest until she was located. She only hoped Captain Whitehead would sail north and stay away from the Normand army. "I need to buy you and your crew's trust not to tell anyone about us. This one additional gold coin will make you rich. I must be able to stay here in Tanger."

She turned and walked next to the rail. She hated her choices. She knew she had to make the correct choice, or her baby would be killed along with these other four children. She had a nostalgic memory of growing up in Cliff Tops as she rested her arms on the boat rail. How easy her life was growing up in Cliff Tops. Michael and Viking walked next to her. She glanced at the two men, "I have a hunch about Tanger, and the one person I have previously met. This hunch will be a long shot. I have no other alternative, and nowhere else to turn. Captain Whitehead has done what he can."

The two guards looked at their Queen. Michael announced, "We understand our risk, and we freely take on the challenge to protect you and these children."

# Chapter 9

The twenty-one men and Zenith had ridden the horses hard for seven straight days. They had cleared their clan's boundary and headed deep into the Midlander's territory. The weather cooperated, and the large winter storms had not struck. Billy Ray ordered the group to go north and stay north of the Midlander's tribes. Dak and Zenith speculated the Midlanders would migrate south for the warmer weather. Billy Ray looked at the river and the distance to cross, "We need to set camp here and then send a scout south ten miles ahead to see if we can stay clear of any Midlander entanglements."

Dak looked at Billy Ray, "I really have no clue when we should go south. I know I would rather not get too close to Merlin since Zenith and I are wanted dead or alive by the Merlin Senate." He smiled and then suggested, "I would suggest we cross this second river and then go south. We will need to slow our pace and send scouts further in front. We might need to travel at night to avoid the Midlanders. My plan had always been to avoid the Midlanders, make the trip through their territory undetected, and proceed around the desert and through the mountain pass north of Tanger."

Billy Ray thought about Dak, and how the two men had hardly spoken since they left Cliff Tops. Billy Ray could sense Dak was upset with him being in charge. He knew he would have to confront Dak at some point. He listened as Dak mentioned his plan as if he was leading the mission. He ordered, "We will cross the river and then camp on the opposite side."

***

The rest was a welcome respite for the weary travelers. Most of the men enjoyed the deer meat and had taken a midafternoon nap. Dak and his group of friends were coming awake and sitting around a fire they had started away from the others. Billy Ray and Samuel walked over to them. "We need to send a scout close to twenty miles south. If it's clear, we will travel tonight. Dak, I need you to scout the area ahead of us."

Hulk and the others looked at each other with sudden glances. Dak was not accustomed to taking orders from someone else. Hulk said, "Dad, you were elected to go on this mission by the Queen without Dak being asked. Dak had planned this mission and set up the path after the contact with our spy in Southern City. Dad, the only reason Dak mentioned this mission to the Queen and others of Cliff Tops was because of the need for Samuel. Samuel is needed because of his experience and his Blueblood abilities dealing with the Rogue Bluebloods . Dak has been our commander for the past two years, and he was in charge of an entire army. I have always been the scout." The group of friends were aware Zenith would not take orders from Billy Ray. They had traveled all over the southern hemisphere with her over the past two years. She would elect to go where Dak went, but she was never ordered by Dak or anyone. Zenith was a Blueblood warrior and her talents for battling with a sword and bow had greatly increased over the last year. She went where her husband, Dak, went. Hulk announced, "I will go south as the scout. If I leave now, I might be able to go as far as fifty miles. I can report back to you as you guys start moving south at midnight."

Billy Ray looked at his son and then at Dak. Hulk stood and looked at Billy Ray, "Dad, Dak does not take orders from you. He oversees the men from Zenith Point which include your two sons, and his friends sitting here. He will also be ordering the men from the New York Tribe and Meadow Bottoms. If you would like to order someone around on this mission, you may order Samuel."

Samuel stood still with a slight grin as he glanced at the ground. Samuel was a Blueblood warrior and at one time had been the general over the army in Merlin. He was now married to Dak's mother, Queen Vicky. Billy Ray looked angrily at Zenith and Dak. He elected to turn his head and not look at his two sons as he turned and walked back to the other campfire.

Hulk said, "I will head out. Dak you are the leader. Give me a two-hour head start and follow the river. I will leave markers for you to follow. Robin Hood will follow the group just like always."

Hulk saddled his horse and took close to a pound of deer meat. He headed south along the second river. Dak stood and said, "I love Billy Ray. That could have been handled a little more delicately. Give me a few minutes to talk to him." He walked to the other campfire.

The men watched as Dak approached, "Hulk is scouting the trail south. We will provide him a two-hour head start and then we will follow. You men need to be ready to ride as the sun starts setting. We should have a full moon, and the men will need to be prepared to ride all night. Our goal is to keep traveling southwest before a large winter storm hits." Dak noticed Billy Ray stared at the fire the entire time, and he did not look at him. Dak then added, "We have shown you men the map. Merlin is located on the west coast and in the Great Gulf area which happens to be the shortest distance from east to west. For all of you who remember the old world, the city of Merlin is located northwest of where the state of Missouri was located on the old North American continent. My plan is for us to travel southwest close to six-hundred-miles before we cut through the mountains and reach the Port of Tanger."

Billy Ray looked at Dak, "I did not volunteer to come on this mission. I was ordered to by the Queen." Zenith walked over and stood next to Dak. Billy Ray added, "There was someone who told the Queen you were great, but you needed help with being in charge."

Dak looked frustrated, "Who betrayed me? I want to know now."

Billy Ray looked at the fire, "No one betrayed you. Dak, you almost lost the battle and the midcontinent territory to King Solman. Being a leader, you receive all the glory when you win, but when you lose you receive all the blame." He stared into the fire.

Zenith spoke, "Dak, it was me. I made the request of the Queen." Dak turned and looked at Zenith.

"It was you?"

"Yes Dak. I made the request to the Queen to send Billy Ray to command this mission." She turned and looked at Dak. "You were so engrossed in your plan fighting against the Normand army, you missed the obvious. They attacked us in the north and several places you had not considered across the front lines. If Veronica had not mentioned the possible attack north of Harpers Ferry Harbor to you, we would have been forced to surrender. You also should have ordered Marshall law which would have forced the farmers and ranchers and all others to fight with us. You should have hung the ones who would not join our army. I tried to explain these things to you, and you were so mad you threw things across the command tent. In my training, as a Blueblood warrior, we spent six months in a classroom evaluating strategies and delegating responsibilities. Dak, you are great at strategizing plans of battle but horrible at delegating the responsibilities to others."

Dak stared at Zenith for a few seconds. He then turned and walked toward the other fire and his friends.

Samuel watched the three from his standing position and could tell the body language by Dak's movement. He was surprised about something being said.

Dak turned and as he walked by, he watched Samuel standing by the fire eating additional deer meat. "Samuel, if you do not mind, ride next to Billy Ray and keep an eye on him. We expect to run into trouble, and I do not wish anything bad happening to him. I am the leader of this mission, and I will lead." Dak watched Samuel eating the deer meat. He did not seem to be concerned. Dak added, "I guess you knew about my shortcomings, and Zenith's conversation with our Queen."

Samual kept eating, "I was made aware. I am also here to help you with your shortcomings."

Dak looked at Samuel, "Who else knows?"

Samuel secured another bite, "Just Billy Ray, me, Zenith, and now you." Dak watched Samuel as he wiped the deer juice from his cheek with the back of his hand.

"Maybe I need to assist you with your shortcomings? You need to eat with some manners."

Samuel smiled at Dak, "Have you or your men fought against men armed with a spear?"

Dak looked at Samuel, "No, Why do you ask?"

"Some tribes along the West Coast favor fighting with spears." He looked at Dak, "We in Merlin trained with spears and fighting against men with spears. A soldier with a sword who is properly trained will win every time."

Dak watched as Samuel took an additional bite of deer meat and then he gently wiped his mouth with a towel. "Trained how?" Dak smiled as he watched Samuel, who was carefully wiping his mouth.

Samuel stood and pretended to have a spear. "Most men elect to place both hands on the shaft of the spear when they jab at their opponent. When the combatant jabs the spear, you simple push the tip out wide with your sword using a backhand motion, and this opens the combatant up for the short knife or second sword and the kill shot. If they have a spear and a shield, your men will need to push the tip of the spear wide and then attack the open space with the short knife or second sword. That is why I trained with my two hatchets. I am so much quicker and once I penetrate inside their attack zone, I am faster to the kill shot. You using the two Sai Swords would also be very deadly against the longer spear."

Dak announced, "You need to make certain the men are properly trained." He then turned and walked off as Samuel grinned and watched him.

# Chapter 10

The boat drifted into the dock as the workers winched the vessel the last few feet and secured the tow ropes to the steel cleats on the dock. Captain Whitehead was the first to exit the ramp as he immediately followed the dock employee to the office to meet the dock master. Veronica stood on the deck next to the rail of the ship and could tell the dock master appeared to be a little anxious as Captain Whitehead exited the boat. She noticed as Captain Whitehead approached, the dock master paced back and forth at the office doorway and rubbed his hands through his hair. Veronica observed the body language of the dock master to be someone who did not invite confrontation and an unscheduled ship heading north hauling people without the passengers being listed on a manifest from the Normand control territory would not be invited to off board at the dock. She noticed the body language of both men as Captain Whitehead and the dock master were not in agreement. She turned to Michael and motioned her head for him to follow her.

Captain Whitehead and the dock master watched Veronica and Michael approach. Veronica looked at the captain, "Have you been able to arrange for me and my family a place to stay for the winter?"

Captain Whitehead turned to the dock master. He was a big man with a long beard. He wore a protective mask as did all the men working on the dock. He looked at Veronica, "I am sorry. We do not have cottages for rent. We do not allow people to stay in our city until they have been in the isolated medical building under quarantine for one week. Our quarantine facility is full, and we cannot accommodate a group of ten. We do not take chances with the B12 virus. Those are our rules. I am sorry, but you are not allowed to exit your vessel." He turned to Captain Whitehead, "Your vessel does not have a manifest with cargo we desire and according to the West Coast Shipping Alliance Agreement 4A which stipulates you must not be allowed to trade those items or allow the individuals not listed to off board. You will need to leave." He looked like he was regretful.

Veronica looked at the man, "I need to talk with Mr. Frank Dupont Jr about business. You need to explain to Frank Dupont Jr. I will be waiting for him in the tavern. He sells cattle, right?" The dock master motioned his head yes. "I need to talk with him about purchasing cattle. I can assure you we will not need to be quarantined. My group has been vaccinated for the B12 virus. Do you know the man by the name of Frank Depont Jr.?"

The dock master seemed to relax but he still seemed to be afraid as he kept looking around and rubbing his hands together, "Yes, I will have one of my men ask the guards to request Mr. Frank Jr. presents. I can assure you everyone knows of him. He sells cattle and has a huge cattle ranch and sugar plantation south of our city."

Veronica and Michael walked past the two men toward the tavern. She whispered to Michael to have Pretty Boy follow them into the tavern and watch our backs. "Tell Viking and Hector to guard the kids and keep them below deck out of sight and make certain Cruise is seen by the doctor here in this city. I do not wish for his leg to get infected." Michael turned at once and quickly walked back on board and followed Veronica's orders. He then returned to Veronica's side as they approached the tavern.

Three guards approached them as they were about to enter the front door of the tavern. The guard in the middle commanded, "Stop right there. You are not allowed to depart your vessel. You will return at once."

Veronica turned to the men, and the three noticed she was pregnant, "I have requested an audience with Frank Dupont Jr. to discuss business. I am waiting for his arrival. You will make certain he is aware I am here. We have been vaccinated against the B12 virus. We will not submit to being quarantined." The three guards each wore a mask as did the other people on the streets. The guards seemed to hesitate when she mentioned Frank's name. She turned and motioned for Micheal to follow her and entered the tavern.

Frank Jr. rode to the town followed by ten of his men and the one officer who had relayed the message. He walked into the tavern and looked around. Several of his men followed him into the restaurant. The officer pointed toward Veronica who was facing away from the door while sitting at the table. Frank walked over and stood. He looked at Michael trying to remember if he had ever met him. He then turned to Veronica. "I'll be damned. I thought you were the one person I would never see again. Lady, you must be like a cat and have nine lives." He smiled.

Veronica smiled back at him, "I noticed you are without a mask. Are you not concerned about me being contagious?"

He smiled and looked around at all the people of Tanger wearing the protective masks. "No. I am not concerned about the B12 virus. You would have symptoms by now after being at sea for three days. I understand your captain has sailed from Southern City, but you are not listed on his ship's manifest."

"I assure you I am no cat. I need to talk to you in private. Michael, please excuse us."

Michael got up and walked to the bar and ordered a drink. Frank Jr. motioned for his men standing nearby to walk away. Frank sat down and stared into the two prettiest brown eyes he had ever seen. "Is that your husband you ordered to leave?"

Veronica looked at Frank, "No, Michael is not my husband. I am sorry about your father and the four other men. I discovered the men hanging in the tree and your father were dead before I arrived. I wish I had been better prepared and arrived earlier. Maybe I could have killed Damon and saved their lives."

He looked mad, "I wished I had never met you. You were the cause of their deaths. Now you have summoned me on the pretense of buying my cattle. I am a rancher. Why do I get the feeling you are not here to buy cattle."

Veronica's forehead wrinkled as she leaned forward over the table. "You, your father, and your men knew of the threat. You could have warned me what was out there. I returned the rig back to your father to the same spot as promised, and I was captured by that monster. I was taken to Southern City and presented to King Solman as a trophy to be imprisoned and repeatedly raped."

Frank Jr looked directly at Veronica, "What do you want?"

She relaxed and seemed sincere, "I need your help. I am on the run. I have no other place to turn."

"Excuse me. Well hell lady. I have lost enough. You brought the world down on us. We live in constant fear. Our port is small, and everyone who is off boarded is documented. There is a record kept."

Veronica looked at Frank, "How many Rogue Bluebloods are there hidden here in Tanger, and where exactly do they live? I might be able to assist you. You help me, and I might be able to help you."

Frank leaned forward on the table and glanced around him to see if anyone could hear what he was about to say. "I do not know how many there are, but me talking to an outsider about them could cause us to be skinned alive. You do not understand. These people will do what the Dark Master orders."

Veronica leaned closer within a couple of inches, "I killed Damon. The man who killed your father. He said he did the bidding of his master. The master lives close and you know where. I am a woman. You are a coward. Why are you more fearful of him than me?"

Frank shifted back in his chair. He appeared to be uncomfortable. He leaned forward again on the table and whispered, "I cannot talk about the cult. They have ears everywhere. I do not trust my own men. I have seen what they are capable of doing. They are pure evil and savagely kill anyone who opposes them."

"I said I need help. This is Merlin gold. It is pure and accepted anywhere in the world." She pulled a bag of gold from her pocket and sat it on the table.

He leaned forward and his eyes narrowed, "Hide that. You do not need to attract attention to yourself. You do not listen. I cannot help you. Why come here? This is the one place you would not be safe that I can assure you."

Veronica placed the gold back into her pocket. "What are you going to do? Live in constant fear for the rest of your life? There is enough gold in this bag for you to sail anywhere in the world. You do not have to stay, but you must help me. You do not understand the world landscape."

"This is my home. My brother, father and I settled this territory right after the Transitional Period."

"The cult killed your father and four of your men. I have no other place to go. I need your help. I need to hide out until spring. I will be hunted, and I assure you, I have no other place to run. Please help me." She thought about telling him about the four Blueblood children. Could she trust him with knowing what was at stake?

"Listen to me." He hesitated and looked around again to see if anyone could hear. "It makes no sense. Why stop here? I do not know you. I met you one time in a field while you were sitting on my wagon being pulled by my horses which you stole from me. You are part of the rebels from the north fighting against the Normand army. We are not involved in the war."

"I am with child. I cannot run any further. I will be giving birth in two to four weeks. I need a place to give birth, hide, and wait until the spring to leave. I am desperate. I was kidnapped, raped and now I have escaped. All this happened to me because of you. You could have warned me about the danger."

Frank looked concerned. He glanced at her mid-section and for the first time realized the lady across the table was pregnant.

He took a deep breath and seemed to be considering the situation.

Veronica noticed Michael glanced at her from the bar as three additional men entered the tavern. They were all carrying swords and bows and dressed as soldiers. They were obviously not farmers. "Listen to me." She reached for his arm. "We can off load in the middle of the night with no one knowing. There must be a place we can hide. You can sell the captain some cattle to transport for you. He is heading north. No one will be suspicious. There are those that will kill my baby if they find me. I am without a choice. I really have no one else I trust, and nowhere else to hide. I am out of options."

He looked like he wanted to ask a question. She could read his thoughts, "Who is the father?"

Veronica looked at him, "You want to know who the father of my unborn child?"

Frank motioned his head, "Yes. I would like to know who you are hiding from, what type of people will be coming after you, why am I sticking my neck out for you?"

She looked directly at him, "King Solman is the father, and there is no one else more dangerous than he. Now you know."

Frank Jr. noticed Veronica's sad eyes as he shifted his view to someone behind her. She turned and glanced at the three men and seemed alert to their presence. She motioned her hand for Michael to stay. He whispered as he stood. "My God. King

Solman. This could not get any worse. Be ready at three A.M to off load from the boat. Captain Whitehead needs to set sail and leave our port at that time. I will bring him ten cows, and he can give me the gold this afternoon. We must make this look like a legit deal. Now, you and your man need to leave before the soldiers place you and him in quarantine which will lead to an investigation. You do not want to be arrested and taken to the dungeon."

"I am traveling with five soldiers and four young children. We will be ready at three A.M." She stood and walked toward the door.

Frank Jr. was surprised to hear of the others, but he knew he had to interfere with the soldiers doing their job. He walked toward the bar to talk to the three soldiers who had entered and were approaching the bar and Michael. Frank Jr. intercepted them as he asked them a question.

Veronica stood at the exit door and motioned for Michael to follow her out the door as Frank Jr. talked with the three Tanger soldiers.

***

Veronica dressed the four kids in warm clothes and hugged each of them. She placed hoods over their heads and kissed each of them on the foreheads. "We will be going on a trip tonight. I need you four to be brave. We will be going on an adventure riding in a wagon in the dark. We will be going to a home to live for a few weeks."

The kids looked at Veronica and Stone asked, "A home?"

"Yes. A home we can stay for the winter and then we will travel across the great mountains. It will be fun and full of excitement." She smiled at each kid trying not to worry about the difficult journey with the kids. She then added, "That sounds like fun doesn't it.?" She smiled.

Michael opened the door to the boat cabin. "There is a wagon approaching on the front road. We will need to hurry."

Veronica looked worried as she took a deep breath. "Michael, verify this is not a trap. We will start that way. If there are any signs of trouble, we will have Captain Whitehead cut the ropes, and we will set sail."

Michael closed the door to the cabin. He motioned for Viking to pick up the two smallest kids. He went down the ramp to the dock. Hector was on crutches and stood next to Veronica as she held the hands of Vaughn and Mica. The group stopped at the bottom of the ramp and waited. The wagon came to a stop at the entrance to the dock. John Dupont Jr was the lone rider in the wagon and appeared to be nervous as he pulled the wagon to a stop. Michael walked over to him and Frank Jr. said, "We need to hurry." He looked toward the tavern and behind him, "The night watchman will be coming any second."

Michael stood still with confidence as he looked around the area. He noticed Frank Jr. appeared nervous as he was looking around the area for an approaching city guard. Michael said, "A nice night for a wagon ride." He then turned and lit a match.

Viking turned, "My Queen. That is the signal. We need to hurry. He carried the gear of the children and Isabel and Stone. Captain Whitehead picked up Veronica's gear bag and followed Veronica as she walked to the wagon and the pier entrance following the men.

The kids were loaded, and Hector took his seat in the back of the wagon, Michael helped Veronica into the front of the wagon. Captain Whitehead looked at Veronica, "I will see you next spring. We have loaded the cattle, and we will head north. I was able to convince the dock master to delay our departure due to the threat of a storm. We will leave now. Good luck."

Cruise walked out of the shadows where he had been watching for a possible trap. He motioned to Michael, "The coast is clear." Michael and the other two guards jumped into the rear of the wagon. The wagon started pulling away as Cruise ran and jumped in the rear of the wagon. John Dupont Jr. looked worried as he shook the reins for the horses to increase their pace as they pulled away from the dock. He glanced at Veronica and noticed she was holding her sword across her lap. She noticed the glance, "How far will we be traveling?"

"I will have to hide you, your men, and those children on my property. The trip is close to five miles. You will stay in the bunkhouse. You waited to mention the other children and the fact you had five men traveling with you."

"You did not ask. There are ten of us. You will be well compensated for your risk."

John Jr. glanced at the back of the wagon and then turned. "There is not enough gold you could pay me to justify this risk. I do not trust my men. Everyone in this community is scared. This city has a deal with the Dark Master. The cult is located at the Low Mountain. Our king will deliver you to The Dark Master if you are discovered. Our king will not hesitate to report you to the Dark Master. And anyone caught helping you will be impaled for all to see."

"The plan should work. Captain Whitehead will sail out of the harbor tonight, and no one will ever know we off boarded."

"How well do you know Captain Whitehead?" He hesitated, "I get the feeling there are a lot of people looking for you and these kids, and why do you have five men who look like they are bounty hunters traveling with you? Their equipment is state of the art. Their swords are crafted by an expert with the highest quality of metal, and their bows are reversible which are only crafted for professional soldiers. The normal person cannot afford their equipment." He glanced at Veronica with a questionable grimace.

Veronica never trusted Captain Whitehead. She could not place her finger on the lack of trust, but she just did not believe him to be honest. "I met Captain Whitehead two and half days ago in Southern City. He came highly recommended. I have paid him handsomely for his loyalty. The five men are my guards. They are loyal to me and very well trained. I trust them with my life. The kids are under my protection, and me and my men will protect them with our lives." She looked at John Jr. and both stared at one another for a second. "How well do you trust your doctor?"

John Jr. looked at Veronica and blew out air. He also raised his hands as he was driving the wagon, "I do not trust him. There are very few people I trust here in Tanger. He looked at your man's leg wound who obviously lied about the cause. We do not believe he fell and cut his leg on the boat winch. The physician commented the injury looked like the damage was caused by a sword and only a very trained and experienced surgeon could have surgically repaired the artery and then sewed him up so cleanly. He was heard to repeat himself, only an experienced surgeon could have attached the artery so cleanly. The only surgeons on the west coast experienced enough to complete such a surgery are located in Merlin or Southern City. He might mention this to the city guards. The guards talk with our king who uses a liaison to communicate with the Dark Master. The Dark Master will demand answers."

Veronica said, "As far as your king knows, we sailed out of your harbor this morning before daybreak."

Veronica could tell John Jr. was concerned. She knew there would be a better time to discuss the future and right now she needed to get the children in a warm home. She knew the next six months were going to be difficult living in hiding. "Was Damon a Lower Mountain liaison?"

"Damon was the devil. He was the enforcer. If we did not do what the liaison instructed, Damon would pay our city a visit. At first, we opposed them. Then, we would find our animals mutilated. He would leave them for us to see hanging in a tree. Then, he mutilated two of our elderly townspeople. Five of our young boys disappeared. As soon as we did as the liaison instructed, the killings stopped. The five boys were never located. We have heard rumors of other tribes losing young men to the cult." He looked at Veronica, "We all fear the Dark Master. He and his men are pure evil. We suspect young boys are traded from Merlin and Southern City by slave traders and transported to the cult."

"And you do nothing to help the boys?"

Frank Jr. glanced at Veronica, "There is no proof. The boys are not brought into our dock. That I know for certain. The rumors are the boys are brought into an inlet fifty miles south of here and transported by wagon in crates."

Veronica looked at Frank Jr, "A rumor?"

"From time-to-time fisherman find the bodies in that bay of young boys. They are not from our city. That is all I know."

# Chapter 11

The group rode at a slow pace in the darkness. The ambient moon light provided enough light for the horse riders to follow one another. Dak knew where to look for Hulk's signs where he had cut the bark off the north side of the trees. He also told Hulk to stay within one-hundred yards of the west side of the river. The group needed intel, and what was ahead of them. They could not afford to miss Hulk as he headed north with an update. Most of the land was flat with fields leading to a vast prairie to the west as the river ran southwest with small trees lining the riverbanks. Hulk's trail was at the edge of the fields and the outside perimeter of the trees lining the west riverbank. Dak knew Hulk would use the cover of the trees to conceal himself traveling on horseback.

Hulk met them at three A.M. as they cut across a small stream leading to the river. Dak saw the silhouette of a man on a horse standing in the open and knew it to be his friend. Dak stopped his horse next to Hulk. Some of the other men rode over to Hulk while others dismounted and allowed the horses an opportunity to drink in the stream which fed into the large river east of them. Dak asked, "What is the news?"

Hulk looked at his father and Samuel as they rode to the stop. "I can see where there have been people, but I did not locate the tribe. The foot traffic along the river has been heavy. I would suggest we cut across the prairie where the journey will be easier riding, and we can cover greater distances. Based on the foot traffic along the river, I believe we are headed directly into a large Midlander camp."

Dak looked at Hulk and turned to the men, "We need to rest for a few minutes and fill up with water. We will head out across the prairie west for a couple of hours. We will find a spot to camp and rest." Dak turned to Trey, "Pass the word."

Dak heard the one large man from Meadow Bottoms speak about being tired, wet, and hungry. Dak looked at Trey, "Tell the weak link in our chain to be quiet and stop complaining." He then thought of his mother forcing him to bring those two men on the mission. Dak clenched his jaw, "Tell those two they will have the first guard duty when we stop to camp." Trey looked at Dak with understanding that Dak did not like the two men.

\*\*\*

The cold rain started in the night and did not stop until close to eleven A.M. The men stayed in their tents with guards switching duties. Once the rain stopped, Dak and Zenith came out and welcomed the sun. Dak took the tent down and placed it on the pack horse. He met Hulk, Tommy Boy, Billy Ray, and others at the fire where the deer was being cooked. Dak noticed no one was talking. He finally said, "We have been lucky with the weather. The rain will help conceal us. I figured we would be stuck in snow drifts. The weather could have been worse." He glanced to see where the two men from Meadow Bottoms were located.

Hulk glanced up, "We were lucky we went south when we did. A few hundred miles north of our location must have got two feet of snow." Hulk then added, "Here comes Robin Hood."

Billy Ray announced, "We have been traveling for fourteen days. We must be getting close to the basin area of the mountains. While we traveled southwest across the prairie, we covered close to two-hundred miles a day."

Dak saw Robin Hood exiting the woody area to the west on his horse. "Where has he been?"

Tommy Boy announced, "While it was raining, he wanted to check the surrounding area. The Midlanders would not be out in this weather, and it would be safe to complete the recon west of us."

Dak glanced at Billy Ray. He knew Billy Ray had requested Robin Hood do this. He also was aware Robin Hood never would have volunteered to ride in the rain. Dak then noticed Samuel coming in from the south on a horse. "Who else has been out on recon?"

Billy Ray announced, "We need to know if we are safe here. We came in and set up camp in the fog yesterday morning." Dak knew they had ridden in the darkness and rain and the men were exhausted.

Dak reached for the deer meat and noticed Zenith was walking toward them. She had been to the creek to wash off and change clothing. The seal fur clothing helped keep one warm in this cold rain. It was great at repelling the cold rain, but the insulated clothing was too warm to wear in the humidity of the woody area. Dax commanded, "We need to make certain everyone is prepared to move out in one hour. We will travel for six hours then set up camp. We need dry weather so our tents will dry out. I packed my tent up wet. We will see what the scouts say and decide on the direction. Pass the word."

Robin Hood rode into camp and dismounted. He tied his horse off, and announced, "I still have not seen a Midlander camp. Where would they be?"

The men waited for Samuel. He announced once he dismounted. There is a camp of well over two hundred thousand people twenty miles south. The camp stretches for miles along the river and then east. The camp is located at the foot of the mountains and is on both sides of the river. The men look like warriors."

Dak looked at Billy Ray and commanded, "That settles our travel plans. We will proceed west." Dak glanced at Zenith as she took a bite of deer. He knew she was tired of eating the same meal daily. He smiled to himself as she looked disgusted with the taste of the meat.

\*\*\*

Billy Ray stood looking at the mountain ranges to the south. Hulk walked up next to him. "Dad, what do you think? Should we now go closer to the coast or keep going south?"

Tommy Boy walked up next to his brother and father. He announced, "Dak has ordered us to go southwest. He believes we should be closer to the coastline before we cut directly south through the mountains. Dak and Samuel both felt we needed to approach the mountains near a low gap in the mountain range. Hulk, they will want you to start using your scanner to check for nuclear contamination once we head into the mountains. The desert and drylands are north which we have avoided."

Billy Ray looked over at Hulk, "We will be going southwest. I do not like the looks of the height of those mountains. We will need to locate a valley leading to the mountain range and a low gap to cross. We will also need to be lucky with the weather. That is snow on some of the peaks."

Dak walked over to the men, "Hulk, I need you to scout us out a trail southwest. We will head toward the end of the mountain range and travel up through the pass." He pointed southwest. "We hope that is the best point to cross through the mountains."

Hulk shook his head in agreement. "I will find us a trail. This is not going to be easy."

***

Hulk crawled up the embankment. He was under the thick underbrush which was covered in a light dusting of snow. He had noticed as they went southwest the last few miles, the area turned thick with new growth of woods. He peered into the meadow and along the river. At first, he did not see the kids. They were somewhat hidden behind the large granite boulders which lined the river. They were standing along the river close to one hundred yards southwest of his location. He could see six young kids playing in the water and jumping into the pool of water from the large granite boulders. He could see the fog lifting from the pool of water near the river. He tried to count the people who were in the swimming hole as he looked for adults. He noticed a valley leading into the mountains a few yards northeast of their location. He thought that may be the best entry point to allow them to travel to the ridge of the mountain and then further west along the ridge line. The mountains would help them stay hidden. He knew at some point they would meet up with Midlanders if they stayed in the open prairie or along the rivers. He decided if he crossed the river, he could have a better view of the valley to determine if the valley is passable on horseback. He also knew he had been traveling slow, and Dak and the others would be close behind him. Most of the woods in the area at ground level along the riverbanks were too thick and too steep to forge through. He crawled back down the embankment and retrieved his bow from his horse. He made certain no one could see him down river as he then crossed the river staying behind the large river rocks when he could. The river current was fast but not deep. He forged through the underbrush along the steep riverbank and positioned himself thirty feet from the pool of water. He noticed steam coming from the pool and knew there was a hot spring next to the river. He noticed several young boys were leaving and heading up the river on a trail located on the riverbank. He then noticed three young girls started walking up the trail. Hulk relocated his position and got within twenty feet of the large granite rock where the boys had been jumping. He listened, and there was no sound except for the rushing water of the river. He needed to inspect the valley and quickly return to his horse. He peered around the large boulder where he was hiding and observed a young lady who was bathing in the pool of water. He was surprised when he noticed her clothing was lying within three feet of his hidden spot. As he peered around the area looking for other people, he noticed movement out of his peripheral vision. The nude lady was walking toward him and her clothing. He noticed the look of surprise on her face when she saw him watching her. She immediately ran for her clothing.

Hulk whispered to himself, "Dammit." He then bolted to his feet and ran for her. She changed direction and then ran back to the pool of water diving headfirst and then swimming under water for the far side. He chased her as he dropped his bow with the case of arrows and dove into the water and swam to the far side of the hot spring. As she swam to the other side, she could feel the adrenaline rush and the rapidly increase of her heart beat. She became scared as she exited the pool and ran across the river rocks barefoot and then toward the trail. Hulk took a shorter route and exited the pool and then leaped across a large rock to another rock taking advantage of the shortcut. He leaped for her and caught her and as they fell on top of a large granite boulder, Hulk tried to protect her and allowed his body to land first and then pull her body down on his as they landed on the large rock. She came down with her fingers and tried to scratch Hulk's eyes. Hulk immediately reached for her arms and held them to her sides and rolled over on her. She bit his left hand as she was pinned under him. He raised up and held her still looking down at her and pulled his hand out of her mouth. She fiercely shook her head from side to side trying to bite his other hand then rotated back to his right hand. She then tried to raise her legs upward from underneath him. His body weight held her down. She then stared into his eyes, "Let me go you filthy, stinking bastard."

She then started trying to break free as she struggled, trying to kick him and break her arms free of his hands. He held her firmly with his hands and his body weight securely pinning her under him. She opened her mouth to yell. Hulk released his left hand and quickly covered her mouth. She swung as hard as she could and hit him in the right jaw. Hulk aggressively moved upward and straddled her, holding her hands down with his right hand above her head and placed his left gloved hand over her mouth. She squirmed for a few additional seconds until she realized her attempts were futile. She then stared into his eyes, a few inches above hers.

Hulk clenched his jaws, "You need to be quiet. I am not going to harm you. We need your help." He cautiously lifted his left hand.

"If you rape me, you better kill me because I will hunt you down and cut your balls off. There is no rock you can crawl back under that I will not find you." Her eyes were cold with hatred and narrow with her stare. She looked enraged.

Hulk looked up and saw Dak leading the group across the river on the horses. The lady looked sideways and saw the riders. She became frantic and tried to pull loose as her fear increased with the presents of additional men, but Hulk held her in place. Once they crossed the river, Zenith jumped off her horse, "Where are her clothes?"

Hulk motioned with his head, "On the other side of the boulder near the hot spring." He then motioned his head back up stream. Zenith smiled as now she understood Hulk was perplexed with his next move.

Robin Hood dismounted and ran to the other side of the pool and picked up her clothes. He ran to Zenith and handed her the clothing. Zenith took her clothes and handed them forward to her, "Let her up. Here are your clothes. No one is going to harm you." Hulk noticed the presents of another female seemed to mitigate the female's fear of being harmed. He then relaxed and rolled to the side and sat on the boulder.

The lady stood and looked at the riders as she noticed they all appeared to be observing her and then slowly put on her underwear and then her pants, socks, and boots. The last item she put on was her shirt as stood facing Dak and his group as she pulled the thick wool sweater over her head. All the riders watched, as she stood and took three fast steps over to Hulk while he was still sitting on the granite rock and kicked him in the side of his ribs, "You perverted bastard."

Robin Hood laughed, "Every relationship starts with a conversation. While you two were lying on the boulder all tied up together, what were you discussing?" Several men grinned at the comment.

Hulk stood and walked away. She pointed to her chest, "I told that bastard, I was the one that would cut his balls off."

"Sounds like love at first sight," announced Robin Hood. The group of men laughed.

Zenith looked at the young lady and sized her up to be an athletic active female. Maybe a warrior of such. The lady looked at the men on horses who had crossed the river, all wearing black leather carrying multiple weapons on their persons. Zenith kept her distance but stepped forward, "We need your help. No one is going to harm you."

The lady looked at Zenith, "Where are you from? Who are you people? You are a war party traveling through my tribe's sanctioned property. You shall be arrested and punished."

Dak punched his horse in the sides and the horse moved forward. "We mean you and your tribe no harm. We are passing through. We will be happy to pay a reasonable toll for our transgressions. We will also be happy to pay you personally for your troubles. My scout did not mean you any harm."

The lady looked mad at Dak, "My troubles. That pervert watched me while I was bathing. He was not looking for passage. He crawled within a few feet of me watching me bathe. He knew what he was doing. My people do not except such behavior. He must be punished. The king will order his balls removed."

Zenith did not like the direction of the conversation. She knew Hulk was not a pervert and was trying to discern a trail for them to cross the mountains. She was getting aggravated and announced, "You are not hurt, and Hulk is no pervert. He will not be punished. You need to grow up and act like an adult. He is trying to locate a path across the mountains and stay clear of you and your tribe. He needed to verify if the small valley up stream leading into the mountains is passable. We are headed for a city on the coast called Tanger."

The lady turned to Zenith, "You do not tell me what to do. I do not care what you are doing. You are trespassing on our sanctioned land without our permission. This is against the basic rules established by all Midlander tribes, which have all been reaffirmed at the Winter Summit."

Dak jumped off his horse. He knew he needed to deescalate the situation. He noticed the young lady was very pretty, and he assumed she had always gotten her way. She seemed to exemplify an attitude of privilege. She had not acted like she was offended he and his soldiers seeing her in the nude as she stood on the large boulder looking at them. She then seemed to take her time dressing after she stared at each of them before placing on her clothing. She was proud of her body, and she knew she was pretty. "What is your name?"

"My name is Boudica."

Dak clenched his jaws, "Boudica, we are not from around here. We are on a mission trying to stop some extremely violent people located near Tanger. We are trying to help your tribe. That is all we are doing. We mean you no harm. The winter snow blocked our passage from crossing the high mountain ranges coming in from the east forcing us to travel through your tribe's territory. Now we are headed to Tanger from the northwest. The Normand Army is blocking the south by land and sea. Can you provide us some information? We need to find safe passage down the coastline around the known nuclear waste pit located on the shoreline or through these mountains. We mean you and your people no harm. We will be gone by tomorrow."

"Are you talking about the fort located at Lower Mountain, the evil Dark Master and his cult?"

Dak was surprised at her question. Billy Ray dismounted and walked toward the young lady, "What can you tell us about the fort located at Lower Mountain?"

Boudica was surprised with Billy Ray's sudden actions and question. He seemed to have appeared energized when she mentioned the fort located at Lower Mountain. She realized this group was seeking out the cult and not hiding from them. "The Lower Mountain marks my tribe's southern boundary. The cult and the Dark Master are pure evil. They kidnap our young men and kill our people." She looked at the entire group. "You will all be killed if you approach them. They have an army of the dead, and they will not stop killing until the Master tells them to stop."

"Army of the dead?" asked Tommy Boy

She looked up at Tommy Boy sitting on the large horse with her jaws clenched. "They took my brother. He has now been brainwashed along with many others. By now, if he has not been impaled on a post and left for all to see, he would be brainwashed and conditioned to follow the Master's orders."

Zenith inquired, "What do you mean conditioned?"

"The males are neutered and then they are brainwashed. They are made to learn to kill without any regret of their actions. They do not take women." She stared at Zenith and then looked away with a sad expression.

Dak then asked, "How large is the army? And why have they not attacked your village?"

"I do not know their size. If the Dark Master decides a boy or young man is not suitable, he is brought back to where he was kidnapped and impaled on a ten-foot post for all to see. I believe he needs us and the other villages located on the other side of the mountains to supply him with soldiers and food. The Master comes to terms with the villages and agrees to live in close proximity to them as long as they stay quiet and supply him what he orders. I once spied down on them and saw a wagon being pulled into the fort with a crate in the back. I watched them open the crate and pull a young man out. The young man stood and looked at the soldiers standing around him and knew he was in for hell. The majority of the boys must come into Tanger by ship and are then transported in crates to the fort where the master has them processed to be soldiers."

Dak said, "They are the orphans being shipped from Merlin in the human trade industry."

Zenith then inquired, "Can you or someone in your tribe help us? We need direction and information. We mean you no harm."

"My father and his council have just returned from the Winter Summit. Our tribe is a small tribe, one of ten thousand Midlander tribes. You can meet with him."

"What is the Winter Summit?" asked Billy Ray

"Where are you from? You should know about the Winter Summit. All Midlanders groups send a representative along with their tribe's contention to meet at the Winter Summit. It is an honor to be asked by your village to attend the Winter Summit meetings. You should know this."

# Chapter 12

Vicky smiled at Dominique's attempts to hit the target. She could hear Little Jimmy's instruction explaining to hold the bow still and not release the arrow until she held her breath for a second. Then she should steady her aim and then release the arrow smoothly without jerking. Dominique held the bow up but was unable to keep the arrowhead from moving. Vicky watched from behind and could tell her left arm was bent inward, and she knew what was about to happen. Dominique released the arrow, and the bow string hit the inside of her left forearm. Dominique recoiled from the sting. The arrow flew over top of the target. Vicky could not help but laugh. She recalled when she first learned to shoot a bow, she had trouble pulling the string back enough to release the arrow. The bow would not bend at her attempt to pull the string. "That was good for the first-time attempt."

Dominique turned to Vicky, "I heard you approach. Why did you not warn me? My forearm hurts." She pulled her sleeve up and showed her the red welt.

Vicky smiled and knew Dominque sensed her presents but knew she had not heard her as she walked in behind the two. She then walked toward Little Jimmy and Dominique, "My first attempt was a lot worse than your shot. I was not strong enough to bend the bow and pull the string back far enough to shoot the arrow." She laughed as she looked at her arm.

Little Jimmy picked up his bow which was twelve inches longer, "You must keep your left arm straight. I knew you were going to hit your forearm. That is the only way you will learn. You will never forget the sting of the bow string." He lifted an arrow and pulled the string back and released the arrow in less than a second. The arrow flew straight hitting the target in the middle. "You must get stronger in your shoulders to shoot an arrow four-hundred yards with a 100-pound combat bow. To master a 100-pound bow one must practice for months."

Dominique handed the bow to Vicky. "I would like to see you shoot."

Vicky took the bow and loaded an arrow and fired the arrow hitting Little Jimmy's arrow sticking in the middle of the target. Little Jimmy said, "Shooting a bow takes practice. Being good with a sword and spear takes practice. You need to be stronger, faster, and more agile which comes with exercising. I will train with you with a sword and hand-to-hand fighting, but you must start working out with weights and running. You must decide if this is what you want. I cannot work out for you. You must set your goals and then achieve those goals. Otherwise, you will just be going through the motions and wasting your trainer's time."

Dominique looked deflated, "How long does it take?"

Little Jimmy looked at Vicky and then looked at Dominique, "You are a Blueblood. You should be able to master all this in a few months. You must get stronger and faster. You need to set your mind to accomplish these, or you will never learn to be a warrior. Then, when Samuel returns, he can complete your training."

Dominique picked up another arrow and the bow. She aimed the arrow. Little Jimmy walked next to her and held her left forearm straight. "You must extend your forearm and keep your arm straight. The string will not hit you, if you do this correctly." Dominique released the arrow which hit the target five inches from the center.

Vicky smiled, "See you are catching on. Remember how high your aim is above the target and then when you adjust your distance you will know how much to adjust your aim. The key to hitting a target is understanding the flight of the arrow. Now shoot twenty-five arrows in a row."

# Chapter 13

Veronica spent time individually with each child each day. The three weeks had passed quickly as they stayed in a small cottage located behind John Jr.'s home. John Jr. would have the maids bring them food and check on them daily. The four children would all sleep in the same bed with Veronica. During the day at lunch two of her guards would come into the home and play with the children. On occasions, Michael and Viking would take the two oldest boys for a walk outside and go on horse rides with them. The temperature was in the fifties during the day and the kids loved the outdoors. In order to blend in with the rest of the men on the ranch, Cruzie and Pretty Boy worked as cowboys rounding up cattle. Michael and Viking would work directly with John Jr. One day they would cut firewood. The next day they would repair the barn. The next day they would assist in delivering cattle to the dock to sell to a boat captain going north or south. Hector slowly recovered from his injured leg and was always on guard. They all were careful not to draw attention to themselves. They also watched and listened for any activity not routine in the town. Every time a ship sailed into the harbor at least one of them would be near the dock watching for Normand soldiers or bounty hunters.

Veronica knew the time for giving birth was quickly approaching. Frank Jr. had contracted with two neighbor ladies to be the midwives to assist in delivering the baby. They tried to keep the number of people who knew about Veronica staying in the cottage to the two women and the maids working in the home. Frank told the two midwives Veronica was his girlfriend, and he implied she had accidentally gotten pregnant. The charade seemed to work.

During the fifth week Veronica sat up in bed and felt the wet sheet. She knew her water had broken. She walked to the bedroom door and opened the door. She saw Michael asleep on the floor near the fire. He awoke and saw her, "It is time. My water has broken."

Michael at once stood, "Please return to your bed and lie down. I will tell the guys. We will summon the midwives." Michael ran out the door to the barn and awoke the other four men.

*\*\**

The birth took place fourteen hours later. She had screamed in pain for the last hour as the two ladies urged Veronica through the birth. Veronica was tired and relieved with the joy of motherhood. She was thankful the baby boy was healthy.

The older lady held the baby out and noticed the child was healthy. She handed the child to the younger lady who was holding a towel to wrap around the newborn. As the older lady started to hand the child over, both noticed the pointed ears, blue eyes, and a trace of blonde hair. The two women looked at each other with the understanding Veronica had just given birth to a Blueblood. They stared at each other, understanding the ramification of what they had witnessed.

The younger lady handed the child to Veronica to hold. The two ladies observed Veronica to see her reaction to the child and the pointed ears.

Veronica kissed the child and started talking baby talk and how handsome her son appeared. She kissed him on the forehead and hugged him. The younger lady announced, "I will get the father." She opened the door and announced, "We have a healthy little boy."

Frank Jr. walked in and held the child and did as he was instructed. He acted like he did not realize the child was a Blueblood. He then followed the two women into the foyer and to pay both women with gold. He needed them to keep the birth a secret. "This payment is for your cooperation and your help. You will tell no one about this birth." He then held the two gold coins up. The ladies looked at the gold. Frank then added, "This is enough to compensation for your service, and you will never speak to tell anyone of the baby being born. Do not mention the mother, her children, or the birth."

The older lady reached for the coin, "Yes. Mr. Frank Jr. We will keep the secret. Thank you." The two ladies walked out the door and past Veronica's guards who were standing on the front porch.

After the midwives departed, her guards all walked into her room and celebrated the birth. Viking announced, "Do not worry. The four kids had been carried into Frank Jr's home and entertained by the maids."

Pretty Boy held the small child and asked his name. Veronica declared, "He will be named Gabriel Solomon Zbar. I will name him after my mother's maiden name, Zbar and Gabriel, the archangel who announced the Virgin Mary and God's plan for the people of earth." She intentionally did not mention the middle name and corrected the spelling to reflect the King of the Jewish people as noted in the Bible and not the spelling of her husband and the father of her child.

Frank Jr. looked at Veronica, "I paid the midwives. They should tell no one of this birth. The maids will assist you."

Veronica was exhausted. She stood with a cotton gown on, and the front opened while her bed had been made and cleaned. She held Gabriel against her breast hoping he would start feeding. The midwives had explained the child's need to eat and the importance of her being able to breastfeed. "I need rest. If all of you could clear the room except Michael and Frank Jr., I need to talk with you."

The guards left and Michael closed the door behind them. Veronica looked at the two men, "I do not know if I can trust the midwives. They both noticed my son's pointed ears. They know. We will need a contingency plan."

Michael announced, "We will stay close and provide you twenty-four-hour security. I believe the threat will come from the sea. We will watch the docks."

Frank Jr. announced, "I paid them with the gold. They said they would tell no one. The greatest threat to all of us is the threat of the dead soldiers coming from the mountain fortress. If our King finds out about you and these kids, we will all be killed. The King's guards will stop at nothing to expose you and these kids. The King will know what is at stake if anyone in his realm has broken the rules as set by the Dark Master. We cannot allow your group to be discovered. If you are discovered." He hesitated, "You will need to run and run far. I trust some of my men to fight with me, but I do not trust everyone here at my ranch. I have tried to vet the two midwives and paid them handsomely. I would suggest when you are able, you all relocate. My biggest fear is word will travel, and you will be discovered."

Michael looked at Frank Jr., "Where could we relocate and still be safe?"

"There is an island two miles northwest with a small shack. Men travel there and fish. I can arrange for a ship to sail you out of the harbor tomorrow." He looked at Veronica, "The living conditions are not like these. It will be hard, but I know of no other alternative. I can have a man watch the dock after you have departed, and we can bring you supplies."

Michael was fast to say, "My Queen, I do not like the deal. We would be trapped on this island with no way to run or hide. We would be at the mercy of someone bringing us supplies. We can leave in five months and cross the mountains. I suggest we stay."

Frank Jr acted as if he did not hear Michael's remark when Michael referred to Veronica as his queen. Veronica said, "I am so thankful for my son, and for both of you." She looked at both men, "I must rest. My body needs to adjust, so I can feed my baby. We will discuss this further this afternoon."

# Chapter 14

Dak was discouraged as he rode along the path. He had heard the stories over the years as he sat around the camp fires while growing up listening to the adults tell of how the Midlander Tribes would kill foreigners if they crossed into their territory. The Midlanders had elected to live a solitary life without allowing foreigners to intervene. Diversity in the religion and not doing as the leaders commanded was not tolerated. Dak thought of the story told by Eric of Newport when he, Little Jimmy and Billy Ray had traveled across the continent over fifteen years prior and killed over a dozen Midlanders trying to return to Cliff Tops. The story was told that every Midlander was required to endorse the same strict religion with no exception. Dak had an ominous feeling about the tribe as he watched the back of Boudica leading the way. As they approached the city, he noticed several men and women watching as they entered the town on the dirt road between the log homes lining both sides. Dak noticed the blacksmith shop with the open front wall with a large man forging iron as he could hear the hammer striking the metal. He noticed to the right of the blacksmith shop the stack of old iron salvaged from the old world stored for further use to be transformed into weapons and other metal products. As they rode the slow pace, he noticed the corral with several horses. Then, as they kept proceeding further into the town, he could see the building at the end of the street where they appeared to be headed. He then noticed the pig pen full of mud-covered hogs located behind the barn. He could hear a sawmill in the distance cutting logs into blanks. He wondered about the energy source to run the sawmill. The Midlanders did not except the energy sources of the old world.

Boudica interrupted his observations when she announced as they came to the last structure on the street, "You may tie your horses here. I will introduce you to my father, the king. You may wait here." She dismounted and walked into the stone building.

Dak glanced at the citizens as Boudica closed the door. Some of the men appeared to be capable hunters as they held their weapons as they walked through the town. He noticed the bows carried by several men as the men were walking into a building to his left. The bows appeared to be made from some light-colored flexible wood. He also noticed the swords and long knives the men were carrying on their bodies looked deadly with the extended blades. The people were well armed.

Boudica looked at the four men in her father's office. She saw her father sitting in a chair behind his desk. The talking stopped as she walked further into the room. She looked at her father, "I met some warriors at the swimming hole who requested our help. They seek passage through the low gap in the mountains in their travel to Tanger."

The large man reached for his dual ax leaning against the center pole. In his deep voice, "Which Midlander tribe are they from? They know better than to cross into our realm without coming to a conference."

"They are not Midlanders."

The King looked at his daughter, "How did these warriors cross onto our sanctioned property? Where are they from? I demand to know now."

Boudica now realized she might have underestimated her father and the tribe. "I have guaranteed the warriors safe passage. Three of the travelers are in the street waiting to meet you. I thought it would be best to introduce them to you. We need to assist them. By us helping them, they will be helping us." She hesitated now realizing her tribe might not be hospitable. The other men in the room reached for their weapons. "They mean us no harm. They request safe passage through our realm." She hesitated again, "Father, I can assure you, they are just passing through."

The King acted frustrated, "You do not speak for me." He rammed his index finger into the desktop as he spoke. She could tell with his jaws clenched he was not going to be hospitable. "You know outsiders are not allowed inside our city. Send in their leader. The other two will remain outside with you. I will decide who can cross our territory, not you."

Boudica turned and walked out the door. The King motioned for his men to be prepared.

Boudica opened the door and announced, "You and you alone may enter the King's chambers. He will see you now." Dak noticed Boudica's mood had changed. She seemed more reserved. Dak felt the pit in his stomach move. He did not feel good about this meeting. He looked at Zenith and then Hulk with a concerned expression alerting them to be on the lookout for trouble. As he dismounted, he whispered, "Keep your guard up. Something does not feel kosher."

Zenith turned her horse around and peered in all directions. They were at the end of the street boxed in on three sides. She knew this was a perfect place to be ambushed while they stood in the open. Hulk dismounted and tied his horse to the post next to Dak's horse. He held his bow in front of him as he looked at Boudica, "We are trying to do the right thing. Why all of a sudden do I not trust you?"

Boudica did not wish to talk with Hulk, but she understood his concern. She turned her back to him as she patiently stood and waited. She now realized she had made a mistake bringing the three into her city.

As Dak walked into the stone building, Hulk looked at Boudica standing with her back to him. He housed bitter feeling toward her as she had kicked him in the side as he was sitting on the rock and then she had also embarrassed him by suggesting he was perverted. "It is one thing to hurt or kill me, but these are my friends, and I can assure you, Boudica, you will be the first to die if anyone tries to harm any of my friends."

Boudica heard Hulk's threat but stood still staring at the door to her father's building. She was already trying to figure out how to resolve the pending issue.

The door was slammed behind Dak by the man standing against the front wall as he walked into the middle of the large room. Two men walked from behind him and demanded, "We will be taking your steel." He saw a large man approach with a two-foot-long dual ax. He noticed the men behind him had swords pulled.

Dak calmly announced as he held his hands out to his side, "I come in peace. This is not necessary." He glanced around trying to discern who was in charge, and how many possible combatants were in the room.

"Boudica indicated I would be granted an audience with her father the king." The man behind him pushed him forward and then held his sword in a threatening manner, "I said we will be taking your steel."

Dak glanced at a man sitting behind a large table and figured him to be the leader. He was older with grey in his beard and seemed to be waiting for his men to disarm him. Dak stared at the man and noticed the dark-skinned man appeared to be in his fifties, and his long hair was pulled back into a ponytail with a few wrinkles under his eyes. The man looked fierce and cruel. Dak immediately did not like the situation and felt an ominous gut feeling something bad was about to occur. He stared at Dak. Dak reached down and released his belt holding his two swords. The other man behind him came up and pulled Dak's knife from his back holster and then pulled the knife from his boot. The man looked at the two Sai swords with interest and then threw the swords and two knives into the corner next to the front door. The other man stepped into the back of Dak's legs forcing him to the floor on his knees. A fifth man came over and wrapped a rope around Dak's neck and then threw the end of the rope over the open rafter. He then tightened the rope. The big man holding the dual ax set the ax down leaning the ax against one of the poles supporting the open rafters. He picked Dak up and placed him in a chair. The man with the rope walked behind the chair holding the rope tight, cutting into Dak's neck making his breathing difficult.

The man behind the table stood and walked into the middle of the room. He turned and stared at Dak for a second, "Where are you from?"

Dak could feel the rope being pulled tighter around his neck and his breathing more restricted. He reached and placed his fingers between the rope and his neck. "We are from the far northeast part of the continent. We have traveled a long way to be here. We mean you no harm. We mean your people no harm."

"So, you and your men are not Midlanders? I would disagree with you. You do mean us harm." He looked closely at Dak.

"We seek nothing from you or your people other than safe passage through your realm. We will be happy to pay a fair toll."

"Why are you traveling to Tanger?"

"We have tried to live in peace with the Midlanders near our village. We have tried to live in isolation from the world, but the wars down south arrived at our sanctioned realm. We were forced to join many others in the wars in the south. The city of Tanger houses some mean people. We seek to serve justice on the evil people hiding near Tanger. This is part of our war effort and has nothing to do with you and your tribe."

The King interrupted Dak, "People like you are the cause of the nuclear war and the B12 virus being released on the planet. Your kind caused Armageddon. You will not be allowed to cause a second Armageddon. We Midlanders will not tolerate aggressive behavior on our soil. You are not welcome on the Midlander's property. All our tribes have agreed, we will not leave our territories and anyone that enters our lands will be punished. You now are being tried in our court. The penalty could lead to you and your men being executed. You trespassed across our land without our permission. You will be sentenced to death."

Dak looked surprised, "We mean you no harm. We seek safe passage across the mountains to the City of Tanger." The man to the left hit Dak hard with his glove covered fist.

Dak turned sharply to the left from the impact of the blow. His first consideration was of his wife and Hulk standing in the road surrounded. The door opened and in walked Boudica. She was surprised to see Dak with a rope around his neck and a man pulling the rope which was hung over a rafter. The guards all hesitated. She demanded, "What is the meaning of this? Release him father. I demand it." She walked into the middle of the room.

She then turned to the man holding the rope, "I said release him. He is not our enemy. He wishes to fight our enemy. Father, actions like this is why there has been so many desertion from our tribe to Merlin. Our people do not wish to live like this."

The King looked at his daughter and trembled with anger as he spoke, "You know nothing of what you speak. His kind is forbidden to be on our land, and they know this. Yet they come anyway. The Winter Summit has ruled on this issue. We will not tolerate or allow outsiders to enter our realm. They will spread their ways of greed, dishonesty, and moral corruption which leads to our death. You do not know the history of the world and how the country in the old world, the United States fell from within by allowing non-believers and morally ill people to lead their country. The Winter Summit has invoked the death sentence for men like these men. Allowing them in our realm will jeopardize our lives. My job as king is to prevent these types of people from spreading the ideological virus which would corrupt our citizens."

Wrinkles appeared on her forehead, "He knows nothing of our customs and laws. Father, they are here to fight the cult led by the Dark Master. You cannot take up for the cult after what they have done. They took your son, and you did nothing."

His face turned red with rage, "How dare you tell me I did nothing? I must answer to our tribe, and we live in peace with the Dark Master. You know nothing of his power. I have allowed you to speak too often. I must demand your tongue girl if you do not take heed of my respect."

She turned to her father, "We live in fear of the Dark Master. You and your men are scared to fight the true enemy. Let these soldiers from the far east fight for us."

Dak could tell the King was not going to provide mercy. He fully intended to execute him and his warriors. He forced his hand between the rope and his neck and positioned his body, so he could leap from his knees to his feet and then push backward against the man holding the rope. He played the fight over in his head how he best could attack and win.

The King motioned for one of the men to go outside. Dak knew Zenith and Hulk were going to be arrested or die fighting. Dak announced, "No wait." He then suddenly stood and pushed backward. With each step, he gained momentum as he stood holding the chair under him. He pushed backward forcing the man with the rope into the large pole holding the rafters in place. The impact of the pole slamming the man hard knocked the breath out of him as the roof framing vibrated by the force of the impact. Dak did not hesitate as he turned and drove his fist into the man's ribs. The man doubled over out of breath and in pain from his three fractured ribs. Dak turned as he removed the rope from around his neck and then moved forward as the big man with the dual ax swung right to left. Dak dodged the swing by jumping backward and then dropped to the floor and attacked with a Karate kick with his left foot pushing the man's right knee inverted, causing him to collapse to the floor. The man stumbled backward hitting the floor holding his right knee. The man at the door pulled his sword and came forward. Dak backed up and lifted the chair using the chair to block the sword swing. Dak moved forward as the sword was stuck into the leg of the chair. Dak grabbed with his left hand the man's wrist holding the sword and then punched the man in the face with his right fist. The man fell backward as Dak took his sword and now held his sword in front of him. Dak turned to the fourth man and blocked his swing. He moved forward and drove his forehead into the nose fracturing the bridge bone as the nose bone moved downward as the bone snapped and flattened out on his right cheek. The man fell to the floor bleeding from his face and was unconscious as he laid on the floor.

Dak turned his attention to the King the last man standing. The King pulled his sword. He was overweight and appeared to be nervous as he took a deep breath. The first man with the cracked ribs stood hunched to his injured side but stepped forward and swung his sword. Dak blocked his sword swing and then quickly pivoted into a spinning circle hitting the man in the face with the broad side of his sword blade. The sound of the slap by the sword was loud as the man dropped his sword. Dak then kicked the fourth man in the chest driving him backward into the exterior wall. Boudica stepped in front of Dak, "Stop. He is an old, scared man. I will be your guide and show you the way. Do not kill these cowards. They are scared little men."

She then turned to her father, "The cult will keep taking from us until we have nothing. You were too frightened to mention the Lower Mountain Master to the Winter Summit. You are a scared coward, and worthless. You cannot see the forest for the trees. You think the cult is going to stop taking from us? They are not ever going to stop until someone kills them."

He interrupted, "Child, you do not understand. I have protected you and our tribe."

She interrupted her father, "You are too scared to be a man. Constantly living in fear is no way to live. You know what the cult will do to other tribes, and you do nothing to help others. I feel sorry for you and the tribe's council. I will lead these warriors across the mountain. You might want to go back to the Winter Council and confess the facts about the cult to the Winter Summit."

The King looked frustrated. He glanced at his four men lying on the floor. He watched as Dax turned his blade sideways and slapped his man standing and could have just as easily decapitated him. He spared their lives. He then looked at Dak holding a sword and realized he could not best the man in front of him. "You may go." He looked at Boudica, "You are not welcome here. Do not return. I banish you from our city."

Dak clenched his jaws as he heard the King tell his daughter not to return. He stared at the King, "The next time I visit this shit hole you call a city; you better call me sir and be hospitable, or I will drag your worthless ass out to the pig pen and force you to bath in the mud with the hogs. Your daughter is correct. You are a scared, worthless piece of shit. You hide behind your fears and your bullshit selfish laws."

\*\*\*

The four rode into the camp next to the river and the hot spring. Dak looked at Samuel and Billy Ray sitting next to the fire pit drinking coffee. He noticed there was no campfire. "We have a guide to take us across the mountain, and a temporary

160

agreement with Boudica's tribe for us to travel through their territory. We need to eat and then leave. I am not certain how long the temporary agreement will last."

Boudica dismounted next to Zenith and tied her horse to the lead rope with the other horses. Zenith noticed several men swimming in the hot spring. She was envious and wanted her turn in the hot water on this cold afternoon. Billy Ray and Samuel both looked at Boudica with skepticism.

Samuel asked, "Do you know the way?"

Boudica answered, "Yes. I know the way. There is a path leading to the mountain. I have been across the mountain once."

Dak walked to the fire pit and sat on a log. "We need to start a fire. What are you planning on cooking?"

"Tommy Boy and Trey killed a couple of groundhogs," announced Billy Ray.

Trey announced, "We are waiting for the men to bring us some matches from Robin Hood's brown saddlebag."

Boudica looked over behind the tree and saw the brown saddlebag, "I will fetch them." She walked over behind the tree and opened the saddlebag and noticed a shirt and then a bag of ground mushrooms. She sat the bag down and then dug deeper into the bag. As she was placing the mushrooms back into the bag, she heard a man's voice from behind her demand for her to close the bag and step away. She stood and turned and the large man from Meadow Bottoms was standing ten feet behind her.

She noticed the clenched jaws and the crease in his forehead as he was staring at her. "You will not steal my stuff." He walked over and grabbed her arm and pulled her from behind the tree. "She is trying to steal my stuff." He pushed her down as she tried to twist back and forward to free herself from his grip.

Hulk walked toward the man and exploded into him forcing him to land on his back. The large man landed hard on the Mountain Laurel undergrowth growing along the open area. Boudica stood and was in shock that someone had pushed her to the ground and announced, "I was trying to locate the matches from Robin Hood's saddlebag. I was not trying to steal your stuff. Why would I want anything you own?" She walked toward the fire pit.

Tommy Boy announced, "Robin Hood's saddlebag is lying inside his tent."

Dak watched the man stand and appear to be upset with Hulk's involvement as he walked to his saddlebag and fastened the leather strap. Dak watched him carry his saddlebag as he walked off into the woods. Dak said, "Tell Tommy Boy and Trey it is rude not to share. They will eat both groundhogs. Tommy Boy says a groundhog is the best tasting meat."

Zenith looked at Robin Hood as he was out of hearing range cleaning the deer down by the river, "I have eaten deer meat every meal for the last ten days. I will nor be eating the rodent for dinner."

Billy Ray smiled at Zenith, "The groundhog tast good."

"I will not eat a rat for dinner."

Bill Ray smiled, "We told the cook to add salt, ground pepper, parsley, lemon juice and other spices to the roasted deer meat while the tender meet slowly marinates over the warm fire. The taste will be exquisite." The group laughed.

Zenith deadpanned her statement as she looked at Billy Ray, "I cannot wait. Parsley is my favorite."

Tommy Boy added, "Zenith, you must have eaten high on the hog in Merlin."

"I was joking. I have never eaten parsley."

Boudica sat on the log across from Samuel and Billy Ray. Hulk sat down then Tommy Boy, and Trey took his seat. Boudica looked at Zenith, "Have you been to Merlin? I always wanted to see the big city."

Everyone got quiet and the mood changed to one of seriousness. Zenith looked at Boudica, "I grew up in Merlin."

Robin Hood walked over next to Hulk and placed the deer over the fire to cook. He then sat down, "Dak also had an opportunity to visit Merlin. He cannot wait to take another vacation to the city. He says the trip is to literally die for." The group all started laughing as Robin Hood used had hands when he talked. Dak glanced at Samuel who was laughing in his deep voice while holding his side.

Boudica looked at everyone, not certain why the laughter, "I think the big city would be glamourous to see the plays, the war tournaments, and dress up and go out to eat at nice restaurants. I dream of going at some point." She smiled as she thought about going to the big city. "I have never traveled, but I hope to see several large cities." She looked at Zenith, "Maybe you can assist me as a tour guide."

Zenith tried to smile knowing she would be arrested if she returned, but also realizing the young lady was trying to fit in to their group.

Dak noticed the large man from Meadow Bottoms talking with his traveling companion behind the trees as he was looking through his saddle bag. He was thinking he did not like the two men. He smiled and added as he turned his view to Boudica, "I truly hope when you visit, your accommodations are nicer than my accommodations. I could not get comfortable in my room. I could hear my neighbors yelling about the discomforts they faced. I was eaten alive by flying insects, and my room was very hot. The room service really could have also been better."

Everyone laughed again with Samuel laughing so hard he could not talk. He finally added, "You should have asked for the full body massage. I am certain your room service butlers would have been happy to provide the massage for you at no additional charge." He then bent over; he was laughing so hard. The group watched him, and all laughed. Boudica looked at the individuals laughing knowing there must have been a story behind the humor. She smiled at Dak and Zenith.

Zenith stopped laughing and pulled her hood back and then removed her cap. She scratched her head and glanced at the hot spring. She could see a couple of the naked men standing on the rocks next to the hot spring as they then walked over to put on their clothes.

Dak looked at Zenith. He smiled. He knew she really wanted to bathe in the hot spring. "After we eat this upscale roasted deer meat, and maybe some groundhog if Trey and Tommy Boy share, we will take our turn taking a bath."

Boudica looked at the nude men and noticed they were dressing. She then glanced at Zenith and was startled as she stared at her ears, "You are a Blueblood!"

Everyone was quiet. Zenith looked at Boudica, "Yes, I am a Blueblood from Merlin. I choose to make my home south of Cliff Tops at a place called Zenith Point. I can never return to Merlin. I would be arrested and most likely executed by the Merlin Senate."

She looked at Dak, "Are you also a Blueblood?" she then added, "I mean the way you handled yourself in my father's chambers. Those four men were our best warriors."

Dak removed his cap, so she could see his ears, "No. I am not a Blueblood. I have visited Merlin on one occasion, and I will never willingly go back." He then looked seriously at Boudica,

165

"Your men would not fare so well if they faced the Normand soldiers. Your people will find out what a good soldier is when the Normand army marches this way. Your soldiers do not fight as a team. They have a lot to learn. Being brave is not enough. I have seen thousands of brave men die on the battlefield. They need training. They will die on the battlefield if they face the soldiers from Southern City."

"We are great warriors. The man with the dual ax won the tournament at the Winter Summit two years in a row." She then looked at Dak, "You got lucky and surprised them. We all are great warriors."

Everyone was silent and then Boudica asked, "Why not go back to Merlin? You seem so certain."

Dak turned and looked at Boudica, "I got in a tussle with Zenith's boyfriend, and it was really ugly."

The men getting out of the hot spring all turned to look at the group sitting around the fire laughing. Zenith announced with a smile, "Apollo was not my boyfriend."

Boudica acted excited, "Do you know Apollo? I understand he is very handsome. I heard from a traveler; Apollo is the best-looking man in all of Merlin. He fears no one and is the best sword fighter on the planet." She then looked at Dak, "I mean I heard the story from a couple of traders who had talked with a sailor. He also indicated Merlin is so glamorous."

Dak looked into the fire, "That may be true, but he now has a scar on his right wrist because of me." The group laughed again with Samuel drowning out everyone else's laugh with his deep sounding voice as his face turned red while trying to catch his breath.

"The roasted deer with the parsley and other seasonings is ready to eat," announced Trey as he smiled, looking at Zenith.

Billy Ray looked at Zenith, "I do not know about the rest of you, but I am looking forward to the gourmet meal." Everyone laughed.

Everyone started eating and drinking water from the canteens. Boudica looked around and finally exclaimed, "I do not taste the seasoning with pepper or salt. This meat is overcooked and tastes very plain."

Hulk looked up from taking a bite and deadpanned his statement, "They were joking." He then took another bite.

The young man from Meadow Bottoms had walked over to the fire pit. He seemed to be hesitant on entering the circle of friends. He sat on a log by himself behind Dak. He said, "We can sprinkle Laetiporus Sulphureus mushrooms on this deer meat and that will make the deer taste like chicken." He took another bite of deer.

Robin Hood asked "Where do we find Laetiporus Sulphureus mushrooms? I would like some chicken right now."

Trey looked at the man from Meadow Bottoms, "How do you know so much about mushrooms? What do you all do in Meadow Bottoms? Have mushroom class?" He smiled.

The man from Meadow Bottoms then added, "We will start looking for mushrooms we can eat."

Boudica looked at Hulk with a scornful expression. The two had not talked since they first met. "Are you also a Blueblood?"

Hulk glanced up from taking another bite as he stared at Boudica. Robin Hood smiled and answered, "No, Hulk is not a Blueblood but talking of being lucky. He is the luckiest man on earth. He is the only man that I know who can lead a group of warriors halfway across the continent through the wilderness and end up in the middle of Bum Fuck nowhere and land on top of a beautiful nude lady after he was forced to watch her bath in the nude." Robin Hood used his hands while he talked and was very animated with his gestures. Everyone but Hulk and Boudica laughed.

Zenith turned her head with a smile on her face and noticed all the men were out of the hot spring. "I am going to take a bath." She set her plate down and looked at Trey.

Trey looked at Zenith, "I got you. I will wash the dinnerware."

Dak stood and looked at Trey, "Hey bro. You got me also? I need a bath." He walked with Zenith toward the hot spring. Trey smiled and reached for Dak's pan.

Hulk looked at Boudica, "Is there any chance your tribe will try to intervene with our plans? Our plans are to initiate a strategy of attack and use surprise as our main tactic. It would be imperative; The Dark Master does not see us coming."

Boudica did not answer, and Hulk stood and took his pan to the river downstream to clean it. Boudica looked at the men sitting at the fire. "Is Dak in charge? Is Zenith in charge? Is Hulk in Charge? I cannot figure out who is in charge. So far, every one of you have asked me questions and not one seems to be giving orders."

Billy Ray looked at Boudica, "While on this mission, Dak is in charge. He is the most experienced and successful soldier at fighting against the Normand army. He is a proven warrior."

Robin Hood smiled and added, "In addition, Zenith goes where Dak goes which provides him with additional leverage in any conflict. I am not certain what you have heard about Bluebloods in battle, but I am glad she is on my side."

Boudica turned and could not see the two in the spring. She suspected they were fornicating. No one else seemed to care. "So, those two are married?"

Tommy Boy smiled, "I hope so because if they are not, they will have a difficult time explaining to Queen Vicky, the parents of her two grandsons are not married." He smiled and then stopped smiling when no one else smiled. Tommy Boy then glanced at his father and then at Samuel. He knew not to mention Dak's family tree. The group of friends had talked in private about Dak and Samuel's relationship and the fact Samuel was Dak's stepfather. The two men hardly talked and did not appear to be close.

# Chapter 15

Wayne's expression reflected a cringe as he hurriedly walked by the guard, Quincy who was stationed at the double doors to the board meeting, "I am sorry I am late." He took his seat to the right of the Queen. The seat represented the second highest ranking officer in the realm, and the seat also represented the job of the realm manager who worked exclusively under the Queen.

Vicky smiled, "That is quite alright. I understand you were making certain the hunters traveling across the glacier to Seal Island were prepared. We have spent the time getting updated on the realm's activities."

"Yes, I have Walter set up to be on watch from the tower and the other men ready to follow the first group in twenty-four hours to haul back the harvested seals. We hope for a good hunting trip. The snow is deep, and the stray cattle are easy to locate and round up. Several dozen men will attempt to locate and round up the strays."

Vicky smiled, "Our newest member of the board, Mr. Barney Simpson, was updating us on the families living at the newly established outpost."

Wayne glanced at Barney as Vicky added, "They are on schedule to send a pigeon daily. Barney has expressed this issue to them and the importance of us being alerted to an attack from the west. We will send riders when the weather is accommodating every four weeks to the outpost."

Wayne did not like the man from Meadow Bottoms. He reminded Wayne of a certain old-world Politician who hesitated before he spoke and never said what he thought, just what he knew others wanted to hear. Wayne said, "We will be shorthanded for a couple of weeks with the men out hunting and others looking for cattle. We are well supplied with wood. The miners are going to dig out additional coal and stockpile the coal. We should have plenty in three weeks. We have a squad of guards watching the bridge leading to the New York tribe. Representative Simpson has also updated me, the men and women of Meadow Bottoms are continuing their training to be soldiers. The squad from Meadow Bottoms has rotated from our border crossing at the bridge last week back to their farms."

The Queen glanced at Barney who tilted his head and smiled at Vicky.

Vicky ended the meeting after additional small talk about the weather.

Barney stood as the board members started dispersing and then turned to Vicky, "I do have one other question. I noticed you did not mention the military mission you sponsored. I understood the secret mission is located on the west coast. We pray the group going to the west coast has a safe mission. They have been gone for a month. When will your son and husband be expected to return from their trip?"

Vicky smiled, "The sooner the better, but I do not expect them until spring. The winter will be too severe to travel. You know it is hard enough for us to travel from building to building here without the ropes connecting our buildings during a blizzard." Vicky watched Barney as he turned and left. She wondered, "Why would he ask only when her son and husband would return? He had suggested the two men from Meadow Bottoms be part of the mission without knowing the details of the mission, and Dak was upset when she forced the two men on Dak. Why not ask about the mission or the two men? Several others had asked about the secret mission." As she walked out the double doors of the church, she noticed Barney was standing in the front yard staring up the incline toward the watch tower and seemed to be looking around the interior city. She walked down the steps and turned to him, "Why did you not ask about the mission to the west coast? Why ask only when my son and my husband will return?"

Barney turned to face the Queen. He seemed to hesitate and think before he answered. She asked, "Do you already know the details of the mission?"

He smiled, "I do know the details. I overheard Wayne and Billy Ray talking about the mission before they left. I believe they thought I must have been aware of the details because I was elected to the board. The mission is such an important mission. I wish your soldiers God's speed. I assure you that is my only concern is your soldiers safely returning after being successful with the mission."

# Chapter 16

Dominique decided she wanted to become proficient at self-defense and training as a warrior. She also decided she liked Little Jimmy as an instructor. He took time to explain the goals of the workout, and how being a great soldier would demand the warrior complete physical training. The body of a warrior would be required to be strong, agile, and mentally prepared. Eating, sleeping, and exercise were the three main elements to obtain the goals.

In order not to become bored and stay inside her guest room, she decided to venture out to the blacksmith building and workout several hours a day. She enjoyed pushing her body physically and marveled at how fast she was getting stronger and better with a sword. She needed to do something during the stay at Cliff Tops, and she could surprise her parents next year when she returned to Merlin. The winter was too harsh to travel by a sailing vessel to return her home to Merlin. She set her goals and exercised close to eight hours a day. She learned to push her body to the limit with the conditioning and the pushups. She also worked on flexibility and quickness. She jumped rope several thousand times daily. She noticed as she got stronger over the past month, she could pull the larger bowstring tight much easier. She also realized the larger bows would shoot with greater force and longer distances. She pushed herself to be able to use the larger bows and longer arrows. She also learned the importance of giving to the community. She provided a pint of her blood, the same as Zenith and Samuel, once a week to someone in the realm to assist in preventing the person from contracting the deadly B12 virus.

Little Jimmy set up a corner area in the Blacksmith Shop with a bail of straw to use as a target to learn how to properly fight with a sword. He would assist in training Dominique with a sword, a spear, and throwing knives. She would stand and pull the string back time after time building up her shoulders on a large longbow. They would practice outside with the bow and a target when the weather permitted. Dominque pushed herself to be able to fire an arrow four-hundred yards, the same as Little Jimmy. She struggled to reach a distance of three-hundred yards and then worked for thirty days pushing to increase to three-hundred-fifty yards.

The heat from the forge would keep the area warm during the workouts. Little Jimmy explained the process of making a steel sword, and he enjoyed the workouts with Dominique. He wanted to reward her as he planned on forging a personalized sword for her if she passed the training goals he established. "I make the swords out of 1080 high-carbon steel. The steel is best for balance, hardness, and edge retention."

Dominque smiled, "I would not know how best to make a weapon. I do not believing in taking life of others."

During their sparring with the wooden practice swords, Little Jimmy would not hold back. He would be aggressive and then explain how she needed to take advantage of her opportunities in a battle and not over think the confrontation. "You need to use your brain when faced with killing another in battle. You need to be fast, agile, and powerful. You need to take advantage of any opportunity the competition presents you." He watched her standing in the ready position waiting on him to start the practice round. He moved very quickly and cut her off from moving to her right. He then reached out with his left gloved hand and grabbed her wooden sword blade. He then rushed her, knocking her down and then stood over her with his wooden sword pressed against her chest. "I will not hurt you, but the other warriors will kill you. You need to concentrate on your training, and how to be better at being faster and not predictable. I have seen unmotivated students spend more time training than others because they horse around and do not understand the importance of the training. There is a limit of time one can spend on training. They never get better with a sword or bow because they will not spend the time to enhance their weaknesses. This is no game. There is no time to fool around, and there is no fair play on the battlefield. You either kill or be killed."

She squared up and her jaws were clenched. They had fought in sparring twenty times, and Little Jimmy had beat her every single time. "I will do better. One more time."

Little Jimmy looked at Dominique. "Keep your wits about you. You left your sword hanging in front of me. Why would I not grab the blade? The sword will not cut through these thick welding gloves unless the sword is swung with force. You need to consider these reasons I keep beating you. When Samuel returns this spring and takes over your training, you need to be better. A lot better with your power, footwork, and conviction to be a warrior. He will spot your weaknesses and exploit them."

\*\*\*

Dominique dressed in her warm attire. The last three weeks of training had been challenging but fun for her. She decided she loved the older man training her. Little Jimmy was like a father to her. He was a gentle giant of a man. She was tired from her four-hour workout in the Blacksmith Shop. Little Jimmy had provider her a long knife and explained she needed to become accustom to carrying her weapons as she jogged. He urged her to run with the knife, her bundle of arrows and her bow. She wanted to jog at least ten miles through the snow and ice-covered ground. Forging through the snow was more difficult than running on a hard surface. "I will see you in two hours and then we can wrap up my sword fighting. I intend to beat you in the next round." She smiled at him as she exited the door into the sunny cold air. The temperature was just a little above zero degrees, and the day was going to warm up to the low thirties in the early afternoon before dropping below zero in the clear cold night. She wanted to run and enjoy the outdoors before another large storm blew through and dropped several feet of snow on the frozen ground.

Little Jimmy smiled as Dominique closed the door behind her and went for her run. He had grown fawned of her. She had a delightful personality, well-mannered, and nice to be around. He also knew she was not going to give up, and she would start beating him at some point. Her natural skills from being a Blueblood would enhance her fighting abilities. He turned to the forge; he was going to surprise her with a sword he was making for her. He thought she had no idea that he was heating the liquid metal to form a special sword for her. The form had been adjusted, so the weight of the sword would match her strength. He was forging her sword as they talked, and she worked out, swinging the practice sword, hitting the bag of straw for hours at a time. She would then do several pushups and jump rope. Her routine was to run ten miles before they would spar. Little Jimmy wanted her to be tired and to learn how to fight the fatigue as she trained with the heavier wooden sword. He had worked on the form for the sword for two days and crafted the sword from iron located in the earth from an old-world train track the men had salvaged the prior year. Now, as she left on her run, he could complete the forging. The metal part of the sword had been completed. The three feet of leather strip had been soaked in seal oil for two days and then heated by being left hanging over the forge the prior day. He figured to wrap the handle with the soft leather and then sharpen the sword to the final product. He took his time as he bent over to engrave her initials, DV, on the blade next to the handle. He was trying to hold his right hand steady as he engraved the letter when he heard someone come into the blacksmith building. "Did you forget something?" He kept his concentration on engraving the V as he was bent over the brackets holding the sword blade in place as he rubbed the sharp point of the harden metal driver into the blade.

The man peered through the front window and noticed Little Jimmy bent over the blade of a sword with his back to the door. He motioned for his partner to follow him and be quiet. He placed his sword back into the sleeve as he quietly opened the door. He saw Little Jimmy working at the table with his back to him. The man reached for the twenty-ounce wooden handled hammer lying on the bench at the door and took the hammer. He slowly walked toward Little Jimmy careful not to make a sound.

Little Jimmy started to turn when he realized no one answered him. The man swung the hammer hitting him in the back of his head. Little Jimmy fell over into the forge which burned him and then fell to the ground bleeding from his skull.

The man replied as he waved the hammer over Little Jimmy's body, "Yeah, I forgot something. I forgot to turn your lights out." He hit Little Jimmy again in the head with the hammer. He looked at the other man, "Signal the others."

The other man smiled at Little Jimmy lying on the ground. He turned to the opened door and flashed his mirror into the sun. He then turned and walked toward the lookout station.

The man was dressed in a large fur coat with his head covered under the fur hood. He walked up behind the elderly man sitting in the lookout chair viewing the ocean. Walter was friendly. He invited company and conversation. He hoped the man was bringing him some hot coffee. Walter announced, "I hope the coffee is hot and bitter." Walter glanced at the man approaching. He could not see his face with the large hood from the fur coat pulled down. Walter did not suspect the man not to be friendly. People in the community were always trying the next best thing in the form of warmer clothing, and Walter had not recognized the large coat. The man pulled his knife as Walter turned his view back to the sea. "Being the lookout has one advantage," declared Walter. Walter then remembered the man was not carrying a thermos. He smiled and turned to look at the man, "People bring me coffee."

The knife went straight through Walter's heart. Walter hunched over and died instantly with his eyes frozen open. The man looked around to make certain the area was clear. He also made certain he stayed clear of the warning bell hanging next to Walter. He wiped his blade on Walter's coat, then picked Walter's lifeless body up by the boots and drug Walter to the top of the cliff. He pushed the body over the rock bluff and watched as the body bounced off the outcropping of the cliff fifteen feet beneath the lookout station and then fell toward the rock covered shore two-hundred feet below. He glanced in both directions overlooking the beach below and did not see anyone as he then noticed Walter's body had ricochet off the rocks and rolled to the edge of the ocean.

Four men led a group of thirty men who walked onto the main snow-covered road leading into Cliff Tops. They were all carrying swords and bows. As they passed the small cottages, two would enter and pull the townsfolk out to the road and force them to walk toward the church. Four of the men went to the front door of the fourplex. Queen Vicky, Delores, Mia, and Casey were drinking coffee. They thought they heard someone yell.

***

Wayne was in the loft of the barn writing a note to be carried by pigeon to Old Thomas' Outpost. He sent messages every day at this time. He heard the familiar screech sound of the iron barn door hinges rubbing as the door opened. He started rolling up the small note, and he knew someone had entered the barn. He heard footsteps ascending the steps to the loft. He heard the screech of the barn door open a second time. He felt something was not kosher as he thought of the possibilities. Most of the men were out hunting, mining, or rounding up stray cattle. The kids and women all elected to stay indoors out of the below zero-degree weather until later in the afternoon when the day warmed. He turned to the stairs and saw the man ascending the top step. Wayne dropped the note and reached for his sword. The man ascended the last of the stairs with his pulled sword. The recognition of the identity registered with Wayne. Sie's son had picked this time to attack when very few men were in the village, and no one was standing guard on the roadways.

Wayne yelled as loud as he could as he pulled his sword and charged the man swinging his sword hard right to left. The man blocked his swings. Wayne yelled a second time as he swung two more times. Both attempts were blocked. The two men had little room to swing the swords in such a confined area. This part of the second story loft of the barn had been converted into the pigeon coup. The small two-foot by two-foot wooden paneled door, located on the second level of the north elevation exterior

183

wall of the barn, could be easily opened to allow the pigeons to fly heading on their journeys.

Wayne hit the man in the mouth with the handle of his sword. The man responded by grabbing his hand and tackled Wayne forcing him backward into the wall and then both men fell to the floor. Both men rolled over on one another as they wrestled across the floor, with both ending up dropping their swords and fighting with their fists. Wayne was able to break free from the teenager as he pushed the man backward as he stood and ran toward the stairs. The man leaped and tackled him from behind. The two men ended up trading punches in their fight. Wayne pushed the man into the pigeon cages. Wayne used this opportunity to flee. He knew he must warn the others. Wayne felt panicked as he was over forty years older than this young man who was in better physical shape to fight. He descended the steps and ran for the barn door.

The second man stood with his back to the interior wood wall as he waited. He listened at the fast steps, descending the ladder from the loft and running across the barn floor. He stepped out of the stable and released his arrow hitting Wayne in the upper back of his shoulder as Wayne reached for the door handle. Wayne suddenly felt something was not alright as the impact was like a hammer hitting him. He felt himself trying to reach for the door handle but could not extend his arm outward as he fell forward into the closed door. As he was falling, he glanced down at his upper shoulder and saw the arrowhead sticking out with his blood running down his arm. The impact caused Wayne to fall forward into the door and then fall to the barn floor. Wayne felt the nauseating feeling and hot flush moment as he tried to stand. He realized the danger and pushed his body to stand, but his vision became hazy as he peered toward the ceiling of the barn as the cold sweat covered his body.

The second man looked at Sie's oldest son as he held his bow out in front of him. As Sie's son cleared the last step of the ladder with his sword held in a threatening manner, the bounty hunter smiled, "Being a bounty hunter from down south, one learns how to do things the easy way. Now sleeve your sword. We need him alive. Notice how he is wounded and can walk on his own. He will be able to tell us what we need to know. Now pick him up and force him to walk to the church."

Sie's son stared at Wayne as he placed his sword in his sleeve, "I will kill that bastard."

"Not until we have the gold."

# Chapter 17

Dak glanced at Hulk, "Lead the way."

Boudica rode next to Hulk as the rest of the squad fell in behind as they rode in tandem. Dak had finally made the decision they would not ride through Boudica's town or stay on her tribe's sanctioned property. He did not desire to have any additional trouble with any of the Midlander's Tribes. They had been lucky and not had to fight the Midlanders as he anticipated while crossing their massive realm which was open country. They had gone undetected on the journey all the way from Cliff Tops until now, and now they could see the gap in the mountain which they should be able to cross and travel out of the Midlander's territory.

Hulk was able to lead the group up the small steep valley which dead ended into the main ridge line. The smaller mountain leveled off before the ascent to the top of the ridge which was steep and difficult. Hulk rode southwest diagonally across the face of the mountain toward a low gap in the range. Boudica had told Dak they would intersect the Old Mountain Trail close to twenty miles and at that point she could lead the way.

Hulk rode his horse through the under growth of small trees and bushes into the open once he arrived on the trail. He was tired of forging through the trees and not being on a maintained trail. As he looked both directions in the clearing, he noticed there were no noticeable horse tracks on the trail. The trail was covered with undisturbed leaves and patches of unmelted snow. He dismounted and walked the trail in both directions looking closer for signs of people. Boudica rode out from the thick underbrush and watched Hulk. He walked back toward his horse, "You made it to the Old Mountain Trail. This is it." She watched him look for signs of travelers. "You do not trust me. You are looking for signs of someone in my tribe warning the Dark Master."

Hulk still had not talked to Boudica and avoided unnecessary conversation with her. He glanced at her as he walked to his horse and pulled his canteen down. He drank some water as Boudica announced, "There is a small creek fed by a high mountain spring a few miles south."

Hulk pulled the bridle off his horse and poured water into his pan for his horse to drink. Boudica looked aggravated at Hulk, "I said there is a creek a few miles south. Your horse will be okay. I thought we were in a rush to cross the mountain."

"We will wait on the others. Dak told me to locate the trail and wait on him. I do not see signs of other riders. When is the last time someone from your tribe has been on the trail?"

Boudica dismounted, "I do not know. The hunting parties avoid this area." She removed the bridle on her horse and provided some grain and water. The two waited in silence for fifteen minutes as the other riders appeared from the underbrush onto the trail.

Everyone dismounted and rested. Dak announced, "Hulk, you, Zenith and I will ride out front. If they have guards, they will be hidden along this trail."

Billy Ray looked at Boudica, "When is the last time you have been this far south?"

Boudica looked at the group sitting on the ground. She noticed the men pulling the two pack horses finally came into the open. Then, Robin Hood rode onto the trail. "It has been sometime since I have been this far. We are still on my clan's property. As a kid, we would come up here and play. We built tree houses, crawled into the caves, and hiked for miles and miles. Then, my brother was taken from us three years ago, and the elders would not search for him beyond our property line. They ruled no one was allowed this far south. They knew what had happened." She then spoke louder, "My father knew what had happened, and no one did anything."

"I ran from the clan and my father and came here to spy on the cult. I thought I could find my brother. Their fortress is across the mountain. I went to the cliff overlooking them and watched for my brother. That is how I know the boys are all cut, and they are trained to become soldiers. Once I thought I saw my brother; his name is Star. I thought I could maybe get his attention, so I crawled to the perimeter wall of the fort. I watched and realized he was too far gone. Their training is so intense. His mind had been conditioned." Boudica stopped talking as she was mentally revisiting the scene. The group watched her face turn sad. They could tell she was thinking about something unpleasant, and what must have happened next.

Dak announced, "We will ride to the boundary line and then camp. We then will send in a four-member recon team. I must see from the cliffs down into this fortress. I have spoken."

\*\*\*

Dak noticed the sun was setting in the western sky and the evening hours were upon them as they allowed the horses to drink from the spring fed creek. He could also tell the group started becoming a little on edge with the anticipation of a battle. Two of the men from the New York tribe had started asking multiple questions about the pending mission. One asked, "How far away are they? Did Boudica say they impale the boys who could not complete the training of being a soldier?" Dak glanced at Samuel who had the look of understanding the men were scared. He and Samuel both were aware there were always men who were frightened when faced with death. The great warriors would think like a Berserker, the old Viking warriors who became intoxicated with killing the enemy and had no fear of death only visualized victory and glory for killing the opponent. Dak also knew once he had presented the plan of the attack the nervousness with his men would somewhat diminish. The part of not knowing made warriors anxious.

Dak said, "You men will stay behind for now. This is not going to be any different than the other battles you have been engaged in fighting the Normand army."

The soldier from the New York Tribe responded, "We have never faced a Blueblood in battle or soldiers that fight like men with Rabies who are without fear of dying."

Zenith said, "Yes, we have killed a Blueblood in battle, Harpers Ferry Harbor. General Cuez was a Blueblood. You men will not worry about the Bluebloods, we will take care of them."

Dak noticed the two men from Meadow Bottoms did not seem to be concerned and smiled at the men from the New York Tribe. Dak knew once the war started that would change. The men from Meadow Bottoms had not been in battle and had not witnessed the death caused in war with other men dying all around. Everyone else was an experience fighter. He understood why the men from New York were concerned and seemed on edge. He watched the one soldier rub his hands together with anticipation and the others also seemed nervus as they set and stared at the ground in front of them. These men had survived the battle of New York and the Battle of Harpers Ferry Harbor. They had seen the dead stacked up like firewood. Dak knew they were fighters, and they would do as they were ordered.

The big man from Meadows Bottom looked at one of the soldiers from the New York Tribe, "You ask a lot of unnecessary questions." He looked at the nervous men from the New York Tribe and smiled with confidence and acted like he was a great warrior.

Dak stepped forward in a harsh tone, "What do you two from Meadow Bottoms know about war? I did not desire for either one of you to join our mission. Both of you are a liability to me and both of you were forced on me. You two better not be cowards in the face of a battle. I know these men from the New York Tribe are great warriors. I have fought next to them. What can you two do for us in battle? When the battlefield turns red in blood, you two better not run, or I will chase you down, beat you like an unwanted bastard from Southern City."

The two men both stopped smiling and understood Dak was not someone they needed to impress in conversation.

Robin Hood sensed Dak's anger and tried to diffuse the conversation. "Are these mushrooms safe to eat? I would like to at least eat something that tasted like chicken."

The men changed the conversation talking about eating some mushrooms. Dak did not want to listen as some of the men disagreed about the type of mushrooms growing on the ground behind a log. As he walked off, he noticed the bigger man from Meadow Bottoms ate some of the mushrooms to prove a point. "See, these mushrooms are harmless. They are "King Bolete. They taste like water." He ate a second mushroom.

Dak thought about the two men. He did not like his mother telling him they were part of the team on this mission. He thought about how he disliked their selfish, overconfident personalities. He then considered maybe he was being hard on the two men because he was forced to accept them on this mission against his will, or maybe he did not like them because of the guilt he felt for decapitating Sie months ago in front of his wife and others in Meadow Bottoms.

***

As Dak and Hulk led the way south, Zenith and Boudica followed. The four rode for three hours and arrived at the old wooden sign which was a carved message in a plank. "Do not cross this line." The sign had fallen to the ground from the post in the middle of an open area. Boudica rode next to Dak, "This is the boundary line. I do not know who claims that property, but our property stops here. The Cult's fort is another twenty miles south."

Hulk turned and looked north along the trail they had ridden and the ridgeline. No one was following them. He glanced at

Dak, "We have gained close to three-thousand feet in elevation since we left the camp. We are close to five-thousand feet total in elevation. We are going to get cold tonight." They could see the higher mountains in the distance with the white snow-covered tops.

Dak looked at Boudica, "So we have close to twenty miles to travel to those cliffs?"

Boudica glanced at Dak, "I hike close to three miles per hour. I run close to six miles an hour on flat land. It took me five hours from here to get to the cliffs. I walked in and ran out." The three could see the terror in her face as she thought of what she saw.

"We will camp here. We are northeast of them, with the wind blowing west, we should be okay with a fire tonight."

The four dismounted with Hulk tying off a lead rope for the horses. He then removed their bridles and saddles. Dak and Zenith picked up limbs and logs for firewood. Dak then announced, "I will set up the tents."

Boudica looked at the fire as Dak was finishing setting up his and Zenith's tent and then Hulk's tent. Dak placed his fur lined bedroll into his tent. Boudica asked, "Where is my tent?"

Zenith answered, "Dak and I will sleep inside our tent inside our fur lined bedroll. I would suggest both of you removing all your clothing, especially anything that is damp. Your body heat will provide you with the necessary heat to keep you alive curled up inside the bedroll."

"I am not sleeping in a tent with him, let alone in the nude inside his bedroll!"

Zenith smiled and was nonchalant, "That is how Dak and I fell in love."

Dak noticed the tension between Hulk and Boudica. He was trying to think of something to say to diffuse the awkward situation, but before he could say anything, Zenith announced, "He has already seen you naked. Remember, he spied on you as you bathed in the hot spring. You do recall how he chased you across the rocks and tackled you on that large granite boulder, don't you? You were nude then." Zenith was the only one who laughed. Dak, at that point, could not hold back his smile and tried to ignore the tension between Boudica and Hulk. He started cutting firewood down to size with a smile on his face.

Hulk looked at Zenith, "You certainly are enjoying yourself."

Zenith tried to stop laughing, "Pay backs are hell." Dak started laughing.

Hulk looked at Dak, "You two think you are funny." They could not stop laughing.

Boudica watched the two laugh, "You intentionally only packed two tents knowing there were only two bedrolls."

Zenith could not control herself. She held her belly as she laughed so hard when she bent over. Dak came over and hugged her while he was also laughing. He tried to speak but started laughing again as Hulk and Boudica watched. Dak finally said as he was trying to stop laughing, "I am tasked with planning a mission against a group of Rogue Bluebloods. Believe it or not, but I have other things to worry about in addition to whether you have a bed roll. But now that you mention it; I will accept full responsibility. I guess I am the leader, and everything is my fault. You two will sleep together. That is an order."

Dak then stopped laughing enough to say, "Maybe, you two could sit next to each other by the fire and get to know one another a little before bed." Both Dak and Zenith laughed until they could hardly stand.

Hulk announced, "I am going to get additional wood. You two are embarrassing me. This lady is going to think you two are crazy the way you are giggling out of control." He walked into the woods to retrieve some firewood.

Zenith stopped laughing and looked at Boudica, "I am sorry for laughing at the situation. It is really funny to me, because I have been in your shoes. I was starving to death, wet, cold, and alone. I had just met Dak and his band of misfits, and Dak announced I would be required to bundle up with Veronica. It was a lot colder then, and I was not dressed for the cold weather. I was literally freezing to death. Veronica is the older sister to Trey. I will never forget the look on Veronica's face. I had to decide my next move, and I literally went and took off my clothes and got inside Dak's bedroll."

Dak added, "Yeah, we've been sleeping together ever since."

Boudica set by the fire, "Is that when you became pregnant? Someone said you had two boys."

Zenith laughed and started holding her belly. She shook her head no and then announced, "No, I did not become pregnant that night. I actually believe Dak was scared to touch me. He did slowly start to rub my legs and feet to warm me, but he was a perfect gentleman."

Dak added, "We had sex thirty-four times in four days while we were trapped by the snow in a cabin in the mountains while we were running for our lives next to a river full of trout. She might have got pregnant during that time period."

Zenith smiled, "I loved that cabin, and evidently the trout are a great source of protein which drives a male sexually." She then watched as Hulk walked into the camp as she started laughing.

Hulk walked back into the camp with a large load of firewood and dropped the load near the fire. "I thought certainly you would have stopped laughing by now. I guess I will go get another load of wood."

Zenith tried to stop laughing, "No. Come here and give me a big boy hug. I am sorry. We were just talking about how great it would be to eat a lot of trout before bedtime."

Boudica watched as Zenith wrapped her arms around Hulk and hugged him. She then pulled away while still holding him, "It is just so funny to me. The fact that all those whores you paid to bed you and now you are in the mountains with this pretty young lady who does not like you and will cut your balls off if you touch her."

Hulk stepped backward, "Dammit Zenith. That is enough."

Zenith and Dak kept laughing while Hulk went to his saddle bag and pulled some dry meat. He looked at Boudica with a humble smile and asked, "Would you like some deer jerky?"

Zenith and Dak laughed more intensely with Zenith saying between laughs, "What a great pickup line. Would you like some deer jerky?" She held her right hand out and acted like she was holding a piece of jerky.

Dak added, "I bet that line works all the time with the women at Harpers Ferry Harbor."

Boudica could not help herself watching the three friends. She started laughing and could not stop either, while Hulk took a bit of deer jerky and watched the three laugh.

Zenith then laughed as she tried to talk. "What was that old whore's name in New Foundland that was older than Hulk's mother? Did you ask her if she wanted deer jerky?" She had tears running down her face. She laughed so hard as she slapped her hand on her thigh.

Dak started laughing, "Her name was Becky the Whore." He looked at Boudica. "You should have seen him walking around the exterior of the tavern, in the winter, without a shirt and his hands tied behind him because Becky the Whore set him up." Dak and Zenith bent over laughing so hard they could not stand.

Hulk remained serious and watched the three laughed, "I believe I have gone camping with three giggle heads. Maybe when we meet the cult warriors, you can distract them with your sense of humor."

The four sat around the fire. When Boudica would turn her head, Dak would motion for Hulk to talk with Boudica. Zenith would start laughing. Boudica would look at Zenith and smile and laugh a little. After they had eaten, Dak asked what does your name mean? I have never heard the name Boudica."

"The name Boudica means victory in battle."

Dak grinned, "We are going to need Boudica with what we are facing." He hesitated, "Boudica, I heard what your father said to you about not being welcome back into your village. You may ride with us if so desire. Like Zenith said, we are a bunch of misfits."

"Why are you doing this? I mean, you have traveled all the way across the continent to fight this battle."

Hulk looked at Boudica and announced, "The Dark Master is controlling the Normand Army, and maybe somewhat controlling the government in Merlin. We know he is a Rogue

Blueblood from an old country called Germany. He means to kill all of us, our tribe, and anyone else in his way. There will be no chance for peace in this world unless someone kills him. We must take him out before he obtains so much power he cannot be touched. There is no other way."

Hulk glanced at Boudica, "What are you not telling us about your brother Star?"

"He was three years younger than I. He was a good-natured kid." She smiled as she thought. The three could tell she was reliving a nostalgic moment. Her expression turned from one of happiness to sullenness. "He was my responsibility. We loved to hike in the mountains. We would sometimes hunt in these mountains, climb trees, and spend time spelunking. I did not know about the cult. We were just told not to ever go off our tribe's property. My tribe, our warriors, and my father were too scared to talk openly about the cult."

She hesitated, "He was taken by three of the cult members. I ran to my tribe and thought they would help me fight for him. The men were too scared. I was told I was a female and too young to understand. The men in the tribe did nothing. At first, they said I was making everything up about the cult, and he got lost when I should have been watching him. There were ten other kids with us. We were playing hide and seek. I rounded the other kids up, and we returned to our camp. The adults at the camp went and looked for him, but they never crossed out of our property. I pleaded with the adults in my city and then I realized they were never going to fight the cult. My family blamed me for him being taken. My father yelled at me, telling me I should not have been in this section of the woods. A week later I went by myself to the cliff and spied down into the fort. I thought I saw my brother. There were several boys in training. I sneaked down to the wood perimeter wall and was trying to get a closer look between the logs around the fort. I was hoping I could get his attention and maybe we could run away together." She cried. "It was my brother who helped hold another boy down along with three others, as two more boys in training impaled him with a ten-foot post. I will never forget the yelling and screaming of the boy being tortured to death. It was Star, but I did not recognize him. He would have never done something like that to another. The master and his four-henchman watched. They all stood in their robes, and their hoods pulled over their heads. I could only see a glimpse of their faces. They are pure evil. That is why I choose to help you."

Hulk looked at Dak and Zenith, "I am sorry to hear about your loss. You three can go to bed. I will take the first watch."

Zenith announced, "It will be too cold. The fire will not keep you warm." She glanced at Boudica.

Boudica said, "I do not desire to die tonight. We will sleep together in your bedroll. This is what we must do to survive."

She stood and walked into the small tent. Zenith walked to the other tent. Dak walked over to his saddle bag and pulled the honeysuckle lotion out and rubbed some on his chest. He walked up behind Hulk and rubbed some on his neck. "You might need this." Hulk reacted by slapping Dak's hand. Dak laughed and went and crawled in the tent door.

Hulk considered his options and hesitated prior to crawling in the tent through the flap of the door. He removed his clothes down to his underwear and crawled inside the fur lined bedroll. They could hear Zenith giggling in the other tent.

Hulk yelled, "We are trying to sleep over here. We need quietness. I hope you can cause the cult warriors to giggle and be distracting with your laughter."

There were a few seconds pause and Boudica whispered, "What is your lifelong dream?"

Hulk was caught off guard as he raised the palms of his hands and then rubbed his forehead. "My lifelong dream. Hell, lady you certainly ask a complicated question." He hesitated, "I would like to live through this mission. I would like for you not to cut my balls off. Maybe have a ranch and kids. I do not know."

"How many women have you bedded?"

Hulk replied, "What kind of question is that? Hell lady, there has been hundreds. I do not know. I do not keep count. Tomorrow morning, we are going to a cliff overlooking a deadly cult for the purpose of planning a battle and that is what you ask me?"

"Okay, I will change the topic. Can Zenith kill the Blueblood Master? Is she that good."

"Not by herself. Dak is better. He is that good. The rest of our group is good. We all used to train for days and days. My father would always suggest we look for the hints of a swordman we were fighting against. He will always repeat his stands when he swings his sword. There are always tell-tale signs of which hand he will lead with, and it is always good to know what your opponent is going to do before they do it. Our squad, except for those two men from Meadow Bottoms, are experienced in battle. We hope their inexperience in battle does not hurt our chances. A good, experienced warrior in battle is worth three inexperienced warriors." Hulk looked perplexed like he was trying to figure out, why them?

"Do you trust them?"

Hulk thought for a second. He did not know those two men from Meadow Bottoms. They had not ever been on a hunting trip with any of the men. Robin Hood had suggested five other men, but Barney Simpson had insisted on those two men. "I trust everyone but those two men. There is something about them. I would not trust them in battle. Why do you ask?"

"Everyone's weapons are used and have wear from practice or battles. The handle on your sword needs to be rewrapped and the handle on Trey's is chipped. Your bow and the bows of your friends are rubbed inward where the arrows rest before being shot. Their weapons on the other hand have not been used. There are no signs of even their bows and swords being used in practice. I assumed they each acquired new bows for this trip. There is no sign of the rubbing caused by arrows on their bows. The taller one appeared awkward holding his sword as if he was not accustomed to the weight. The younger one I believe, would have trouble pulling back the string on a good quality large bow. He has no calluses on his fingers or hands. They do not appear to be someone I would desire to have watching my back in a battle."

"Wow, what made you notice something like that? What else have you observed?"

She rolled over and placed her breast against his upper arm and leg against his leg. Hulk could feel her nude body rub against his. He felt a little aroused knowing he was physically attracted to her body. She whispered, "Midlanders live and die with their weapons. We notice the enemy. I also noticed your father, Billy Ray, does not pray. Everyone else was praying, and he did not participate." She pushed her body harder against his body and placed her right leg over his left leg forcing her crotch against his thigh.

"My father has helped others for years. That is who he has chosen to be. He loves his God. An angel never prays. What do you make of the two men from Meadow Bottoms?"

"If they were women, I would check them for poison. Poison is a passive female's tool for killing. When I was looking for matches in the wrong saddle bag, I discovered ground up powdered mushrooms in an unopened bag. Why have they not opened the bag, and why have they not eaten the mushrooms by now? Yet they pick up mushrooms from the ground and eat those. It does not make sense."

"Why did you not mention this before now?"

"I thought all of you liked and respected each other. I did not realize those two were foreigners to you." She leaned in closer with his lips near his ear and hesitated, "You know, I have never been with a man. I was hoping to experience the feeling before I die. I do not intend to come back from this mission without my brother. If I cannot save him, I choose to die in the battle." She rubbed her hand down his chest across his belly and then lower. "I am so sorry to ask you this, but can you please help me out? We can do it as many times as you desire."

# Chapter 18

Mia jerked her head and looked at Vicky, "Was that Wayne? There it is again."

Delores, Mia, and Casey scrambled to the door of the kitchen with Mia leading the way. After she opened the front door, they saw the approaching four men. Delores was the third one in the line and noticed the four men on the front porch dressed for battle. She immediately realized the mistake of sending most of their men away from Cliff Tops at one time and leaving the city unprotected. Vicky heard Delores, "We are under an attack." The arrow fired by the man in the brown fur coat hit Mia in the chest, and she fell to the floor of the porch in front of Casey.

Vicky dropped her coffee and knew what she must do. She ran through the kitchen interior doorway and across the foyer. She took two steps at a time climbing the stairs. She saw Delores position herself between herself and the doorway, blocking one of the men. She then could hear Casey yell in pain as a man hit her and pushed her out of the way as he entered the door and chased after her up the stairs. Vicky slammed the door locking the latch. She quickly pushed the dresser in front of the door and then turned the dresser over with the top colliding with the opposite interior wall blocking the door from being opened. She heard the man turn the knob and try to force the door forward.

The dresser was wedged against the door and the wall and could not be forced open. At first she was scared and then she was angry. She knew she must protect her kids and two grand kids.

Vicky could hear the man pushing again and again against the door. She heard him say, "The door is blocked from the inside. It will not open."

Vicky looked at the two maids. "Get the children in the bedroom and block the window with the dresser. We are being attacked." She pulled her bow and strapped her hatchets to her hip. She knew she must block the balcony door. She ran to the balcony and looked out on the street. She could see some of the townspeople being forced to the church. She noticed her two-night guards were half dressed and being forced to walk to the church with others. One did not have boots on and neither had on coats. She saw movement on the deck of the balcony as a man's hand appear on the side of the balcony under the rail. He was trying to climb up from the lower level. She opened the door and quickly swung her hatchet downward, cutting off the tips of four of his fingers. The man yelled and fell to the snow-covered ground holding his hand, cussing in pain with blood spreading over the white snow-covered ground. Vicky stepped backward, loaded her bow and waited.

As Vicky stood watching the open balcony doorway, she considered her next move. How could she find help? She then positioned herself low on the floor sitting on one knee with her bow loaded as she wanted to minimize herself in case someone shot from the street through the door. She turned on one knee as she heard someone trying to break through the door. She stayed low as she was on one knee. She wanted a firing zone. She spoke softly, "Wilma you and Nancy keep the window blocked with the dresser and the door blocked with the bed. Make certain the bed is over in front of the door, blocking the door from opening. They are after the kids. If I ask you to open the bedroom door do so, but do not open that door for any other person. I may die out here, but you will protect those kids. We will have help soon." She then realized someone must have known about their city not being properly guarded. Her nearest guards were watching the gorge bridge leading to the New York Tribe.

She heard Nancy answer, "Yes, my Queen. Who are they?"

"I do not know, but we will find out soon enough. They are organized and this attack has been planned."

Vicky stepped backward and placed firewood into the wood burning stove. She heard a voice call out, "We only want the gold. We can do this the easy way or the hard way, but either way, we are not leaving here without the gold."

"What gold?"

"The gold your son stole from King Solman. Please do not act like you do not know."

"Who are you?"

Vicky knew if he answered identifying himself, their intentions were to kill everyone. She heard another voice coming from the street below. The young man clinched his jaws and in a voice riddled with revulsion, "Let me give you a hint. You had your son murder my father in the street in front of his home. My father was the legally elected authority of this territory. I am going to personally set things right for your treason."

Vicky could tell by the tone the young man who answered was full of hatred. She responded, "So you are not here for the gold."

The first man waved his hand at the son of Sie and told him to be quiet. "No, we are here for the gold. You need to tell us where the gold is hidden, and we will leave. I promise you this."

Vicky knew she needed to buy time. Maybe some of the coal miners would return, but she knew no one was scheduled back until later in the week when the men trying to round up stray cows would return home. She then wondered what happened to Wayne and Little Jimmy. "Just like that. You will leave."

"That is true. We will leave. All we want is the gold."

"Allow me time to consider my options."

She heard the son of Sie yell, "She is stalling, and she needs to send the Blueblood children out first."

The other voice replied, "Certainly. We will provide you fifteen minutes to consider your choices. Then, we will march your citizens into the street for you to watch us execute them. After all, we have no other choice. What kind of Queen are you? One that loves her gold or her people?"

Vicky crawled to the balcony doors and saw the man at the tower. She knew Walter must have been killed. She could not see the Blacksmith Shop from her window. She did not hear anyone talking. She had no way to know how many men she was facing. She had no food, two maids, and four Blueblood children to protect. She thought, "These men would have to kill her and everyone here to get to these kids. There would not be a place on earth Dak, Zenith and Samuel would not travel to seek their revenge if the kids were harmed. These men would be aware. She knew her only hope would be to hold out. They were going to kill all the witnesses."

***

Dominique thought of the beautiful views as she jogged through the mountain area on the horse-riding trail. She could see the ocean to her left as she was returning. She knew she needed to act surprised with the sword Little Jimmy was making for her. Who else would have the first initial, D. He would inscribe the V later today. She smiled as she thought about Mia sewing the sleeve for her new sword. She saw the sleeve while eating dinner with them. Mia did not realize who she was making the sleeve for and left it lying on their table. She knew Little Jimmy had worked hard on the sword and wanted very much to surprise her. She noticed he had spent extra time making certain the metal in the sword was the high quality that would not chip and hold an edge. He had spent extra time crafting the blade with an inscribed design on the top of the blade. He always was so positive with her work ethic and her improvement. He seemed to take personal pride in her becoming better each week. He explained what to expect in the competition in a sword fight. He would talk about the untrained versus the trained soldier, and how each would have a different skill set. He would provide her examples of what to expect in combat, and how to remain alert to opportunities. "The best warrior does not always win the fight. Sometimes the smartest warrior wins the fight. The one who takes advantage of the opportunities presented during the battle."

She came around the curve in the trail and was approaching the end. She thought, "I am going to run to the right and take the trail leading to the mines and then cut back and take the other trail leading to the back of the Blacksmith Shop. I will sneak a look through the dirty old window and spy on Little Jimmy working on my sword." She smiled to herself as she thought about his statements on how he also preached about surprise being a great equalizer in battle. She would surprise him and show him she listened to his advice.

Dominique cut off the horse trail right on the next trail. She pushed herself as she jogged up the incline on the trail then cut left down the decline toward the Blacksmith Shop. She heard someone yelling about something, but she could not understand what was being said. She stopped running and tried to control her breathing. She stepped very quietly through the evergreen Hemlock pine trees to the rear of the shop. She eased over to the window and quickly peered through the dirty glass. Her anticipation was spiking with seeing Little Jimmy bent over the forge or maybe the anvil, working on the sword.

The window had not been cleaned in years, and she could not see anyone inside. She moved back behind the wall, so no one would see her and then looked a second time. She could see a man standing at the door looking out to the street. She kept staring at the man. He was holding a sword, and she then realized she did not recognize him. She stood on her toes to raise up above the dirt on the glass and peered around the interior of the shop. There was very little smoke coming from the forge. She then saw the toe end of a boot lying on the floor. She recognized the boot of Little Jimmy. Her heart sank with worry. She then heard someone yell, "Your fifteen minutes are up. You will need to come on out with the four kids and tell us where the gold is located. We do not wish to harm anyone."

Dominique eased over to the other side of the window to obtain a clearer view of the floor of the Blacksmith Shop. From this angle, she could clearly see Little Jimmy lying face down on the floor. She could not tell if he was still breathing. She strained to hold her position as she tried to discern if his back was moving from him breathing.

Dominique listened. She recognized Queen Vicky's voice coming from the fourplex. "I need more time. You did not mention anything about the kids being forced to come out. Having the gold is one thing, but the kids are not going to come out."

Dominique noticed the man in the doorway walking into the street. She pushed the glass and frame over to the side and quickly opened the window. She pulled herself up and crawled through headfirst. She inched down to the workbench with her hands holding her position until she could pull her legs and feet through the window opening. She went to the side of Little Jimmy and noticed the indention in the back of his head and the blood pooled up on the floor. She rolled him over. She felt for a heartbeat. Her heart sank when she verified there was no pulse. Little Jimmy was dead. She reached over and closed his eyes. She became mad with rage and picked up the metal sword lying in the brackets with her initials. She noticed the metal handle had holes in it so the leather grip could be installed. She then picked up Little Jimmy's large bow from the stand located at the right of the front door. She started to pick up several of the practice arrows but instead she reached for the combat arrows in the stand near the front wall. She slowly peaked around the door jam and saw the man who was standing close to ten feet in front of her and then looked beyond him and saw four additional men. They were talking to someone just outside her peripheral vision. She then glanced to the church and saw two guards standing in front of the church doors with the doors blocked off by a horizontal board. She quickly leaned back behind the wall and took a deep breath. She noticed there was no one else on the street. She realized some of the men were dressed similar to one another in uniforms, and those men looked like warriors with expensive appearing weapons. The other men who seemed to be leading the group were dressed in large fur coats, hoods, and the clothing did not match. They all looked like killers. She thought, "Are these men Normand soldiers with some dressed to blend in with the common person and some dressed as Normand soldiers?"

When she heard the young man yell, "Bring me one of the guards. Then, we will wait ten minutes and then bring me the black female council member. I will show the Queen we mean business," she snapped back to her position hiding in the Black Smith Shed.

Dominique stood to the side and hid behind the wheelbarrow full of iron. She backed herself in between the stands holding the stored spears lining the wall and the stored arrows. She threw a piece of iron toward the back wall near the window. The guard heard the sound and turned and walked to the door and peered inside. He noticed the body on the floor had been rolled over. His first thought was that Little Jimmy was not dead and had somehow rolled himself over on the floor. He eased in with his sword out looking to the rear of the shop. He took three steps toward Little Jimmy and then noticed the window was opened. He walked forward toward the open window. Dominique was angered and without any difficulty she pulled the string back all the way on the large bow as she stepped forward. She released the combat arrow and watched as the man turned to face her with his sword extended in front of him. She at first thought she missed. The arrow had disappeared. He turned to the side, and she noticed the arrow was not sticking in his back. She pulled her sword and was prepared to fight when the man took two steps toward her. She noticed he was covered in sweat, and his face was flush. She stood as he leaned backward and then fell face first to the floor. She then noticed he was dressed like a farmer from Meadow Bottoms. Her eyes then looked at the back wall and she saw her arrow sticking in the back log wall of the shop. As she turned her gaze to his back, she noticed he had blood on the rear of his coat with a hole in his coat right where his heart was located.

Dominique quickly climbed out the window. She peered around the corner toward the church. She could see one guard in a uniform and another one in a large fur coat. She knew the town's people must have been forced into the church. She went to the other corner of the Blacksmith Shop and peaked around the corner and saw one of the night guards walking without any shoes to the middle of the street in front of the fourplex with four men walking around him. He had a rope tied around his neck with one man pulling the rope tight as he was forced to follow the man as he walked barefoot in the snow-covered ground. His hands were tied behind his back, and one of the men behind him would push him if he slowed his pace. There were two men standing in the middle of the street in front of the fourplex waiting for the prisoner. She saw two guards at the doors to the church. She now knew there were at least nine men.

She considered her raging feelings and then thought of her options. She considered what Little Jimmy would do. He had been matter of fact in his teaching. "He taught me to always reflect on my training and the mental aspect of a battle. He has taught me his main responsibility in the tribe was to protect the Queen and the Queen's family." She now figured her next move. If she could go back into the woods and then approach the fourplex from the rear entrance, she could take out the guard posted on the rear and maybe the front and rescue the Queen and kids. She could protect them in the woods with her bow.

She peaked around the corner a second time and saw the Cliff Tops guard being forced to the ground in the street. "You need to come out. We just want the gold. You need to tell us where the gold is located," the man yelled.

Dominique ran into the woods and turned on a small trail. She knew there would be at least one guard located at the rear of the fourplex. She listened as she ran and noticed Queen Vicky never answered the man's request. She then heard the young man yell, "Bring out another one. We will up the ante. This time bring the black female council member."

Dominique walked through the thick Hemlocks and got as close as she dared without being seen. She tried to stay behind the trunk of the tree peering through the thick ever-green pine branches as they spread out circular over ten feet from the trunk. She peered through the branches and could see a man standing at the rear exit door in a fur coat, fur hood, and red scarf. He was looking into the woods. She said to herself, "This is number ten." She needed him to turn slightly to the left away from the porch post as she lifted Little Jimmy's bow very slowly and pulled the string tight and held her breath and waited. The man stepped forward trying to move a little to stay warm as he walked back and forth. As she aimed, she tried to estimate if the man was thirty or forty-feet in distance from her. She did not know how much the combat arrow would drop at her distance, and how different from the practice arrows the combat arrows would travel. She recalled how Little Jimmy explained the additional time it took to make the combat arrows with the razor-sharp tips. The tips were three prong sharpened like steal razor blades where the practice arrows were pointed and capped with a dual aluminum tip. She started to question her abilities. "How much drop should I consider?" She then considered the training from Little Jimmy. She reflected back at his clenched jaws as he told her, "I know you are a sweet young lady, but you must listen. You do not wish for the animal to suffer. Always aim for the heart in the middle of the chest. The area is unprotected by bones unlike the skull. The arrow is less likely to ricochet and miss the heart or lungs. If the arrow is shot at an angle, the arrow can glance off the skull bone, miss the brain, and make the adversary mad." She shifted her aim lower from the head to the middle of the chest. She took a second breath and then held her breath. As he moved into her firing zone, she released the arrow with the arrow traveling through the evergreen branches. The four-foot-long arrow hit the man in the center stomach. He was standing in the clear area of the rear yard. He took three steps backward and fell against the rear of the fourplex. She rushed forward as she ran through the tree limbs. She knew she hit low. The man fell to the ground and seemed to be in shock. The arrow traveled all the way through his midsection and was sticking out his back. She ran up to him and recognized him to be from Meadow Bottoms and a teenager. He glanced up at her with a bewildered expression. She placed her sword to his throat, "How many men are there?"

"What?" He looked at the blood on his left hand and seemed to be confused. He seemed to know something bad had happened to his body but had not been able to realize the danger.

"How many men are with you?"

"Twenty-four from Meadow Bottoms. I promise we do not want to harm the children. We just want the gold. We do not want to harm anyone, but if you force us, we will kill a person every ten minutes until the Queen complies with our request. We have a team of bounty hunters from down south. They know what they are doing. You need to tell us where the gold is located."

"I recognize the puke smell of you scum from Meadow Bottoms. Why ask for the four Blueblood children to be led out of the command center if they are not wanted? Who are these other men?"

He reached behind him and felt the arrow and then seemed to realize he had been shot. "They are from down south. They will help us negotiate a settlement with the Normand army once the Queen hands us the four Blueblood kids. They are led by Bloody Bill. Oh my God. You shot me. Please help."

She could tell he was confused and seemed to be going into shock. She rammed her sword through the man's chest. She then opened the door very carefully. She saw the back of a guard watching the street. He was standing inside the foyer at the bottom of the stairs. She listened and did not hear anyone else.

She set her bow down in the corner and walked through the hall, taking small soft steps. She walked into the foyer and glanced up the stairs to make certain no one was at the top foyer area. The man never turned. Dominique switched her sword for her knife and then carefully took ten additional steps as she approached him. As she took the last step, she rammed her long knife through the man's back with the blade sticking out his chest. She reached the man before he fell and pulled the dying man into the kitchen. She retrieved her bow and then went to the front door. She could see the headless body of the city night guard lying in the street with his bare feet lying in the ice and snow. The ice and snow were covered in his blood. She counted four men with swords watching the front street area. The younger man was talking to someone standing at the small cottage. Out of her peripheral vision she caught a glimpse of the two other men. She recognized the one man. He had been to the city council meetings with Queen Vicky and Wayne. She thought, "He is the new councilman, Barney Simpson. He has betrayed his Queen."

Dominique reached for the doorknob and then hesitated as she thought back to her training and listening to Little Jimmy. He would explain the importance of the mental aspect of fighting and being patient and picking her battles. Having the element of surprise and allowing the opponent to underestimate your abilities were a couple of the most important tactical advantages in fighting. She stepped back and released the knob. She walked up the stairs and knocked on the door. "Queen Vicky. Queen Vicky. It is Dominique." She gently knocked on the door a second time.

Vicky heard the knock and then the whisper. She recognized the voice. "Dominique, is that you?"

"Yes. I have killed the two guards. You and the kids can escape out the rear and hide in one of the caves. Queen Vicky, I am sorry to tell you, but those bastards killed Little Jimmy." She heard the dresser being moved. Vicky opened the door and stepped into the hallway with her bow tight with an arrow locked in place. She looked down the stairs and could see the blood on the floor of the foyer.

Vicky looked at Dominique and noticed the sword in one hand with the unfinished handle and blood on the blade of her long knife. She knew Little Jimmy was making her a special sword just for her. "Dominique, I need you to lead the children and the two maids to the Bat Cave. You will be safe until help comes."

Dominique replied, "I do not want to be safe. I saw your newest councilman, Barney Simpson, standing in the doorway of the small cottage on the right. He is one of them. He means to kill everyone. There are now twenty-one men from Meadow Bottoms. There were twenty-four. There is additional group of bounty hunters from down south."

"Listen Dominique, we do not have much time. The people of our village are being held in the church. They are going to kill them until I release these kids to them. They say they want the gold, but I believe they want the Blueblood kids to trade to the Normand command. They are going to bring out one of my friends next. I must stop them. I need you to take the kids."

Vicky ran to the bedroom door. "Nancy, open the door. You will need to take the kids and hide in a cave. You must hurry. Vicky heard the bed being moved. She watched the two ladies gather the four kids and walk out of the bedroom. She felt saddened to think of the kids who were almost three-years old facing this.

Dominique picked up one of the kids and told the ladies to follow her. They ran out the back door with one lady carrying two kids and the other one carrying one. Once they were close to one hundred yards away, Dominique turned to the two ladies. The Bat Cave is about a quarter of a mile in that direction. Go there and wait."

Nancy turned to Dominique, "I have been to the Bat Cave years ago. I believe I can find the entrance, but our Queen told you to stay with us."

"I must protect the Queen. They will kill the Queen if I do not protect her. You will protect the kids." She handed Nancy the long knife.

# Chapter 19

The four crawled out of the two tents in the darkness of the morning. Dak and Zenith tried not to smile at Hulk and Boudica. Zenith finally broke the ice, "I slept great last night. Hulk, how did you sleep?"

Hulk smiled and then his smile turned to a serious expression, "The sun will be coming up in an hour. I did not sleep. There is something bothering me. I believe Boudica and I should return to the men at camp. You and Zenith can walk to the cliffs and complete the recon on the fortress. Boudica said you need to walk up the east side and around the top. You should have a clear view at that point."

Dak looked concerned as Hulk and Boudica were saddling their horses, "What has you upset?" Dak could tell Hulk was concerned about something the way he was rushing to reach his bridle.

"The two men from Meadow Bottoms. They do not fit. Neither one is a warrior or even a hunter. They should not have been allowed to be on this mission. The big one is soft and clumsy and worked in the general store. The young one has been a stable boy for years. The only reason they are here is because of Barney Simpson. Your mother gave in to him, and I am betting those two were related to Sie's wife."

Zenith said, "If they are not warriors, what is the concern? Why else would they be riding with us?"

Boudica responded, "Poison is their weapon of choice."

Dak was shocked, "Poison!"

Hulk started putting his saddle bag on his horse and Boudica was taking down the tent. Hulk announced, "I knew something was bothering me, and the though became clear. They knew the difference between the mushrooms. Remember when we were camping at the creek, the tall one ate the mushroom growing on the log. And then the short one ate the other mushrooms. Robin Hood thought he was eating a Destroying Angel mushroom. Both walked over and picked a few, smiled, and ate them. Robin Hood was certain they were the poison Destroying Angel mushrooms. The man then explained the small difference. He has a saddle bag full of dry powder mushrooms which they have wrapped up in a bag. Why would they not eat the mushrooms in their bag? Why would they not show fear in the face of our battle? The rest of us know what we are facing, and we all are scared. They are not scared. My father and brother will be sitting next to them at breakfast. We will ride back and arrived before breakfast."

Zenith asked, "How do you know they have ground up mushrooms?"

Hulk fastened his saddle tight, "Boudica accidently opened the large man's saddle bag as she was looking for matches. Remember how mad he got? He knew she was not trying to steal his stuff. She saw the poison." He hesitated as he started to mount his horse, "What about our families in Cliff Tops?"

\*\*\*

Dak and Zenith watched the two as they rode away at a fast gallop heading back to the camp. Dak looked at Zenith, "There is more than Hulk's sixth sense, and if Hulk is correct, Barney must be leading a revolution. They will attack Cliff Tops. Dammit. I hope Little Jimmy and Wayne are paying attention. I wish Eric of Newport was not leading the seal hunters."

Zenith said, "Hulk should be able to return to the camp before breakfast. We need to get going. We need to keep our attention on this mission. This is going to be hard enough without being distracted."

The two fed their horses and left them tied up. They packed their tent and backpacks and before he loaded his backpack, he opened his backpack a second time making certain he had what he needed, "Boudica indicated the hike is close to seven hours from this spot. We will run and cut the time in half."

Zenith could tell Dak was apprehensive. She knew when he repeated the facts of the mission and took a second inspection of the contents in his backpack, he was uptight. She had heard Boudica tell them the cliff overlooking the fortress was twenty miles. She said, "We need to stay focused and get moving."

Dak followed her, "We are lucky we were able to ride the horses this far. These mountains are all covered with new growth from the earth reshaping. These mountains are all newly formed. If these mountains had been like the mountains back home, there would have been trees blown down across the trail. The newer growth in the forest is not blocking the trails like the older forest."

Zenith knew he was worried. She remembered when he was in the jail cell in Merlin, and he thought he was going to be executed, he would talk with a nostalgic viewpoint of Cliff Tops. "Look Dak. I know you are worried. There is a lot to be worried about, but you must stay focused. You cannot control what happens in Cliff Tops or back at the camp. We can only work to control what happens here and now. I need you to be dialed into what is in front of us. We both need to clearly understand what we are facing. There is a significant reason the other Rogue Bluebloods take orders from the one Dark Master. This is going to be dangerous and challenging." She jumped over a small limb and kept the pace as she jogged south.

\*\*\*

The two trotted through the snow along the ridge line over the rough but level surface for close to a mile. Then, the trail followed the ridge line upward along the top of the mountain range. Dak and Zenith both were tired after the fast pace having to forge through the snow and ice. Dak stopped, "I believe this is the point where we need to loop around the back side of the apex of the summit and then we should be able to view down into the fortress. My best guess is we are at seven to eight-thousand feet in elevation. We need to hurry. We do not need to be up here if a winter storm hits. Our spikes should hold us as we cross the ice cliff." He pointed to the cliff, "This is solid ice."

Dak kneeled in front of Zenith and made certain her spikes were attached to her boots and were not loose and would not become ajar. He noticed the area was quiet except for the wind howling as it blew across the ridge and the occasional fall of the icicles around the base of the rock cliff. He smiled up at her. "You know I love you."

Zenith could tell something else was on his mind. "What is bothering you?"

He placed his spikes on as he sat on the snow-covered rock, "We are a long way from home, and I wonder if this is worth it?"

"I believe it is. Cults must be stopped or at least held in check. When could the brainwashing of people ever be acceptable?"

"But why us?"

She looked at Dak and did not answer. He put his backpack on and led the way off the path. The spikes held them as they dug into the ice as they crossed the side of the ice-covered bluff one foot at a time as the area was noticeably steeper with each step closer to the large ice cliff. Dak pulled himself up to the rock ledge and peered across the face of the mountain. He helped Zenith to his spot, "We need to lay under the white tent over there on that rock bluff." He pointed thirty feet further around the apex of the mountain side. We need to make certain the sun does not create a reflection from our equipment."

Dak glanced at Zenith. He could tell she was tired from the journey across the face of the bluff. Each step had been risky with the danger of falling several hundred feet. Zenith tried to smile, "Let us get this done."

Dak said, "I will tie this rope to my waist and then I can pull the packs over to me. Then you come over."

Zenith watched as Dak used his knife to create a place to hold as he crossed the cliff to the rock ledge. He would force the knife into the ice and then dig the spikes on his boots into the ice and pull the knife out and then move a few inches across the cliff and then repeat the process. Zenith held her breath as she watched him try to hold his position and remove the knife to reset the blade into the hard ice surface. She increased her grip on the rope and positioned her feet with her spikes into the ice and snow leaning backward just in case he faltered. She glanced at the safety spike she had driven into the ice-covered rock and tried to picture how the spike would hold if Dak fell. She wanted to be braced in case Dak slipped, and the spike failed. She repositioned her spikes in the ice and held the lifeline as she watched as Dak slowly crossed the ice cliff.

She watched as Dak pulled himself over the ledge and laid on his stomach resting. He then jabbed his knife into the snow/ice ledge and motioned for her to send over the pack. Zenith tied off the first pack and Dak pulled the pack over to himself. Zenith left the other pack and then used the rope as a security catch as she had to climb across the ice cliff the same as Dak.

After Zenith crossed over to the rock, Dak removed the white tent from the pack and then set the white tent on the rock without raising the tent. He positioned himself lying on his belly with the binoculars. Zenith positioned herself next to him and pulled her binoculars out of her backpack. They both studied the men inside the wooden fortress over four thousand feet below. The men were involved in extensive combat training. Dak saw one man receive a broken arm and another appeared to be killed with a sword in practice. He counted two guards at the front gate. Zenith finally announced, "I count fifty men in training. One possible Blueblood standing on the balcony watching. I only see two guards at the front gate. What do you think?"

Dak hesitated and then announced, "They are preparing for war. They could have twice that number of men. I do not like what I see. Veronica did not report this many combatants. We cannot beat them with us attacking the fort. There are too many of them."

"We cannot return across the Midlander Territory. We must engage them here and now."

"I believe for us to be successful; we need to entice those soldiers out of the fort into the open. I bet their stables are full of horses. We need them to chase our men out of the fort. I will sneak into the fort and attack the Blueblood Master."

She looked at her husband with a questionable expression, "You will not attack the Blueblood Master without me. There are too many soldiers. We cannot win fighting them in the open. Boudica indicated she counted at least three maybe four Rogue Blueblood warriors and then the Master. We must use stealth and assassinate the Master."

Dak did not respond for a couple of seconds, "You and I then need to sneak into the fort and catch the Blueblood Master in our trap. He will stay behind. Veronica did not report this large of an army, or there are three maybe four Rogue Bluebloods in addition to the Master. We do not have the time to spend with surveillance to establish a plan to assassinate the Master."

"How would we entice them out of the fort?"

"We would entice the Master with something he fears, and something he would chase. Something he must eliminate."

Zenith smiled, "So that is why you asked Samuel to come?"

"The cult would have heard of him and fear him. The plan, as I see it, will be some of our men arrive at the door of the fort with Samuel and act like they are attacking. The soldiers will be ordered to attack. The men will fall back close to a half-mile and hold the line while you, me, Billy Ray, and Hulk sneak into the compound and assassinate the Blueblood Master."

"What! Dak there are at least three other Blueblood warriors. Killing them will not be easy. What if they do not come out of the fort?"

"See the livestock. They are in a corral outside the fort walls. We will run off their food supply. I am betting they do not have an ample supply of food stored, but I am counting on the Master seeing his number one adversary sitting on a white horse out front. He will order the gates opened, and his men will attack. He will be fearful the Blueblood empire in Merlin will find his location. Senator Dale would not be able to protect him. The Master will be aggressive and order his men to attack and then he will relocate. He cannot stay here now that he knows the world has located him. So, we must kill him here and now. This is the best I can do. I give us a twenty percent chance of winning."

Zenith looked at Dak and smiled, "Twenty percent? That high." She knew Dak had already made up his mind and if they could isolate the Master the two of them could kill him. "I was thinking about nineteen percent. Boudica will wish to go with us. Her brother is in that fort. She has helped us, and she should have the right to choose her destiny." Dak smiled to himself at the remark of nineteen percent as he kept looking through the binoculars.

Zenith and Dak stayed on the ledge for close to five hours watching and talking about their plan of attack. Dak announced, "We have watched for close to five hours. We need to leave and head back to the main camp. I count two maybe three Blueblood warriors. I fear we cannot defeat them."

Zenith could tell Dak was concerned about what he might find when they returned. She also knew he was worried about his mother and the children. Zenith could hear the excitement in Dak's tone, and how he was animated when he discussed the details of the upcoming attack. He really liked the tactical part of planning an attack and then carrying out the battle plans. "Dak, we must attack now. We cannot afford for the Master to become stronger. I agree the risk is great. I was hoping he had not formed an army this size. I wished Veronica had told us we would face this many Blueblood warriors and soldiers. I am not certain nineteen percent is a real assessment of our chances, but we have no choice."

# Chapter 20

The guard from Meadow Bottoms arrived from the New York Tribe the prior year. Wayne recognized him as he opened the double doors. He was nothing but trash. Wayne had not agreed for him to seek sanctuary in their realm, but others indicated they needed young working age men. He watched as the guard approached Casey and her daughter, Jesse. The man looked down at Casey sitting on the floor holding her ten-year-old daughter. Wayne could not hear the man, but he feared what he might do. Wayne looked at the other guard stationed at the interior double doors. He had on a uniform and appeared to be a soldier from down south. He was a professional soldier and seemed to understand the importance of following orders, but the man from Meadow Bottoms was worthless. Wayne watched as the soldier turned and walked out the double doors, and this left the one guard standing over Casey.

The man stared down at Casey. He stood still with her eyes fixed on the floor holding her daughter. "You certainly are a pretty thing." Casey did not respond. She kept her arms tight around her daughter. The man then said, "Your daughter is a pretty thing just like her mother."

Casey looked up with clenched jaws, "Don't you dare. She is a child."

The man smiled, "One of you will go in the backroom with me. I need some loving. You choose, you or your daughter."

Casey glared, "Neither one of us are going anywhere with you." Casey looked back at the floor. Wayne and the others watched the man reach down and pull the daughter's arm. Casey fought back and the daughter cried out. The elderly man sitting near them yelled, "Leave her alone."

The guard turned and walked over to the man sitting against the exterior wall and hit him hard with the broad side of the sword. The man held his arms up to protect himself as the sword hit him in his left forearm. He rolled over from the impact and cried out in pain. "I have been nice, but I am not going to be nice any longer. Your daughter will go with me."

Casey stood, "I will go with you. You will leave my daughter alone."

The man smiled, "I can assure you. I am a gentleman, but how this plays out is all based on your behavior and your loving effort." The two walked into the back room as the daughter cried for her mother. One of the ladies crawled over to her to comfort her.

Wayne waited for the guard and Casey to exit and then motioned for Benny, the older man sitting next to him. Benny hurriedly bent over and walked to Wayne's side. Wayne ordered, "Break the arrow and pull the damn thing out." Benny did not waver as he reached for the back end and snapped the arrow. He then pulled the broken arrow through Wayne's shoulder.

Wayne almost blacked out from the pain. The man placed a rag over his shoulder. Benny whispered, "They will be back. I believe they will kill all of us. They cannot afford to leave witnesses."

Wayne gritted his teeth, "You are correct. They mean to kill all of us. They cannot afford for any witnesses to survive."

He looked at Benny. His jaws were clenched from the pain radiating from his shoulder down his arm. "I helped build this church. Under the altar, there is a tunnel which leads to the barn. You need to pull the altar to the side, crawl through the tunnel to the barn and climb the ladder up in the pigeon pen. The sixth cage from your right is the pigeon set to fly to the gate of the gorge. Send a message, we are under an attack from men of Meadow Bottoms. Need help. Can you do that?"

Benny looked around at the tied-up night watchman on the other side and the females sitting in the pews with the children. "I will do it."

Wayne reached his arm with his teeth clenched, "Bring me back a knife. I need a weapon."

Benny shifted the altar to the side, lit a candle, and dropped through the floor.

Wayne, with the help of one of the ladies, shifted the altar back in place as the guard at the front door opened the door and walked into the church. He was followed by another guard. The one guard stayed at the door while the other guard walked to the back of the church. He looked down at Wayne lying next to the altar with the arrow removed and blood on the floor. "Fifteen minutes after the lady is beheaded, it will be your turn. It really is a shame the doctor went seal hunting or otherwise he could help you right before you are executed."

Wayne was holding his right arm. He tried to move it, but it would not move. The pain was excruciating. Wayne had never known the throbbing pain like this. With each breath, pain would register in his shoulder and down his right arm. "You will not get away with this."

The guard kicked Wayne in the stomach. "We already have gotten away with it. Where is the gold?"

Wayne turned over and was now lying on his injured arm. He gritted his teeth, "What gold?"

The guard clenched his jaws and kicked Wayne again and again. One of the women started crying and the guard went and picked her up and slapped her. We need the gold, or we are going to kill every one of you. Now, where is the gold?"

The young lady shook her head as she was crying, "I promise I do not know anything about any gold. Please let us go." He slapped her, knocking her to the floor. Another lady crawled to her side and held her.

***

The guard smiled at Casey, "You better be good to me. I mean, you'd better be really good to me."

Casey smiled as she started removing her clothing. "I used to be a stripper in the old world. I believe I know a thing or two about pleasing a man. You know you are very good looking." She pulled her coat and top off and allowed the man the full view of her chest. She then removed her pants and underwear. She stood still and smiled, "What now?"

The guard started removing his clothing. He quickly pulled his boots off and then his pants and shirts. Casey could tell the man was going to be easy to manipulate. He was young and stupid. He reached for her, and she turned him around, and allowed him to lie on his back. She quickly straddled him, and he gasped with the sudden pleasure. She rotated her hips and then slowly leaned over him as she smiled down on him. His eyes closed as he was experiencing the pleasure. She reached with her right hand and pulled the sharp metal hairpin from her hair and quickly shoved the hairpin into his temple. "I am sorry, but I must protect my child." She glared down at the dead man as she felt his orgasm inside of her. She then stood and started getting dressed as she turned and noticed the blood dripping down his head onto his shoulder.

***

Vicky knew she needed to reposition herself and buy time for Dominique to secure the four children and the two daycare workers. The two women would be slow to travel to the cave. She looked in the air and noticed a pigeon flying from the barn toward the New York Tribe. Her guards at the gorge were fifteen minutes away. She thought, "I must buy some needed time. The men would be watching the fourplex." She ran out the rear door and into the woods. She knew she needed to rush to get in position behind the Blacksmith Shop. There she could go unnoticed and pick off one, maybe two of the soldiers.

Vicky watched from the west rear corner of the Blacksmith Shop. The four guards were watching her balcony and standing behind Delores. They forced Dolores to the ground next to the decapitated night watchman. She looked to the side of the fourplex and saw Mia's lifeless body.

Sie's oldest son commanded, "What will it be? You have a few more minutes before we kill her then bring out the next citizen. We have your friend with us. You need to tell us the location of the gold. We are not going to harm the children."

Vicky loaded her arrow. She knew the smart play was to stall for time. She could hide with the kids and unless they had dogs to track them, they would not be able to locate them. She also knew she loved her friends. She said to herself, "What a better way to die than to die trying to save a friend?"

Vicky waited and watched from the corner of the Blacksmith Shop on her knee, hiding behind the thick evergreen rhododendron bushes. Sie's oldest son yelled, "Okay, enough time has expired. Off with her head." He waved to his thirteen-year-old brother. Vicky noticed the teenager had no reservation in killing another person. Matter of fact, he seemed eager to be the one to swing the sword. Vicky thought to herself, "A young person with that much hatred, who looked forward to killing another person would have psychotic issues and needed to be stopped."

He stepped next to Delores and lifted the sword. Delores kept her head bent down facing the ground. She seemed to understand she would be sacrificed for the four children. She was brave and knew her Queen loved her.

Vicky, in one fast motion, stepped out from the rear corner of the Blacksmith Shop and sent the arrow toward the target. She ran forward as she loaded another arrow and aimed while running into the street and released another arrow.

The first arrow hit the teenager in the ribs driving the sharp point into the lower part of the left lung. The kid coughed up blood and fell over in the street on top of the snow as he dropped his sword. The second arrow hit the guard standing to the right of Delores. The other soldiers raised their shields and turned to fight Vicky.

Vicky dropped her bow and pulled her two hatchets. She ran straight for the first guard and swung both her hatchets right then left. Both were blocked by the guard. She then dropped to her right knee and went low with the hatchet in her right hand and under his shield hitting the soldier in the left knee. He buckled over in the street and fell into the fetal position. Vicky now watched as several guards surrounded her and Delores. She positioned herself in front of Delores, "Are you alright?"

"Cut these damn ropes off me, and I will show these cowards. Dammit. You should have fled. You are the Queen, and you do not need to martyr yourself for me."

"You are my friend. I do not know of a better way to die than die for a friend. They have us surrounded. How many of our people have been killed?"

"They have killed at least eight. They will kill all of us. You should have fled."

Sie's youngest son laid on the snow-covered street while he was bleeding. "Help me." He started crying as he coughed up blood and then died.

"You bitch. You killed my brother. He was a kid. I will kill you."

The man's voice boomed over the fighters, "You will do no such thing. We need her."

Vicky and Delores both looked at Barney Simpson and an unknown man standing next to him. The two stepped out of the small cottage, west of the fourplex. Vicky carefully worded her statement. "After further consideration of your actions and your chronic bad breath, I have declared you a coward and a backstabbing bastard. I have decided to revoke your position of City Councilman on Cliff Tops Board of Directors. Barney Simpson, you are fired."

Barney stepped into the street and told the young man to hold off. He then smiled at the statement and looked at Vicky, "Yes, I guess you would fire me, but I really do not care. You have more pressing issues. I know your men are out hunting seals and will not return for a week. The other men are out at the boundary of your realm looking for stray cattle. Your best soldiers are clear across the continent and might already be dead. You see, the men I sent were no warriors, but they know how to mix mushroom poison." He smiled at Vicky. "You have no help coming and now you have walked into the street in front of us where we can overpower you. I figured you were smarter than this."

"I do not recognize your murderous acquaintance. Have you told him he will be killed for listening to you?"

Barney smiled. "I am sorry. Allow me to introduce you to Bill. His friends call him Bloody Bill. He fought next to your son, your sons' friends, and Billy Ray in the Battle of Harpers Ferry Harbor. After the battle he decided to go into business on his own. You see, Bloody Bill has his own acquaintances who have contacts with the bounty hunters working for King Solman. I found it in my best interest and the best interest of folks living in Meadow Bottoms to work out an agreement with these men. We will take the gold with us. I promise you we will not harm your children, but we will also take them with us. You know those children are worth as much as the gold is to the Normand Army. They will be please to deal with us. I also would like to update you on the trip west. You see my two men are experts dealing with mushrooms. At the right time, they will kill by poisoning everyone of your men on that mission. You see, we need your son to make contact with the supreme leader of the newly forming government on the west coast." He smiled at Vicky.

Bloody Bill walked further into the street, "I was told you were wise. Yet, you freely ran into the street to fight us trying to protect this one person. You are gravely outnumbered. I can assure you; my men are all experienced and great soldiers. Why would you do something so stupid?" His face turned red with anger. He seemed to realize the reason, "Check the house for the kids." He motioned for one of his men to enter the fourplex.

Vicky looked at the men she was now facing. She did not doubt Bloody Bill was a killer. He and his men had the look of warriors. They each had multiple, good quality weapons and watching her guard being executed and now lying in the street did not faze them. The men with Barney from Meadow Bottoms did not look like experienced warriors. The man she had just taken down was no warrior. He did not move while she approached him with the hatchets, and he allowed her the opportunity to take his leg out from under him. Sie's sons were killers but not warriors. Vicky looked at Bloody Bill and announced, "You are a fool if you think for a second that you can make a deal with the cult leading the Normand army, his men, and the bounty hunters from King Solman cannot be trusted. They have no intention to share anything with you. Barney, you are a fool. Bloody Bill, your men will be killed after we are all killed."

Bloody Bill's man turned and jogged to the front door and as he entered the front foyer, he immediately noticed the guard from Meadow Bottoms lying face down in the kitchen entryway. He ran to the back door and peered to the right and saw the second guard from Meadow Bottoms with his eyes frozen opened and an arrow sticking through his stomach. He turned and ran back to the front of the hall and up the stairs. The door to Vicky's room was ajar. He stepped by the dresser lying across the floor and then went into the bedroom and looked inside. The upstairs was empty. He ran down the stairs to the front foyer to report what he had discovered. As he approached the front door, the arrow hit him in the middle of his back and drove through his protected padded protector and out the front of his chest. His momentum carried him out the front door, across the front porch, down the stairs, and landed him motionless in the street.

Dominique stood behind the evergreen trees and watched the man appear in the rear door entrance as he noticed the dead guard. He then turned back into the fourplex and quickly disappeared inside the home. She ran to the rear door and heard the man coming down the stairs. She raised her bow and waited for him to clear the bottom of the stairs and come into her firing zone. She held her breath and gently released the arrow.

The other men looked at their fallen comrade as he fell out the front door and down the stairs. He laid at the bottom of the stairs in the street, dead. Bloody Bill yelled, "Secure the building."

Dominique stepped to the northwest exterior rear corner of the home and rushed toward the front. The man ran around the corner and was surprised to see a Blueblood facing him with an arrow pulled tight in her bow. He instantly reacted and raised his shield to protect his face and upper body. Right before she released her arrow, she adjusted her aim, and the arrow flew under the man's shield and hit him below his waist. He buckled over as Dominique ran past him to the street.

Vicky looked at Sie's oldest son holding his sword. She pointed at him with the hatchet in her right hand and smiled, "You want me? Come and get me."

The young man rushed with anger as he yelled carrying a shield and sword. He swung as hard as he could with his right hand as he was running toward Vicky. She blocked the swing with the hatchet in her left hand, then dropped low, cutting his left ankle with her right hatchet. The hatchet hit in the joint of the ankle and the blade drove deep. The young man fell, dropping his weapons in the street yelping in pain as he rolled over in the street.

Vicky rolled in the street and stood facing the other men. Bloody Bill motioned for his three archers to hold steady. Vicky figured at least one of them would be taking aim with a bow, and she picked up the shield lying on the street near Sie's son. The men looked surprised when a Blueblood came around the corner of the building with an arrow loaded, aiming at them. Dominique fired the arrow hitting the man closest to her with the arrow through his stomach. She loaded another arrow as she ran toward them.

Barney yelled, "Kill them!"

Vicky used the opportunity to run behind Delores and cut the ropes holding her wrist and ankles. Delores crawled to the dead teenager and picked up his sword. As she stood, her expression turned to one of a demonic expression. She looked full of rage.

The two men with the bows loaded, aimed at Vicky and fired their arrows with one hitting her shield. The other missed her. As she rolled onto the ground, she was able to dodge the arrows. The one then turned to face the immediate threat, Dominique. The second man fired his second arrow, hitting Delores in the back, upper shoulder as she stood with a sword. She fell over in the street, wounded.

Dominique turned and aimed her bow and shot the man who turned to her.

Barney yelled a second time, "Kill them!" He looked at Bloody Bill. "Why are your men not attacking?"

Barney pulled his sword and ran toward Delores.

Vicky was attacked by three men from Meadow Bottoms. She rotated from the first man blocking his sword. She rolled on the ground and then stood quickly blocking the swing from the second man. She knew she must keep moving and tried to keep them occupied. She hoped the untrain men would present her an opportunity to take one of them out at a time. She spun away from the third man and swung her right hatchet at the first man. He blocked the swing, and the third man moved forward to cut her off from escaping from the middle of the circle.

Barney kicked Delores in the side. He then stepped on her arm, forcing her to drop the sword. He reached with his left hand and pulled Delores's head back holding his sword at her throat as he now looked at Vicky. "Drop your weapons."

Delores was in pain from the arrow. She clenched her jaws and looked at her friend, "Kill this bastard and then root out all those in Meadow Bottoms and hang them. You will not drop your weapons."

Barney pulled his blade across her throat, killing Delores in the street.

Bloody Bill stepped forward. He held his hand up for his men to hold still. His three archers had now surrounded Dominique, and Vicky was facing three swordsman from Meadow Bottoms and two bounty hunters. Bloody Bill said, "It is over. You two need to lay down your weapons. I do not wish to kill you."

# Chapter 21

Dak and Zenith rode toward the main camp. Zenith knew Dak was afraid for his friends. He rode faster than normal through the woods and along the ridge line. They both had an ominous feeling, knowing the two men from Meadow Bottoms had been sent to poison them. Dying by poison was a horrible way to die. Sometimes the time to die would take days for the body to shut down and the heart stop pumping. Poison was no way for a warrior to die.

Dak and his horse came into an open area in the trail, and he could see his men gathering around a fire. He felt relief when he saw Samuel and Billy Ray drinking coffee and talking over to the side of the camp. He and Zenith both slowed their pace, then walked their horses the last few steps into the camp. Zenith, like always, scanned the area around the camp to verify if there were any dangers, and noticed the big man from Meadow Bottoms hanging by his neck from the tree limb approximately fifty feet deep in the woods. She noticed the big man was hanging still, three feet from the ground, and barefoot. She turned her attention to Dak and noticed he was staring at the other man sitting on the ground and appeared to have his hands tied behind his back lying next to a tree. Zenith then motioned her head for

Dak to look over to the right at the barefoot man dangling from a rope.

Dak and Zenith dismounted and tied their lead ropes off to a tree. Tommy Boy walked over and said he would take care of the horses. Dak walked toward Hulk who was sitting on a log next to Boudica, "I see you made the journey back to camp in time."

Hulk motioned his head up and down, "They confessed they were sent to poison us with Amanita Phalloides also known as the Death Cap Mushroom. The mushrooms had been ground to powder, which is in the saddle bag." He pointed to the saddle bag sitting next to the tree. "We hung one man. The other one was a little more talkative."

Dak looked at the dead man hanging by the rope and his bare feet, "He died without his boots. Why remove his boots?"

Trey smiled and held up the boot, "Look at his right boot. This is so cool. The man's father is a leather bootmaker in Meadow Bottoms. He made his son this right boot with a hidden knife that can be activated by the touch of the ball of the foot. The three-inch knife flips out of the toe of the boot." Dak watched Trey stick his hand into the boot and the blade came flipping out. "I discovered the deadly weapon once he activated the blade and tried to kill me. The knife is deadly, but he was no warrior. He was big and slow and once I grabbed his foot and twisted his leg, he fell to the ground. I beat the shit out of him."

Dak smiled, "His boots might fit me. I need a pair of new leather boots."

Dak walked over and stood in front of the man from Meadow Bottoms, "Your friend hanging in the tree, his father worked as a leather worker. What did your father do?"

The man looked down as he talked, "My mother's first husband died years ago right after the Transitional Period caused by the virus. My mother was raped by men in a tribe down south as she traveled north. Nine months later my mother gave birth to me. The people in Meadow Bottoms helped my mother. I felt I owed them."

"You are a bastard, and your mother was a whore. Do not lie to me. You came here to kill every one of us with the mushroom poison?"

The man still would not look up. Dak commanded, "You are a bastard. Look up at me when I talk to you, you bastard."

He slowly looked up, "Hulk and Billy Ray agreed if I told them the truth, they would not harm me. I have rights."

"Why would you conspire to kill us?"

The man looked at Dak with his red face and stern look. "We were told if we took the gold back and offered the gold to King Solman, he would not attack. The newly formed government would work out the details with the Normand empire. Barney Simpson told us he would be a leader in the future, and we needed to act now or never. He expressed the men of Cliff Tops were either seal hunting, looking for stray cattle along the outskirts of the realm, or mining. The city would not be protected, and once we had control, we could defend the city until the Normand army took over."

Dak reached down and picked the man up from the ground, "And you believed his bull shit was going to be that simple? You are so stupid. You believe King Solman would trust you and your fellow conspiratorial assholes? What about my kids and two nieces?"

The man hesitated and looked scared. Dak could tell he was trying to think of something to say. Dak pushed the man down on the ground. "Your plan consisted of killing my family and my friends."

The man looked up from the ground while lying on his back, "Not the kids. The kids were going to be traded to the Normand sympathizers. The gold was going to be split between us and the bounty hunters from Southern City and some mercenaries from the middle of the continent. The leaders felt they could work out a trade with the Normand Empire for the Blueblood kids."

"Why did you wait?" Dak realized the answer to his question. "Damn you, you were waiting for us to locate the Dark Master. Those bastards were going to work out a deal with the devil. That is why the other man is here. He was here to broker a deal with the Dark Master once we located him." Dak looked angered as wrinkles appeared in his forehead and his eyes narrowed.

Billy Ray walked over and stood next to Dak, "He gave us the names of all who were involved. The men have been praying our community is still standing when we get back to Cliff Tops."

Dak thought of his kids. He looked at Hulk, "So you have a list of everyone involved, including the bounty hunters?"

Hulk stood and looked at Dak. Hulk could tell by the look in Dak's eyes what he was about to do. "Yes, we have a complete list of everyone in Meadow Bottoms guilty of insurrection and the mercenaries from down south. The mercenaries are led by Bloody Bill."

Dak said, "Bloody Bill. I will kill that bastard, Bloody Bill." Dak walked over to the saddle bag and opened the flap and pulled the bag of the mushroom powder out and held the bag up. He walked over to the man on the ground holding the bag in front of him. Billy Ray stopped Dak by reaching his bicep and held him. "I gave him my word; he would not be harmed. He is our witness. We can use him to prove our case."

Dak pulled his arm free and bent down in front of the man. "I did not give my word, and I do not need a witness to carry out my judgement. Remember we live in a Monarchy, and what I say is the law. You and your co-conspirators may have killed the two people ranked ahead of me which now makes me the King of Cliff Tops. You do have rights. You have the right to swallow and then die of mushroom poison." Dak reached into the bag with his gloved hand and pulled out some of the powered mushroom. He pushed the man backward on his back and forced the man's mouth open and stuffed mushroom powder into his mouth. The man with his hands tied behind his back and his feet tied together, could only move his head from side to side. Dak then repeated forcing the mushroom powder four additional times into the man's throat with everyone watching. The man was crying and begging for mercy. He had tried to spit out the powder, but he could not help but swallow some of the powder as he took a breath. Dak had forced his left hand, holding the man's nose closed and his right hand over the man's face with his finger rammed into the man's mouth with his right hand full of powder. When the man took a breath Dak would force the powder down his throat.

Dak turned to Samuel, "We do not have enough time to return to Cliff Tops to protect our loved ones. We will assume the best for them. Zenith and I have worked out the details for an immediate attack and a plan to assault the Dark Master. We should be able to surprise them. If we are successful, we hope to sail a ship north past the Normand Army and dock at Harpers Ferry Harbor and then ride north. We came here for this purpose. We will assume the leaders in Cliff Tops were prepared. We have come too far not to keep to our mission." Everyone could tell Dak was aggravated as he glanced at the prisoner lying on the ground on his side with the mushroom powder all over his cheeks, nose, and mouth. "If he does not die tonight, I will hang him at first light. I cannot stand to see someone suffer."

Tommy Boy looked at him, "He got what he deserved. Justice has been served."

Zenith then announced, "We need to have everyone ready for battle tonight because in the early morning we need to be in position. Then, we will strike at noon."

Dak looked at the group, "My plan is simple." He bent down as he pulled his knife. "We are here. The fort is here." He made the drawing on the ground. "All of you men except for Zenith, myself, Hulk, Boudica and Billy Ray will ride to the ocean and then proceed south along the beach. There should be a trail leading south. You will take the trail." He marked the area with his knife as the others looked on. "We are not worried about people of the small villages seeing you as you ride south. It should not matter. When we are set at the top of the mountain, we will signal you with a mirror. I need Trey and Tommy Boy to run off their livestock located outside the fort. There are two guards. Here and here." He pointed to the ground to the west of the fort. "Samuel, you and Robin Hood will slowly ride to the front gate and shoot the two guards." He pointed to the ground and drew the area in the front of the fort, the road, the corral of animals. "Samuel, you and Robin Hood will remove your hood once you kill the guards. We want them to charge you. We must provide them a reason to charge you from the fort. I am counting on the Dark Master to order his men to charge as he prepares to relocate." He hesitated, "You must keep the soldiers occupied in a battle while my group will wait on the soldiers to attack you. Then we will descend the mountain and enter the fort from the rear." Dak pointed to the rear of the fort. "We will seek out the Dark Master and destroy him."

Samuel looked at Dak, "You are using me as bait to lure them out!"

Dak looked at Samuel, "There are more soldiers than Veronica reported. I am not certain the number of Blueblood warriors, but I counted two for certain and maybe four. There could be more. We must manipulate the Dark Master to send his soldiers out of the fort, and there is no better way than to make them believe we are going to wait them out. There is only one person the Dark Master will fear and that is you. He will sacrifice his men. He will stay behind to plan his escape. You men will retreat across the field and back track on the road close to half mile. There you will make your stand. The men will need to keep your hoods on. We want them to suspect there is more than one Blueblood riding with you. We want him to send his Blueblood soldiers out of the fort." He looked at Samuel, "Your skills will be tested on the battlefield."

Samuel looked at Dak and then Zenith, "How many soldiers?"

Dak looked at his men, "We counted fifty in training. There were at least fifteen others standing guard and working within the fort."

Trey looked at Dak, "One-hundred! Dammit, That is more than we considered."

Dak glanced at Trey and the others, "I do not see another alternative. We attack now or never. I will be honest with you; we might have bit off more than we can chew."

Samuel said, "I like your plan, but I should be the one assaulting the rear of the fort and killing the Dark Master. Killing him is my unfinished business and my responsibility."

Dak stepped forward, "We need you to entice the army out of the fort. He will not expect us to scale down the cliff this time of year. I am counting on him not fearing us. He has us outnumbered four to one. The Dark Master is arrogant, he will want to kill us and that will be his undoing. We do not have time to wait them out. We must return to Cliff Tops." Dak looked at Trey, "You Trey are in charge. You men will do as Trey commands. This is my order to you as the King of Cliff Tops and the commander of this mission. Trey, after your battle, you will lead the men around Tanger south, close to fifty miles and wait until spring at the base of the mountains near the river where we crossed before at the large oak tree. The tree will be the rendezvous point. If we do not meet you, you will know we failed in killing the Dark Master. You will head home without us on The No She Trail. You will not come looking for us. Our tribe cannot afford for all of us to die here. The people in Cliff Tops will need some of us to survive for the future battles." He turned and made eye contact with Samuel, "If we meet you, at which time the weather warms, we will cross the mountains together and head home. The other path for us to travel home would be by ship, but we have no contingent plan for us to travel by sea. This is my plan, and I have spoken."

Tommy Boy looked at the others and at Dak, "What has you so concerned? We have been in battles before against greater odds."

Zenith stepped forward, "We have never fought against a team of Bluebloods. If they fight as a team, this could be tricky for all of us. Plus, we watched as their soldiers trained. They will show no fear and no mercy. They will die for their master. This is not going to be easy, but you must keep the main body of soldiers occupied while our group assassinates the Master." She turned to Samuel. "If we fail, we fail. Samuel you will need to retreat and leave us. We cannot forget about our homeland. The kids in our village need you to protect them and train them. This is the best shot we have." She looked at the down trotted faces of the men. She then turned to her husband, "This is not a good plan, but this is the best plan we have. There will be no one second guessing our plan. You are soldiers, and soldiers die in battle."

# Chapter 22

Veronica looked at Frank Jr. She could see the worry in his expression as he rubbed his hands together. He intentionally avoided eye contact as he stood in the open room and walked over to the window. "There is nothing else I can do for you. I have allowed you to stay in my bunkhouse as a guest at my residence with your children and guards. Our King will order his guards to eradicate all of us. I have risked everything for you and asked nothing in return. The King will turn you over to the Dark Master. It is part of our King's agreement with the Dark Master. The King and his soldiers will find out that I have helped you. It is unavoidable. There are too many people here that are related to the sheriff and his men. Someone will talk. They will order me to be executed along with anyone who works for me. They fear the Dark Master and his army more than doing the right thing. You must understand what it is like to see a man impaled and left hanging alive on a pole screaming until he can scream no more. Those images are forever imprinted in a person's memory."

Veronica looked at Frank Jr., "I understand your town and the people who live here are all cowards. Your kids and grandkids will always live in fear and give into the cult. The cult will take everything from you, not just your property but your dignity. They will keep on taking until there is nothing left to take."

Michael stepped forward, "My Queen. We will die for you in battle." Michael looked at Frank Jr., "Let them try to arrest her and take these children."

"You asked me what concerns me. I have told you. The people of Tanger do not speak of the unspeakable. You are correct, they are scared. We all live in constant fear. I will travel to the city and see if there is any chatter about you living here. I pray I hear nothing."

Frank Jr. walked toward the exterior door and Pretty Boy stepped in front of him blocking his path. Veronica noticed, "Let him go. He has helped us. He speaks the truth. There are too many maids and workers who know I am here. We must leave and stay hidden." She looked at Frank Jr., "Where is this island where we must live like refugees?"

"I will return tonight, and we can talk. Like I said, I will verify if the farm hands, maids or anyone has mentioned you to the authorities. I will check to see if the sheriff and his men are on to us. I know a deputy in town that I can trust. He will tell me." He opened the door and left, closing the door behind him.

Michael turned to Veronica, "My Queen, I do not trust that man. I urge you not to trust him. He will do what he must to protect himself and his riches. We will be ready. I will station

Viking on the road to watch for the soldiers of Tanger. We will fight as you trained us."

Veronica considered what Michael was suggesting. She thought back to her interaction with Dezie, the elderly lady who worked in the castle, who knew how to manipulate men. She thought of Dak and the last meeting when she met Dak and Zenith. She wondered, "Where are they?" She then looked at Michael, "There army has too many soldiers. There sheriff has too many deputies. Everyone in Tanger is scared of the cult. I noticed the fear in the people's eyes when we first came ashore. We have very few options. Please have the maids fill my tub with water. I will bathe, and I must bathe these children."

***

Veronica awoke and was surprised Gabriel had not awoken, crying wanting to be fed. He seemed to need to be fed every three hours. The nurse maid explained the child would sleep longer once he ate solid food. Her instincts forced her to crawl out from under her warm bedding and go to the crib to make certain he was breathing. She looked at her baby boy and smiled. She thought, "He slept for five straight hours as she looked at her watch." She picked up the bottle of soybean oil and rubbed the oil on her dry legs. She pulled her shirt over her head and rubbed the oil on her arms, back and chest. She then reached

down and rubbed the oil on each foot. She placed her shirt on
and turned to the crib as she heard Gabriel stir. She smiled and
picked him up as she glanced at the other sleeping children. She
eased the door open and walk to the fireplace. She placed
additional firewood on the hot ashes. She carried her baby to the
area in front of the fire and sat him down and started changing
his diaper on the floor in front of the burning fire. She then
positioned herself next to the fireplace in the rocking chair. She
pulled her shirt down over her shoulder to the side and allowed
Gabriel to start feeding. "You are such a good boy. You are
growing so fast. Mommy loves her big boy."

Frank Jr. walked into the living room. He watched Veronica
sitting on the floor with her legs bent under her as she changed
the diaper and then she stood and moved to the rocking chair
feeding her son, talking to him. He noticed her legs shined with
the ambient light from the fire reflecting off her as she had one
foot placed on the rung of the chair. He noticed on her other leg
one streak of oil on her shin leading down to the foot positioned
on the floor. Her white shirt was thin cotton material, which was
loose fitting, hanging down past her waist to her mid upper
thigh. He stared at her as he walked into the room. He then stood
in the middle of the room and tried not to be obvious as he
watched her feed her son. "That chair was my mother's. She
died during the Transitional Period."

Veronica was surprised at hearing the male voice and looked over at Frank Jr. "The chair is comfortable. I like a warm fire. Where I am from, the weather is so much colder than here. My body is acclimated to the cold freezing temperatures." She looked back at her nursing son.

Frank Jr. took two additional steps to the opposite side of the fireplace as he faced the fire. "My father would sit near the fire in that chair every night while he smoked, and then he would fall asleep. I could hear him snoring at the other end of the home. At some point, he would awake and go to bed. He also loved a warm fire." He glanced at Veronica feeding her baby, "He seems to be hungry."

She smiled as she changed breasts and repositioned his head, "My baby boy is so hungry. He is going to be a big boy soon." He stepped closer as he watched Veronica peering down at her son. He felt his throat become dry as he noticed she was covered in oil with her right leg propped against the arm rest and her right arm resting on her knee as she held her child bundled in a blanket. He noticed she was wearing no panties as she repositioned her leg. "I did not hear you come home last night. Was there any news in town?"

Frank Jr. watched, "No. I believe you are still safe. I trust my contact. He is a good man."

Veronica changed her position as she placed the child over her shoulder and started lightly patting his back. She yawned, waiting for the child to burp. "Can you burp for mommy?"

Frank Jr. fought himself trying not to stare at Veronica in the thin white shirt that was now wet around both breast areas. He could not help but stare at the thin transparent wet material and be attracted to her. He felt the warm fire as the heat radiated off his pants and slightly burned his leg when he moved with the pant leg rubbing against his skin.

Veronica kept patting her baby as she thought about Frank Jr. watching her every move. She wondered if other women enjoyed attracting the attention of a man. She listened and heard the voice of a child coming from the bedroom.

Veronica stood and looked him in the eyes, "It is good news your source did not report anything about me. I am ever so grateful for your help. I will compensate you when this is over. I am going to place him back in bed. Mr. Gabriel is finished eating, and I need to check on his brother who just woke. I will be back to sit by the fire with you, and we can talk more about compensation for your risk and troubles."

Frank Jr. waited by the fire as he thought about bedding Veronica. How he desired to touch her. He had several different images go through his mind as he fantasized about being with her. His thoughts quickly changed a few minutes had passed as he realized she never returned. He walked over to her bedroom door and peered into the room. He held his candle in front of him and could see from the candlelight her eyes were closed with Vaugh's little head sticking out from under the cover lying next to her. Both asleep.

# Chapter 23

Bloody Bill looked at his men and then stared at Vicky. "I know your son and his group has more stolen Merlin gold than we can count. I have talked to the men who were asked to guard the gold in Harpers Ferry Harbor. I personally do not like the Normand army, nor do I trust them. I am not interested in kidnapping the four Blueblood kids and selling them to Normand bounty hunters. That was his plan not mine."

Bloody Bill turned and looked at Barney, "You did not tell me you were going to work out a deal with a Rogue Blueblood cult. I am here for the gold." He turned back to face the Queen, "He is here for the gold, the children, and the power." He pointed toward Barney.

Vicky looked at Bloody Bill. "He is going to trick you and then kill your men. I will pay you and your men ten pounds of gold to leave. I will have the gold delivered to you at the entrance of the tunnel on the Continental Trail south entrance in two days."

Bloody Bill looked at his men and then back at Vicky. "Why would I trust you? I need a guarantee we will not be hunted by your men, and you will deliver the gold."

"You will have my word, and you might want to consider the alternative of leaving here with nothing." She then pointed toward Dominique, "Or not leaving here at all."

"Have the gold brought to New Foundland."

Vicky realized Bloody Bill's plan and would take the gold and hide out in the Midlander territory. She knew her son had contacts in that area with a man named Vulture. "Like I said, I will have the gold delivered to you at the southern entrance of the tunnel on the Continental Trail in two days. This is an open area which is safe for all of us."

"I have lost one man lying in the street. I need additional compensation. I demand twelve pounds of gold." He pointed at the man Dominique shot in the back.

Her jaws were now clenched, "I have lost more than you. He is collateral damage. My husband and daughter-in-law are Bluebloods the same as Dominique." Vicky had just realized that Bloody Bill did not know Dominique was an untrained Blueblood warrior. She pointed toward Dominique, "You will lose all your men and maybe your own life, but if you do survive, you also might wish to consider, my son was the general over the Northern Army. He fought next to Midlanders. There is no place you can hide that they cannot find you." She knew she needed to bluff. "I do not believe Barney's two men will be successful in poisoning my men. My husband is one of the few Bluebloods that was gifted the soothsayer ability. He will see through the scheme. You need to consider my next offer very carefully. I will pay you nine pounds of gold and meet you at the south entrance of the Continental Trail. This is my final offer."

Bloody Bill smiled at Vicky realizing her offer had dropped by a pound. He then considered her statement. "It is a deal. We ride south." He motioned for his three archers and the other men standing guard around the city and at the church to leave. The three-swordsman facing Vicky also walked toward their horses.

Barney Simpson yelled, "You cannot leave. We had a deal. She knows where the gold is located. I will share the profits of the sale of the kids. I swear this to you."

"We just got a better deal. Her soldiers on the mission in the west will return. They will hunt all of us down and kill us. You never mentioned kidnapping kids, or the fact there was a Blueblood in this village we would have to kill." The men with Bloody Bill walked to their horses and rode south.

Buna, a dark skin man, came from behind the fourplex. Vicky had heard a man cry out, and she turned to see a man standing with blood on his shirt, "My son is dead. He is lying in the snow dead. You lied to us. You said the gold would be given to us, and no one would get hurt. Yet you brought him and his brother." He pointed at Sie's two sons, one of which was dead and the other injured. "You knew what they were capable of doing. You did not mention kidnapping the kids. I am going to bury my son. The hell with you." Buna threw his sword to the ground and walked back to the rear of the fourplex.

Vicky looked at Barney and commanded, "It is over."

The other soldiers looked around and lowered their weapons. They dropped them to the ground to surrender. Barney yelled, "It is not over. Her men on the mission west will all be killed by now. They will all be poisoned and dead. They will make contact with the newly forming government in the west, and I will reach an agreement with them."

Vicky was now staring at Barney who was standing over Delores. She clenched her jaws and ran toward him. She swung her right hatchet and then her left hatchet driving Barney backward as he recoiled from the swings. As he stepped backward from her and the recoil of the hatchet, he could not stop her momentum. He kept blocking her multiple swings. On her fifth swing, she acted as if she would swing for a mid-body strike but ducked low and swung her right hatchet low connecting with his ankle, forcing him to the ground. She then raised up and swung her left hatchet hitting him in the right forearm. She stood over him as she held her right hatchet in a threatening position as he could no longer raise his arm to defend himself. He dropped his sword. "Go ahead and kill me."

Her jaws were still clenched, "I am not going to kill you. I am going to arrest you, and you will answer for the crimes you have committed. I will show you I do grant people a fair trial, but do not get your hopes up asking for mercy. The newly forming government you are referring is a cult led by people designed in a lab with ability and desire to kill all of us. You have confessed to treason."

Vicky could then hear horses running as she looked to the south and saw ten of her guards returning from their watch at the gate on the gorge trail leading to the New York Tribe. She yelled, "Arrest them." The guards immediately jumped from their horses and forced the men from Meadow Bottoms to the ground.

One of her guards searched the men and made certain the injured combatants did not have additional weapons. He forced Barney and Sid's son onto their stomachs while forcing them to stay on the ground.

Vicky went to Delores's side and held her while crying. Her friend was dead. She looked up and saw Wayne and others walking out of the church. She could tell Wayne was injured as Casey and her daughter, Jessie, were holding him as they walked toward her. Wayne was hunched over to one side holding his right arm as the three walked. She could see the blood stains on his shirt and was thankful he was alive. She glanced at the north side of the fourplex and could see her other dead friend, Mia, with an arrow protruding through her chest and out her back. She then glanced at the Blacksmith Shop and felt for the loss of her old friend Little Jimmy.

***

Wayne noticed the guards returning from the gate at the gorge between the New York Tribe territory and Cliff Tops and knew the pigeon carrying the message had in fact delivered the note. He felt relief for the realm. As he announced to the prisoners in the church, "They are lying down their weapons. We must defend our Queen."

Casey opened the door to the church and held the dead soldier's sword in front of her as she walked out the doors. She then motioned for her daughter to assist Wayne as she watched the Queen attack Barney Simpson with Barney falling to the ground and then the Queen standing over him with her two hatchets held firmly above him. One of the elderly men rushed by Casey toward the open area and picked up a sword from a dead guard and stood over Sie's injured son.

# Chapter 24

Queen Vicky felt her rage at the thought of the insurrection led by men from Meadow Bottoms. Her son had tried to warn her about the people in that community and told her she needed to confront them with force. She thought, "I have accepted the death of my citizens and was force to make the speeches to the survivors. I have disliked the uncomfortable emotional process of going to eleven separate accepting of friends ceremonies and eleven separate funerals. All this happened because I did not listen to my son. Being kind does not always work. Being unprepared for the attack was all my fault."

Wayne stood with his arm in a sling at the cemetery next to the Queen. The people had gathered and now were disbursing after paying their respects for the last person to be buried. Wayne noticed the Queen was in deep thought. "My Queen, the community is grieving for the death of our citizens. Eleven people were killed by the revolutionary men from Meadow Bottoms. The burial service is now complete for the dead. The guilty have been interrogated and other names have been provided on who conspired with the murderous scum who lived in Meadow Bottoms. We know who they are, and where they live. What are your orders?" Vicky watched the men lower

Delores's body into the grave. She remembered what her friend had said right before she died. "Round up the guilty and hang them." She placed her hand gentle on Wayne's back and could tell he was in constant pain from being shot. She had noticed his face reflected a cringe from the pain every time he seemed to move. "I must make some decisions. Some you will agree with and some you will not, but I expect them to be carried out." She turned and walked toward her home.

\*\*\*

Vicky looked at Quincy once they were near the end of the large tunnel as the sunlight was beaming into the entrance, he turned and peered behind them to verify if anyone was following them. He then shifted trying to see further ahead of them as they approached the exit. "Quincy, there is no reason to be nervous. Bloody Bill is the one who should be nervous, not us."

"Yes, my Queen, but according to the report from Zorro, Bloody Bill has over one hundred men under his control. He and his men have killed thousands of Normand soldiers during the war. They are killers."

The two rode slowly out of the south end of the tunnel leading to The Midnight Hole. The sunlight was bright as several people were working with the livestock pulling wagons of lumber. Two teams of mules were lined up preparing to transport lumber north through the tunnel to the New York Tribe. They both adjusted their eyes to the bright sun as they emerged from the darkness of the tunnel. Vicky noticed men dressed like bounty hunters to her left with bows hanging over their backs and swords strapped to their sides, and then she recognized Bloody Bill slowly emerging from the congested corral area over three-hundred yards west of their location near the large herd of cattle and cowboys. She recognized the dark brim hat as Bloody Bill was riding his black horse forward toward her. She motioned for Quincy to stop and wait next to her.

Bloody Bill and three of his men came forward and stopped their horses facing Vicky. Vicky could see additional men stationed at several locations near the corral, the lumber yard, and the road leading west to New Foundland. At first no one spoke, as Vicky was staring at Bloody Bill. He finally said, "I am glad you made the trip."

She responded, "You look surprised that I am here."

Bloody Bill considered the statement and hesitated as he gestured with his right hand he was surprised. He studied Vicky and then glanced at the one rider next to her, "I am surprised you did not ride with a patrol or maybe the Blueblood. Did you bring the gold as you promised?" He glanced behind her and then around looking for a trap. "Did you have any problems coming through the New York territory?" He just realized the Queen was with only one other man. She was not guarded, and word would have spread about her traveling with the gold. Talk of the attempted coup had spread through the north region. He studied the situation and concluded the people of the area respected her or feared her. He set his gaze on her and noticed her beautiful appearance and how her riding clothes were tight and appealing for a man to notice. He also noticed she seemed confident and unafraid. He then also reaffirmed his future position of having to become a fugitive in the world.

"I have kept my word. I did not have any issues with my travel. I do have the gold promised to you. However, Bloody Bill, you might wish to reconsider the terms of the agreement before you accept the gold, and also Zorro wanted to accompany me with his army. We have an alliance, and he very much wanted to kill you and your men. The Blueblood you speak of is awaiting further orders. She likewise wanted to attack you and your men and kill every last one of you." She stared at Bloody Bill.

Bloody Bill looked at the saddlebags on the back of her horse. He hesitated, "You and this one soldier rode here to meet me alone carrying all this gold without a patrol escort? Why?"

"Because I could. We did come alone. I know you used the hidden trail from Meadow Bottoms to the Midlander Territory and then traveled down the road southeast from New Foundland. You might want to consider your next decision very carefully. I brought you the gold as I promised." The two stared at each other, "These people know my husband is a Blueblood. I am protected at all times. His wrath would be unmerciful if he is provoked. In addition, my son knows who you are and what you look like. My son, as a matter of fact, knows Midlanders and fought next to them in the wars of the south. They will be beholden to him. You will not be able to spend this gold because my posse will be able to track you. You will not be able to hide from my men. You might wish to consider the fact that you and your men will be tracked down and killed at my command. You cannot hide in the Normand controlled territory and if you are caught spending Merlin made gold in their territories, they will kill you. So, unless you are willing to relocate to Asia, I would suggest another alternative."

"You are assuming the bastard Simpson did not have your husband and son killed. They might already be dead. You know I knew nothing about his plan to sell the kids to the Normand army, or a plan to kill your son and his men. I swear this to you. My men knew nothing of this."

Vicky glanced at the other three riders and then the two stared at each other. He then asked, "What are your terms?"

Vicky did not lose her focus. "My terms are straight forward. You and your men will do what they do best. I will give you the nine pounds of gold, and in exchange, you and your men will work for me."

Bloody Bill could not hide his surprise, "You are hiring us?"

"Yes. You and your men will fight for me and with my army against the Merlin Army as they approach from the west through the Midlander Territory in the spring of next year. This money is payment as a retainer for your services as mercenary soldiers to fight in Cliff Tops Army. In return, I will make certain you and your men are not hunted and killed by my people."

# Chapter 25

Wayne was in constant pain as he sat in Doc Johnson's home. "I believe, as I was falling forward toward the door, I lifted my arm to brace for the fall and must have damaged the rotator cuff in my shoulder. Being shot by the arrow felt like someone hit me with a hammer, and now I cannot move my arm. The pain runs all the way down to my fingers." The Doc raised and lowered his arm and moved his arm back and forth. Wayne endure the pain with each move of his arm as his face reflected a cringe expression. Wayne said, "Give me the news in plain terms."

Doc Johnson looked sadly at Wayne, "The cause of the pain is not a rotator cuff tear in the shoulder. I am sorry. The Axillary Nerve has been lacerated. I do not have the ability to repair the nerve damage. Your arm is dead. It will hang to your side, and you will not have use of your arm. You must learn to deal with the habit of pain."

Both men looked sad at the news. "I understand. Dammit, I must wear this sling to hold my right arm in place. I am right-handed. I wish my left arm had been the one injured. The nerve hurts. I always have a throbbing pain."

Doc Johnson was watching Wayne and observing his mood and understanding the news. "The sling will hold your arm in position. You will never have the use of your arm. Keeping the arm still and in place will keep the shoulder from movement which moving your arm could cause you to have phantom pain. The nerve in your arm is dead, but the nerve running through your shoulder still sends the pulse sensation. You will always have to deal with the phantom pain. If you can keep your arm stationary in a sling and do not move your shoulder, this should lessen the nerve pain. Movement will cause the nerve in your shoulder to try to send impulses down your arm even though the nerve is lacerated."

Wayne walked out of the Doctor's home and headed to the fourplex. He tried to accept his horrific news. As he walked into the kitchen, he looked at Vicky, "The arrow fired by the soldier cut the Axillary Nerve and damaged the muscle. The nerve in my shoulder is permanently damaged, and I will never have the use of my right arm."

She hugged him, "I am sorry, but I need you. I have lost three of my best friends, and I pray my son, his friends and my husband are alright. I do not know what I would do if I lost you."

"I know what you would do. My Queen, you are my friend, you would survive and raise those grandkids and your two daughters. They will be your legacy."

***

Three days later Wayne walked into the church. The folks all looked upset and were still recovering from the insurrection. Vicky looked at Wayne. She felt for her friend. He had been through a lot over the years. "It has been three days. I plan to pass my sentence on these seven men."

Wayne looked mad, "I hope you provide them no mercy. They all should be tried as an adult and hung. We do not have the resources in our jail to house them for an extended period."

Wayne then announced, "We have the names of the people in Meadow Bottoms who supported the insurrection. A few of the captured prisoners have cooperated with a little bit of persuasion." Wayne knew how Vicky felt about brutalizing prisoners.

Vicky waited for Wayne to complete his report, "First, I will place Casey on the board in the vacancy created by the loss of our friend Little Jimmy. I have promoted Quincy to supervisor of the guards and the protection of Cliff Tops. He will also be on the board replacing Delores. Quincy is the surviving city night guard, and I trust him. I will delegate him the responsibility to hire additional guards to protect us. His title will also be the sheriff, and he and his men will keep order in my realm. Quincy and I agreed, he would be paid a gold coin every month for his service and the guards he hires will be paid on a lesser schedule. I will double the tax rate for Meadow Bottoms and spend the money on establishing a full-time army with all the men and women in my realm supporting the army in a temporary manner. We will also increase the selling price of our items being sold to the New York Tribe. I will tell Zorro to use the money to maintain an army and that army will also be used to assist him if they are ever attacked. Now, as far as my judgement on the guilty men, we will move them to Meadow Bottoms where we will hang them by the neck until they are dead. This will take place at four P.M. tomorrow. The people of Meadow Bottoms will be forced to bury the guilty. Their people."

Wayne asked, "What about Bloody Bill?"

Vicky looked at Wayne. "Quincy and I met with Bloody Bill. He took the gold. I in turn, hired him to fight for us. He will be an asset."

Wayne could not hold back his surprise. He blurted out, "He was part of this murderous plot. He needs to be hunted down, tried, and hanged."

"He knows, if Dak and Samuel are still alive, they would hunt him down and kill him. We still have a war to fight, and I need soldiers. His men are true warriors, plus he will hire additional men. Together we will forge a large army. He has contacts with Midlanders, and we need their assistance to fight on their soil. I was forced to make concessions. Those terms were agreed upon when I told him he could not hide."

Wayne looked perplexed, "What about Dak?"

Vicky looked at her friend of many years, "I will name Dak as the king in waiting for my realm. I will expand my board of directors to include Hulk and Trey. I will make Robin Hood and Tommy Boy employees of the court and Federal Marshalls in my Realm. I will grant them the ability to be lethal when they deem the action necessary."

Wayne knew Dak had made his home south at Zenith Point and his friends were his business partners. He knew the Queen would have considered those facts. "Yes, my Queen."

***

Wayne announced, "Most of the men have been called back to our city. The twenty men stationed at the gate and the gorge to monitor the security of the passage have returned. The gate has been closed, and they are not allowing anyone to cross into our territory. The men who went seal hunting have returned. The miners have all returned. The city is protected."

Vicky ordered, "We will leave at once."

The fifty soldiers rode in tandem with Eric of Newport leading the column followed by Vicky and Quincy. The seven men from Meadow Bottoms who were found guilty of insurrection and murder were sitting in the wagon with their hands and legs bound. They had not been told their sentence, and a couple looked hopeful when they heard the news they were being returned to Meadow Bottoms. Only the city council members and Quincy, the newly promoted sheriff and his deputies were aware of Vicky's plan. Quincy had been fast to hire five additional deputies, and each understood the punishment for the men in the wagon. He had also hired forty additional men to assist with the hanging of the prisoners and the pending arrest of the guilty. The soldiers accompanying the group were given the names of the other people that would be arrested, and they were going to apprehend them after the sentence of the seven individuals was carried out.

As they rode into the city of Meadow Bottoms, the town's people came out of the cottages and store fronts to watch the soldiers. No one was aware of what to anticipate. The wind was cold, and the day looked bleak with dark clouds. The people in the community heard stories of what had occurred in Cliff Tops, but the punishment of the men being arrested was all kept quiet. While in Cliff Tops, the prisoners were kept in isolation without being permitted an opportunity to have visitors.

The soldiers all took their position at the exterior of the circle around Meadow Bottom's interior city, and the sheriff and deputies rode next to Vicky. Vicky did not dismount from her horse and announced, "These men from your community have been found guilty of murder and insurrection. I have buried my friends and citizens. Now I must deal with the ones found guilty of murder." She looked at the faces of the audience. "Ladies and

Gentlemen, you might choose to take your kids inside. My court will carry out the punishment for these men, and since these men are from your village, they will be punished here in your village. I want you to see what happens when laws are broken in my realm."

Quincy walked to the oak tree and threw a rope with a noose around the tree limb. He held the noose and then tied the long end of the rope to the bottom of the tree. The other city guard who was decapitated was Quincy's best friend. The two men had survived the wars, the B12 virus, and the rest of the mayhem which occurred in the Transitional Period. Both men had felt blessed every day and now Quincy's best friend had been killed. He was not interested in being merciful. He felt anger for the loss of his friend being executed in the snow-covered road in front of the Queen's residence.

The four newly hired deputies forced the men to stand in a line in the wagon and then step down to the mud-covered ground. The wagon was then taken and parked in the open area. Quincy motioned for the first man to be escorted to the noose. Vicky recognized the dark skin man, Buna, who had lost his son. She felt sad for his loss, but she had lost several friends. He was forced to step up on the bench and then stand on the three-foot-high stool. Quincy looked at Vicky, and she motioned her head. The deputy pulled the stool from under the man and the drop broke his neck.

The townspeople were surprised with the first hanging, and how fast the hanging took place. The deputies released the rope, and the body was dropped to the ground. The next man was motioned to walk forward. He was the man who had tried to climb to the balcony, and the Queen had cut off four of his fingers. He tried to fight back as he resisted walking to the noose. The three deputies carried him to the stool and placed the noose around his neck. The fourth deputy pulled the man off the ground in the air, and the stool was placed under his swinging feet. He was gasping for a breath. When the hanging man stabilized himself on the stool, Quincy looked at Vicky. She again motioned her head. The deputy pulled the stool out from under the man and the drop of three-feet broke his neck. The man was left hanging until he was dead and then the next man was forced to the stool.

Vicky watched this man walk toward the noose as he was the man who stabbed Walter and then threw his body over the cliff. She thought of Walter and how he was the oldest resident in her community, and he tried to help the people working as guard. He also contributed to the community in the church and was a helpful beacon for the people with his faith in the Lord. She was glad to watch him hang.

Sie's widow walked into the street and started to approach as her oldest son was then led to the stool. He was assisted by the guards with him limping on his injured leg. Sie's widow yelled,

"You have no right." She turned and started to protest and was turning to seek help from the community. Vicky ordered, "Arrest her for treason, and she should be placed on the stool after her son. She deserves to watch her son die first."

Two of the soldiers ran into the street and forcibly grabbed her. She was forced to watch her son die while hanging on the end of the rope. She was then led to the stool and stepped up without fighting back or crying. Vicky watched her as she thought she had acted as if she accepted her death and seemed to be relieved, she was about to die. Vicky motioned her head, and the deputy pulled the stool out from under her.

The quietness was very noticeable in the crowd as they watch the people being hung. The last man was Barney Simpson. He limped to the stool and cried as the rope was placed around his neck. Vicky nodded her head for the stool to be removed, and his neck broke on the drop.

Vicky turned to the people. We have confessions from all these men. We know there are others. When I call your name, come forward, so we can hang you. Some of the people tried to run. The guards were watching the ones on the list and positioned themselves to arrest them. They were carried and pushed to the street. Each had their hands tied behind their backs. Six additional people were hung, including the preacher.

Vicky turned to the citizens. "Because of this crisis, I have elected a sheriff and deputies. I will establish an army where the citizens of my realm will serve as I command. I have passed the laws that will be obeyed. Your taxes have just doubled because of this increased burden you place on my government. You do not own any of this land. I own the land. I own all the cattle and sheep. You will pay rent for these homes. If you do not like the rules, you need to leave. If you do not pay, you will be placed in jail. I will name a custodian to be in charge of Meadow Bottoms, and he or she will govern you. You will be required to work, or you will be forced to leave. Now, you may bury your dead."

# Chapter 26

Zenith looked at Dak, "I hope this works the first time. I do not want to stay here any longer than we must. I very much would like to take a warm bath, eat at a nice restaurant, and sleep in a warm bed."

Dak glanced at Zenith as they walked toward the apex of the mountain, "I wish we could have spent additional time observing their habits. They have us outnumbered maybe as much as four to one. We are not certain how many Bluebloods we must kill. Everyone is having trouble with staying focused. We are all worried about what has happened back at Cliff Tops. I just do not know if we are ready for the assault. We need more intel on the Dark Master. He would have an escape plan and an alternative living arrangement. He knows the first-generation Bluebloods would force a coup in Merlin and hunt him if he is discovered. This situation is similar to the second battle south of Harpers Ferry Harbor with King Solman after we lost the Waldo Bridge. This plan is not a good plan, but this plan is the only plan I have. I am certain I will be second guessed with this plan just like I was with the Battle of Waldo Bridge."

Zenith smiled at Dak knowing he was jabbing back at her, "I do not believe you will be second guessed by anyone with this plan. This strategy is so bad, I doubt there will be any of us left alive to tell the story."

Dak smiled at his wife. She then said, "I bought your speech to the men not to worry about things we cannot change. The group we left in charge at Cliff Tops were highly trained agents from the old world. They should have handled the conflict."

Dak turned to Zenith, "I am thankful you like something I did. Also, I Thank God for Boudica. She observed the obvious which the rest of us missed. That would have been my fault. The assassins were holding out until we located the Dark Master, so they could have worked out a deal. They would have killed every one of us. Do the people of Meadow Bottoms hate me and the Queen so much they would make a deal with the devil?"

"I believe they hate you and your mother because they desire the power and wish to control her realm. They are greedy and power hungry. They keep telling the others the same story and finally the good people of Meadow Bottoms started believing them. That is the way propaganda works." Zenith looked forward along the trail and then at Hulk who had just caught up with their pace, "We will ascend the backside and then cross over the gorge like we did yesterday."

Dak announced, "We released all our horses. There is no turning back. What a great plan I have." Zenith smiled and kept walking.

Hulk pulled his hood off, "I am burning up with all these clothes. As we move along the backside of the mountain we will be out of the direct wind."

Dak looked at his friend as he walked faster trying to lead the way, "You will need those clothes once we lie in the cold wind and wait on the mission to start. We will have to wait on the others to proceed to the ocean and then cut across the open area to the front of the fort. My friend, you need to stay warm." The five walked out the east side of the ridge leading to the cliff. Dak led the way and followed the path he and Zenith had used the prior day. Dak used the rope he and Zenith had left and dug his spikes into the ice and crossed over to the same position he laid the prior day. Boudica watched as Dak had to pull himself over the ice-covered ledge while his boots held his position on the ice-covered cliff. "This is not the route I took years ago. I was up here in the summer. There was no ice."

Hulk and Billy Ray looked at the frightened eyes of Boudica. As Zenith dug her spikes into the ice and grabbed the rope, Billy Ray asked, "Can you do this?"

Billy Ray knew the answer before he asked the question. He recognized the fear of heights and falling with her facial expression, and her body was stiff, and her movements were insecure. Hulk asked, "Which route did you take? Dak's plan is for us to repel down the face of the cliff. He figures that is the fastest path, and we must be in position quickly as the other men are moving forward with the mission."

"I must do this." She started to fall on the ice-covered snow. Billy Ray held her. "You will not be able to cross." The three watched as Zenith pulled herself over the ledge.

Hulk looked at his father. "She can hang on my back, and I can get her across to the ledge. Dak can then reach her and pull her over the top." He then looked at Boudica, "Once you cross over you must repel down the face of the cliff. There is no way for you to come back across by yourself with the face of the cliff covered in ice. I would suggest you return to your village."

Her expression turned to determination, "I am not returning to my village." She clenched her jaws, "You can assist me with crossing this ice cliff and help me to the landing. I will repel down the cliff."

Billy Ray said, "We must hurry." He looked at Boudica, "Do not look down. I will tie a rope to you and hold the rope. If you lose your grip, you will not fall. I will have you." He then waved to Zenith and signaled that Boudica would need assistance.

Boudica closed her eyes as she held tightly to the straps on Hulk's backpack. She could feel Billy Ray tying the rope around her waist. Hulk had turned his backpack around, so the pack was in the front and his straps were on his back for her to grasp. He knew he would need to move fast across the gorge. He knew his strength could not support both of them hanging on the cliff longer than a couple of minutes.

Dak watched from the perch on the top of the mountain as his warriors took their position. Dak pointed out the route to Zenith they would take as they descended the cliff part of the mountain. "We will be in the open as we descend the cliff. We must hurry and hopefully will go unseen as we approach the fort. We hope the guards at the rear will move to the front, or we will have to scale the wall of the fort and fight our way inside. Once we are at the bottom of the cliff, we can stay hidden in the trees and large boulders. Here we go." Dak held the small mirror in the sunlight and gave a quick response with the reflection. He then noticed the signal from Trey.

Zenith dug her spikes into the ice as she also drove her knife into the snow-covered ice and held her position as she watched Hulk take his first step. Zenith could tell Hulk was trying to compensate for the extra weight on his back. "Hulk, you need to dig your spikes in and try to step where we have already created foot holds." Hulk's front foot slipped, and he struggled to hold his position.

Dak noticed no one had responded to his announcement of his plan. He turned and saw that Zenith was over twenty-feet away from him and now lying on the side of the top of the ledge holding onto her knife with one hand as the knife was wedged into the ice-covered slope. The spikes on her feet were dug into the ice below her. "What are you doing?"

Zenith looked at Dak, "They are having trouble."

Dak moved over next to his wife as he peered over the ledge. In a harsh tone, "We Must hurry. I have flashed the signal."

Billy Ray kicked his spikes into the ice and drove his knife into the ice at chest level and moved quickly into the gorge and repeated his movements and eased out and grabbed Boudica. "Hulk, I got her. You need to place the spike on your front foot into the ice and secure your position. Then move forward. I will move next to you and then you can reach back and pull Boudica to you. Do not waste time. You must hurry. Hulk felt the body weight of Boudica shift from his back. He immediately kicked his spike into the ice and maneuvered across the clear ice cliff. He dug his other foot into the snow-covered ice once he cleared the clear ice spot. He turned and reached back for Boudica's hand.

Billy Ray in a gentle voice, "Sweetheart, you must reach for Hulk. He will pull you across to him and then he will be able to proceed a few steps to Dak's position." Boudica opened her eyes and looked down at the five-hundred-foot drop. She initially froze in place as she looked close to twelve feet away at Dak lying above Zenith waiting on her. Billy Ray said, "Do as I say. You can do this. Sweetheart, reach now for Hulk." She could feel the freezing-cold wind blow into her face. Her hands were so cold her fingertips were hurting inside her gloves. She could tell Billy Ray was straining to hold her with one arm as he must have been holding himself to the side of the clear ice cliff with his other hand, his knife wedged into the ice cliff.

She slowly reached her left hand toward Hulk. He reached her wrist and said, "Boudica when I pull you, you will need to grab the straps on my back and hold yourself in place. We can do this."

"I cannot do this. Let me drop. Please let me drop."

Billy Ray whispered in a calm voice, "Sweetheart, on three. One, two, three."

Boudica reached for the strap with her left hand and as Hulk pulled her between himself and the cliff. She reached for his left shoulder and then placed her right arm around his neck and pulled her right leg around his back and was now facing Hulk. Hulk glanced at her face and noticed her eyes were now closed, and her face was red from the bitter wind. Her expression was one of apprehension. Hulk had predetermined his next two steps before Boudica ended up in his lap. He immediately took two fast steps to his left as he moved toward Dak. "Keep your eyes closed," he whispered. Hulk tried to look down to verify the next good step as he was looking for the foot faults Dak and Zenith had created. Boudica was blocking his vision of being able to locate the next step.

Dak noticed Hulk could not look down because he could not lean back any further as he held tight to the knife. "Hulk, move your left foot two inches further. There is a solid step," Dak announced.

Hulk moved his foot and wedged the spikes on the toe of his boot in place. He then repositioned his hand and moved across the cliff another fourteen inches. "I cannot look down. I am flying blind. Where is my next step?"

This time Zenith announced, "You have a step at six inches and then one at two-feet." She watched Hulk move six inches. "You got it." Hulk moved another six inches. He then stretched his foot two feet and was trying to locate the next foot placement. Dak announced, "You got it."

Hulk made the next four steps and was close to the ledge. As he tried to reposition his knife, his right foot slipped. Hulk felt the fear as he started to slide. Boudica yelped in fear as Hulk suddenly moved. She could tell they were about to fall. Hulk was straining with his boot and the spike on his left boot to secure his position. As Hulk was desperately trying to dig the spikes on the right foot back into the ice cliff and also slam the knife into the ice cliff above him, he lost his grip on his knife as the knife blade ricocheted backward from the wall of ice. He dropped the knife. He tried to ram his fingers into the snow and ice desperately trying to locate something to grasp to stabilize himself. He was now holding on with only his fingers dug into the cliff as Boudica was preventing him from moving closer to the cliff.

Hulk heard the gentle voice of his father, "Boudica, I got you. You need to switch back to me. I have a good hold. My spikes are dug into the ice. I am a little below your position which will make it easier on you." Hulk heard the uninspected direction of his father. He did not realize his father had not waited. Hulk felt his left hand about to slip.

Boudica opened her eyes and looked back at Billy Ray. He was close to one foot below their level. She did not hesitate as she could tell Hulk was about to fall. She reached for Billy Ray and wrapped her arms over his shoulders and held on the straps of his backpack as she positioned herself high on his back. "Okay. I got her. Hulk you can reach back and retrieve my knife. I have a second one. Hulk knew his left hand would not hold him. He also knew he must reach back with his right hand and grab his father's knife. Hulk turned his head looking for the knife and as he moved his left hand to hold where his right hand was holding, he simultaneously moved his right hand back across the ice wall and grabbed the knife handle wedged into the ice wall. He then held his position and took a deep breath but knew he must hurry. He pulled the knife and moved across the ice wall and over the ledge. Billy Ray said, "With her on my back like she is now, I can see to make the steps. I will get her to the ledge."

Hulk pulled himself over to the ledge and Dak helped him over the top lip of the rock. Hulk crawled over next to Zenith and laid on his back and rested. Billy Ray moved across the Cliff and Dak reached down and pulled Boudica over the ledge. He then helped Bill Ray over the ledge. Dak did not waste time he crawled over next to Zenith, "What is happening?"

Zenith did not change her position holding the binoculars, and in an urgent tone, "They are moving forward ahead of schedule. We need to be ready. Trey and Tommy Boy are closing in on their position at the corral. I can now see Robin Hood. He and Samuel are walking their horses toward the front gate. They are not waiting for our second signal."

Billy Ray crawled next to Dak, "Let me see." Zenith handed the binoculars in front of Dak to Billy Ray. He lifted the Binoculars and held them steady as he moved his vision to the exterior. He noticed Samuel riding a pale horse as he and Robin Hood approached the front road heading to the castle. "Dammit. I never thought I would quote Revelation. 'I looked, and there was a pale-colored horse. Its rider was named Death and Hell followed.' We need to prepare ourselves for death. That is a damn army we have elected to fight today."

Dak said, "May our Lord be with us."

\*\*\*

Zenith watched through her binoculars, "Here we go. The start of the mission. Tommy Boy is in position." She watched as Tommy Boy raised up from behind the bushes and fired his arrow hitting the cult guard watching the cattle. Trey likewise eased through the cattle herd and shot the other guard as he was distracted by Samuel and Robin Hood as they approached the front of the fort. A twenty-foot section of the fence along the outskirts of the field, away from the fort was then pulled down as Tommy Boy threw his rope around the rail and post and then rode down the hill pulling the fence. Trey chased the cattle and horses forcing a stampede out of the corral.

"I can now see Samuel and Robin Hood riding to the front gate. Both have pulled their hoods back and have fired their arrows, killing the two front guards stationed outside the closed front gate."

The lieutenant inside the fort walked into the inner office, "Sir, our guards have reported we are under attack. Our cattle and horses have been stampeded, and the two guards stationed at the corral are dead. What are your orders?" He bowed his head and waited.

The Master looked up from his lunch. He was surprised. "How many combatants?"

Sir, there were two men who killed our men watching the livestock and ran the livestock toward the shore. They have ridden around to join the other men in the front of our fort.

There were two more men who rode up close to our front gate and killed the two gate guards. There are several men who appear to be waiting to attack out of range of our arrows. The gates are locked." The lieutenant bowed his head.

The Master looked in thought as he turned to his two Blueblood guards. He started to give an order when the lieutenant announced, "Sir, the one man in front appears to be a Blueblood." He bowed his head.

The Master jumped up and slapped the lieutenant as he reached for his sword. "The next time you will mention the part about the Blueblood first. Now follow me."

The four men walked quickly to the second story platform around the front of the fort which provided a view over the road leading to the fort. The Master glanced down and saw the two gate guards lying dead from arrows. He noticed the livestock were missing and a portion of the corral fence was destroyed. He could see Samuel sitting on his white stallion in the front of the men. He counted eighteen men. "They know where we are. They are going to try to starve us out." He turned to the Blueblood warrior on the right. "Send a rider to Tanger to notify the sheriff, we need his help. Have them send their army. Take the men and crush them. I want their heads, and the body of the Blueblood leader."

"Yes sir. The men are in the barracks resting from the morning training. Sir, most of our horses have run off. So, you are ordering us to attack on foot?"

"Yes. Take the rest of the horses in the stables, but you must attack! Crush our enemy." The two Rogue Bluebloods ran to the ladder and quickly descended to the ground and ordered, "Sound the alarm."

Once the men came out of the barracks, they lined up for inspection. "We will kill all who have attacked us. Bring their heads to the Master." The ten front linemen mounted the horses, and the rest marched out the gate. They lined up and stood in attack position. The Rogue Blueblood ordered, "Attack."

The horse soldier ran the horses toward Samuel and the others followed on foot. All were screaming the battle cry.

Trey ordered, "Load your arrows. We need to make this look good."

Trey waited for the horse riders to advance to forty meters, "Fire." All the men released their arrows.
The arrows hit the shields of the riders, and the horses. A few of the men fell off the horses when the horses buckled from arrows.

Trey ordered, "Reload and fire at will. Take the horses out. We want them on the ground." Robin Hood, Samuel, Tommy Boy and the other soldiers all aimed for the horse's front legs. Once the arrows hit the legs of the horses, the horses would buckle and fall with the riders falling headfirst onto the ground.

The men kept firing the arrows hitting the men fast approaching. The Blueblood leader stood from the ground as he watched his horse limp away. He yelled, "Attack. The Master has ordered you to kill these soldiers." The foot soldiers were closing in as they fast approached across the open area.

Trey saw the horses start buckling from the arrows. The soldier in front of Trey stood and ran toward him while yelling the battle cry. Trey had never heard such a loud high pitch scream. He loaded his bow and fired his arrow, hitting the soldier. Trey quickly loaded another arrow and was preparing to locate another target. He could see the large number of men approaching on foot across the field. He quickly rotated back to the soldier in front of him that stood and came at him with his sword pulled, still screaming the loud pitched scream. Trey noticed the man appeared to be psychotic with a very determined, demonic expression. He fired his arrow hitting the soldier in the chest. The soldier did not fall but still kept pushing forward toward Trey. Trey extended his bow like a sword and swung his bow and hit the man in the neck with the end of his bow. The man fell to the side and started bleeding from his neck. With two arrows and a wound to his neck from Trey's bow, he turned toward Trey and ran toward him screaming. Trey pulled his sword, stepped forward and decapitated the soldier. He looked at the soldier's head as the face turned upward with the eyes frozen open. Trey heard Samuel order, "Retreat."

\*\*\*

Dak looked at the others, "We need to be prepared and in position at the bottom of the cliff. He tied the rope end to the rock and dropped the rope to allow the rope to be unrolled down the face of the cliff. He looked at Zenith, "Let me know when they rotate the guards to the front of the fort." Zenith kept her focus watching through the binoculars.

Dak looked at Billy Ray, Zenith, Boudica and Hulk, "Our Lord be with us."

Hulk said a quick prayer and then looked at his father. He noticed his father never bowed his head in prayer. Hulk proclaimed, "I asked our Lord to watch over all of us. An angel never prays. Right, Dad?"

Billy Ray looked at his son, "We are going to do what is right. That is the way I raised you and your brother. You need to do what is right, always in life. You know what a sin is, and you know when you sin. Do not be loath with your actions. The Lord Jesus came to us to serve and not be served. You know I love you."

Boudica was lying still on the slope of the ice with her hands pressed against the snow holding herself in place. She was scared to move. She looked at Billy Ray and Hulk, "Thank you for helping me."

Zenith announced while scanning from the top of the mountain, "So far so good. They have charged out of the fort." She looked to Dak while taking her binoculars off, "Go ahead. The guards are all facing south. I see the Dark Master. He is watching from the top of the fort facing Samuel and our men. Your plan seems to be working. However, there are two additional Blueblood warriors that just appeared standing next to the Master."

Dak thought to himself his wife was joking with him about his plan and being second guessed and having nineteen percent chance of working. He smiled and then did not hesitate and descended the cliff. Hulk moved into position and started down the same rope before Dak had landed. Billy Ray did the same as Hulk and did not hesitate to descend the cliff. The three men dropped the two hundred feet in a few seconds. Zenith felt rushed. She noticed Boudica did hesitate. "Have you repelled?"

Boudica looked perplexed, "I can do this, but no I have never repelled."

Zenith jumped in front of Boudica, "Watch me. Straddle the rope and then bring the rope back around one leg and across your hip, then up over the opposite shoulder. Then, bring the rope across your back. Your left hand will be the brake hand. You need to position the left hand beside your hip." Zenith pushed off with her legs and let the rope slide through her gloves. She then stopped. See how the brake hand stopped me? I must hurry. The window for us to slip by their guards is small. You can stay here. My husband will not wait on me, and he will need my assistance. I cannot allow him to move on the Dark Master without me. You should have stayed behind. You are becoming a liability, and we cannot afford to babysit you." She backed over the side of the cliff and disappeared from Boudica's view.

Boudica did not move. The fear she felt had frozen her in position. She at first tried to move her left hand over and then she brought it back holding onto the knife wedged in the ice. She cried. "I cannot do this." She then glanced below and saw her feet with the spikes holding her in place. She then tried to lift her left foot and dig her spikes into the ice, but she was too scared to move. She was too terrified to look down at her feet again. The snow was lying above an ice-covered rock cliff. The slope was about thirty degrees down toward the cliff. She froze in position and struggled with the fear of falling as she laid on the slick surface, too scared to move. She cried as she thought of what Zenith had instructed her on the placement of the rope. She thought, "Why do I not just let go and slide off the cliff. Who would care if I died. My father mentioned he would cut my tongue out and my brother is now a soldier of the dead. I want to die." She started to release her hold and pick both her feet up. She then thought, "Dying be suicide is the cowards way out. I must die in battle. I came here to save my brother."

Zenith quickly descended the cliff. Billy Ray and Hulk were waiting on her. She unlaced the rope from around her and looked at Hulk, "She is staying at the top. She is scared. I must keep up with Dak. You know he is not going to wait on me."

Dak ordered, "Her staying at the top is for the better. Follow me. We must hurry. Our window of opportunity is closing."

Billy Ray said, "After the mission, I will come back up here and assist her getting down."

Hulk glanced upward toward the top of the cliff and could see the rope hanging down but could not see Boudica. He turned as they jogged down the trail jumping from rock to rock as the trail descended close to fifteen hundred feet in elevation. The trail turned back and forth at switchbacks leading to the fort. They followed the trail to within one-hundred-yards of the rear wall, staying hidden behind the large number of spruce pine trees and boulders. Dak could see the guards standing on the upper platform viewing from behind the top of the fort wall into wilderness. When the guard turned to walk the opposite direction, he motioned with his hand. Dak ran down the embankment and slid down the hill with the others following him. The four ran to the wall of the fort unnoticed. Wasting no time, Hulk threw the rope with the grappling hook, tested the rope, and bent down to hold the bottom of the rope tight. "The hook is holding." Dak did not hesitate as he ascended the wall.

He crouched down and looked for the enemy before he leaned over the wall and motioned for Zenith and the others to advance.

The guards were intrigued by the battle going on in the front of the fort. The two guards stationed on the rear of the fort heard their soldiers and the battle cries as the soldiers charged the combatants. The two walked to the eastside and then walked to the front and were observing from the top platform over the fort wall.

Once on the platform, Billy Ray led the way with Hulk following him. They loaded their bows and approached the guards on the west side of the platform. Billy Ray motioned for Hulk to stop next to him. Both men released their arrows hitting the two men in the back as they were watching the battle out in front of the fort. The arrows flew true, and the guard near the interior buckled and fell to the ground from the second level. The guard stationed on the ground level under the platform sounded the alarm when the one guard fell from the second story walkway with an arrow sticking through his torso.

Billy Ray then led the way toward the ladder and quickly approached the other guards on the platform. Suddenly, in front of Billy Ray, a man appeared climbing onto the balcony wearing a cape. He pulled his sword with his right hand and with his left hand he pulled back his hood, revealing his tattoo covered face, yellow teeth and pointed ears. Billy Ray released an arrow, which the man blocked with his sword. The man stood still and smiled a sinister smile. Billy Ray recognized he was facing a Rogue Blueblood warrior. He instantly took three steps backward, away from the Rogue Blueblood. Dak rushed by Billy Ray and took the position in the front, facing the Blueblood.

Zenith announced, "There is another one."

Zenith turned and walked behind Hulk with her sword pulled. She was now facing the second Rogue Blueblood.

Hulk ordered, "Over the rail." He jumped, then Billy Ray followed. The two Rogue Bluebloods approached with their swords pointed forward toward Dak and Zenith from the opposite ends of the balcony walkway.

*** 

Boudica took a deep breath, smiled, and decided what she must do. She quickly moved across the face of the sloped area to the rope and once the rope was in her hand she felt confident. She wrapped the rope around her waist as Zenith had explained and backed off the cliff. She was no longer scared. She removed the rope once at the bottom and ran down the path. As she approached the fort, she saw Hulk climb over the top of the wall. She tried to run faster as she knew she must hurry.

Hulk turned when he heard Boudica announce, "Star, I am Boudica, your sister. Do you remember?" Hulk saw the man standing between them and the door to the building. Boudica removed her hood and smiled with a gentle tone in her voice. "Star, I have come for you. I am sorry. I am going to take you home."

Hulk was surprised Boudica had caught up with them and she had come down the cliff by herself. He at first thought Star did not recognize his sister. Hulk said, "Stand back Boudica. He is lost." Hulk considered killing him if he approached her. The young man lowered his sword. Billy Ray, facing the other way, fought one quick moving guard and killed him with his sword. The second and third guard pressed the attack with additional men headed their way. Billy Ray whispered, "We need to do something, We cannot stay in the open. They have bows."

Boudica lowered her sword and walked to her brother, standing three feet in front of him. As he held his sword in front, she reached for his sword. He at first acted like he would release the sword. He then reacted aggressively and raised his sword and swung the sword right to left. Boudica reacted and pulled her sword in front of her and blocked the swing. Hulk did not hesitate and rushed Star, blocking the second swing of his sword. Then using his shoulder, he rushed Star, knocking him to the ground. Boudica yelled, "No!"

Hulk held his sword at Star's throat and turned and looked at Boudica.

"No. Let him up."

Hulk stepped backward watching Star. He knew he needed to keep up with his father. He then turned and followed Billy Ray, who had walked into the doorway behind Star. Boudica rushed to her brother's side. He did not respond. Hulk turned and ran back into the compound and grabbed Boudica's arm and pulled her through the door, closing the door behind them as two arrows stuck in the door. "We must leave. There are too many of them." He placed the wooden board across the face of the door locking the door shut.

"I am not going to leave my brother."

Hulk clenched his jaws, "He did not recognize you. He is gone. It is not him. We have a mission. I thought you were staying on the cliff. We were going to come back for you."

Star laid on the ground and his fellow guards attacked the door and tried to force the door open. A couple of the guards glanced at Star and noticed he appeared to be in a trance. His eyes were not blinking as he laid still on the ground, fixated on the sky above.

Boudica turned to Hulk with a determined look, "That is my brother. I came here to die for him. I overcame my fear because my fear of failure was greater. Now stay out of my way. I must do what I must."

Hulk looked just as determined, "He is too far gone. They will kill you. I cannot allow you to be killed. You are special." He stared into her eyes. "We must support Dak and Zenith."

Hulk then added, "I am sorry. He has been hypnotized. The only way to break the spell is to kill the master and provide the victim professional help."

Billy Ray then looked at Boudica, "Sweetheart, all these young men have been hypnotized. They will do what their master directs them to do. They are totally under his power. I have seen assassins in the old world placed under a trance, and this is the manner they behave. They are brainwashed and do what they are told to do." Billy Ray tilted his head toward the rear of the room. He thought he heard a noise from the hallway. He turned and disappeared as he ran through the interior door to the hallway.

Hulk could tell the door was about to give way from the men beating on the door with an ax. The last swing, the ax head could be seen cutting through the wood door. He pulled his bow. "We will need to make our stand here."

Billy Ray returned through the other door entrance. He raised his bow with a loaded arrow, "That leads to another room. The hallway is clear. I agree we make a stand here and then retreat into the other room which leads to the compound out front. Boudica, stand to the side and unlatch that door."

Boudica ran to the door and pulled the board lying across the backside upward and jumped into the corner as another swing of the ax hit the backside of the door. The door flew open. The soldiers were surprised and not prepared with their shields raised. Hulk fired his arrow and hit the young warrior in the forehead driving the arrow out the back of his head. Billy Ray released his arrow while aiming through the door opening and hit another man in the chest. Several men rushed through the door opening with their swords and spears. Hulk fired a second arrow hitting the third soldier as he was close to a foot away. Billy Ray dropped his bow and pulled his sword. He attacked the fourth man to break through the door opening. The men looked like mad dogs with their expressions and their demonic desire to kill. Additional men rushed into the room. Billy Ray traded swings with two men blocking each of their swings. He rotated fast and killed the one on the left and turned to the one on the right.

Hulk pulled his sword in his right hand and his long knife in his left and tried to take on the next three men. Hulk swung his sword and blocked the young man on the right. He then pivoted and stuck his knife through the man's chest. He stood and watched as the other soldier was about to release his spear when suddenly, the man took an arrow in the temple. The soldier fell dead. Hulk nodded to Boudica his thanks as he charged the third warrior. Billy Ray killed the soldier fighting him with a swing to the man's arm cutting to the bone and then his second swing hitting him in the neck. The last man held his spear straight and tried to stab Hulk. Hulk blocked the spear as the spear was being jabbed at him and then Billy Ray drove his sword through the man's neck.

***

Zenith could not force the Blueblood backward, but she refused to give ground. They stood toe to toe swinging and blocking each other's swords. She could sense the opponent's swing, whether the swing was right to left or left to right. She also could tell by the way he held his head where his next swing was coming. If his head shifted to the left, he would swing with his right arm and if he was going to swing with left arm, his head would shift to the right. Her training to be a Blueblood warrior had taught her to watch for the subtle hints of a warrior's techniques. She, however, could not penetrate past his sword. She knew she was in a stalemate and was concerned about Dak. She heard Dak and the other Blueblood fall from behind her from the six-foot-high-platform walkway to the compound dirt floor below. She swung three quick times right to left, left to right and then right to left and then retreated backward when all the swings were blocked. She saw Dak and the other Blueblood fighting to the death with neither getting the upper hand. She jumped to the compound below and waited for her adversary. Once he landed, they fought as hard as they could with both swinging their swords and long knives.

Billy Ray announced, "Follow me." Billy Ray started to leave as Hulk turned to Boudica. She announced, "I am going to check on my brother. Star needs me." Billy Ray ran past Hulk out the door and entered the main room of the interior building.

Hulk said, "Boudica." She turned and stared at him. "Please be careful. They will show no mercy. I must support Dak and Zenith. If they lose, we all will lose." He started to say no, but he realized she had made up her mind. He stood and watched as Boudica ran back out the door into the compound. He watched her go as he heard a thud sound. He turned to follow his father. He said, "Dammit. Wait on me."

Boudica bent down over her brother. She held him tight while she placed his sword out of his reach and then announced, "Let me take you home. Come and stand for me, little brother. I will show you the way out. He stood, and she helped him to the ladder. As he climbed the ladder, she turned to see if there were any threatening combatants. She saw Zenith and Dak fighting two men and other guards seeing her and Star standing on the upper fort walkway. She knew they needed to hurry and hoped no one would follow them. She tried to force Star to climb over the fort wall faster as they crossed the top of the wall and headed into the forest. She pulled him along the trail toward the mountain. "Please hurry. We must hurry brother. We will need to climb the cliff." She turned to verify if they were being followed.

After ascending close to fifty-yards, he turned and looked at her as if he did not remember who she was. The expression was one of someone confused as he stared at his sister. "Come on little brother. Please. I will take care of you." The arrow from the guard drove through Star's back and out his chest. He fell into Boudica's arms. Blood started to spill out his mouth.

Boudica cried and held her brother. He looked at her with his last breath, "Sister. Thanks for coming for me, but you must run. My time has come to an end."

She jumped behind a tree and then ran up the steep path. She could hear the soldier following her. She looked at the large mountain and decided to run no more. "It is time someone fought this evil. This man just killed my brother." The flash back of her father hiding behind his words as he and the tribe were too scared to fight rushed through her memory. She stepped behind the boulder and raised her sword while she waited. Boudica could hear the man as his feet stepped on the rocks and debris on the trail. As the soldier was running up the path his breathing became heavier. She knew he no doubt was pressing himself to cut her off before she made it to the cliff. Once she crossed the cliff, he knew he might not be able to catch her. He wanted a fast kill to impress his master. Failure was not acceptable, and he pushed harder as he could feel his lungs straining to take on air with each step. She could hear his steps getting louder and then she could hear his breathing. He appeared around the corner; she jumped out swinging down and struck him with her sword across his left arm. He seemed to be surprised with her decision to fight. He dropped his bow and pulled his sword with his right hand. The blade had cut deep to the bone in his forearm and the blood was dripping to the ground and across his shirt as his left arm hung limply.

Boudica pressed the attack from the high ground, forcing the soldier to back up as she swung her sword downhill with force. He lost his footing as he stumbled over the rocky ground and fell against the large boulder. She stood over him and hated him for killing her brother. She saw the look in his eyes of the realization he was about to die. Without hesitating, she swung her sword with enough force to drive her sword into his skull. She then looked at the dead man and felt vindicated. She thought she would be scared or feel sorrow, but she was surprised how satisfying she felt killing the soldier.

She immediately picked up the bow and arrows from the dead man and ran back down the fifty-foot steep trail to her brother and held him as he was now dead. "Please forgive me little brother. You were my responsibility. Star, I am so sorry." She cried, hugging Star.

# Chapter 27

Frank Jr. hated the thought of forcing the kids and Veronica to the island. He hated living in fear and the anxiety of hiding Veronica, her kids and guards from the sheriff of Tanger. "I have been to the island on fishing trips. The island is not more than a large rock sticking out of the surf with a small amount of shelter built from floating debris arriving from the ocean surf. The seagulls frequent the island, along with other birds. There was no shelter from the weather except the small shed-like structure." He also knew what his king and sheriff would do. "The sheriff will kill your guards and present as a gift you and the kids to the Dark Master."

Frank looked at Veronica, "I have risked everything for you and have asked nothing in return. I have watched you feed your baby. I have allowed you to take over my bedroom. I have provided your kids and your guards sanctuary."

Veronica looked at Frank Jr. "I have provided you with gold. What else would you have me do?"

Frank Jr. looked at Veronica, "I desire for you to share my bed with me."

"I am married." She could tell he did not care. As he was standing in front of her, he lifted both hands with his palms up.

Veronica knew she had no choice, and she did not hesitate. "I will be your concubine as long as you protect my kids, my guards, and myself. You will need to make certain your workers keep the secret. You will need to be honest with your employees and make them fight with you. I will pay them for their co-operation."

***

Frank Jr. looked at the men and women in the compound in front of his home, "We need to do what is right." He pointed his index finger to his chest, "I need to do what is right. I have kept something from you. I have kept something from all my employees. I have placed you in danger." He looked at the men and women. Some had worked for his father for years. Most had survived the Transitional Period and one way or another ended up in Tanger. They were happy to have survived with some family members who had also survived and relocated in Tanger. A few were younger men and women in their late teens and only knew of the old world from the stories of the survivors. Frank Jr. was not certain what they would do, however, he knew he had to tell them the truth. He announced, "My father, my brother, and I were the first to sail to this area and picked the best land to farm and ranch. Others heard of the area and soon the city grew, and now there are close to three thousand citizens. No one knows when the Dark Master arrived with his five Blueblood soldiers. The fort was built and then he started taking from us what he desired. The Dark Master set up treaties with the villages all the way to the Midlander camps on the other side of the great mountains. You know he had his men take our boys as soldiers. Yet, we did nothing to stop him. The villages and small cities in our district have learned fast how cruel and vicious the men were in the cult. We must fight this monster. I can no longer run. One of them killed my father and four of my friends. I am going to fight our king and not force a mother and her five children to run. I have kept this information from you. You may leave, or you can stay and fight with me." He looked at the men and his brother. "I have kept hidden, five small children and their mother, from our king and his sheriff. I have elected to fight for what is right." Veronica walked out on the front porch with her sword in the sleeve and stood facing the people.

One of the men said, "I have heard there are five Blueblood children you are hiding in the bunkhouse."

Michael, Viking, and Pretty Boy walked out with their battle clothing, armor, and weapons and stood next to Veronica. Hector and Cruzie walked out of the barn carrying their bows, with their armor on and swords in hand.

Veronica looked at the people, "My men and I killed Damon in Southern City. He was the Blueblood who killed your boss and four friends. What I ask of you will not be easy. I am the wife of King Solman. He is a renegade Blueblood, the same as the Dark Master. I am in hiding because I gave birth to his son. I need to hide until spring at which time I will be able to flee across the mountains with my son and his three half-brothers and half-sister to my homeland. I am willing to pay each of you one Merlin gold coin to fight with me and my men until which time I can flee. I need your help."

The men seemed to be contemplating the offer. Frank Jr. stepped forward, "Our king will order her arrested. You will have to take sides. I choose to be on her side. This is about doing what is right. We cannot live in fear from our king and the Dark Master anymore. There is a time to stand and fight, and this is it. Our king has turned into a monster in himself, and he must be stopped. What we have here is worth fighting for, but we must fight."

Another man asked, "What will happen to us once she and her guards leave? We are not soldiers."

Frank said, "We must fight for each other. My father, my brother, and I settled this land. You all were hired and helped us build this ranch." He looked at the man, "I was present when your daughter was born. My father gave you and your wife a home to live. My father cared about all you men and your families. It is time we fight for this ranch. It is time we fight for what is right."

"What about the Dark Master? You know we cannot defend ourselves against him and his men. They are Bluebloods." He looked at Veronica, "Are you suggesting to us your men are good enough to kill Blueblood warriors?"

"As a team, my men working together killed Damon. There is a reason the Dark Master is in hiding. Once he gains enough power, he will hide no more, and he will not tolerate your freedom. You will become slaves in his empire. My men will leave with me. We cannot fight your battles. There are others who have committed to hunt and kill the Dark Master. The Dark Master needs you to keep him hidden. Once the Blueblood army in Merlin knows he is hiding here, they will come for him. That is his weakness."

Frank Jr. stepped forward, "The Blueblood warriors may never know. We need to keep these people in hiding, a secret. I do not trust our king and his henchmen. You know what they will do. This is no way to live. We are in constant fear and knowing others are losing their boys to the army of the dead. Our king will send his henchmen here to this ranch. You will need to be careful and prepare to fight. I will summon help from others who do not agree with our king, but I must start with you. You need to make your decision."

# Chapter 28

Billy Ray faced the double-doors to the compound. He glanced around looking for a second door and combatants. He could hear Hulk talking with Boudica and then he could hear him approaching from behind as he entered from the hallway. He looked a second time at the front double doors leading to the outside compound. Billy Ray noticed the workout equipment along the left wall. He stepped further into the room when he heard the noise from behind and assumed Hulk was the source of the sound. He never saw who hit him in the back of the head as he fell further into the large combat training room. He fell face down as he blacked out.

Hulk tried to catch up to his father as he rushed in the hall toward the door opening, he peered through the door and saw his father lying on the floor. He carefully stood in place as he rotated his head to view around the dark room for the adversaries and then looked back at his father and felt relieved when he could discern his father's back move, caused by his lungs expanding and then contracting. He entered the room further with his sword in front of him and walked to his father's side. A small amount of sunlight was beaming into the large room around the edges of the front blinds covering the front windows, as he tried to peer into the shadows and a second doorway. He knelt on one knee and checked his father for a pulse with his left hand while holding his sword in his right hand as he kept rotating his head watching for the enemy. He could not see clearly in the dark corners and in the dark hallway leading to another room. All the windows were covered with blinds and there was no artificial light and very little sunlight in the room. Most of the light was the ambient light coming from behind him from the doorway he had just entered. He then shook his father to verify if he could awaken him.

"I like to see warriors who care about each other. It is so touching but also reflects a weakness in the character of the warrior. My warriors I train would never be allowed to demonstrate such a weakness."

Hulk was startled at the harshness in the deep tone of the voice coming from behind him. He quickly turned and saw the shadow of a large man standing in the back doorway where he and his father had just entered. The silhouette of the man took up the entire doorway. Hulk realized there must have been a hidden passage. The man was huge with a deep accented voice. He was holding a long sword to his side. Hulk realized the adversary to be confident and cerebral in his mannerism.

"I assume you are the one we seek. You are the mentally ill, sociopathic monster who buys young boys and then butchers these young children, turning them into your soldiers. You hide behind the children and force the kids to do your murderous bidding."

"I know once a young man has been physically separated from unnecessary desires, I can better train them to be mentally conditioned. Once they are freed from their worldly, sin driven appetites, they can then become true soldiers. The most normal activity for a man is to kill, and I am a teacher of death." He smiled and took a step forward, "I have not killed your friend, but I will in time. Both of you will die an ugly death, but first you will do me one favor." Hulk was concerned with the action of the man, who stood still with confidence glaring at him with a sinister smile.

Hulk stood and cautiously looked around for other possible combatants, "The only favor I will do for you is kill you and put you out of your psychotic misery." Hulk moved in front of his father with his sword pointed at the large man.

The man stepped forward faster than Hulk thought possible. He was now standing in front of him four feet away. Hulk swung his sword, and the man blocked the swing. The Dark Master smiled at Hulk, "You are weak and slow. I hope the Bluebloods that travel with you are more adapted with sword fighting against a Blueblood master than you."

Hulk swung two quick times and braced for an attack. The large man blocked both swings. He stood still waiting for another attack by Hulk. Hulk could sense something was not kosher. The man seemed to be buying time. Hulk rotated around the man watching him. He kept Hulk square in front of him and was waiting. Hulk, at first wanted to drag the fight out until which time Dak and Zenith could arrive. Hulk knew he could not beat a Rogue Blueblood trained in fighting. "You mentioned a favor."

The man pulled his hood back and dropped his cape. The man was hideous looking with four incisor front teeth and a bald head with pointed ears. His arms were huge with muscles and his chest was well developed from working out. His fists looked to be twice the size of a normal man. He was very powerful with a deep, harsh accented toned voice. "Yes, I need you to draw your friends in here, so I can kill them. This is my domain and the place where I feel most comfortable."

Hulk responded, "That is not going to happen." He then attacked the man. The man blocked his swings and in one quick motion, stepped inside the sword while holding Hulk's right arm out to the side. As Hulk tried to stab the man with the knife in his left hand, the man blocked his left arm and pushed the arm away from his body. Before Hulk could react and move backward to reposition himself, the man head-butted Hulk, knocking Hulk backward to the floor. Hulk flew from his feet with the rear of his head colliding with the concrete floor first, then his body. His eyes rolled back inside his head as he blacked out.

Hulk awoke, lying on the floor, tied up with his hands bound together in front of him. His vision was at first blurred and his head was throbbing in pain. He slowly understood there was one rope running to his ankles and then looped three times around his ankles, tied in a knot he could not reach with his bound hands. He tried to focus his mind to remember where he was. The throbbing pain coming from his forehead at first prevented him from being able to concentrate. He tried to move his hands to his hurting head, and he could not rotate them. He then realized he could not reach the knot in the rope restraining his feet. He tried a second time and could not pull his hands-free. They were tied in front of him with the rope wrapped around his waist. The rope was so tight his feet were tingling from lack of circulation. His fingertips did not have proper circulation and had turned purple due to the rope being pulled so tight around his wrists. He looked ahead of him and tried to clear his vision. His head was throbbing, then he realized someone on the floor was slowly standing and stumbled as he tried to walk toward him. He was seeing double vision and tried to recall who would be in front of him. He then recalled where he was, and that the Dark Master had hit him. Hulk cried out, "No. Dad, run!"

Hulk noticed movement from his left as the big man appeared and kicked Billy Ray knocking him into the wall. The large man walked over to the wall and picked up Billy Ray and lifted him above his head and dropped him across his knee, breaking Billy Ray's back. Billy Ray coughed as the air escaped his lungs.

Hulk yelled as loud as he could. "No!"

The man drug Billy Ray in front of Hulk. He lifted his head into the fold of his forearm, stared at Hulk, and then jerked his head hard to the left. He forced Hulk to watch his father's neck being snapped. He knew his father was now dead. Hulk cried out, "No. Damn you. You Bastard."

\*\*\*

Zenith had been fighting the Blueblood for over ten minutes. The temperature at the top of the mountain at seven thousand feet higher elevation had been freezing and the wind chill factor had been below zero. Her clothing was not suitable for the warmer weather at the bottom of the mountain where there was little wind and sunshine with temperatures in the upper sixties. She was exhausted from the heat and the heavy clothing she was wearing. She was battling a man with a thin shirt who was more acclimated to the heat and humidity. She had been fortunate and cut the man across his lower right leg and his left bicep. The Blueblood had shown no signs of being injured.

Dak likewise was in a fight to the death. He ended up dropping his sword and forcing the Blueblood to drop his weapon as both men traded numerous punches as they wrestled each other, rolling around on the ground. Finally, Dak pushed the man backward, tripping the Blueblood over the wooden water trough, causing him to fall into the horse trough. Dak placed his body weight on the man, his knee pressing the man to the bottom as he held him around the neck with his left hand forcing his head under water for over a minute, while the man was reaching with his right hand trying to strangle Dak. Dak knew he could not release his grip as the Blueblood struggled. Dak clenched his jaws and as he felt his muscles giving way, he forced his arms to hold the position. He could see the panic in the facial expression of the Blueblood with his eyes open under the water as he held him tight. The man stopped moving as an air bubble came to the top of the water as he finally drowned, his eyes still wide open.

Dak stood and removed his warm heavy shirt and looked across the compound at Zenith. Both heard the scream from Hulk. Zenith motioned for Dak to check on Hulk. "I've got this." Dak noticed the blood on the Blueblood's leg. She then swung her sword three times fast, driving her combatant backward. He countered and drove her backward as Dak picked up his swords and ran through the double doors into the room and saw Hulk lying on the floor, tied up with his hands pulled in front of him and the same rope used to restrain his ankles. The sunlight beamed through the double doors as they now were wide open. Dak, at first was confused, looking at Hulk tied up with his face red in anger and then noticed Billy Ray's head was twisted backward as his body was lying limply on the floor. He knew immediately by the limp body of Billy Ray, he was dead. His head was twisted backward in an unnatural manner. Hulk, with tears in his eyes, yelled, "Watch out!" Dak saw something large in his peripheral vision to his left. He rotated just in time to block the sword with his left hand and attacked with his right hand. The large man was fast to block both swings and then he countered as Dak rolled backward and quickly stood now facing the monster. He placed both his swords in front of him and observed his opponent. The man was huge and covered in muscles. He had pointed ears on his bald head and a sinister looking smile.

The man kept smiling at Dak, "You walked into my trap. My two men were instructed to wear you down but not kill you. They were instructed to allow you to come to me."

"One of your Blueblood warriors is lying in the water trough, dead. My wife will kill the other and be in here momentarily. I doubt you wanted your men killed. You are a liar."

"We will truly see about that."

Dak smiled at the big man, "Did you know General Cuez? He lost his head in a battle with me. You are in my trap. I can sense you are scared of me."

The Master studied Dak and noticed he was confident, without fear. The large man did not react to the news about General Cuez. "Unlike your two friends here, your reflexes are that of a Blueblood, but I do not sense the presence of a Blueblood. Why is that?"

Dak responded, "I can sense your fear, and I can also sense I am in the presence of a psychotic evil entity. One not born but made by a mistake of another man. One I must kill."

"I can guarantee you, I do not fear you. I however am a little confused about why I cannot sense your presence." He looked perplexed and studied Dak. "You choose the way you prefer to die. I would suggest you need to choose your weapons carefully."

Dak thought to himself, "My advantage is that he has never fought a man with two Sai swords." He also thought he needed the man disarmed. Zenith then might have a chance when she arrived with her sword. He also thought of something else. Dak stood straight and held his swords to his side, "I elect hand to hand. I believe you to be a clumsy coward."

The large man smiled as he placed his sword to his side as if he would drop his sword if Dak dropped his swords first.

Dak threw his two swords to the side, along with the belt he used to hold them. He then removed his boots and socks. He acted like he was indifferent where he threw the items.

# An Angel Never Prays

*** 

Zenith was so tired she could barely hold up her sword. She had tried swing after swing in order to try to break through his defenses. Likewise, her enemy had done the same. Both were tired to the point of total exhaustion and dropping to the ground. Zenith had cut him on the leg with her last swing in the battle, but this had not seemed to slow the man. She was aware she could not hold out much longer. On top of the mountain, the temperature was cold in the shadows with the constant freezing wind. At the lower elevation inside the fort, the silk shirt and the seal pants and seal vest were too hot. The humidity was stifling, there was no shade, and she was too tired to keep fighting at this pace. At this point, she needed a fast victory. She dropped her guard acting like she was done and exhausted. The man advanced and tried a hard downward kill shot. Zenith responded quicker than her opponent thought possible. She knew she had to take a chance. She blocked the swing with the sword in her right hand, and instead of reaching for his body, she used her left hand holding the knife to reach for his sword hand. She then rolled backward to dodge his second swing with his left hand holding his second sword. She jumped to her feet and turned to face her enemy. She noticed three of his fingers lying on the dirt next to his sword. She placed her knife in her boot and reached for the abandoned shield lying on the ground and held the shield.

He looked at his bloody hand and became enraged. He then yelled and immediately threw his second sword at her face as he charged her. She had not expected the charge and blocked the sword with her shield. The impact from the collision forced her to drop the shield as she flew backwards and landed on the dirt ground with him on top. She initially had the breath knocked out of her lungs, and she struggled to capture her next breath. He grabbed her sword hand and repeatedly beat her hand and arm against the ground, forcing her to lose her grip as her sword fell out of her reach. She was able to capture her breath and reached for the knife from her boot with her left hand. He noticed her left hand had slipped low and instinctively reached for her wrist and pulled her left arm above her face and started forcing the knife toward her neck. She strained with every muscle in her arms, trying to dig her heels into the ground for leverage. She reached out with her right hand and squeezed his now amputated fingers. He did not respond to the pain. She broke her right hand free and pulled her right hand to the inside of his left arm and was now pushing upward with both arms. He, likewise, was using the leverage from being on top with both hands and his body weight pushing the knife blade down. The blade was now within an inch of her neck. She could only accept her fate. She saw the blade move closer as she grunted with all her strength to push upward. Her mind shifted to her two sons and her husband. She knew she would die as she laid on her back pushing him upward.

He suddenly tried to jerk away his arms from above her as she held his wrist tight. His body suddenly jerked, and he tried to pull the knife away from her throat as she held his right wrist with her right hand. She sensed his body weight was no longer pushing downward as she watched him try to rotate to the side as an arrow suddenly appeared sticking through his heart. Zenith, at first could not comprehend what had happened. She used all her strength to push the man to the side of her and crawled out from under him. She struggled to force her body to sit up as she looked toward the fort wall and saw Boudica standing with her bow aimed in her direction. She now realized the Rogue Blueblood had sensed the danger from the rear and tried to turn and block the incoming arrow.

# Chapter 29

The men retreated on horse back to the far side of the open field. Tommy Boy and Trey led the group of men, as the horses were pushed for the half mile on a full run. Trey thought as he kept kicking his horse in the sides, pushing the animal to run faster, they were going to be in for one hell of a battle. The men they were facing were not normal. The acted as if they wanted to die. Even with arrows in the soldiers, they would still attack. He and Tommy Boy pulled back on the horse bridles, dismounted, and tied them around a low hanging tree limb. He waved for the men to line up in position as the men rode to the tree line to tie off their horses. Samuel announced, as he peered across the field, "This is good land for us to make our stand. We need to take out as many as we can as they cross the open field with our arrows. They will be using shields so preserve your arrows. Once they get within twenty feet of our line, drop your aim and shoot low for the lower legs. We must slow them down."

Trey ordered, "Robin Hood, you and two men stand behind us and provide us cover fire." He reached for his pouch of arrows and threw the pouch toward Robin Hood, "Here are some extra arrows. I only need a few." Trey looked at Tommy Boy with his bow up and ready, "This is going to get really ugly, really fast.

Our arrows are not going to penetrate through their shields, and they have spears."

Tommy Boy could tell Trey was a little nervous. Trey had clinched jaws and announced, "These men we are about to fight will not show fear and will not let up until either they are dead, or they have killed us. Listen to Samuel. Aim for the lower legs. We must wound them as quickly as we can, before they cross our battle line." Tommy Boy glanced down the line to his right and then to his left. He could see the fear in the eyes of the men as the anticipated battle coming toward them. He counted eighteen men. "We make our stand here. We eighteen men stand together. Trey, you need to turn into a Berserker." He then yelled out loudly, so everyone could hear him. "We are Berserkers. We will destroy our enemy." The men all yelled, "We are Berserkers."

The enemy appeared at first one and then two and then multiple men approaching on foot, coming out of the woods carrying their spears and shields. They were running directly at them with no signs of slowing down. The commanders were on horses allowing the foot soldiers to attack as they approached from behind the running men. Samuel yelled, "We will release one round of arrows at one hundred meters. Then we will hold our arrows for the short shots aiming for the lower legs below the shields." Samuel looked at the men he was fighting with and wished he had a unit of trained Bluebloods by his side. He was concerned about these men and their abilities. He knew the battle was going to be brutal. The men attacking were under a trance and would not stop until one side was killed. He, however, noticed these men showed no signs of backing down and appeared to be listening to his orders. He noticed the one man holding his position with his bow held in the ready, and he could see the man was nervous as he took a hard swallow as his throat shifted as he stared at the approaching combatants. He yelled, "Ready your bows on my signal."

Samuel waited and then he released his arrow, "Now." All the men released their arrows. Samuel watched as most of the arrows either missed a target or hit a shield. He saw two combatants drop from the arrows. He yelled, "Ready your arrows. Make it look as if you are going to aim high but drop your aim at the last second. We must get off two rounds of arrows."

Samuel heard Tommy Boy yell, "We are Berserkers. We are Berserkers." They all held their bows with the arrows leveled, waiting as the men fast approached.

Samuel yelled, "Fire at will."

Several of the charging men dropped to the ground once the arrows hit them in the legs. With no regard for the wounded men, the men approaching from the rear, trampled their injured comrades lying on the battlefield. Tommy Boy and Trey were in the middle of the defensive line, and both fired two shots each before they pulled their shields and swords. The initial push by the combatants was brutal, with three of the New York men being killed by spears on the combatants using their shields to slam into their defensive line. Robin Hood and two other two men had positioned themselves behind the line of defense and fired round after round of arrows. Once the combatants started engaging their spears, they would drop their shields slightly, and the three would fire their arrows trying to take out as many men as they could.

Trey saw the line of soldiers fast approaching him. The soldiers were staggered in their approach. He fired his second arrow low, hitting the man in the right foot. Trey dropped his bow and prepared for the battle. He watched as the soldier behind the man he shot, did not try to avoid the injured soldier. Instead, he stepped on him and kept moving forward. Trey waited for the first approaching soldier to cross his imaginary battle line. Trey had noted a spot in the weeds where he had predetermined would be his line of assault. When the first man crossed the line, Trey moved forward while swinging his sword, hitting the tip of the spear. Trey swung with a back hand swing which pushed the spear tip wide. He then braced for the impact of the soldier running into him with his shield. Trey used his shoulder and slammed into the shield, causing the smaller soldier to not only stop his momentum, but actually knock the man to the ground. Trey instantly swung downward with his left hand driving his sword into the man's stomach, slowly killing the man.

Trey had no time to waste as he confronted another combatant and then another. There was no stopping Trey as he swung his swords and blocked the deadly blades of the combatants. He would kill one man and then go to the next and then the next.

The man to the right of Robin Hood fired an arrow, hitting the combatant in the side below the rib cage as the battle line was divided by the two Rogue Bluebloods attacking the defensive line and then attacking Samuel. The combatant kept his momentum as he was running toward the archer. The archer fired another arrow hitting the shield of the approaching combatant. The archer dropped his bow at the last instant when he realized he did not have enough time to fire a third arrow at the fast-approaching man. He pulled his sword and swung hard, hitting the shield. The soldier pushed forward with the shield and then drove his spear into the man from Cliff Tops. Robin Hood loaded another arrow. He was pulling arrow after arrow from the satchel. He knew if he could not aim for a kill shot, he might be able to hit the combatants in the hand or even a foot. The arrow would slow the soldier. Robin Hood also knew he had to protect Samuel. If Samuel was killed by one of the Rogue Bluebloods, they would lose the battle. He and his friends could not kill two Rogue Bluebloods. He was firing his arrows at the soldiers approaching Samuel. However, Robin Hood noticed from his peripheral vision, movement from his right as he was loading another arrow and saw the soldier kill his comrade with the spear. The man turned toward Robin Hood as Robin Hood quickly adjusted his aim. Robin pulled his arrow and aimed upward, away from the shield protecting the man's body. He knew the arrow could possibly deflect off the metal helmet if he tried a head shot. He released the arrow and hit the man in the neck. The arrow missed the cervical bones and the windpipe but was sticking through the man's neck tissue and muscles. Robin Hood saw the two arrows in the man as he was still fast approaching. He noticed the man's eyes as he looked possessed with pure evil. He was not going to stop. Robin Hood dropped his bow and pulled his sword. He knew his training. He and his friends had worked almost every evening before dinner on how best to defeat a combatant with a spear as they trained for hours at a time. The spear was longer but a liability fighting against a man with a sword. He waited for the man to jab with the spear and then he used his quickness with his sword with a backhand motion pushing the spear tip away from his body. Then, he pulled his knife in one motion while holding the spear out to the side with his sword. He lunged forward with quickness, and he reached over the shield as he rammed his knife into the front of the man's face. Robin Hood pushed the man backward as he was now a falling dead man. Robin Hood quickly picked up his bow and immediately looked for other targets. He also realized these men would not stop fighting until they were killed. He noticed a few of the combatants were archers and had positioned themselves behind the line of their assault. They were indifferent in firing their arrows as they fired into their men who were engaged in fighting. He aimed and hit one archer as the man's arrow flew through the air and hit Tommy Boy in the left thigh. Robin Hood was quicker at loading arrows than the combatants and more accurate with the placement of the arrows. He aimed at another archer and hit him as he was about to release his arrow. Robin Hood did not hesitate. He fired his arrow hitting the archer who had shot Tommy Boy. He then saw Trey have an arrow glance off his head as he was swinging his sword at two different combatants. He noticed his friend did not stop fighting as the arrow glanced off the side of his head, and the arrow fell to the ground. Trey killed another man approaching him with a spear. Robin Hood fired two arrows within two seconds, hitting two additional archers. He then saw a spearman fast approaching Tommy Boy, and he fired another arrow hitting the man in the chest, killing him instantly.

Samuel pulled his hatchet in his left hand and his sword in his right hand and, like Trey and Tommy Boy, met the attackers head on. All the men were swinging their weapons and then going to the next target. The Rogue Blueblood commander spotted Samuel and spurred his horse for his position. Samuel saw the man and moved out into the battlefield. Samuel lunged to the side and cut the front leg with the sword on the horse as the rider was trying to trample him. He dropped his sword from the forceable contact with the running horse. Samuel rolled to the side as the Blueblood combatant fell forward to the ground, over the top of the stumbling horse. The Rogue Blueblood stood quickly, and the two men squared off, both blocking the swings of each other. Samuel spotted the second Blueblood as he killed two men from the New York tribe in his path, as he also was preparing to attack him. Samuel swung with great force with the hatchet in his left hand and pulled his second hatchet in his right hand. The three Bluebloods had moved into the battlefield away from the other warriors. Samuel then ducked under the sword and swung his other hatchet with great force, striking the Blueblood in the shin. Samuel turned to block the second Blueblood warrior's swing and then gave ground to reposition himself. The injured Blueblood had fallen and then stood on one leg. Samuel attacked by swinging both hatchets at one time, forcing the second one backward. He pivoted and noticed the Blueblood had pulled his sword to the right and deflected an arrow. He advanced and turned his hatchet backward so the spike in the curved handle of the hatchet could penetrate the helmet. He swung his hatchet high, hitting the injured Blueblood this time in the head with the spike on the backside of his curved hatchet driving through the helmet. Samuel realized someone had fired an arrow and distracted the Blueblood, allowing him an opportunity to finish him. Samuel could not immediately pull his hatchet free from the skull, so he pivoted to the right and held his other hatchet in front, blocking the sword of the second Blueblood.

Robin Hood had a less than a second to make his decision and a small exposed area with the shield being held in front of the combatant. He aimed and released his arrow, hitting a soldier approaching him in the arm. The arrow hit the man in the exposed right bicep as the man held his shield in front with his body and left hand. The man was bent over charging him with the shield held in front of him. The man fell, holding his injured arm. Robin Hood loaded another arrow and started to shoot the injured man but instead shifted his arrow, shooting at the head of the standing Blueblood that was fighting Samuel. Samuel saw the arrow deflect off the sword of the Blueblood and then almost simultaneously swung his hatchet and hit the Blueblood in the head, killing him. Samuel rolled to the side to dodge the other Blueblood's swing, as he blocked the deadly sword with his hatchet. He then picked up a sword from a dead combatant and threw the sword, hitting the next soldier as he approached. Samuel picked up a spear and rushed the second Blueblood and swung the spear hard and downward as the Blueblood blocked his swing. Samuel countered and spun in a circle with the hatchet in his left hand and drove the hatchet deep into the man's chest. Samuel pulled his hatchet from the man's chest as he watch the Rogue Blueblood fall backward. He then walked over and pulled his other hatchet from the skull of the other dead Blueblood. He turned to look at the others. He saw a soldier come at Trey with a spear as Trey had blood running down the side of his face. Trey used his right hand and backhanded the spear, blocking the spear with the sword in his left hand. The soldier was off balance and left his right side open and unguarded. While pushing the spear away, Trey swung hard with the sword in his right hand, cutting the man completely in half. Then, without hesitating Trey rotated to another advancing soldier. Samuel then noticed all the dead bodies lying around Trey and Tommy Boy. He noticed all the arrows in the dead combatants lying in the middle of the battlefield. The battle was now winding down, and there were now only a few wounded men left. He saw an arrow fly by him ten feet away as Robin Hood shot another man as he was limping forward to fight. The arrow hit the man in the middle of his chest, causing the man to tip backward as he fell to the ground, dead.

Robin Hood loaded one of the few arrows he had left, as he rotated back to his left. He saw Rofel, a man from his tribe who had relocated his family close to ten years prior to Cliff Tops. Billy Ray and he had become friends as the two men would hunt and fish together.

Robin Hood saw Rofel run forward to assist one of the New York fighters when a soldier, who appeared to be dead, raised up

from the ground and stuck his knife in Rofel's belly. Robin
Hood pulled the arrow back on his bow, aiming as he raised the
bow. He released the arrow, striking the soldier in the back as he
was attempting to crawl toward Rofel who was lying on the
ground. Robin Hood hoped Rofel would be okay. He pulled
another arrow and looked for additional targets as the last of the
army were now dead or defeated.

Tommy Boy sat down next to a couple of the New York men
who were wounded. Tommy Boy yelled, "We need to help our
wounded!" as he reached for a bandage and tread to sew up a cut
to repair the laceration on the man's arm. He held the bandage in
place with pressure trying to stop the bleeding.

Trey announced, "We will grant the enemy mercy, but we
will take no prisoners." He and three men walked out to the field
and started killing the wounded combatants lying nearby.

Samuel observed the carnage on the battlefield and considered
the next move as Trey rammed his sword into the back of a man
lying injured on the battlefield.

***

The men helped each other apply bandages and carried water
to the wounded. Samuel sat leaning over Rofel and carefully
sewed the wound together. "I stitched your intestine, and you
will heal. The wound will be allowed to drain, so you need to

change the bandage daily. You now will have a scar to tell your kids about the story and the battle here today." Samuel washed his hands, cleaning the blood from them. "Rofel, I will provide you with a pint of my blood to assist in your recovery." He then pulled the hose and the syringe and started the process as Rofel laid on the ground next to Samuel.

Tommy Boy and Trey both observed another side of Samuel as he took his time and assisted in providing medical help to their men. They listened as Samuel told Rofel and the six injured men from the New York tribe, how well they had fought. "I have fought with several men in several different battles, and you were some of the best soldiers I have fought next to. I was happily surprised with your abilities, and how well you men fought here today. It is my privilege to assist you brave men with bandages. I am happy to say none of you appear to have life threatening injuries."

Trey noticed that Rofel was relieved and smiled as he looked down at the bandage on his midsection. The other men also seem to take pride in the complement and the personal message provided by Samuel. Trey held the bandage in place on the side of his head as Robin Hood pulled the wrap tight.

Tommy Boy did not reveal the pain as Robin Hood pulled the arrow from his leg. Robin Hood placed a bandage over the wound and then encircled the wrap tight around the leg.

Samuel walked over and sat next to Trey, Robin Hood, and Tommy Boy. They were discussing the plan and wondering how Dak and his group had fared in their part of the mission. Samuel announced in an alarm, "Listen." The group of men looked around and could tell the sound of the horses was coming from the south and the direction of City of Tanger. They heard the unmistakable sound of horses running. The sound was getting louder and louder. The men glanced at each other with a confused expression. Tommy Boy stood and walked into the battle field and quickly picked up some bows and handed them, along with some arrows, to the other men.

The man riding next to the sheriff asked, "Should we not wait on the rest of our men?"

The sheriff was a big man and a bully. He had always enjoyed pushing folks around and intimating them into submission. The King of Tanger liked the fact that his sheriff was a bully and had promoted him to be the Sheriff of Tanger. The sheriff led his men over the rise of the hill on the trail and could see the battlefield as he approached battle area. He motioned for his men to slow the pace as they observed the area as Trey and his men were sitting on the ground. "We have them outnumbered with several more men. They will give up and do as I say. Look at them. Most are injured." The group galloped their horses toward the battlefield.

The man riding next to the sheriff scrutinized the battlefield as he rode forward and noticed the dead men from the fort lying in the field and near the resting soldiers. He glanced back at the sheriff with a questionable expression. "There are a lot of dead men lying on the ground. Maybe we should wait."

The horse riders appeared from the south. Tommy Boy yelled, "It is the militia from Tanger." Samuel pulled his hood on and sat still. The others stayed seated while gripping their weapons and seeming to be disinterested in the approaching militia. They watched the riders ride in a column of two. The front of the column stopped at about thirty yards, and the men on the horses spread out facing them. The sheriff looked at the battlefield and then stared at Samuel wearing a hood with his head tilted down as he was viewing the ground in front of him. He then looked at the other men sitting on the ground and noticed most were injured. "You men are under arrest. You will lay down your weapons."

Trey was surprised at the request of the militia leader and then he became frustrated with the dire situation. Dak had not considered the men from Tanger would be willing to support the cult and the Rogue Blueblood leader. He looked at the man in disbelief as he sat still, "Who the hell are you?"

In a loud commanding voice, "I am the appointed Sheriff of Tanger, and these are my appointed deputies. By order of the King of Tanger, you will drop your weapons. You do not trespass on the King's property and then commit murder. We have a standing treaty with those men from the fort. They summoned our help, and we will provide them that help by orders of our king." He raised his voice as he spoke, "Now lay down your weapons and stand to be arrested. You will march to our holding cell."

Trey looked frustrated, and he motioned with his hand for his men to stand and take a defensive position. Even the wounded men stood and created a semi-circle. The men pulled their bows and loaded their arrows. Trey looked at the Sheriff, "Today we fight like a Viking warrior. Today we fight like Berserkers."

The group yelled, "We are Berserkers."

The sheriff was surprised with the response. He hesitated and glanced at his men. Trey leveled his bow and released his arrow hitting the sheriff in the chest. The man fell backward off his horse to the ground. Samuel raised his bow and released his arrow hitting a deputy in the chest and reloaded and fire a second arrow before most of the men fired their first arrow. The rest of the men released their arrows and then reloaded a second time and then a third time. The men with the sheriff were surprised they were being attacked by these men. The deputies on horses were discombobulated and without shields the arrows hit several of them. With the sheriff lying on the ground dead, they had no second in command. One of the men yelled retreat and another man yelled attack. Some retreated and some attacked.

After the attacking group realized most of their men had retreated, they then turned and fled the battlefield with arrows hitting some of them as injured deputies were hunched over their horses as they rode toward Tanger. Trey walked out into the field and stood over an injured deputy. The man looked at Trey and pleaded for his life. Trey rammed his sword through the man. "We came here to free you, and you try to arrest me. The hell with mercy." The others walked out among the injured and finished killing the wounded with their swords.

Samuel was impressed with Tommy Boy and Trey and their ability to wage war. He walked over to Trey. "They will return and be better prepared."

Trey looked angry, "I hope so."

Samuel smiled at Trey and Tommy Boy. "You men are very gifted with a bow and sword. Sometimes though, we need to use wisdom. It may be better to back down."

Tommy Boy looked surprised as he turned to Samuel, "You are saying we need to allow them to arrest us?"

Samuel hesitated and allowed his hands out to his side with his palms turned upward, "Maybe we should retreat to the fort. We did not travel all this distance to kill the men of Tanger. We need to stay focused. We need to support our assassins. We do not wish for them to be arrested. These men of Tanager are not our enemy."

Trey knew Dak placed him in charge, and being the leader, he was going to make the decision. He knew he was responsible for these men. They had just fought one battle, and most were wounded. He glanced at Rofel standing with blood on his bandage. He was apprehensive about the battle at the fort, but he also knew Dak had ordered him to ride south around Tanger and wait on them at the base of the mountains. Dak and Zenith were to kill the Dark Master and that was not going to be easy. The long-term plan was to wait out the winter and cross the mountains and head north to beat the possible army from Merlin which would be attacking their homeland in the spring or maybe sail around the horn and Southern City to Harpers Ferry Harbor. Both plans were stacked with perils. They had not considered having to fight the Tanger Militia. "Men mount your horses. We will retreat to the fort and check on our friends. If they try to arrest us, we will fight. We cannot outrun them. The fort might provide us our

# Chapter 30

The rider slammed his heels into the horse's sides pushing the animal to the limit as he came into the straight away on the dirt road. He pulled back slightly as he turned the curve in the road and then dug his heels in the sides of the animal again pushing the animal. As he approached the ranch, he could see some men out in front of the barn as he rode as fast as the animal could run. He knew the news he was he carrying was urgent. He had to warn Frank Jr. what was happening.

Frank Jr. heard his foreman yell. He feared the worst as he saw the man through the glass window racing toward his home. He picked up his sword, his shield, and ran out the front door looking for his men. The man ran the horse into the front yard and pulled back on the bridle, forcing the horse to an abrupt stop. Several hands working close by ran to hear the news.

Michael looked at Viking, "Get the men. I will go tell the Queen." Viking turned and ran to the barn and yelled for Pretty Boy and Cruzie. He turned and ran toward the home as the messenger was jumping from the horse.

Michael entered the bunk house, "My Queen, a messenger stationed in Tanger is delivering a message to Frank Jr. We need to get prepared. I have sent Viking to retrieve both Pretty Boy and Cruzie. I will wake Hector. I believe we need to be prepared for war. This is urgent."

Veronica looked at the maid. "Keep the kids in the back bedroom. You will not allow anyone in the room. You will protect these children with your life. Michael, you need to have all my guards prepared for battle."

"Yes. My Queen." He turned and ran toward the other bunk house.

Veronica turned and went to the cabinet and retrieved her silk shirt and placed the shirt on and then her padded vest. She picked up her weapons.

As Veronica walked to the front of the bunkhouse with her sword in the sheath and her bow strapped to her back, she considered the worst. She felt the despair, and how she should have listened to Frank Jr. and moved herself and the kids to the island where they could have stayed hidden. As she approached the main home, she could see Frank Jr. standing with his sword and bow as he was talking with the one messenger. She was somewhat relieved and felt maybe they now would have an opportunity to run and hide. As she approached, Frank turned to her, "The news is not what I suspected. Our King has ordered his army assembled to attack insurgent at the Lower Mountain Fort. The Sheriff and a few deputies have already responded to the fort, which is under attack."

Veronica looked at the men gathered around Frank Jr. She walked in front of him, "We need to stop the army from Tanger. Those who are attacking the Dark Master are doing us a favor. We need to assist the men from Cliff Tops."

Michael, and Veronica's other four guards arrived and were standing behind her. They were all fully dressed and ready for war. Frank Jr. looked perplexed, "Who has attacked the Dark Master? I do not understand what is happening." He stared at Veronica. "You know who is attacking the fort?"

Veronica replied, "I do know. They are part of the northern army. I was not certain if they would make the trip through the Midlander Territory in time. Evidently, they made the trip. If you ever are going to be free, you and your men need to seize the opportunity with me and my men now and fight for your freedom. This may be the only opportunity you will ever have."

# Chapter 31

Boudica ran across the balcony walkway to the descending ladder and across the compound to Zenith and held her. "Thank you for coming back. You saved my life, and for that, I will always be grateful." Zenith then felt exhausted, and her body felt faint. "Please find me some water."

Boudica ran to the water trough and saw the dead body. She reached for a canteen full of water hanging on the pole and returned to Zenith. "Here is some water." Zenith drank the water and poured some over her head. Then, Boudica helped Zenith stand as she drank additional water. She then handed Zenith her sword. "Where is your brother?"

"He is dead. Killed by cult soldiers. I have no reason to live. I choose to die with you."

Zenith drank additional water and turned to look at Boudica, "I am not dead yet. I am sorry to hear of your loss." She then turned to the main building. She had heard Hulk yell twice, "Dak entered the building close to seven minutes ago. He has not returned. Here, you drink some water. We will fight."

Zenith had an ominous feeling as she and Boudica slowly walked toward the building. Boudica drank some water and then dropped the canteen to the ground as she glanced all around and made certain the area was clear as she kept her arrow loaded watching for other combatants. Boudica looked at Zenith and noticed she was so tired she could barely walk and raise her sword. "Maybe we should retreat. You are too tired to fight another battle."

Zenith took a short step toward the stairs leading to the double doors of the building. "My husband is in that building. I will have the same fate as he. You may run and save yourself."

"I will not run. I will fight with you. I choose to be your friend. I will die with you."

***

Hulk watched as Dak walked in a half circle around the Dark Master with the Dark Master slowly turning and now had his back to him. Dak announced, "I do not understand why everyone has trouble locating you Master Rogue Bluebloods. All I had to do was ask where the man lives that is uglier than hammered shit."

Hulk immediately started stretching his tied legs to use his feet to reach the boot. He strains to extend his tied hands toward his feet, so he can extend his foot another few inches. He reaches for the right boot pushing his tied feet toward the right boot and then he uses the toe of his left boot to reach the boot lying on the floor. He knew if he could place his heel over the boot, he could pull the boot between his legs and then reach the boot with his tied hands. He kept using his heels trying to edge the boot closer.

The man answered Dak, "I will show you who is ugly after I break your back like I did your friend. I will cut your pretty face off your head while you are still alive. I will paste your face on a pole for all to see, with your live body impaled next to your face."

Dak approached and both men traded punches. Each was trying to anticipate the other's movements. Dak tried a Karate kick to the man in his ribs, and the man blocked the kick with his forearm. Dak then repositioned himself and tried to keep the large man squarely in front of him. He then blocked an aggressive attack with the man throwing combinations. The man's left jab connected twice to Dak's right cheek, driving Dak backwards. The man had the advantage with his longer reach and more rest over the past few days. Dak jumped backward and to the side and fought off the aggressive swings as he was forced backward to the front wall. He absorbed the hard jab and then he timed his right swing with an uppercut, which caught the man in the chin forcing the man's head to tilt backward from the force of the blow. Dak hit the man in the throat with his left fist and knew this should be the turning point in the fight. Dak pushed the issue, thinking the upper cut and the jab to the throat would have stunned the man. The man backs up, blocking most of Dak's punches with his forearms in close against his midsection.

Dak moved in close and kept swinging both right and then left fists, hitting the man in the stomach and ribs. The man suddenly grabs Dak by the upper arms, turning him and driving Dak into the wall and then uses his body weight to hold Dak firmly against the wall. Dak started to feel trapped and tried lower body punches to the man's private section and then his stomach. Nothing seemed to be working. The man did not seem to feel the pain of the punches. Dak had hit the man as hard as he could, and the man did not recoil from his fist and being hit. He now realized the man was congenitally insensitive to pain and anhidrosis. Dak immediately felt a sense of desperation, knowing he couldn't hurt the man with body blows. He needed to injure the man to win. Dak tried to push the man backward and create space between them to move to the left, away from the wall and back into the middle of the room. The man held Dak in a stand-up-neck-hold and then drove Dak backward as the two were holding each other trying to prevail in a wrestler's grip. Dak tried to position his left foot inside the man's right foot and then tried to throw the man to the floor. The man shifted his weight and held Dak's head in the chokehold. Dak was able to trip the huge man, and the two men fell to the floor with both trying desperately gain the advantage.

As Hulk pulled the boot toward his hands, he looked up to verify if the Dark Master knew he was about to reach the boot with both hands. He then pictured in his mind how he would turn the boot and open the blade. He knew he had to release the hidden blade and start to cut the rope leading from his hands to his feet. He knew he must hurry as he glanced at the back of the Blueblood Master. He saw Dak fall to the floor with the large man on top. He felt the sweat run down his face as his nerves started to react to the panic feeling caused by his possible failure to reach the boot in time. He knew he would also die as he would be tortured the same as Dak if he did not cut the rope and attack the large man.

Dak pushed the man's arm upward and broke out of the choke hold as he slid his head free but in doing so he could tell the man was starting to obtain better leverage as the large man reaches for Dak's neck with his left hand and holds Dak tight with his right hand while he is on top. Little by little the man starts to pull his hands free and then with a massive right, he punches Dak in the left temple as they were lying on the floor. Dak is stunned from the punch as the sweat from his scalp flew into the air to the floor and wall. Dak releases his grip on the man's left arm and tries to grab his right wrist. Dak attempts to roll the man off him, but the man braces his position with his feet and legs. He then reaches down and places both hands on Dak's head. Dak grabs each wrist, fighting back with all his strength. Dak's head is pulled back and forth, hitting the back of his skull on the floor. Dak reaches up with both hands and strains to hold his forearms in place, but he now knew he had lost the fight. The man was too strong and too big. The man had absorbed the punches without reflecting pain. Dak now knew he should have tried to injure the man and then take away some of his abilities. The man could not be distracted by inflicting pain with mere punches.

Dak could barely see the man's face through the blood running into his eyes. He knew the next punch would kill him. He closed his eyes, grinding his teeth as he held the man tight against his body trying to prevent the man from having room to land another hard punch. He suddenly felt the man trying desperately to pull his arms free where Dak was holding them tight against his body. He felt the man jerk his arms backward away from Dak as Dak held him firmly against his body. Dak then heard the grunt from the man. He opened his eyes as he saw one of his Sai Sword blades protruding through the man's chest. He held the man up, then pushes him to the side. He could barely see through the blood and sweat in his eyes, Hulk is standing ten feet behind him with his hands still tied together looking down at him, holding his second sword.

# Chapter 32

Trey and Tommy Boy rode side by side slowly through the fort's opened gates, with the rest of the men following close behind. They were careful so that they would not ride into a trap. They stopped their horses and looked around at the dead Blueblood in the middle of the compound and another man lying on his back with his torso in the water trough. They also noticed the other dead soldiers lying around the compound. They were relieved to see their two friends sitting on the steps and rode over toward the main building where Dak and Zenith were sitting. Zenith was wiping the blood from Dak's face as he drank water. Both looked exhausted. Tommy Boy asked, "Where is my father and brother? Dak motioned his head behind him as he glanced up at his two friends, "I am sorry Tommy Boy, but we paid a huge price."

Tommy Boy immediately jumped off his horse and ran into the building. He saw Hulk holding Billy Ray's body. Tommy Boy saw the dead Blueblood lying on the floor. Hulk looked up at his brother and shook his head no with tears in his eyes as he held his father.

Dak looked at Zenith, "We are done. Both of us have given enough for the cause. We need to go home and be with our family. Our two sons need us, and we need to be parents."

Zenith sat next to him, "We could have just as easily died here today. Boudica saved my life, and Hulk saved your life."

Dak looked at the ground in front of him. His thoughts drifted from his battle inside with the Dark Master and the fact he left his wife outside to fight a Rogue Blueblood knowing he could have helped her first. He felt the remorse of leaving his wife and the sadness of losing Billy Ray. "Hulk and Boudica saved all our lives. A person's actions have consequences some intentional and some unintentional. Samuel tried to warn me; we were going to have losses. Billy Ray was like a father to me."

The soldier from the New York tribe yelled, "Here comes the army from Tanger." Dak and Zenith didn't move. They were tired and baffled. Trey ordered, "Battle stations. Robin Hood, you and a couple of men set up on the top platform with your bows. The rest of you prepare to shoot them as they come through the gate."

Trey watched as the army approached. He then glanced back at Zenith and Dak and neither responded. Both sat on the steps. Tommy Boy and Hulk were still inside, grieving over the death of their father. Trey knew he needed help. Samuel walked into the middle of the gate entrance and instead of holding his two hatchets, he held is curved sword out in front of him. Boudica climbed the ladder to the platform and loaded her bow. Samuel positioned himself and looked like he was inviting the Tanger soldiers to battle him. He pulled his hood back and exemplified a Blueblood warrior who is ready to fight to the death.

This time the King was leading the men. The King stopped his men just out of the range of the arrows. "You are all under arrest for murder. You invaded by realm. You will be taken to the jail and processed through our court. I can guarantee that you will be provided a fair trial. This is my word as the King of Tanger."

Trey looked next to him as Dak, Zenith, Hulk and Tommy Boy appeared as they stood behind Samuel. They all stared at the men lined up, all on horses. The men, this time, all holding spears with shields in front of them. Dak whispered, "We need to close the gates and force them to break through. We need to buy time."

Trey then noticed to the far-right territory another group of sixty riders heading toward them. He, at first thought his eyes were playing a trick on him. He then exclaimed, "I would be damned. That is Veronica leading them. Hold your fire." Dak and Zenith looked in the direction of the riders.

Frank Jr., his men, and Veronica, along with her five guards, ride their horses down the long sloping hill in front of the fort and turn to face the King and his soldiers. Frank Jr. stares at the King. "These brave soldiers have saved us from the cult. There is no more cult. We owe them gratitude. My men and I have decided to fight alongside them to protect Tanger. What are your intentions?"

"I am your King. These soldiers have entered my realm and killed my sheriff and his deputies. You will arrest the soldiers in the fort and bring them to me."

"You will not be arresting anyone," yelled Frank Jr.

The King was caught off guard. "There is a warrant for their arrest. They murdered our Sheriff as he was trying to serve a warrant. They killed ten of his deputies, and these others are common outlaws. There will be a warrant for your arrest for treason if you do not comply with my mandate. This is the law. Now, lay down your weapons and step aside."

Veronica looked at the men facing her, "I am the Queen of the Normand Army. At best, some of you men might survive the pending battle today, but you will not survive the Normand army when King Solman finds out you killed his Queen and his five guards. My five guards individually are better than any four of your men. There are two Blueblood warriors standing behind me. You are the ones who needs to lay down your weapons and surrender to us."

"I said you are under arrest. You will be provided a fair trial. I will contact King Solman and advise him I have his Queen. You have no other choice. My army will crush you. Now drop your weapons."

Frank Jr stuck his spurs into the side of his horse, forcing the animal into a fast gallop heading to meet the King face to face. Frank Jr. slowed his horse as he came to a stop in front of the King. Frank Jr took a second to peer at the men next to the King and then looked at the King. "I wonder what these men will do once I cut your fucking heart out."

A wrinkle developed on the King's forehead and his face turned red. Frank Jr. announced, "My family settled this land after the Transitional Period. There was no one else here. We allowed others to move into Tanger and live. Matter of fact, we invited others to move to our town. People needed a place to live, and we tried to accommodate others. You arrived here from the north and took control. Then, the cult showed up one day without my family knowing they were here. We would have fought them. Now the cult has been rooted out and killed. The evil that you conspired with has been annihilated. Now is your time to be gone. You are no longer welcome in Tanger."

The King yelled, "Arrest him. I am the King, and this is treason." The King noticed no one moved, and his soldiers were watching. He demanded, "You know nothing of what you speak. The cult will return. There are others. I said to arrest this man."

Frank Jr. pulled the knife from under his vest and threw the weapon. The knife sank to the hilt, hitting the King in the neck. The King fell from his horse to the ground gasping for air as the men watched him bleed to death.

Frank Jr then looks at the soldiers sitting on their horses nearest to him. He loudly announces, "This land has always been our land. These warriors fighting for us here today hunt down and kill rogue Bluebloods. If you men want to die fighting to steal my land, I will be waiting in the fort for you." He turned and rode back to the fort.

# Chapter 33

Hulk and Tommy Boy buried their father, Billy Ray Claiborne. The two sons were both trying to accept his death as a warrior dying in battle with pride. Dak spoke to the group at the grave site about how much Billy Ray had meant to him as a friend and a father figure. "He died doing what he did best, which was fighting for his family, friends, and his way of life. He taught us the moral and the goal in life is to do the right thing. He was a man that never prayed. In my opinion, an angel never prays." Dak's speech lasted for close to five minutes and then the body was lowered into the ground at the graveyard located in the City of Tanger. Hulk placed the marker over the grave, "Billy Ray Claiborne, An Angel Never Prays."

His two sons, with tears in their eyes, received hugs from Veronica and Zenith and handshakes from the other warriors and visitors as they stood next to the grave. The group of visitors walked away from the grave, leaving Hulk an opportunity to say his goodbye while he stood by himself at the grave site. Hulk asked himself as he was looking at the mound of dirt, "Dad, what must I do to continue your legacy?"

\*\*\*

Trey was happy to reunite with his older sister, Veronica, and meet his nephew, Gabriel Soloman Zbar. He held Gabriel and hugged the child. Veronica showed Trey how to change a diaper, and the three had an opportunity to bond as a family as Trey proudly held his nephew. Trey was also introduced to the other four kids and enjoyed spending time with them.

Zenith and Dak also spent time with the four Blueblood children learning their interests and playing one on one with the kids and playing chase with the older boys. Zenith was surprised as she watched Dak position himself on his knees and act as if he was a wild horse. When Mica and Vaughn would fall to the ground, Dak would then act like a horse trampling the child, but he was actually tickling the child as laughter ensued. The two boys would rush to be the next rider with the younger brother, Stone, being tickled by Dak. The City of Tanger was transposed from a city where the people lived with fear, to one of hope and grace. The war had ended the eleven years of the tyrant.

Boudica buried her brother, Star, on the hill side where he died. She covered his body in rocks in a shallow grave. She did not cry, looking at Star's last resting place. "I am sorry little brother for the hell you received. I live with quilt of not watching you closer, and I will correct my short coming in the future."

Frank Dupont Jr. overnight became the governor of Tanger and hired a new sheriff. He established the election for the new government and established land deals for the people to consider. He had the people who benefited and worked for the now dead King to be arrested and striped of their property. He set up an affordable tax rate for the residents and a sales tax for the animals and lumber being shipped from the harbor to other locations. The dead King's property was going to be sold or gifted to the citizens to start farming and ranching. All of the citizens were excited about the opportunities Frank Jr. had supported.

Mark Spence, one of the men from The New York Tribe, felt relieved to have survived the battle from the previous day and the journey across the continent. He had fought hard and done as he was ordered. Trey had assigned him and two other men the duty to bury the dead soldiers from the cult inside the fort. The men in Tanger were assigned to bury the soldiers in the field and also guard against any hidden soldiers of the Dark Master. Mark and the two other men were tired. They had dug a trench four by six feet and buried the cult members located inside the fort. Mark and the two men then walked through the gates of the vacant fort and noticed the guards from Tanger walking the upper platform watching for combatants. Everyone was on alert for a possible attack from a Rogue Blueblood soldier and possible combatants from the fort that might have escaped. Mark walked up the stairs to the main building and into a rear room.

He and his two men noticed a desk, "The spoils go to the victor. This must be the cult leader's room," announced Mark.

Mark lit a candle and glanced at the other men as he pulled the chair and sat behind the desk. He was tired and enjoyed the opportunity to relax. "I wonder if there is a hidden bottle of whiskey in this fort?" He knew the two other men were tired. The two men leaned against the wall and watched with disinterested expressions.

Mark looked at the desk and then pulled a drawer open. He pulled some papers out and noticed they were written in a foreign language. He then pulled open the other drawer. "No whiskey yet. Don't lose faith. Certainly, that dead bastard had some whiskey for medicinal purposes." He laid some additional papers on the desktop, "These papers are in a foreign language. I'll be damned. It is our luck, there is nothing of value in this forsaken place. You would think the poor bastards would have something of value. If no whiskey, maybe some gold." He places additional papers from the drawer to the side on top of the desk. He then noticed an eight by ten photo slip from between the pages and fall to the floor. The two men watch as Mark nonchalantly picks up the photo.

One of the other men walks to the desk and looks in the other drawer. He announces, "If we cannot locate gold, maybe some whiskey. We could not be so lucky to find a bottle of Black

Label Jack Daniels. The good old stuff from the old state of Tennessee."

The other man smiled, "If no gold and no whiskey, you would think between all these men, at least one would have some old photos of a naked female."

Mark had not seen a photo in years. He smiled and held the photo, "Well shit. This photo is not what you want. There are no pornographic photos of females here. I can remember before the Transitional Period in the old world, the photos with my family and friends. Photos always had a way of stopping time, and one could reminisce about the period when the photo was taken. Taking photos is a lost art. It is old technology, and no one has been able to bring the technology forward to the new world." Mark stares at the photo of a group of men and women taken at a spot in front of a stone wall several years prior to the Transitional Period. Mark recognized the photo was maybe twenty years old. He thought, "Why would a cult leader live all the way out here in this fort, isolated from the world?" He then asked, "Have you guys ever considered why the cult leader would live all the way out here in the middle of nowhere? Why hide?"

The man at the door replied, "I am glad he is dead. Our friends are damn good warriors. That was one hell of a battle we survived. Robin Hood is deadly with his bow. He fired most of those arrows taking out several of those damn soldiers."

Mark kept staring at the photo. "Hell, I killed several of those nutless bastards." He noticed the photo was taken maybe ten years prior to the Transitional Period during the time period before the demise of the old world. "I believe this photo was taken maybe ten to twenty years prior to the Transitional Period." He stared at the photo. "I wonder if this photo is significant." He then repeated, "Why would a Rogue Blueblood live here to begin with? Why not live in a city?"

The other man listened as Mark repeated himself and became interested in the photo. He walked over behind Mark as both men stared at the photo. He then asked, "Are there additional photos?"

Mark looked to the faces in the photo. He, at first could not recognize anyone as he studied the photo. Mark moved the photo closer to the candlelight sitting on the desk.

The man leaning against the wall noticed the crease in Mark's forehead as he peered at the photo. He then stated, "I wish we could find a bottle of whiskey. I know I am looking forward to drinking the town dry. Trey mentioned the first three rounds tonight are on him."

The man then noticed Mark and the other man were both staring at the photo. The man at the door asked, "What have you discovered?"

Mark then looked closely at the big man in the middle of the photo. The man had longhair which hung down over his ears and fell over his forehead to his eyebrows. His mouth was closed in the photo and all the others were smiling. He studied the eyes of the man in the middle. He pointed to the large man, "This man is the Cult Leader. This is the same man we buried." He looked closer at the photo and noticed the man next to the now dead cult leader had pointed ears. He noticed the man on the bottom row has pointed ears. He then scanned the photo, and where the men were standing to the right, he could make out the pointed ears. He counted twenty-two men and four women.

Mark suddenly burst out, "My God! There are twenty-four Rogue Bluebloods in this photo. You two need to gather these papers and protect them. Dak's mother, the Queen, can read this language." He stood and ran past his buddy and out the door. He ran to the stable and jumped on a horse and headed out of the fort's gate on a dead run.

He rode at a fast gallop into Tanger, and he stopped the horse at the door to the motel and did not bother with tying the horse to the post. He abruptly entered the double doors and ran across the foyer. The people in the lobby and the front desk employees watched Mark ascend the stairs while running. He knocks on Dak's door and then waits. He knocks a second time and still no one answered. He turns and notices the maid watching him in the hall. "They went on a picnic and then they went to the dock with the children."

Mark turned and descended the stairs two at a time, dodging a couple walking into the motel as he ran out the doors. He ran to his horse and immediately jumped on the saddle and headed toward the dock.

"Where is Dak?" he asks the soldier stationed at the dock entrance. The soldier points to the end of the dock. Mark ran by several workers on the dock unloading a vessel.

Dak and Zenith saw Mark coming as they were showing the four children the view from the end of the dock and talking about the different sailing vessels. Veronica was holding her baby and talking as they were enjoying the sunny day. Mark approached and slowed his pace. "What is the rush?" Dak smiles.

Mark was out of breath, "I found this photo at the fort in a desk in the back room under some papers. The papers are written in a foreign language." He hands Dak the photo.

Dak looks at the photo and his face reflects his displeasure. Veronica walks over to him while still holding her son and peers at the photo. Zenith looks over at Dak as she kept the kids from getting too close to the edge of the dock. Veronica was the first to say with alarm in her voice, "Oh my God. They are all Rogue Bluebloods created in the old world. That stone wall must be located in the old country of Germany. The writing on the building is the old German language."

Dak asks, "Where could they all be? Could they have survived the Transitional Period?" He then stares at the photo and at the man on one end. "Dammit, that is Senator Dale. The bastard over the Merlin Senate."

# Chapter 34

The festive dinner and party at the City Tavern were a joyous occasion with most becoming intoxicated while eating and celebrating. The City Tavern is located on the bottom floor of the hotel with rooms for guests taking up the second floor. The hotel had been used to quarantine ship's crews in the past as the crew would trade with the store owners and the ranchers for commodities. Dak and Zenith sat at the head of the table next to Veronica and Frank Jr. The tavern was standing room only around the walls with tables full of food and joyous customers. Dak watched as Veronica stood and walks over to the table with her five guards. He observes her as she says something to the men and then reaches for a pitcher of ale from the next table over and pours them each a drink. He smiles to himself knowing the guards are still on duty, and she desires them to relax and have a drink. She then walks over to the other side of Zenith and the two women engage in a conversation.

After several individuals standing and toasting others, Dak felt the effects of the alcohol. He watches as Zenith is talking with Veronica and both seem to be discussing something important as he drinks from his mug of beer. Dak looks at his friends and is envious he is not sitting at their table as he notices they are laughing and drinking. The pork has all been consumed by his men, and there are several empty mugs of beer at their table. The entire room is full of smiles and festive drinking. He pushes his chair back and stands. He immediately feels the effects of the beer as he walks from behind his table through the crowd and out the front door. Dak looks up at the sky and the stars and felt the cool breeze and the relief of walking out of the warm building. He considers his trip home. He glanced around him for any possible threat as he embraces the cool breeze blow across his face. He wonders if he should have had the last mug of beer as the effects of the alcohol are noticeable when he tries to peer at the stars. He blinks his eyes in an attempt to try to stop the appearance of the stars flying in circles in the sky above. He then notices Samuel is standing next to the exterior wall and appears to be enjoying his solitude while chewing some tobacco. Dak walks over to the end of the building out of the light and urinates. He then walks back to the front of the building and stands next to Samuel. The two men had never talked as friends. It was always awkward when they tried to speak. Dak smiled, "The city is well protected. There are guards posted on the pier and all the roads leading into the city. We pulled the guards out of the fort. There was no sign of any other threat. You do not need to be standing guard watching for the Rogue Bluebloods."

"You know those guards are no match for those Rogue Bluebloods." He reaches to hand Dak some tobacco.

Dak motioned his head no, "Get that shit out of my face."
Samuel smiles at the comment. As Dak stares at nothing,
thinking about the photo. "Did you have a drink? Maybe you
should relax."

Samuel did not show emotion. "Yeah, I had a couple of beers.
The beer has a ten percent alcohol level, and the wine is higher
in alcohol. I did not ask about the bitter ale, but everyone who
drank some appears to be drunk," He smiles and places the
pouch of tobacco in his pocket, "I have never been one to
overindulge."

Dak turned serious, "We did damn good. Although you were
correct, and I am saddened by the loss of Billy Ray and our
other men. Not all of my hunting party will return with us to
Cliff Tops."

Samuel spit the tobacco juice to the ground, "There might still
be a few Rogue Bluebloods out there close by which we need
guard against. They will want revenge."

Dak looks at Samuel, "Yes, I believe there are. There could be
as many as twenty-one men and four women. It is hard to tell if
those other Bluebloods we killed are in the photo."

Dak then adds, "Veronica is married to one in the photo."

"My understanding it was a forced marriage, and she was
raped. We need to kill him if for no other reason than the rape of
Veronica."

"I cannot sanction his execution. He is married to one of my best friends. Besides, I have killed enough. I hope my family is okay back at Cliff Tops. I will see if I can find a ship and sail us home. You and I need to be home with our kids. This is my last crusade. There is a time to retire, and this is it for me. I have given all I need to give."

Samuel looked at Dak, "Wars and conflicts always follow men like us. This won't be your last or my last battle. This is what we live for. War is in our blood. You will grow to realize this. I have retired twenty times over the years and then the next day I accept my position as a soldier. There is only one way out and Billy Ray showed you the path of a warrior. You cannot run from your destiny." The men turned to the door of the tavern as the door opened.

***

Zenith was surprised with the conversation with Veronica. Veronica had requested she and Dak take the four Blueblood children and her son to their home at Zenith Point to raise them. Zenith sat still in thought. She turned and noticed Dak was in his chair and seemed to be getting tipsy. He stood and toasted several men in the audience, and she knew he was starting to feel the effects of the alcohol. She observed Frank Jr. was constantly talking to the people of his community as they approached his table as he and Veronica greeted them. Some people were thanking him for becoming the governor while others were asking for favors with the proposed land deals. Zenith observed Veronica's guards watching everyone who approached her table. She had also noticed Samuel had finished eating and was one of the few not drinking or smiling. He then stood and walked outside. A few minutes later she realized Dak was nowhere to be seen, and Veronica had returned to her seat next to Frank Jr. after she had suggested to her guards, they needed to have fun. The party was starting to get loud, and more folks were starting to overindulge with wine and beer. The waitresses were constantly bringing beer mugs to the tables. She watched the table with Robin Hood facing her, Hulk had his back to her, Trey and Tommy Boy were sitting across from one another. She smiled when she heard the stories of how Tommy Boy and Robin Hood had each hired females to entertain them in their rooms the previous night and now the young ladies were visiting them at their table, with all drinking and laughing. She watched as Frank Jr. subtly reached his hand under the table and touched Veronica's left thigh just above her knee. Veronica turned her head and faced him. Zenith smiled to herself as she was watching the festive crowd and the flirting occurring next to her.

Zenith acted like she did not hear as Frank Jr. leaned over and whispered, "Your guards are on duty. Must they always watch you?"

Zenith then looked around the dining area and into the bar, observing the people. She saw Veronica shift ever so slightly and smile as she invited his right-hand to edge up her leg and rub her leg inside her dress. "At my request, I can ask for privacy. They are obedient."

Zenith, at that point, could not hear the conversation but suspected the content as both seemed to be romantically invested with one another.

Frank Jr. leaned over further, "I have done a lot for you, your guards, and the kids. I was hoping for a special, more personal type of reward." He then squeezed his four fingers on his right-hand tighter into her the skin on her inner upper left-thigh.

Veronica reached under the table with her left hand and grasped his right-hand. She took his hand in hers and squeezed firmly, pushing her four fingernails into the surface of his skin on the palm of his hand as she turned his hand over and pulled his hand toward her upper inner thigh. Zenith noticed an older, intoxicated gentleman approach their table and thanked Frank Jr. for fixing the government. The older gentleman was starting to go into an extended statement, and the elderly lady pulled her husband away toward the exit door knowing this was not the best time to talk to the new governor. Zenith noticed Frank Jr.

was leaning into Veronica's space and she heard Veronica announce, "These people love what you were able to accomplish. They all seem excited about the new opportunities for commerce. You do deserve to be well rewarded. I was planning to give you additional gold for helping me unless you have something else in mind. I mean, is there anything I could personally do for you?" She smiled at him and pushed his hand further toward her most upper thigh.

Zenith looked around, trying to figure out where her husband had disappeared. She thought he must be in the restroom, but another man had entered the men's room and then came out. She looked at Veronica and started to ask the whereabouts of Dak. She noticed Veronica was sitting close to the table with her feet apart, her hands holding Frank Jr.'s right-hand between her legs. She immediately turned her head away and smiled to herself. She watched as Trey stood on a table and started singing, "Once I had a girl on Rocky Top. Home Sweet Home To Me." Zenith started laughing as she stood and walked toward the exit door. As she walks through the crowd she stops and asks one of the New York soldiers if he has seen where Dak has gone. The man points to the front door. Zenith listens to how Trey is making up the words to the song as he is yelling them out while he drinks beer and enjoys himself. Folks in the room start trying to sing the song with very little success.

Frank Jr. feels the back of his hand rub against her body. His mind hesitates and his mouth becomes dry. He then smiles at the people getting drunk in front of them, "May I suggest something?"

Veronica looks at him with a stern expression as she bites her lower lip and holds his hand pressing against her upper thigh. "You may make a suggestion. If there is anything I can do to repay you, please state your desires now."

"Why do we not go back to my home alone, without your guards and discuss my desires?" He stared into her eyes as the back of his hand rubbed upward and downward again across her. He smiles and gasps for a breath as the back of his hand becomes moist.

She pulls her right-hand from under the table and places her right-hand over her forehead and covers her face and then takes his hand and rubs the back of the hand again against her crotch up then down, "Why return to your home where I will be interrupted by one of the five kids. I have a room upstairs and there are no kids. Meet me in my room in five minutes. Room number four. Please do not make me wait. I will not like you being late." She pulls his hand out from under the table and kisses the moisture on the back of his hand. She straightens her dress and then stands and walks around the tables and ascends the stairs.

He watches her walk across the room in her perfect fitting dress. His anticipation has become difficult for him to control. He notices several of the men and women in the room watch as Veronica walks to the stairway. She is confident in herself, and her attire is well considered and accents her figure. He could not place his finger on why she was so attractive. He recalls watching her hold her baby after the birth, and how she would sit in front of the fire in a rocking chair at night in a short tee shirt with the shirt pulled over to the side while she breasts fed her child. Her legs and feet were covered in soybean oil which made them shine in front of the fire. Her long hair was hanging freely on her shoulders, down her back and across the top of the chair. Now, he watches every step as she ascends the stairs. He checks his watch for the time and clenches his jaws as he anticipates the encounter.

Zenith approaches the front exit door. She smiles to herself and could not help but turn and glance at Veronica and Frank Jr. sitting at the front table with the long tablecloth hanging down covering the lower extremities. She notices Veronica is straightening her dress as she stands. She starts walking toward the stairs and then she glances back at Frank Jr. who seems to be in a trance watching Veronica leave. Zenith thinks to herself, "Those two will meet later in her room." She smiles and opens the door. Zenith walks out in the cool air and notices Dak and Samuel talking, "Well, there you two are. I looked around and both of you had disappeared. You left me in there with all those drunks. Trey is standing on a table singing some song he does not know the words. For heaven sakes, they're getting drunk."

Dak smiles, "We were talking about going home, and I might also be drunk."

Zenith looks at Dak, "Speaking of which, Veronica has asked me to take the children with us. Frank Jr. may have a ship lined up with a captain that can get us past the Normand Naval blockade. The captain has a Certificate of Passage signed by King Solman." She looks concerned at Dak, "She has asked me to take Gabriel with us. She intends to return to Southern City with her guards."

Dak is shocked. He tried to become sober. "I am flattered she would trust us to raise her kids, but I am going to talk with her. I do not understand. She cannot go back to Southern City. There is a Rogue Blueblood in that city who is in charge."

Zenith looked at Dak with a smile, "You will need to wait until tomorrow to meet her. Veronica has excused herself from dinner. The children are all staying at Frank's home in the country under guard with several maids. She has retired to her room upstairs." Zenith raises her eyebrow while looking at Dak. She realizes he does not seem to make the connection with Veronica having a room upstairs and her child and the four other children being kept for the night at another location. She had assumed her husband would have noticed the sexual tension between Veronica and Frank Jr. as they appeared to gather at several of the meetings over the past couple of days.

Samuel announces, "Veronica understands the mission is not over. She would like her son, and those children protected from the Bluebloods in Merlin and their father. Those children will never be safe until such time they can be trained to be warriors and defend themselves. Zenith, you will need to make certain they are all indoctrinated to be a Blueblood warrior. Otherwise without our training, a Blueblood is a target. Word will spread of the Dark Master being killed. One of the other Rogue Bluebloods will assume the command position. There is so much unknown in dealing with the secret cult." He waves his hand in front of him, "There can be only one king of the Rogue Bluebloods, and he died here. You can be assured another will take his place."

\*\*\*

Hulk had not planned to get drunk, but he desired to forget the painful scene of watching his father die. He sat at the table with Robin Hood, Trey, and Tommy Boy and listened to Robin Hood and Tommy Boy talk about the females they each had bedded the prior night. All four men ate the pork meal with two additional servings. They ate more than they should have and drank twice as much as everyone else. The other soldiers and townspeople seem to be watching them from the other tables and the bar area as they were laughing, telling jokes, and being festive. There were single women that would come over and visit their table and flirt with them. The waitresses were overly friendly as they kept them supplied with beer. The entire room was loud with talking and laughter. Trey then presents a toast to Billy Ray, "An angel never prays." The four men stood, bumping their beer mugs together and repeated the phrase and downed the mugs of beer.

After the toast, Tommy Boy seemed to become melancholier than Hulk. He kept telling stories of growing up with their father who always was seen helping other people, and how he would miss him. Hulk listened and knew his younger brother was trying to adjust to the death of their father. He, however, had accepted Billy Ray's death. He tried to forget watching his father take his last breath with his neck being broken and his father's eyes staring at him in vain, while he was helpless, being restrained and forced to watch. He did not wish to discuss his father but out of respect for his brother he sat and listened. Hulk glanced around from time to time and could see Boudica sitting at the bar with three of the men from the New York Tribe and one from his own tribe. People were moving back and forth from the tables to the bar with everyone enjoying the meal and the alcohol drinks. Boudica seemed to be eating and having fun. Hulk passed on the last round of drinks and started to watch

Boudica more and more as the evening passed. From time to time, she would glance at him, and their eyes would lock on each other. He noticed her pretty smile and thought about her athletic body. She was honest, intelligent, brave, and Hulk respected her as a warrior. On the other hand, he knew she was not sophisticated like the women from Harpers Ferry Harbor or Tanger. She had never traveled and was forced, as she was growing up, to live under the strict rule of the Midlander guidelines with only whispers and glimpses of the outside world through the Westcoast traders. He had listened to her talk with excitement in her voice of traveling and indicated she wanted to see the world and live beyond her tribe. She had expressed how she especially wanted to travel to Merlin and other large cities, even go to Israel in Asia. He had observed her with the four small Bluebloods kids playing with them and holding Veronica's son. She was at ease with the kids and viewed life through their eyes. She wanted to be more than a Midlander. Hulk knew the Midlanders were forbidden to associate with outsiders. Hulk noticed the one man placing his arm around Boudica and pouring her another drink. He then held the mug up for her to drink. Hulk's anger spiked as he was watching Boudica, while he was also trying to listen to Tommy Boy tell another story. He quickly stood and walked over to the bar, staring down at Boudica and the men at the bar. All stopped drinking and laughing. The one man then toasted Hulk, "Here is one of the greatest warriors on the planet."

Hulk smiled at the five men. He respected them. They had performed with admiration in battle, and he had gotten to know them on the long journey from the far north. They, after all, had a right to celebrate with each of them being injured in the battle and then surviving the battle with each registering several kills. Each man had performed admirably in the face of the overwhelming numbers of combatant soldiers and Rogue Bluebloods. They were friends with the dead men from the New York Tribe and the Cliff Tops Tribe who had been killed on the battlefield. He did not blame them for trying to get to know Boudica, after all, she was very pretty, brave, smart and had a loving heart. A man watching her from behind could not help but notice her round buttocks in her tight-fitting leather pants and when facing he would notice her beautiful eyes and smile with her dark complexion. She was also very confident in herself and was aware men liked her appearance. He looked at Boudica, "May I have a word with you in private?"

Boudica was obviously drunk. She turned and looked at Hulk and tried to raise her mug to toast him a second time as she inadvertently spilled some of her drink on Hulk. The five men laughed as the beer was pouring down Hulk's leg. Hulk quickly reached for her arm, pulling her to her feet. "Please, may I have a word with you." He took her drink and placed the empty mug on the bar. He then walked her toward the front door of the tavern.

"Here, allow me to wipe your leg." She grabs a cloth napkin as they pass by a table. "What is the hurry? Stand still, and I will wipe the beer off your leg. There is no reason to be upset because of the beer on your crotch. I will wipe it off. I am really good at cleaning up my messes." She laughs, "One might think you wet yourself."

Hulk opened the door, pulling her across the door threshold. "My crotch and leg are okay."

"I am sorry. I was just trying to help you. There is no reason to get your panties in a wad. Where is my drink?"

Hulk walked with her across the street to the sidewalk and the railing over the ocean. "Where are my friends?" She then looks Hulk in the eyes, "Where are my drinking buddies?"

He smiles, "Boudica, you are drunk, and my panties are not in a wad."

"I am not drunk. Matter of fact, I just started drinking. I can drink all night. We need to celebrate you being the best warrior on the planet. What a great compliment from my drinking buddies."

He smiles at her, "Where are you staying? I will take you home."

"Home? I am never going home. I have no gold, and nowhere to live. I have burned that bridge. My brother is now dead because of me, and I buried him on the side of the mountain. I do not desire to live in the same village with my father. I trusted him to protect us kids as we grew up. That is the way your father raised you and your brother. You said he was an angel that never prayed. My father was no angel, and he did pray. He was scared to be a good father. I wished my father had been like your father. Now, I wish to have another drink."

Hulk watched her trying to stand straight without wobbling. "I mean where is your room?"

She points toward the tavern. "It is over there. I cannot remember the room number, and I am not certain what I did with my key. I cannot afford to pay for the room for another night, so I am going to drink myself into a state of mind to forget about my life worries. I have hit rock bottom." She spreads her hands to emulate the bottom of a flat surface.

Hulked looked frustrated. "Come on." He turns her toward the back stairway of the tavern and takes her hand as they walk back across the street to the side of the building.

"Where are we going? I would like to drink more and be more festive." She stumbles as they walk. Boudica feels Hulk pull her upright and then she intentionally falls into him while rubbing her right breast against his elbow. She smiles, "Well, excuse me."

"Do you not think you have had enough to drink? You can hardly stand. I believe those men were trying to get you drunk to take advantage of you."

"I was taking advantage of them. They paid for all the drinks. They are my drinking buddies." Hulk glances at her with a smile as she tries to walk a straight line across the street to the back stairways of the tavern.

"All the drinks and food were free. Frank Jr. paid for the party." He glances at her, "We need to be quiet as we go up the stairs."

She laughs. "That Frank Jr. knows how to make friends."

"Hush. Be quiet."

"Why are you helping me?"

"Because you are a hero. Zenith would want me to help you. You saved her life. It is the right thing to do."

"I saved your life also. Remember the arrow I shot and killed the soldier in the room? He was about to throw his spear right through your heart. You do owe me a life credit." She wobbles as he holds her steady as they both make eye contact.

Hulk smiles, "A life credit? Where did you hear about a life credit?"

"I heard the joke you guys played on Zenith when you first met her. My drinking buddies were telling the story as they heard about the joke from Trey and Robin Hood and now, I am playing the joke on you." She sticks her index finger in his chest.

Hulk smiles to himself as their eyes meet. He then reflects back to over two years ago when his friends were traveling in the cold northwest to Merlin and Zenith, in order to stay warm, was forced to sleep in the tent and bedroll with Dak.

Hulks steps forward and gently position Boudica to the first step of the hotel. The two ascend the stairs with Hulk positioned behind her on the lower step as they slowly stepped on each step while he is holding her from behind with his hands resting on her hips to balance her as she moves in front of him up the stairs. Hulk enjoys the view of the form fitting thin leather pant material covering her backside as she is in front of him located higher on the steps as she slowly steps on each tread on the stairway. Hulk steps around her once they both step off the top step onto the porch entryway. He gently opens the exterior door. Boudica trips over the door threshold, falling into the door facing, forcing the door to open with force. Hulk pulls her hand backward and rushes across the door threshold to hold her as he steps into the dark hallway. Hulk bumps into Frank Jr. standing at the end of the hall next to the exterior door they just entered. Hulk wonders what Frank Jr. is doing standing in the hall in the dark on the second floor. Boudica smiles and as she starts to say, "Excuse us," the door to room number four opens. All three people standing in the hall stare in the open door and see

Veronica standing in the room, with a smile, in the nude, holding the door wide open. Veronica's smile turns to a frown as she slams the door shut when she sees Hulk and Boudica staring at her. Hulk reacts quickly and tries to pull Boudica to his room number three. She hesitates, "Was that not your friend the Queen? Oh, my! That was Veronica." She tries to glance backward to see Frank Jr. as Hulk rushes her to the door of his room. She says loudly as Hulk is opening his door, pushing her into his room, "Frank Jr., thanks for all the free drinks."

Hulk whispers to Boudica, "Please be quiet." He looks back at Frank Jr. and smiles. He hurriedly opens his door and gently pushes Boudica into his room. Boudica started laughing and could not refrain from being tickled. He smiles at her. "Would you be quiet? They will hear you."

"The Queen was naked. What happened to her clothes? Why would she open the door naked?" She then points at room number four, "Where is the King?" Hulk starts to smile as he watches Boudica trying to stand without wobbling. She then adds, "Oh my. Do you think the Queen and Frank Jr. are?" She holds up her index finger on her right hand and starts pushing the finger in and out of the circle of fingers in her left hand. She stops talking in the middle of the sentence and starts laughing. "The Queen is up to no good. Oh my, oh my, oh my. That Frank Jr. is slick, and we caught them. You may not realize what they are doing, but I know what they are up to." She holds her right finger up a second time and rams the finger in and out of her circled fingers on left hand. Hulks laughs and tries to refrain from being heard outside his room. He does not wish for Frank Jr. to hear him laughing.

"I believe I understand the concept of what is going on in room number four." He stepped forward and held her, watching her laugh. He leans forward kissing her on the forehead, trying to control her loud talking and laughter. She stopped laughing and looked into his eyes and was ready to return the kiss. He held her tight against his body and started to push her hair back out of her face. She finally pushed back from him and seems to sober. "I am sorry. I am a Midlander. I know you do not desire to date someone like me. These other women wear dresses, makeup, and such. I thought I was going to die on that mountain, and I asked you as a favor to bed me. Now, I am sorry. I did not realize I was going to live. My intentions were to save my brother and then show the people of my tribe how corrupt my tribe leaders are. My brother was sacrificed by my father, and I hate my father. I honestly thought I would never see you again." She stared into Hulk's eyes.

"You are right. The other women do wear dresses, make up and such, but you are here with me. I picked you, not them."

"Are you leaving tomorrow with your friends? I understand the captain has the paperwork to sneak you to Harpers Ferry Harbor. At least that is what my drinking buddies were saying.

They asked me to go north with them. I have no money to purchase a ticket. My life is in such a mess."

"I want you to come with me. I will buy you a ticket. Remember you are a hero. If I did not pay for your ticket, Zenith would be happy to pay your way." She seemed additionally sober and kissed him. She broke off the kiss.

"Please do not lie to me. I know you do not agree with the way of life the Midlanders have chosen. I also know I am drunk. I do not wish to be mistreated and lied to. Is this real for you? Will you be my friend?"

"For a man like me to confess my feelings for a woman is difficult, a true confession is hard for me to make, but I will show you how real this is for me. When you wake in the morning, you will know the feeling of a man who is truly in love with you and thinks you have a perfect body. I believe you are perfect. If I was God or had the power of a God, I would not change you." He leaned over her, holding her tight as he kissed her.

She broke off the kiss and stepped backward and stared into his eyes as she started to remove the rest of her clothes. She then stood naked as she modeled her nudity for him as he pull off his boots and remove his pants, "Hulk, you do know perfection is an illusion? I am far from perfect." She held her arms out to her side as he stared at her from her feet to her smile.

Hulk stood and prolonged the moment while he admired her. "I think you know you have a perfect body. I think that is one reason you are so damn pretty. You are so confident in yourself. You know I love watching you, especially when you are naked."

\*\*\*

Frank Jr. hesitated as he watched Hulk close the door. Hulk had held his smile while assisting Boudica, as she was laughing, when she crossed the door threshold to his room. He took a deep breath thinking how upset Veronica might be with his secret rendezvous. He then stared at the door as he reached up and knocked on door number four. He stood still staring at nothing but the door and no one answered. He waited close to five seconds as he looked down the hallway to see if anyone else could see him. He then knocked a second time. The door opened and Veronica stood in her sheer, long maternity gown. The front was open revealing her cleavage. She looked at him with a stern expression, "May I help you?"

"Yes, you may. I deserve to receive a reward for helping you. Those two in the hall are not my fault. They came through the back door as I was knocking."

"You do realize I am married, and people talk? My husband is a control freak. I have changed my mind. I will pay you with gold. You will not bed me."

He walked into her room, closing the door behind him and backing her over to her dresser forcing her to sit on the top of the dresser with her legs spread. He started kissing her on the mouth and then her ear as she tried to push him away. He was persistent and kept getting lower and lower until he was on his knees, listening to her moan with pleasure as she started rotating her hips with her hands holding the back of his head in place. As she gasped, "Do not stop. You are an animal."

# Chapter 35

The Blueblood captain does not make eye contact with the guards or other people as he walks with purpose into the Senate building past the guard station. The guards noticed the red patch with three white stripes outlined in a black border sewn on his left sleeve that signified his rank and position in the Secret Police. The guards stepped to the side and allowed the captain to pass without questioning him as he refuses to acknowledge the guards. He took the steps to the third floor and walked past several people as they moved to the side to allow him passage. He came to the door at the end of the hall and did not hesitate to open the door. The secretary asked, "May I help you?"

His voice was stern, "I must see the Senator."

She glanced at his left sleeve and noticed the patch. She thought she should be stern after all, she works for the senior Senator, the most powerful man in Merlin. She announces sternly, "The Senator is in conference. He is not to be disturbed."

With his jaws clinched he commanded, "Tell the Senator, Captain Spielman from the Secret Police is here. This is urgent."

The secretary was intimated, and she tried to smile, "I told you he is not to be disturbed. You can leave the message with me. I will make certain, Captain Spielman, he receives your request. Otherwise, we can set you an appointment. I will check his calendar for an opening."

Captain Spielman noticed that the secretary is an older lady, with glasses, short hair and a stern looking body. He walked past her and opened the Senator's door. "Dammit. I do not wish to be interrupted." The nude lady rolled off his desk, stood up, and gathered her clothes. She rushes away into the back room. The Senator raises himself from his knees and stands. He starts to dress as he notices the captain standing in his office. The captain peers through the hallway into the back room and watches the lady dress.

Captain Spielman commands, "I will meet you on the Courtroom Balcony. We have much to discuss. Do not make me wait." He turns and walks out of the Senator's door and past the secretary into the hall.

***

Senator Dale hesitates at the glass balcony door watching Captain Spielman standing with his back to him. The captain is a strong man with a fierce reputation for being aggressive. The Senator knows he does not like or trust the captain, but was thankful the captain, like himself, had pledged their lives to the same master. The two Rogue Bluebloods were brothers full of hatred toward each other but held together by the common bond to the Master. The Senator was also aware Captain Spielman had killed hundreds of people in the pursuit of his job, with most of the killings taking place behind the closed prison doors, and the public was never informed of how someone died in prison. The news media is controlled by Captain Spielman's office, and he consequently controls the information being released to the citizens. The Senator had an ominous feeling as he finally reached for the door latch, opening the door and then walking onto the balcony. He noticed Captain Spielman was standing at the rail looking over the city. "What is so damn urgent? Do I need to remind you who is in charge, and you work for me." He walks over next to Captain Spielman, as he also takes in the view of the city.

Captain Spielman despised the Senator for him becoming rich and using his office to gain wealth and power. He hesitated and forced the Senator to wait on his response. "I have the updated news from the south. The man known as the Dark Master has been killed."

Senator Dale could not have been more surprised, "General Thieves is dead? Who could have killed him?"

"According to the news, General Samuel was present, but he did not kill General Thieves. He was killed by the drifter who fought Apollo here on our senate floor a couple of years ago."

"General Samuel! He is dead. He was reported killed by Midlanders and so was that drifter."

Captain Spielman turned, "You're an incompetent idiot. I told you I should have killed General Samuel when I had the chance. It would appear he has changed sides. Now he is your greatest threat. He will be coming for you."

"Back then General Samuel had friends, and we cannot kill everyone that opposes us. There is a time and place. I felt we should be cautious. There are several hundred First Generation Bluebloods in this city. They will stick together. Are you certain General Thieves is dead? How accurate is your information? There have been no reports from our office of Army Intelligence."

Captain Spielman turns back to his view overlooking the city. He always presented himself to be calm, stern, and confident with a direct, to the point, type of personality. "My spy is correct. Who else would be so bold to ride up to the gate of General Thieves on a white stallion and kill two of his guards. He then killed two of our Blueblood brothers that were conditioned to fight for General Thieves. It was Samuel, and he knows of you. They will be coming for you, while I, on the other hand, will enjoy anonymity. I choose to live in the shadows while you, on the other hand, are sinfully proud and now you have a large bull's eye on your back." He stood silent and then added, "You will pay for your sins of pride, gluttony, envy, and hatred. You will be next. I will try to protect you. After all, you are my brother."

The two stood looking over the wall, down on the city in thought. Senator Dale thought about the man standing next to him and the fact that he was so bold to have had a spy working under General Thieve's roof, without the master knowing he was being spied on. Captain Spielman said, "One other thing. Zenith was also present and killed another one of our brothers. I have sent some men to locate Aquarius. So far, no one knows his location. He will answer for his daughter's actions. I told you I should have also killed Aquarius years ago. From this point on, you will be doing by bidding, or I will carry you out in the beautiful city in which we live and impale you for all to see. Do you understand how our relationship has evolved?" The captain turned and stared at Senator Dale as he placed his left hand on his knife while his right was resting on the handle of his sword.

Senator Dale slowly turned and faced the captain. He had never considered the Dark Master would have been killed. The natural order in the Rogue Blueblood clan was for the next in line to take his place. The question though was who was the next in line? General Thieves had never named his successor. Senator Dale now understood his situation. He was now standing on a balcony without a weapon next to a cold-blooded killer. He knew he only had one decision if he was to survive, or he would be killed. He then voluntarily got down on his knees. The captain reached his hand forward, and Senator Dale kissed the back of his hand. "I swear to you, my master; I will serve you well."

"Good. Now stand. Your first order is to have the female Blueblood that was just in your office report to my office. I believe she might be able to assist in locating Aquarius. She was married to Aquarius, was she not?"

Senator Dale was looking at Captain Spielman with a questionable expression, "Yes Master, but I can assure you that she does not know her ex-husband's location. I granted the two a consensual divorce over one year ago in my senate chambers. Aquarius was thought to be linked to the secret gold shipment being stolen. I can assure you we are looking for him and are still investigating the theft."

"I will take over the investigation into Aquarius, Samuel, Zenith and the drifter. There are spies at every level of our government, which I will handle. You will no longer be seeing her. I understand she has a very unique appetite for men. She will report to me, and I will assist her with her needs."

To Be Continued